LAVISH ACCLAIM

Some Deaths Before Dying

SELECTED ONE OF THE BEST BOOKS OF THE YEAR BY
PUBLISHERS WEEKLY

"In SOME DEATHS BEFORE DYING, that daredevil stylist Peter Dickinson sets himself the formidable task of solving an undisclosed crime whose principal players are dead, near-dead, or dotty. He executes this feat with extraordinary grace and skill...but there is more to his artistry than technique."
—Marilyn Stasio, *New York Times Book Review*

"Leisurely layered in the grand English tradition, there's plenty of pleasure to be had in watching Dickinson put together the pieces of his well-crafted puzzle."
—*Chicago Tribune*

"This beautifully crafted and highly original English mystery should bring new fans to an exceptional writer."
—*Publishers Weekly* (starred review)

"No one is more subtle, elusive, and suggestive in this quietly insidious prose than Dickinson....He is at the top of his form...superb."
—*Providence Sunday Journal*

"A rich and stylish story that is at once haunting, touching, and provocative, Dickinson's latest will capture the reader's imagination from beginning to end."
—*Booklist*

"Dickinson is one of the few grandmasters [of the English country mystery], as his novels are always deep, entertaining, and highly original. Only an author of his talent could take a seemingly helpless individual and turn her into a dynamic detective within a realistic and exciting tale. The best seems to get better."
—*Midwest Book Review*

SOME DEATHS BEFORE DYING

PETER DICKINSON

THE MYSTERIOUS PRESS
Published by Warner Books

A Time Warner Company

For my mother,
who suggested that I
write about rooks

 Mysterious Press books are published by Warner Books, Inc., 1271 Avenue of the Americas, New York, NY 10020

Visit our Web site at www.twbookmark.com

 A Time Warner Company

The Mysterious Press name and logo are registered trademarks of Warner Books, Inc.

Printed in the United States of America
Originally published in hardcover by The Mysterious Press
First Trade printing: July 2000

10 9 8 7 6 5 4 3 2 1

The Library of Congress has cataloged the hardcover edition as follows:
Dickinson, Peter
    Some deaths before dying / Peter Dickinson.
       p. cm.
    ISBN 0-89296-696-3
    I. Title.
  PR6054.I35S66   1999
  823'.914—dc21   98-37535
                                      CIP

ISBN 0-446-67612-8 (pbk.)

Cover design by Rachel McClain
Photo-illustration by Richard Fahey.

I

Cleaned, changed, propped inert on her pillows and now waiting for her breakfast, Rachel studied the rooks.

First she counted the nests. Ten, still, but the two new ones had grown appreciably since last evening. She had known that serious building had been going on, from the particular type of racket the birds had been making almost from first light, beyond the closed curtains. Indeed, she was disappointed to find that an eleventh nest had not been started. It was in the earliest stages, when the half-completed nest didn't already conceal the process, that she had most chance of seeing how it was done.

It was strangely frustrating. Last spring she had lain here, watching until the young leaves hid the almost completed nests—fourteen of them. Her long sight was remarkably good. She could make out the individual twigs as they were carried in. But she still hadn't been able to see how the birds had achieved structures firm enough not just to endure rearing boisterous young but, all bar one, to stay put through the winter. Then, in early spring, with a lot of yelping and squawking and what looked like real fights, four had been destroyed and rebuilt while the rest had been merely refurbished.

How did they do it? Rachel was far from sure that, if one of the nest sites had been at ground level and she had been given a supply of twigs, she could with two deft-fingered hands have woven a nest to withstand twelve months' weather. Yet the birds did it with no more than a beak. She had seldom seen one use a foot for anything other than to grip the tree. And they worked to some kind of plan. She remembered, years ago, watching one wrestle a twig off a bush down by the churchyard gate, a good two hundred yards from the copper beech where the nests were. Apparently no other twig in the garden would do. It was like Jocelyn embarking on a bit of carpentry by going to the timber store and sorting through a stack of apparently identical planks for the three that suited him.

And only some nest sites were acceptable. Thirty-two years ago Jocelyn had decided that the big beech behind the stables had to come down. It had developed an extremely handsome bracket fungus, over a yard across by the time of the first frosts, then collapsing into slimy pulp. Rachel had taken a truly satisfying series of photographs of it over several years, until Jocelyn had got a tree expert in to take a look at it. *Merulius giganteus* it had turned out to be, a relative of dry rot, and the tree had better come down before the next northeasterly toppled it onto the stables.

"What about the rooks?" Rachel had asked.

"There's plenty of other trees," Jocelyn had answered.

But there hadn't been, not in the rooks' eyes. The copper beech had looked entirely suitable, and indeed in some years an outcast pair had built a solitary nest on a particular side branch, but only three more moved in the first spring after the old beech was felled, and another couple the spring after that. Rachel had paid less attention to them in those days, and in many years didn't bother to count the nests, but her impression was that it had taken a surprising time for the numbers to build up to the dozen plus that they had been since she was first confined here, with time to study the nests and wonder how they were made.

No, "wonder" was too feeble a word for the serious effort and attention she put into it, a tactic in her long and steadfast campaign to keep hold of her mind. Almost everything else was gone, the provinces of her body lost for good. Four years ago she had first been aware of the invaders as an awkwardness in standing and walking, with a tendency to stumble—messages received at the centre of government but then for a while just pigeonholed. It had taken her nearly two months to decide that what was happening to her wasn't fairly normal in the elderly, and that she should go to Dr. Cherry about it.

A fortnight later she had learned, from a London specialist, the barbarous name of the invaders, and that they were irresistible.

The illness followed its expected course, with the head the last to go. By now parties of the invaders were inside the undefended walls. Though taste still functioned, thank goodness, swallowing was starting to be difficult, as was speech—both varyingly, on some days almost normal, on others a willed effort, extremely tiring. Meanwhile signals persisted in arriving from the abandoned provinces—a bit of the bureaucracy still pigheadedly trying to function, but to no purpose because without muscular control, Rachel's sense of her own body was haphazard. If, while her eyes were shut, something touched her hand, she would be aware of the touch, and that it came from her hand, but not which one, nor how it was disposed on the bed. When her lungs went, she would die. (A ventilator? What was the point?) So a few months more, at most.

But until then her mind was hers, untouchable, holy to her, *hagia sophia*. She was determined to die knowing what was happening to her, and aware and confident of the reality of anything in the field of her remaining perceptions.

This was a decision she had come to while she could still walk with two sticks, play bridge, set the shutter speeds on her cameras, be reasonably amusing company. She had made it on what turned out to be her last visit to her elder sister, then in a home. Tabby had not been felled by anything as specific as Rachel's illness, but, it seemed, by something in her own nature. She had kept a good deal of physical control—more, Rachel suspected, than she admitted, preferring to be helpless—but she had given in. That afternoon she had seemed delighted by her visitors at first, but within ten minutes had returned to her TV, switching channels every few minutes but seeming to regard all she saw—soaps, advertisements, news bulletins, horse races—as a single series of events in which she herself was taking part, and all of it somehow continuous with the dream from which they had woken her when they arrived.

"She can't be bothered to distinguish," Rachel had said as Flora drove her home. She had heard the distress and disgust in her own voice. Different though they were, Tabby had always mattered to her.

"Oh, Ma, why should she?" Flora had protested. "What's really happening to her is pretty bloody boring. She has much more fun making it up."

This was true, and very much Tabby's style. Make her live in a pigsty, Jocelyn had once said, and she'd show you proudly over it and tell you that the man who came to change her straw was a real sweetie. But Rachel had found such willing acceptance of mental death impossible to bear, and had, there and then, made her vow not to let it happen to her. Better the dreariness of endless real hours than any escape into fantasy. There was no honour in fantasy, no respect, no decency, none at all.

So now she chose one busy nest, watched a bird depart and counted the seconds until its return. Three hundred and seven. Call it five minutes. Had it been searching for the precise twig? Would it now locate it in a preselected position? Not this time. Several trials at different angles . . . but then, ah, back to a lot of pokings and thrashings and flappings which looked like mere frenzy, looked indeed certain to unsettle the whole structure.

The bird's partner, meanwhile, watched tolerantly from a nearby branch. One needed to stay by the nest the whole time, because if both left, neighbours would nip in and steal material.

The thrashings must have been purposeful, because when the bird desisted the partner hopped up, gave a perfunctory tweak to something, and then both birds cawed vigorously for a while before the nest-builder flew off.

As it did so the door opened and Dilys backed in, fuzzy already as she entered and no more than a talking cloud by the time she reached the bed.

"Here's our breakfast then, dearie. Nice scrambled eggs she's done us. That'll put roses in our cheeks. Still comfortable, are we?"

Code, answered by Rachel with a brief smile, also code, meaning no, she didn't believe her pad needed changing yet. It was probably damp already, but it would have to become really sopping before it began to discomfort her.

"There's a good girl," said Dilys, putting the tray down. "I'll just get the coffee going, shall I?"

She crossed the room and returned to a human shape. The sturdy blue pillar was her uniform, the silvery blob was the back of her head, and the white fuzz was her cap. Rachel listened with satisfaction to the sounds of her folding the filter and measuring grounds and water into the coffee maker. She came back, cranked the top section of the bed to a steeper angle, folded the duvet aside, slid her arms under Rachel's shoulders and thighs and effortlessly eased her into a half-sitting position, wedging her into place with bolsters and pillows. She handled the wasted and useless body with gentleness and dexterity, as if it had been fully sensate.

It had at first appalled, but now after two months merely amused Rachel that somebody so skilled in the essentials of her craft should be so inept in how she spoke of them—that awful "we" and the baby talk, and the coyness about physical functions. Dilys dealt with diarrhoea or a suppurating sore in the most matter-of-fact manner, but couldn't bring herself to name them. Jocelyn would have detested her for that, and manifested his dislike in exaggerated politeness. But already Rachel, though never given to instant friendships, liked her better than any of the other nurses who had cared for her in her helplessness. Nursing skills apart, there was not simply a human warmth about Dilys, there was a strong sense that she in her turn liked and respected the real person inside the stupid inert carcase, and thought of her not as the painful leftover of a life, but as a fully human citizen, with human rights and responsibilities and needs. She was supposed to have weekends off, when Pat, the retired midwife in the village, took over; but when on only her third weekend Pat had had the flu, Dilys had stayed on not just willingly but with something like eagerness. Rachel guessed she would rather be nursing.

"Open wide," she said. "There's a good girl. Not too hot for us? Sure?"

Dutifully Rachel masticated, swallowed and opened her mouth for more. The eggy pap was in fact tepid, fluffy with milk, undersalted and overcooked, everything that scrambled eggs ought not to be, but there was no point in complaining to Dilys. Dilys had no leverage in the kitchen. She was employed by the Trust, and her loyalty was to Rachel. Cooks were Flora's concern. This one was new, and would be busy establishing her own rights and territories. She might well react to any complaint from Dilys by sending up even worse meals.

Still, a fuss must be made. It wasn't just that taste was the only physical pleasure remaining, but the making of a successful fuss, the achieving of a result, would be good for morale, a foray from the citadel to prove that Mind could still accomplish something beyond those walls. The coffee maker had been such a victory, and so had the rejection of the microwave. Again, it wasn't only that it was not Dilys's job to prepare meals. It was that if they came up from the kitchen all ready for the microwave, though they would then at least be hot the machine would have no effect on texture or flavour. No, this cook must be made to provide real scrambled eggs.

Rachel ate as much as she could bear to, then a few fingers of toast and marmalade, the toast from a presliced loaf, a disgrace to the household, but the marmalade homemade by Dora Willmott-Wills and brought by her on her last visit. Finally, redeeming everything, hot, strong Java coffee with a little cream and sugar. Incense in the cathedral.

"Bliss," she whispered as Dilys lifted the cup clear.

"There was a shop in Bangor used to smell this way when you walked past," said Dilys, giving Rachel another sip. "Before the war it would've been of course. They had this machine in the window turning the beans over and over, roasting them. Don't know when I last saw one of those."

"How old?" said Rachel.

"Me? Nineteen thirty-three I was born, so I couldn't've been more than five or maybe six. Funny how clear you remember some things and others are all gone. I don't remember my dad at all from those days, not till he was back from the war and we'd got to look after him. I'd've been twelve or more by then, of course. He'd been a Jap POW, dad, and he was never right after. Mrs. Thomas was telling me it was the same with her dad, being a POW, I mean."

"Yes."

The subject had not come up before in their one-sided conversations. Rachel wouldn't herself have mentioned it, and most of Dilys's talk was discreet trivia about patients and families she had worked for.

"Looks like he came through it better than my dad," said Dilys. "Judging by the picture of him."

Rachel made a questioning murmur, misunderstood by Dilys.

"That one on the bureau, I'm talking about," she said. "You must've took it yourself. Show you, shall I?"

She went to the other end of the room, returned and slid Rachel's spectacles into place. The room unblurred. Dilys acquired a face, round, pallid, with soft brown eyes, a rather spread nose and a deep-dimpled chin. Rachel glanced at the photograph unnecessarily, so well did she know it. It had stood on her worktable or desk for almost fifty years.

It was a snapshot only, but as characteristic of Jocelyn as anything that she had ever persuaded him to pose for. Nineteen forty-eight, and the Rover almost new. He'd been adjusting the timing—no garage could tune a car to his satisfaction. She'd stalked him, called when she was set. He'd straightened and turned, allowing her to catch him before he'd realised what she was up to. She could read his expression perfectly—pride in his machine, confidence in what he'd been doing, mild irritation at the interruption—Jocelyn to the life. To the loved life.

"Big man," she whispered. "When he came back, seven stone ten."

"My dad too, he was a skeleton all right, and like I say he never got it back, not really. Looks like Colonel Matson did a bit better for himself."

"Yes," said Rachel, smiling inwardly as she took another sip of coffee. The phrase was so exactly right to describe what he had done.

"Yes, I'm a bit of a mess at the moment," he'd told her, when she'd failed to conceal her horror at the thing that tottered down onto the platform at Matlock and took her in its arms. "You must have got my letter. Told you I'd lost a bit of weight."

"Yes, but . . . oh my darling, what have they done to you?"

"Oh, I'm not so dusty, compared to some of the others. No point in going back into the hospital now that I'm home. I'll sort myself out sooner here, with you."

Rachel learnt later that he had discharged himself directly from the hospital ship, against doctors' orders and in defiance of military discipline.

There had actually been talk of a court-martial. But at Cambi Road reunions veteran after veteran, some of them still half-broken men, had taken her aside to tell her that they wouldn't have made it through, but for the Colonel. By those times he had his weight and strength back, using his own regime of rest and exercise (the rest, of course, much more of an effort of will for a man of his temperament than the exercise) and food from the garden.

"Tell Thwaite to plant a lot of spinach," he'd said.

"You hate spinach."

"Course I do. Filthy stuff, but I'll get it down somehow. And broccoli and cabbage and that kind of muck. Spring greens, whatever they are. I'll make a list."

"I'll need to stand over Mrs. Mears to stop her boiling them to shreds. She must have been trained as a laundrywoman and got into cooking by accident. I'll look in the library for books about growing vegetables."

"See what you can find. There was an M.O. in Singapore with his head screwed on about this sort of stuff. Interesting chap. Won't get anywhere in his trade, of course, with the self-satisfied clowns they've got running it. Don't worry, Ray, we'll do it between us."

He wasn't trying to cheer himself up, or her. He was stating a fact.

They would do it between them. And they had.

The men at the reunions seemed not to envy Jocelyn his return to fitness. One of them, still in his wheelchair, said as much to Rachel once.

"Good to see the Colonel looking so grand. I'd hate to see him stuck in one of these things."

For his part Jocelyn would have preferred to miss out on these meetings. The war was over, and he was in any case almost wholly uninterested in the past. He went, really, because the men wanted him there, but that was something he would have refused to acknowledge. He did it, he said, because he needed to talk to the men and check whether there was any way in which he could help them, write references, arrange job interviews, cajole, bully, plead, argue, on their behalf. "What's the point of having been to a bloody expensive school where they didn't teach you a thing worth knowing if you didn't pick up a bunch of friends in high places whose arms you can twist in a good cause?"

There was no way now that Rachel could explain any of this, so she simply smiled, accepting that Jocelyn had done well to regain his fitness, and sipped her coffee with relish. Before she had finished there was a knock on the door.

"Come in, Mrs. Thomas," Dilys called. "We're just finishing our breakfast."

She stood out of the way as Flora came bustling in, permed, pink cheeked, scarlet lipped, bright eyed.

"Morning, Ma," she said, bending for a peck at Rachel's cheek. She was wearing that boring scent again. Why bother, if you finish up smelling like last year's potpourri?

"How are you this morning, Ma? Sorry about the eggs. You'd have thought somebody who can manage a perfectly respectable *faisan normande* would have the right idea about scrambled eggs. Da would have dropped them out of the window. And thrown the toast after them. Dick's coming to lunch. He wants to talk to you."

Rachel reacted slowly, though she was well used to her daughter's sudden transitions of subject. No need for a foray about the eggs, then, she'd been thinking with some disappointment.

"Dick?" she whispered.

"That's right. It'll be nice for you to see him, won't it? He says he's been busy. Now, don't be naughty, Ma—Devon is a long way."

As far, in fact, as the detestable Helen could take him. But busy? Flapdoodle.

"What about?"

"He's got someone to see in York, apparently."

More flapdoodle, and judging by the "apparently" Flora thought so too. M5, M42, MI, AI—Matlock wasn't more than a few miles out of his way, but he wanted something all the same. Money, probably. How bad a mess was he in this time?

"All right," she whispered.

2

"Hi, Ma. You're not looking so dusty."

He bent and kissed her with a passable imitation of affection. She smiled. He had of course come in without knocking, but nothing demeaning had been going on. She'd had her elevenses early, and then Dilys had cleaned her up and done her hair and makeup with cheerful enjoyment, taking pride in her patient's appearance, much like that of a breeder preparing a favourite pony for a show. She had slipped out as soon as the visitor was in the room.

"Specs," whispered Rachel. "On the table."

He shoved them into place and she looked at her son with all the old muddle of feelings. It was extremely tiresome, she thought yet again, how when almost everything else was gone the emotions still raged on—worse, perhaps, now that there was no input from the limbs to distract them with trivia. All Rachel's rational self despised her son, but the rest of her, that other self beyond reason, persisted in adoring ... adoring what? There had been a child, yes, but ... Surely, surely, surely, somewhere inside the middle-aged boor by her bed ...

Why did he have to look, speak, laugh, carry himself so like his father when any stranger, suppose one could have met both men at the same age, would have seen at once that Jocelyn was honest timber and Dick was plastic trash? It was detestable. Dick would be sixty next year. He exercised himself at best casually, smoked, drank too much, ate with a boy's greed, but he hadn't run to fat. He hadn't drilled or born arms since the JTC, but he stood and moved like a soldier. Look closely and you saw that the pinkness of the skin wasn't the flush of health. Look into the blue eyes ...

Jocelyn had glanced up from his book, keeping his place with his thumb, and said quietly, "I think we'd better face it. Dick's no good."

This had been apropos of nothing. Four days earlier Dick had driven back to Cirencester for his last term at the agricultural college. They had barely mentioned him since. Rachel was at her worktable, masking negatives for enlargement.

"Oh, dear. I can't help hoping. But . . ."

"Maybe if I'd been home during the war . . ."

"No. It was always there. He was a lovely little boy, but in some of the photographs . . . You couldn't be expected to see it at the time, but you can now. Do you want me to show you?"

"No point. I'm sorry, Ray. It's worse for you."

"Don't let's talk about it."

"Anyway, we have to do the best for him we can. Maybe he'll find a woman who'll make something of him."

"Let's hope," Rachel had said.

She'd had her wish, but in the manner of some moralising fairy tale, in which the princess gets all the gifts her parents asked for, but which then turn out to be the last thing they wanted. For all her many-faceted dislikability Helen had had both the wit and will to make something of Dick, kept him out of both gaol and bankruptcy, organised a life for him, seen to it that he had a job, and held on to it, made not merely something but perhaps the most that could be made out of such material.

Yet, despite such knowledge, even now as she gazed up at him Rachel remembered an eight-year-old wolfing the lardy cake she had found for him in Matlock. Lardy cake had been as good as unobtainable in wartime. He hadn't remembered to say thank you, hadn't understood the achievement, but her body had brimmed with satisfied love at the sight of his pleasure. So now. Though the visit was sure to be uncomfortable and might well be painful, as she looked at him her main emotion was happiness that he had, for whatever reason, come back to her.

"Well, what have you been up to?" she whispered, making the effort to talk in full sentences, as if for a stranger.

He grinned.

"Sweating and suffering, if you want to know," he said. "This stupid beef scare's still playing havoc with the business. Farmers haven't got any money to pay for the stuff, and haven't got any cows to feed it to supposing they had. Not to mention they're pointing the finger at us for starting it. Of course we were cutting the odd corner, but who wasn't? Anyway the rug's been pulled from under us with a vengeance, and unless something happens PDQ to turn the ship round we're all going down the tube. No fun at all."

"So you're going to York?"

"Just scratching around. Not much chance of it coming to anything, but it's better than sitting on my backside waiting for the roof to fall in."

"How are the children?"

"Little monsters. Belinda's got another on the way. She's due to pop next month. Helen must've put all that in our Christmas card, didn't she?"

No shame, none at all. In most years the only communication Rachel received from her son was the annual news roundup that Helen composed on her PC and sent out with the Christmas cards, often signing the card on Dick's behalf. Not that Helen would have allowed any greater contact, but suppose Dick had married a wife who felt drawn to the family rather than repelled by it, he would still have let her do all the work.

Now, though, came a small surprise.

"I've brought you some photos, Ma. Toby's a camera nut, like you, and he sent us a sheaf of the things from last time they were down. Want to see?"

"Please."

Toby was an affable, dull planning official, married to Dick's other daughter, Harriet. (Charley, Belinda's husband, was a Devonshire GP.) Dick shifted his chair to lean over the bed and show her the photographs, mumbling names as he went. Rachel could hear that the process irritated him but that he was trying for as yet undisclosed purposes to please her, presumably to put into her mind that she had these descendants to whom she still owed duties. She barely listened, concentrating on the images.

Winter scenes. Michelin tots—woolly hats and snow suits—poking sticks into bonfires, confronting one of Helen's Shetlands at a fence . . .

"Wait. Back one. Who . . . ?"

"That's Stan again. He's supposed to take after me."

"Yes."

The pang was appalling. Rachel gazed at the small figure absorbed in stamping an icy puddle into splinters. She had a photograph—black and white, of course—of Dick at that age, wearing the then standard tweed coat, leggings and furry cap, but standing in the identical pose to study something on the ground before him. This was the self-same child. Suppose in the winter of 1905 someone had captured the image yet again, Jocelyn aged two and a half, wrapped against the cold, absorbed in some fragment of the universe that lay at his feet . . . Ah, which way would this child go?

"Very, very like," she whispered.

"He's a grand little wretch too," said Dick. "Look, that's him again."

But this picture was not of her lost son, only of a rather similar infant. That was part of the treachery of the frozen image. By insisting on the pure truth of the isolated instant it denied the shift and dither of reality. Jocelyn, anchored in his certainties, could never accept this.

"Why must you take such a lot of the things?" he would grumble. "Can't you make sure you've got what you want before you press the button?"

(It wasn't the cost he grudged, or the loss of her time, but the sense of sheer waste, waste for waste's sake.)

"It isn't like that, darling. I can take two pictures of something—a boulder or a tree trunk—one after the other, with the same settings and everything, but they'll never be quite the same, not when you know how to look."

"It's the same rock, isn't it? And anyway we aren't just talking about a couple of pictures. You take a spool of film and rough-print it—how much of it do you bother to print up? One picture in eight? Ten?"

"Something like that."

"And how many of those do you put in an album? Same again, and that's a generous estimate. They're all just as real as each other, Ray, but only about one in eighty of them makes it into your version of reality."

"You're shifting the argument, darling. And anyway the film's all there in the attic. If I wanted I could go back and make an album of every picture I took of you on Dinah at Meerut."

He had laughed at the memory, but for his next birthday she had in secret got out the old film, stored in acid-free paper, labelled and put away on their return to England almost twenty years earlier. She had needed to contact the celluloid onto fresh film, but from those negatives had printed up forty-three reasonable shots of Jocelyn on his favourite pony during that marvellous fortnight when the regiment had so very nearly won the All-India, and night after night they had danced till the stars faded, and he had proposed to her loping beside her window as her train steamed out. It had been the second best present she had ever given him.

Dick started to put the photographs away.

"May I keep the one of Stan?" she whispered.

"Sure you can. This one?"

"No. Breaking the ice."

"Right, here you are then. I thought you might get a kick out of them."

There was a smugness in his tone, as if he had conferred a major benefit on her and could now expect her to reciprocate. She postponed the moment.

"How is Helen?"

"Firing on all cylinders, including some she'd never told me about. God, what a woman for a crisis! She's found herself a job, dogsbody in a locum agency, but they'd better watch out. Six months and she'll be running the show."

"You've lost your job?"

"Sharp as ever, Ma! But no, I'm still hanging on, though I can see which way the wind's blowing. It's always been a family firm, and I'm the only senior bod left who isn't one of the clan. If they've got to choose between me and some useless little twerp who married the boss's niece, you know darn well who it's going to be."

"Diffcult. I'm sorry."

"Don't worry, Ma. Something will turn up. It's just a matter of having enough irons in the fire and tiding things over meanwhile. By the way talking of irons, do you know where Da's pistols are? The Laduries?"

The suddenness of it was like a physical blow. Dick didn't seem to notice the pause. Perhaps, since she always needed to summon the resources for speech, it hadn't been markedly longer than usual.

"In the bank, I think. Why?"

"They're really mine, you know. He left them to me in his will."

"He changed it."

"Yes, but that was after his stroke, when he was a bit gaga, poor old boy. I bet I could have contested it at the time, but it wouldn't have been worth the rumpus."

It was astounding that he didn't perceive her fury. Surely her eyes at least must blaze, blaze shockingly. The downright falsehood, compounded by the perfunctory sympathy. If she could have moved a muscle she would have struck him. As it was, her anger supplied the energies for a longer answer.

"His first stroke. The same time he set up the trusts. Was he gaga then, Dick?"

"That was old Bickner. He did a pretty good job on the trusts, and I'm very grateful."

"Jocelyn told Bickner exactly what he wanted."

"Well, that's as may be, but—"

She could stand no more and cut him short.

"What about the Laduries? Why?"

He shrugged, glanced out of the window, then back at her, smiling, confident in the cloak of candour. It didn't fit.

"Funny coincidence," he said. "Here I was, coming to see you anyway . . . Do you ever watch a thing on the box called *The Antiques Roadshow*, Ma?"

"Sometimes."

"Helen makes a point of it, so I do too if I'm around. Last Sunday . . . You know how it goes. They have these experts, and they set up shop in the town hall somewhere, like Salisbury, and people bring their heirlooms in to ask about—pictures, furniture, knickknacks, whatever, and then some old biddy who's had a Rembrandt hanging in the loo all these years pretty well has a heart attack when they tell her what it's worth. Right? Well, this time one of the pros was doing arms and armour, and some young woman—never seen her in my life before—showed up with a pistol, just the one of them, but I knew it was one of the Laduries the moment I clapped eyes on it. It had the initials even, J.M. 'Hey! That's one of Da's,' I told Helen. And the fellow who looked at it really knew his stuff. He spotted it for a Ladurie at once, and got very excited. Said it ought to be in a museum, and all that, and it must be one of a pair, and if the woman had had the other one and the box and all the fittings it would've been worth getting on fifty thousand quid—more, if it had belonged to someone famous, which it easily might have, judging by the workmanship. He even got it right that it could've been made for one of Napoleon's marshals. The trouble was she'd only got just the one, and it hadn't been properly cleaned last time it was fired, which knocked the value down a bit, but even as it stood he said it might fetch a couple of thousand. Are you listening, Ma? Do you understand what I'm telling you?"

Rachel had closed her eyes, rather than gaze any longer into the countenance of Greed. Lardy cake, she thought. I might have guessed, even then.

"Yes," she whispered. "Go on."

"There isn't anything more. That's it. The question is, How's this woman got hold of one of my pistols? And where's the other one, and the box and stuff?"

"Not yours."

"Ours, then. When did you last see them? Where are they now? In the bank you said."

"Don't know. I'm tired. Can't think."

"But listen, Ma . . ."

"Sorry, darling. Tell Dilys . . . nurse . . . need her."

He drew breath to persist, but then gave in.

"Oh, all right. I'm sorry, Ma, if I've upset you, but I've got to be on my way in any case. I'll have a word with Flora about it. She's got power of attorney, hasn't she? See you soon."

He squeezed her hand—she could feel the touch but not the compression—and kissed her on the forehead, but didn't think to remove her spectacles. Her fury was now mingled with shame as she listened to his footsteps crossing the room. The door opened. She heard both voices from the corridor, footsteps returning, a murmur from Dick and a thank-you from Dilys, the door closing behind her as she crossed to the bed.

Good heavens, Rachel thought, Helen's been teaching him manners. The notion was bitter.

"How are we then, dearie? Mustn't wear ourselves out, chatting away, must we! Done with our specs, then?"

"No, leave them. Lock the door, please. Need you."

"Now what's this about?" said Dilys, coming back and feeling Rachel's pulse. "So we've got ourselves excited, haven't we? Tsk, tsk."

"Do something for me. Important."

"Well, well, well, aren't we being mysterious? Out with it, then."

"Don't tell anyone, Dilys. Not Flora. Nobody."

"Cross my heart. It's all right, dearie, it's just my manner of talking. I can see you're dead serious, and I shan't let you down. There's secrets I've heard over the years from patients of mine—not like you, dearie, because maybe they'd lost their grip a bit and you're all there and no mistake—but anything they told me like that, it'll go with me to my grave. It wouldn't be right any other way, would it?"

She spoke earnestly, with pride in her professional reticence—nothing that she'd ever taken an oath to, but she was a confidential nurse, and for her the word meant what it said.

"Thank you," said Rachel. "Bottom drawer of bureau. Take everything out. Pull drawer right out."

"Got you. My, isn't this exciting!"

Dilys bustled off. Rachel listened to the slither of the drawer, and the movement of packages. While she waited she thought about the trusts, one for the as yet unborn children of each child. Jocelyn had begun to set them up a fortnight after his first stroke, when he could still barely make himself understood, and then only to her—just as she had at first been the only person who believed that Jocelyn himself was still there, locked inside the mumbling wreck in the wheelchair, all his intelligence, all his pride, all his immense willpower. Mr. Bickner had come and sat with them in the study, stiff and uncertain. Jocelyn had mumbled, she had interpreted, Bickner had answered pityingly, patronizingly, speaking to her, not Jocelyn, until she had been forced to interrupt him in mid-sentence.

"Stop. This won't do. You must talk to my husband, not me. Look him in the eye—it's what he expects you to do. He understands every word you're saying, better than I do, in fact. And listen to him. You can hear what he's saying, if you really try. Think of it like a very bad line on a telephone, but you've got this important message coming and you've just got to catch it, somehow. Please. You've been a very good friend to us over the years, so do please try. Now, darling, just a few words at a time, so I can help Mr. Bickner understand what you're telling him."

And stuffy, unimaginative old Bickner had genuinely tried, and by his third visit was making something of it and answering Jocelyn direct, without waiting for Rachel to interpret. That had been wonderful for Jocelyn, just knowing that there was someone other than his wife and one daughter who was prepared to make the effort to reach him . . . Dick couldn't be bothered, and Anne, alas, had stayed away, furious and frightened . . . only Flora . . . Did she ever think how unfair it had all been? Anne always Jocelyn's darling, Dick Rachel's, but Flora, decent, impulsive, conscientious Flora, simply taken for granted, given her due of parental concern and affection, but never that extra element of passionate love?

There was a rap and creak as the drawer was pulled free. Dilys came back.

"That's all done, dearie, but there's nothing I can see in behind."

"Put a lamp on the floor. Knothole at back on left. Put your finger in. Push left, till it clicks. Pull panel out. Package behind. Bring it."

"Oh, a secret compartment, like in a Victoria Holt! I knew it had to be."

Almost exhausted now, Rachel lay and waited, willing fresh energies to secrete themselves. She watched the rooks without attention, just letting them come and go . . . The panel clicked. Dilys gave a tweet of excitement. There was a scrabble as she eased the package free. It had barely fitted when Rachel had wedged it in against the back panel of the bureau . . . and then Dilys was by the bed again, her eyes bright, her mouth slightly open. She showed Rachel a large buff envelope with a flat rectangular shape inside it.

"Well done," Rachel whispered. "Box inside. Undo catches. Tilt it so I can see. Then open it. Please don't look. Sorry."

"That's all right, dearie. A secret's a secret only till you've told it, I always say. I promise you I'm not bothered."

Dilys followed her instructions to the letter. While she studied the catches Rachel looked at the box. It was just as she remembered, about nine inches by eighteen, polished rosewood with a silver coat of arms let into the top.

"Ready," said Dilys, sliding brass hooks free. "You don't think anything's going to fall out?

"All in its own little beds."

"Right, here we go then."

Dilys tilted the box into position, crooking it on one forearm, ostentatiously closed her eyes, and opened the lid with her other hand.

Rachel had not seen the contents for almost forty years, since the night when the young man came, but she remembered exactly how it had looked. The purple baize lining, indented with shaped slots and pockets. All but one still held the specific item for which it had been made. The two cleaning rods, brush and plunger, spanner, screwdriver, keys, oil phial, cap-flask, mold, cartridges, slugs and a single pistol, its dark metal lightly chased, its ebony butt inlaid with the two silver initials—expensive, beautiful in its precision and its dormant power, a tool to use. The other pistol was missing. The wrong one.

Perhaps her eyes were failing her.

"Closer."

Dilys obeyed.

No, there was no mistake. To the casual eye the pistols had seemed identical, but trying them in his hand Jocelyn had decided that one was lighter than the other, and weighing them on his postal scales had found this to be the case, though the difference was barely half an ounce. The discrepancy was evidently deliberate. Concealed in the chasing below the firing hammer, unnoticeable unless you were searching for it, was a single letter, a D for the heavier weapon and an S for the lighter one. Ladurie had been a Swiss, working in Paris. *Droit. Sinistre.* The lighter gun was intended for the left hand. It had been natural for Rachel to use it when she and Jocelyn had been doing target practice together.

She had been expecting one gun to be missing, since the mysterious woman had apparently shown up with one on *The Antiques Roadshow.* But it was the wrong gun.

Not hers. His.

"Thank you," she whispered. "You can put it back."

Dutifully Dilys kept her eyes closed until she had the box shut and fastened. She slid it back into the envelope and carried it out of sight. Rachel listened to the rasp of it being wedged back into its hiding place, the rattle and click of the panel being fitted in, then the deeper rattle and slither of the drawer. Before Dilys had finished replacing the contents there was a knock at the door.

She hurried across, unlocked it and opened it.

"Not a good moment?" came Flora's voice.

"We're just making ourselves comfortable, Mrs. Thomas. We'll be three or four minutes yet."

(To Rachel's ears Dilys sounded wholly unconspiratorial.)

"I'll be back in ten minutes then, if you think she's up to it."

"I don't know. She was a wee bit tired after Mr. Matson."

"All right. Give me a buzz. I'll be in the morning room."

Dilys closed and locked the door and returned to the bureau. When she'd finished she came back to the bed.

"All done," she said. "Now, up to seeing Mrs. Thomas, are we?"

"Yes. Want to talk to her. Tell her half an hour."

"And we'll have a bit of a rest so we're ready for her? That's the ticket. Off with our specs, then, and a little drinkie before I settle you down? There's a good girl."

Rachel smiled assent and sipped at the barley water. Slop, of course, nothing like Mrs. Moffet used to make, but welcome still. Then she lay with closed eyes and tried to think about the missing pistol. It must have been missing when she had first hidden the box.

She would have been too distressed to notice the difference in weight. If it had been hers that was gone, that might have made sense. But Jocelyn's, and badly cleaned after its last firing . . .

Her mind refused to grapple to the task. From the corridor came the sound of Dilys's voice, speaking to Flora on the in-house system. Half an hour . . . The pistols . . .

October 1949, a fortnight before Jocelyn's birthday. She already had his presents, a pullover knitted by Jennie Walters, a book about British India, a slashing tool for nettles, a card of trout flies. Though they were wealthy enough by most people's standards, they didn't go in for expensive gifts and she wasn't looking for anything else. Petrol was still rationed, so she had come by bus to Nottingham for her dental appointment and now had over an hour to spend before she could return. There was a street near the bus station that contained not one but three junk shops, and on such occasions she used to go along there and poke around. Two years earlier she had found a Victorian half-plate camera, battered but complete. It was now restored, and she used it with great satisfaction.

Two of the shops made little claim to sell anything but junk, but the third had pretensions to the antiques trade. Indeed, its proprietor, a Mr. O'Fierley, dapper, elderly, chirpy, appeared to know a good deal about porcelain, in particular the simpering figurines that many people liked to keep in display cabinets. His main trade was in these, and his shop—dark, cluttered, smelling of dust and leather—was a sort of by-product, stocked with odd items which he had happened to pick up, mainly, Rachel guessed, to conceal his real interest from other, more ignorant dealers. The box had been under a pile of books beside his desk. Rachel had asked to see it.

"Well now . . ." he had begun, doubtfully, and then with a twitter of amusement in his voice. "Care to guess what's in it?"

"I was hoping it might be lenses."

"Oh no. Oh no."

"Not just fish knives, anyway, or you wouldn't . . . I give up."

He had opened the box with a flourish. The moment Rachel had seen the pistols she had known that she had to have them.

"Why! Those are my husband's initials!"

"You don't say. They're duelling pistols, but it's not my field. An unpleasant custom, really."

"Are they for sale? How much do you want for them?"

"Well now. As I say, it's not my field. In fact I'd put them aside to show to someone, but . . . My guess is that they're rather good. What would you say to four hundred pounds?"

"Oh dear. I'll have to think."

"Would three hundred and seventy-five assist in your cogitation?"

"That's very kind. Oh, I don't know . . ."

"Shall I put them aside for you, then?"

"Oh, yes, please! Look, I'll be in Nottingham next week, and . . . Oh, I'll give you my telephone number, just in case somebody else comes in."

"There's no need. The gods send signals to us, you know. They don't bother to tell us what they mean, but it's unwise to ignore them. These are meant for you, my dear."

He was teasing, of course, and Rachel laughed as she thanked him and left. But already on the bus home, with her face still tingling with the after-effects of the anaesthetic, she had known that she would have bought the pistols if he had asked her double what he'd suggested. It wasn't simply that she knew Jocelyn would enjoy them. He had various shotguns and sporting rifles, which on winter evenings he would sometimes fetch out and clean, not because they needed it, but for the pleasure of handling them, of deriving—though he would never have thought of it in such a way—aesthetic delight from the caress of their functional craftsmanship. But for Rachel there was more to it than that. Mr. O'Fierley had been right—the gift was meant. Suppose Jocelyn had been the woman and she the man, and suppose the woman had been forced to spend several years away, enduring hideous privations and sufferings and had then come home to him with her health and strength gone forever, but by her own willpower (and with a little help from the man) had made herself sound and whole, as Jocelyn had, then the time would now be ripe for him to give her some special token in celebration, a ring, a bracelet, a necklace, to be a seal of their love and a sign that all was well with them. Almost unconsciously she had been hoping to find or think of some such object—a new fishing rod, perhaps—but no amount of deliberate searching would have produced anything as exactly right as the pistols.

Jocelyn had undone the wrappings and looked at the box with puzzled interest. He had opened it and stared. She had never before seen him speechless with pleasure—could not have imagined that such a thing was possible. Even now, as she lay waiting for Flora's return, her arid tear ducts attempted to water at the memory. All day, in any vacant few moments, he had the box out and was playing with one of the pistols, loading and unloading it, aiming, feeling the balance in his hand. He carried the box up to bed as if he intended to sleep with it under his pillows, like a child, but he merely put it on his bedside table.

Next week, going up to London for one of his committees, he left early. That evening at supper he said, "Do you mind telling me what you paid for those guns?"

"I don't think I'd better. It was rather a lot."

"Four figures?"

"Goodness me, no!"

"Then you've done well. You remember Gerald Mackie, used to be a beak at Eton? I got to know him because in my day he helped coach the Eleven. He left after the war and got himself a job at Christie's— He'd always been interested in china and stuff, and they were glad to have him."

"Didn't you introduce me to him on Fourth of June? He had a Hitler moustache."

"That's right. He's still got it. Had it before anyone took any notice of Adolf, he used to say, and he was going to hang on to it. Anyway, he couldn't help me himself about the pistols, but he put me onto a chap in Ebury Street who deals in that sort of thing. I looked in this morning, before the committee. Wonderful shop. I could have spent a week there poking around. The fellow who runs it, Grisholm's his name, is a rum little gnome with a club foot, but he obviously knows his stuff, and he got really excited about your pistols. They

were made by a fellow called Ladurie—he was a Swiss, but he worked
in Paris and Grisholm said he'd only once had another pair through
his hands, nothing like as good as yours—it was just the guns, without the box or the trimmings—and they'd been knocked around a bit,
and they were Ladurie's ordinary stock-in-trade, whereas yours are obviously custom built for somebody pretty swell . . . Like to guess what
Grisholm says he sold his for?"

"I don't know. A hundred pounds?"

"Three fifty."

"Oh my goodness."

"The thing about Ladurie, Grisholm says, is that he was the first
person to make a truly modern pistol. Most of the elements were
around already, but he put them together, rifling, cap, powder cartridge, breech loading, firing pin—the only thing still to come was
getting the slug and cap and powder all together into a single round.
There were a couple of other fellows trying to do much the same
thing, Frenchmen too, in the early eighteen hundreds, with the
Napoleonic Wars in full swing, and they were all trying to interest the
French army in taking their guns up. Ladurie's were the best, but he
didn't get anywhere with them. His problem was that his craftsmanship was just too damn good. You can see that, can't you—see it the
moment you open the box. You'd need a workshop full of Laduries if
you were ever going to turn out more than a handful of guns as good
as what he made himself. So that's why there aren't that many around,
and Grisholm's never heard of anything this quality. Ladurie would
have tested them in the workshop, but Grisholm says it looks as if
they've never been fired since. Black powder's desperately corrosive, of
course, so you can usually tell unless they've been cleaned at once by
someone who knows exactly what he's doing."

"Does that mean you can't use them? I hope not. I thought we
might be able to get some fresh ammunition made, somehow. Those
won't still fire, will they, after—what is it?—a hundred and fifty
years?"

"Getting on that. I don't know. When we were in Bangalore—'38,
wasn't it?—the Quartermaster came up with some ammo which had
been around since before the first war, and we tried it out. There were

just two duds in a hundred rounds. That was thirty years old, of course, but a craftsman like Ladurie . . . at a guess I'd say about one in five of the caps might fire, and the cartridges look sound and dry. But if the set's a museum piece, which Grisholm says it is, they're all part of it. No, I'll ask Purdey's. There's bound to be someone there who can tell me how to get fresh ammo made, and how to clean the guns right, and all that, and then we'll have some fun together . . . What's the matter, Ray? Don't you . . . ?"

"No, I'd love to try, darling. It isn't that. To tell you the truth I'm worried about Mr. O'Fierley. I feel as if I've swindled him out of several hundred pounds."

"Oh, I don't think so. You take the rough with the smooth in his line of business. He'll have made what he regards as a decent profit already."

"Yes, I know, but . . . I mean, they're so perfectly right, I don't want anything spoiling it. Did I tell you, Mr. O'Fierley said they were meant for us?"

"That's poppycock. Look, next time you're in Nottingham, why don't you look in and tell him about it, and see what he says? It was a fair sale, so if he tries to be greedy you can just offer him a couple of hundred more and leave it at that, but if he's decent about it then you can work it out between you."

"All right."

"And see if you can take a worthwhile picture of the coat of arms, and I'll send it to Joe Popplewell at the College of Heralds."

"It'll be French, won't it?"

"Yes, of course, but he should be able to look it up."

The answer came back before Rachel next had reason to visit Nottingham. The arms were those of Joachim Murat, Marshal of the first Empire, later King of Naples. Ladurie had presumably made them as a presentation gift, in the hope of persuading this influential soldier to take an interest in his weapons. Jocelyn telephoned Mr. Grisholm, who told him that such a provenance perhaps doubled the already considerable value of the pistols, but Jocelyn, typically, was far less impressed by this than their having belonged to a brave and successful soldier.

*   *   *

Mr. O'Fierley's eyes had barely widened at the news.

"I'd been wondering," he said. "When you've been in the trade as long as I have . . . well, well, well. But you've no need to worry, Mrs. Matson. A sale's a sale, and I've been in the other ends of deals like this often enough in my time. If I had to go back now and make it up to all the people who've sold me stuff when I knew what it was worth and they didn't, I'd be bankrupt ten times over. No, I'm delighted for you, and I haven't made a loss on them—quite the contrary."

"I thought you might say that," said Rachel, "but I know I don't want to leave it like that, so I've brought you these. I've no idea what they're worth, if anything, but they've been sitting in the back of a cupboard since an aunt of mine died, and you might as well have them."

While she was talking she took the cardboard box out of her bag and unwrapped the little china figures, a man and a woman, idealised peasants, far too elaborately dressed for real work, he with a sickle and she with a hay rake. Mr. O'Fierley looked them over with great care.

"Well, well, well," he said again. "The boot is now perhaps on the other foot. These are rather nice, you know. Chelsea, red anchor period, 1753 or so, pretty good condition—there's a tiny chip here, and a flaw here, do you see? Unusual, too . . . Care to know what I'd offer you for these if you brought them in off the street?"

"No, and please don't tell me. If they're worth something then I'm delighted, because I won't have it on my conscience not paying you enough for the pistols. And the same with you about these, I hope. Is that all right?"

"Indeed it is, Mrs. Matson. I believe this is what the economists call the Ideal Transaction. Both parties believe themselves to have done well out of it. *O si sic omnia.*"

"Well, that's all right, then. I'm so relieved."

So they had parted, and rather to her own surprise Rachel had found herself reluctant to return to Mr. O'Fierley's shop when she had spare time in Nottingham. The episode was over, sealed, and could now be put away. The pistols were Jocelyn's, unsullied by any sense of debt. She was still thinking about this when Flora knocked.

"It's all right now, Mrs. Thomas," Dilys called.

Flora, as usual, was speaking before she was through the door.

". . . don't need to lock me out, Dilys. I always knock, and I don't mind waiting." ·

"Oh, it wasn't for you, Mrs. Thomas, but Mr. Matson didn't knock and I didn't know if he mightn't come back."

"Blast him, and I gather he wore Ma out too. You're sure she's up to this?"

"Well, we are a teeny bit tired, Mrs. Thomas, but she's insisting she's got to talk to you. So I'll be in my room if you need me."

"Thank you, Dilys."

"That woman's a jewel," said Flora as soon as the door closed. "You're sure you're not too tired?"

"Yes. Dick gone?"

"Forty minutes ago, in a foul temper. He wouldn't stay for lunch, which was a relief in the circs. We had a proper up and downer about Da's pistols. He said they belonged to him."

"No."

"That's what I kept telling him. He tried to make out that Da was past it when he changed his will, but I wasn't having any. He was completely all there, only he had a bit of trouble making himself understood. I was bloody furious with Dick. As far as I'm concerned, I don't care if he never sets foot in this house again."

"Tell you about TV?"

"Yes, and I don't think he was inventing it, though I wouldn't put it past him. Isn't it extraordinary? Did you have any idea the Laduries were worth that sort of money, Ma? I mean, I knew they were pretty special, belonging to old Murat and so on, but Da and you used to pop away with them on the terrace as if they'd been toys, of course Da was like that, it never bothered him what things cost or didn't. But don't you think we ought to look into this a bit? I mean, if some total stranger has somehow got hold of one of them. Dick says you told him they were in the bank, but I've just checked the list and they aren't. When did you last see them, Ma? I've been trying to think. I remember Da showing Jack how to use them—that'd have been when we were engaged—and then I remember after his first stroke thinking it might do him good to play with them, but they weren't on the table by his desk, where they used to be . . . Didn't you tell me you'd put them away?"

"Did I?"

"Or was that after he'd died?"

Rachel didn't respond, relying on Flora to rattle off in some other direction.

"And another thing—according to Dick the fellow on the box said the pistol he was looking at hadn't been cleaned right, and Da always made such a fuss about that. I must say it's all very baffling. I wonder if I couldn't get hold of a tape of the programme, I'll ask Biddy Paxton, her brother's something fruity in the BBC . . . All right, Ma, you're worn out and you need a rest. I'll push off. I just wanted you to know I'm not going to stand any nonsense from Dick, and I won't do anything without your say-so. There was just something you wanted me for, wasn't there?"

Rachel managed to smile. Her chief worry had been that Flora might try to appease Dick by conceding some kind of right over the pistols to him, but that obviously wasn't now in question. She should have known Flora would do the right thing. She almost always did, though because of her manner those who didn't know her very well tended to take her minor acts of virtue for a lifelong series of flukes. This was what made the coming deception oddly painful.

"Tape," Rachel whispered, as if that had been what was on her mind. "Good idea. But don't tell Biddy it's about pistol. Or anyone. Only Jack. Private. Family."

"Yes, of course, Ma. I know they were pretty special to you both, weren't they?"

"Thank you. No, wait . . . Just this. I want you to know you're very good to me, darling. Much, much better than I deserve."

"Nonsense, Ma, you're just tired. I'll send Dilys along, and then you must have a good rest after your lunch. It's *truite au beurre noir* for supper, and you'll want to enjoy that."

3

Rachel's midday meal was usually little more than a snack, and then Dilys would put some familiar novel onto the machine and she would lie for an hour or two and half listen to it and nap off for a while into dream and wake and half listen again. Henry James was particularly good to doze to, but Jane Austen too insistently soporific.

Today she was too tired to swallow more than a couple of mouthfuls, and then asked Dilys to close the curtains and leave her in silence, so that she could attempt real sleep.

She succeeded, but woke weeping, ravaged with sexual expectation suddenly cut short. The setting was already vague. A boat, rocking on warm waves. Nighttime. The tock of the lanyards against the mast. The man not Jocelyn, not even some particular stranger, just depersonalised man, hands, mouth, weight, member. But herself, her own body, real and solid, not young, no identifiable age, but with senses vivid and focused . . .

Her pad was sopping, of course. Her sheets might need changing.

Why now? It was the first time since—oh, long before she'd been nailed to this bed.

Within a few seconds the physical sensation, so intense in the dream, was mere memory, memory that thinned and became disgusting and absurd as it encountered the reality of her body. But she continued to weep, not now for the lost dream, but the lost years, the years after Jocelyn had come home.

They had both been virgins on their wedding night, but Jocelyn, unlike many of his apparent type, had not been straitjacketed by his culture and upbringing; she in fact had started off the more squeamish and apprehensive, thanks to her mother's embarrassed explications. But they had given each other confidence to explore the possibilities, discover what pleased them and then make the most of it.

This hadn't, in those days, been the kind of thing one talked about to even one's closest friends, but one evening, about two years married, they'd been dining with the Staddings, and she and Leila had left Jocelyn and Fish to their cigars to sit out on the verandah with the punkah swaying softly overhead, its slow draft heavy with the scent of a nearby lemon tree. Beneath the silk of her dress and petticoat her skin felt like sentient velvet. It was that kind of night, but she was in no hurry to get home. The small hours were often the best.

Now Leila decided that she wanted a chartreuse to bring her evening to full perfection, and demanded that Rachel should keep her company. Rachel had already been drinking with care, knowing her own needs and balances. When she refused Leila tried to insist.

"Honestly, no thanks, I've had enough."

"But you're pretty well stone cold sober. What's the matter with you?"

"If you must know, I'm feeling just right for when I get home with Jocelyn. If I drink any more, it'll take the edge off it."

"Oh," said Leila as if this had been something she couldn't have imagined. And then, after a pause, "Tell me more, Ray. I'm not being nosy. Please. It sounds as if we've been missing something."

It had been Rachel's turn to be surprised, though she was long used to the contrast between Leila's exotic looks and her straightforward inner self. But Fish? Rachel knew him far less well, but looks, style and everything else about him made it impossible for her to believe that he had not come to the bridal bed already an experienced lover.

"Please, Ray," Leila had said again, so Rachel had done her best to communicate the nature of her pleasure and the means of it, and Leila had thanked her, telling her later that some of what she'd said had been very useful. Strange, at the time, and in hindsight differently strange.

For the rest of their time in India her pleasure and Jocelyn's in each other had been barely interrupted by the birth of children and by the jerky slither of the nations into war, continuing through the scramble of departure, and his brief leaves from various camps and barracks right up until his eventual sailing for what had seemed the comparative safety of Singapore.

In the years of his absence Rachel had woken night after night aching with longing for him. Occasionally she had felt physically attracted by other men but had not for an instant thought, or even fantasised, about carrying it any further. She was wholly Jocelyn's. She felt that for her any other man would have been, literally, impossible.

Then he had returned, and she had once again slept curled in his arms, though it had been months before he had been well enough for anything beyond caresses. At this point, slowly, she had started to realise that she had not got all of him back. He could, and did, satisfy her physical need. He would initiate the performance and carry it through. But it was a performance. Not that he actively disliked what he was doing. He made the sounds and motions of enjoyment. But after a while she had to accept that what they had had before the war, what they had been so completely and passionately to each other, was now gone.

She had tried to tell herself that it was only natural, that they were older now, and such passion is the province of the young. Her own body gave her the lie. The loss was hers, but it was in him and it had nothing to do with age. It was the result of what had been done to him on the Cambi Road. For his sake, then, she learnt to suppress and control the need, telling herself that if this was the price she must pay for having him home she would pay it ungrudgingly, heavy though it was, because it was worth it, worth it a hundred times over.

She succeeded too. The ache came less often and when it did she was able to order it back to its lair. Sometimes they still made love, gently, without any fuss, like going for a walk together on a fine autumn morning. Thus all was fundamentally well and she loved him as deeply and strongly as ever, and was confident he did her. She had never in these years wept for her loss.

She did now, acid little droplets that were all the withered ducts could wring out beneath the wincing eyelids. They had not ceased when Dilys crept in to see if she'd woken.

"Awake at last? My, we've slept, haven't we? Why, what's up dearie? We've been crying."

"Nothing. Stupid dream. Pad needs changing. Sorry."

"Bound to after this time. Never mind, I'll have you comfortable in a couple of minutes. Let's just dry our poor face off first. Tsk, tsk, naughty girl, getting herself into such a state. Nice happy patients, that's what I like. There. That's better. Now let's see to you."

With her usual sturdy deftness she did what was necessary, chatting away as she worked, a kind of professional tact on her part, a way of making it seem that this was a pleasant social occasion, and the indignities to which she was subjecting her patient were subsidiary and irrelevant.

"Did I say, I got a letter from my niece yesterday? She's the one who married a Yank, took her out to live somewhere in the middle where there isn't much of anything except more of the same, and after a bit she couldn't stand it any longer so she walked out on him, which wasn't very nice of her, I'm afraid, but she always was headstrong. And then she went to live up in the top left corner—you can see the Pacific Ocean from her bathroom, she says—that's when you can see anything because mostly it rains and rains like Scotland, she says, but without the bagpipes, though there's a lot of wet sheep. Well I sent her a snap I'd taken of this house in the snow—just after I came, it was, if you remember, we had that snow—so she could see where I was living. But she didn't answer and she didn't answer and then, like I say, yesterday, I got this letter, fourteen whole pages on a typewriter, which is why I've only just finished reading it. I'm going to have to read it again, mind you, because it's a muddle to sort out what she's saying. She's always flying off at an angle and going on to something else, and then, no warning, you're back where you were before only you've forgotten where that was. Anyway, like I was telling you, I'd sent her this snap of the house and now she's wanting to know all about it, and how old it is, and everything. Victorian, I was going to tell her, and didn't Mrs. Thomas say it was Colonel Matson's grandfather that built it, him having done well out of his cotton mills, and with all these children to house, like families used to be those days—getting on a dozen, wasn't it? Poor women, you can't help thinking. I remember my mum telling me about some old aunt of hers who was a farmer's wife, and her saying how she always loved the springtime, when the evenings were longer and the fields greener and there was milk in the cows and the baby was born. Almost done, dearie. There now, that's better, isn't it?"

"Thank you. Albums."

"Out in the passage? Right you are. Which one? Look in the card index, shall I?"

"No. Different from others. Top left. Blue ring binder. Show me. Something I want to see."

"Righty-oh, I'll just get rid of this wet stuff and put a kettle on for our cup of tea, and then we'll settle down and have a good look."

The folder was one Anne had put together for a Social History project. She was in the Sixth at the time, so it would have been 1952—a good year, Flora in her first job, in a tiny flat just behind Harrods; Anne in her last school year, intelligent, pretty, already a little tending to detach herself from the family, but not yet into the desperate withdrawal that came later; Dick at Eton, and according to his tutor showing signs of pulling himself together.

"Would you like me to take a few photographs?" Rachel had suggested.

"That would be super, Ma. Only if you want to, you know? You don't have to go to town."

"Nonsense. It'll give me a chance to play with the half plate."

Not the least of Dilys's virtues was her enjoyment of looking at photograph albums. She slid the reading desk across the bed, laid the folder in place and opened it at the beginning.

"My, what a big picture! And doesn't it look handsome like that."

Yes, the clear summer light and the motionless subject had suited the half-plate very well. There, on the first spread, opposite a page of Anne's neat italic handwriting (still then showing the self-consciousness of a newly acquired skill) was the view of Forde Place from the main gate, with the monkey puzzle to the right and the stable block to the left. Almost nothing had changed since the afternoon when Rachel had first seen it.

Jocelyn had stopped the car at the top of the drive.

"Oh dear," she had said.

"I told you it was an eyesore," he'd answered, and driven her on down to meet his parents.

Anne's researchers had tended to confirm the family legend that old Eli Matson hadn't employed an architect, but had told his mill foreman to build him a house. The man, after all, was responsible for a couple of perfectly adequate mills. Certainly the house had that look. There was a vernacular style, still to be seen along these valleys: severe façades of brickwork, undecorated apart from a change of colour for the surrounds of the ranked, flat-arched windows; sweeps of narrow-eaved slate roof, soaring stacks; proportions, achieved by eye and instinct rather than theory, that were often strongly satisfying. When Rachel had realised how many demolitions were likely to come she had spent eighteen months systematically recording what still stood, and years later had given her collection to the local record office.

These virtues didn't tame easily to domesticity. Forde Place hadn't the look of a mill in miniature, but of one somehow compacted—drop it in water and it would then expand into a mill. Even the chimneys appeared to be lacking their upper sixty feet. The stables too—they should have housed bale-hoppers, not traps and horses. In the early years of her marriage Rachel couldn't have imagined that she could bear to live here. Now she could hardly remember having wanted to live anywhere else.

Dilys turned the page. Ah. Rachel had forgotten how beautiful. Almost pure abstract. The near-dead lighting of a cloudy noon. Course after course of dark unweatherable bricks, and the lower corner of a window. She and Jocelyn had once come round the corner of the house and found an old builder, there to repair one of the greenhouses, actually caressing a stretch of wall. At their footsteps he had looked up, unashamed. "Lovely work that," he'd said. "You wouldn't find a brickie to touch it, these days. Stand a thousand years, that will, and a thousand after."

Another page. The fire escape. Anne had told the story opposite, how Eli as a young man had worked in a factory that had been gutted by fire, and workers, some of them as young as eight, had died, trapped on the upper floors. All his mills had fire escapes, and so of course did his house, good solid cast iron, painted dark industrial green, zigzagging brazenly up the west facade to the nursery floor. Jocelyn's parents had buried it in Virginia creeper, whose autumn blaze clashed hideously with the purple bricks of the house, but this had got honey fungus and died during the war. On taking over the house Jocelyn had had the ironwork scraped down and repainted, and Rachel had realised that she actually liked the fire escape for the same reason that she had learnt to like the whole building, that it was, emphatically and uniquely, itself.

More pages. Views and details. The stable clock; the bell in its little turret; the boiler shed for the greenhouses. Not many interiors. The main staircase, of course, but few of the actual rooms, as they fitted in less well with Anne's thesis, being surprisingly light and lively, though often oddly proportioned. Jocelyn's parents, on moving in in the nineteen twenties, had redecorated in a nondescript but not unpleasing way; too late for arts and crafts, too early for art deco. Jocelyn, often radical in practical matters, was deeply conservative in his tastes. If a room needed to be done up, he didn't see that it needed to be done differently.

Tucked in at the end of the folder was a large plain envelope.

"More photos," said Dilys, peeking in. "Want to look, dearie? Here you are, then."

Spares. Other interiors. The greenhouses. The laundry. The fire escape again, looking dizzingly down from above. The old nursery— this very room. Last of all, Jocelyn at his desk in the study.

"You're supposed to be taking pictures of the house, aren't you? You don't want people in them."

"I need a focal point."

(Liar. She wanted a picture of him at his desk. It would be her fee for taking all this trouble for his Anne.)

"Oh, if you must."

"You're going to have to sit still when I tell you. It'll be a long exposure because I don't want to bring a lot of lights in. That's why the sitters in some of those old photographs look as if they'd been stuffed."

"I can look stuffed as well as any man I know."

And, of course, he'd stayed as still as a tree stump while she counted the thirty seconds. You could see every wisp of his sparse, sandy hair. His hand, poised above the letter he was writing, had not quivered. His head was bent into the soft glow of the lamp, the rest of his body in shadow. Glow and shadow patterned the room. She had waited till the evening, because this was the hour she had wished to celebrate. Though there were more obviously comfortable rooms in the house, this was where they always sat when alone, a habit begun in the feebleness and chill of his homecoming, because coal had still been rationed and the study was simpler to make snug than anywhere else. She had moved two easy chairs in, and a worktable large enough for her to spread her photographs on. The result was a clutter, but he hadn't once grumbled, even in jest, about her invasion of so male a sanctum. Though by his second winter Jocelyn had regained his robust indifference to temperature, and then fuel had become available and a modern oil-fired boiler had been installed, they had without any discussion stayed on here. As with so many things, they had grown to the shape of their discomforts, and would for a while have felt awkward anywhere else.

Still, it was a strange room to have chosen, a kind of left-over space, all its proportions dictated by whatever lay on the other side of its walls. The chunk out of the corner opposite the door was the back stairs, whose existence also meant that there was only one window, looking out onto the kitchen yard. The fireplace was off centre in the left-hand wall, because the position of the flue was dictated by the dining room fireplace beyond. The fireplace wasn't visible in the photograph, but part of the window was, and the intrusion of the back stairs.

Rachel gazed at the picture. It was exactly as she had remembered, unsurprisingly, as it had stood on her worktable from the day she developed it until the morning after Jocelyn's death, when she had taken it from its frame and put it back here. She had not then expected ever to want to look at it again. It was, in its way just as expressive of Jocelyn's nature as the one of him with the Rover, just as full of the instant, but at the same time seeming to throb faintly with the movement of the web of time around it, invisible threads linking instant to instant, the whole life, the whole memory of that life, right up to this instant now in which she was looking at the photograph after an interval of almost forty years.

It told her nothing that she did not already know. Half the box was clearly visible by the light of the desk lamp on the small table at Jocelyn's right elbow. The further half was in shadow.

"Thank you, Dilys," she whispered. "Copy it for your niece. Copier in office."

"Lovely," said Dilys. "I'm not that much of a writer, you see, and I feel stupid sending her just a page or two back, so it'll be just what I want. Now, I'll change our specs, shall I, and see what's on the telly? Oh, Thursday—it'll be that cooking programme you liked that last time."

"All right."

Dilys swung the bed to face the television, a large screen, mounted well up on the further wall, so that Rachel could watch it more easily. The cooking programme would do, anything would do that would distract her from thought and memory. She would have to face it sometime, sometime soon but not now, she was too tired, too disturbed . . .

It wasn't enough. As Dilys said, she usually enjoyed cooking programmes, despite the tendency of the presenters to thrust their personalities, always so much less pleasing than they seemed to imagine, at the viewer. Rachel herself had never been much of a cook—she had had no need—but she enjoyed watching the process, and the imagined taste seemed to help her to salivate, moistening her mouth for a while. But not today.

Deliberately she had buried patches of memory, though not in the manner she had read about, where the person in question is no longer superficially aware that some hideous event took place. She had always known, just as she had known where she had hidden the pistol box and put the picture of Jocelyn at his desk. At any time in the past forty years she could, if she had chosen, have related in outline most of what had happened on the night that the young man came, but she had never chosen, never intentionally recalled any part of it. Sometimes, unwilled, a fragment would insinuate itself, but as soon as she was aware of it she would push it away, muttering angrily to herself about something irrelevant, until she could force herself to concentrate on the here and now.

But today she lacked the willpower to do that. She would watch the programme for a little, lapse into a snatch of unwanted recall, drag herself clear, watch, and lapse again. Senility must be like this, she thought. Please God may my stupid body go first.

"We're still tired aren't we?" said Dilys as the programme ended. "We must really have overdone things today."

Rachel attempted a "yes" smile, but her lips seemed not to respond and her mouth was too dry for speech. Dilys leaned over the bed, all blur, but her voice revealed her anxiety.

"Worse than that, is it, dearie? Something's really bothering us. Tsk, tsk. But you'd tell Dilys, wouldn't you, if there's anything I can do."

Rachel felt something happen, an actual physical event taking place in the citadel of her mind, a mine sprung, a crack opening in a rampart. To her shame and anger she was weeping again, those strange dry tears, the squeezings from an almost juiceless citrus.

"Jocelyn's pistol," she heard her lips whisper. "She's got Jocelyn's pistol."

I

Jenny carried the portable phone round the house as she bustled to be ready to leave. The moment it beeped she pressed the button and said "Hi."

"Mrs. Pilcher?" said a man's voice—the wrong man.

"Sorry. I can't talk now. I've got a call coming. And if you're selling something, no thanks. Bye."

In a few seconds the handset beeped again. This time she answered more cautiously.

"Hello."

"Mrs. Pilcher. This is important—it's about your pistol—"

"It's not mine, and it's not for sale. Goodbye."

Brusquely she prodded the buttons. How the hell . . . ? They'd promised the thing was absolutely confidential, no addresses passed on, no telephone numbers, not even names. And he was bound to try again. Yes.

"Hello."

"That doesn't sound very welcoming."

"Oh, hi, darling, thank God it's you. I'm being persecuted by some dimwit. How's it going?"

"Dire. We thought we'd got the breakthrough last session, I told you? Now they've got back to Alma-Ata overnight and been told to try and squeeze us some more."

"I want them dead. How long is this going on?"

"You aren't going to like this. The Kazakhs came in all smiles this morning and announced that they're postponing the auction, so we've got a new deadline. Thursday."

"I can't stand it. I won't stand it. I'm coming over for the weekend. I'll get on the Chunnel tonight somehow . . ."

"Oh, God! I wish you could."

"Champs-Elysées, here I come."

"No use, darling. We've been here four days and I've barely set foot out of the hotel. I haven't been in a real restaurant, even. Billy loathes Paris . . ."

"He probably thinks the French don't take him seriously. He wouldn't like that."

"Right. We're only here because the Kazakhs wanted a go at the fleshpots, but if any of us isn't under his eye Billy decides we're hatching something up, so we all eat together in the hotel and then sit around in his suite all night pretending to go over the figures again . . ."

"You must get to bed sometimes."

"Three o'clock, this morning."

"I'll be waiting for you. In a terrific Paris nightie."

"Mmmmmh . . . I could chuck the job up, I suppose . . . I'm tempted . . ."

She could hear that he meant it, and it wasn't fair on him. Working for Billy Cochrane was already frustrating enough.

"All right," she said, "I'll let you off the hook. Next time you're taking a doctor's certificate with you and you can show it to bloody Billy and tell him that sexual frustration is bad for your mathematical abilities and it'll cost the company billions if you get your sums wrong."

"I'll try it if I get the chance. Look, what about next weekend? I could book us into a real hotel, not this plastic—"

"It's Barbara's wedding. Besides, it's you I want, not Paris. Got that? You."

"Mutual. Bloody hell . . ."

"Let's talk about something else."

"All right. What kind of a dimwit? Double glazing?"

"No, I'm afraid it was about Uncle Albert's pistol."

"I thought we'd got away with that. Some kind of dealer, I suppose. Didn't they tell you they kept everything confidential? How did he get hold of you?"

"I've no idea. He didn't sound like a dealer, somehow. If he calls again, I'll tell him to piss off. Don't worry. Provided Uncle Albert himself didn't see the programme. Anyway, don't let's waste time on that now. Are you all right? You don't sound—"

"I'm dog tired but still functioning. The breakouts are the worst. Billy keeps us at it trying to guess what the Kazakhs are up to, so we explore all the blind alleys only he can't see they're blind alleys until he's taken us down them . . ."

"Your problem is you're too damn quick."

"Maybe, but it's no use telling him in advance, because it makes it look as if I thought the lot of them were dead thick, but I've got to keep listening in case Billy swings on me suddenly and says 'How does that work out, Jeff?' and I've got thirty seconds flat to come up with the answer. How's things with you though?"

"I'm fine, apart from being miserable without you. But I've got piles of work to bring home because Trevor's had to go into hospital and Jerry's told me to go through his desk and sort out anything I can deal with—Trevor's always behind with everything, anyway—and that's on top of all my own stuff, so I haven't got time to mope. There's one of Trevor's files which is bothering me a bit. I'll tell you when I see you . . . and I'm on a crash diet so that I can really hog it with you when you get back. Duck and champagne?"

"Spot on."

"They're not going to change your deadline again?"

"Not without postponing the auction again, which . . . anyway, if they do, I'll tell Billy you're coming over for the weekend, and they're giving us time off together, and the company are paying your fare and hotel bill, or I'm chucking it in."

"You don't have to, honestly."

"Yes, I know, but I've just about had it with Billy. Anyway, I think it will work this time. He can't replace me that quick. It might be a blot on my copybook with the company, but Billy's riding for a fall in any case. It's more his fault than anyone else's that the deal's got screwed up the way it has, though given the chance he'll wriggle out of it."

"As far as I'm concerned Billy could shit for the universe. I've got to go now. Same time tomorrow. You're going back to bed, I hope?"

"For thirty-nine and a half minutes, I make it. Look after yourself, darling."

"You too."

She slammed her finger onto the off-button so hard that she broke the nail, and threw the handset onto the floor. Cursing at the top of her voice she flung the pillows across the room, ripped duvet and sheets from the bed—almost undisturbed after a night of sleeping single—swept Jeff's pile of computer mags off the bedside table and kicked them across the carpet, rushed into the bathroom, tipped the empty laundry basket on its side and lashed at it with her feet, and finally, satisfyingly, stood on it, scrunching it flat, and then jumped on it until the wickerwork was splinters. Though nothing like this had happened for years, she was well aware what was going on. The rage was semi-deliberate, a tantrum, Norma-stuff. ("Now, this isn't my sweet little Jenny. This is horrid Norma. I'm not interested in what Norma wants. She isn't my daughter.") Meanwhile Jenny herself—the Jenny people met and talked to and thought chilly and reserved—hovered aside, controlling the fit just enough to prevent any damage she would later regret. She had long disliked the laundry basket, enforced on Jeff by an earlier girlfriend.

Now, as Norma stood panting amid the wreckage, Jenny whispered in her mind.

"Better stop. I've got a client at nine-fifteen."

She took a deep breath, let it go with a whoosh and was Jenny again. For the moment her main superficial emotion was surprise. Why now? For years she had known how to control these angers, keep them rational, channel and focus the pressure onto a target—a jet, not an explosion. Why this sudden loosening? She stared at the wreckage of the laundry basket, sensing it to be an omen, but baffled how to read it.

Turning to the basin, she caught sight of herself in the mirror, a

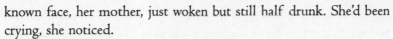

known face, her mother, just woken but still half drunk. She'd been crying, she noticed.

"You're disgusting," she told the image.

Furious again, but this time with her normal efficient Jenny-anger, she cleaned herself up and dressed in her grey suit, with pearl earrings and pin. No time for breakfast—she couldn't have swallowed it anyway. Her briefcase and laptop were ready in the hall. She slipped a banana into the case and left. After locking the door she paused and gave the inner pillar of the absurd little portico a pat, a pat for the whole house.

"It wasn't your fault," she told it, as if speaking to a pet dog, made anxious by a spat among the humans. "You're all right."

2

By dusk there was a chill drizzle slanting from the northeast, more like February than late March. The timer had turned the lights on, as if the house was doing its best to look welcoming, but this evening that wasn't enough.

Anyone coming new to the house would have noticed only—as Jenny herself had, first time—the Ashford Road roaring and stinking by, and then, once inside, would have been mainly impressed by the view across the Weald, with the roofs of oast houses poking above the treetops. One large defect, one medium asset, the little house a sort of null value in between. It had taken Jenny herself several weeks of living in it to appreciate the quirky personality to which she had spoken so affectionately that morning. The line of the road must have been changed after it was built, but before the terrace of basic nineteen-twentyish houses to its right, so that it stood at an obstinate slant both to them and to the bramble-tangled belt of scruffy woodland to its left. And it even more emphatically asserted its indifference to their respective regularity and wilderness because its builder had apparently been determined to cram all the stock ornamentation he could onto its frontage—a kind of flattened portico, with barley-sugar pillars; above that an iron balcony too narrow to stand on; at the southeast corner a squat spire with an elaborate lightning conductor, and, best of all, the pairs of cherubim on either side, apparently supporting the upper windowsills. They had sulky expressions as if the weight gave them headaches. (Jeff, of course, hadn't bought it for any of that. It had been what he could then afford, because of the road.)

This evening Jenny's affection wasn't enough. She couldn't summon up the personality. The house was dead, empty, because Jeff wouldn't be home for almost a week. She had spent most of the day on Trevor's leavings, and had brought her own work back to fill the dismal hours, but that would make them no less dismal. And worse, she would spend them thirsting for a drink. She and Jeff usually had a couple of glasses of wine each with their supper and she was now habituated to that, but she had long ago recognised in herself the risk of going the same way as her mother—it was in her genes, she thought—and had made and kept an inner promise that she would never drink alone. She would keep it still, tonight, and for the next five nights, but it would be hell.

Numbly she let herself in, switched off the alarm and went upstairs. The bedroom was a strewn chaos. She'd forgotten that she'd left it like that, but clearing it up was something to do. She changed into jeans, but had hardly started on the mess when the doorbell rang.

She went down, put the front door on the chain and opened it a crack.

"Mrs. Pilcher?"

She recognised the voice at once.

"Oh, it's you. You called this morning. I'm sorry, but I'm really not interested. The pistol doesn't belong to me, and I know the owner doesn't want to sell it."

"I'm not trying to buy it. Please. I just want to talk to the owners."

"I'm sorry. I've been asked not to talk to anyone about it. I should never have taken it to the show, but I didn't know."

"Please, if I could explain to you, then at least you could pass the message on. May I come in?"

"I don't let people I don't know in, especially at night. Sorry."

She started to close the door. He resisted.

"Stop. Please. You've got to talk to me. Thing is, I've got the other pistol. And the box and all the trimmings."

"You've got them with you?"

"They're in the bank. Listen, I'm absolutely with you about not letting strangers in if you're on your own. I've been waiting for you over at the pub. Suppose I went back there. Would you come and join me for a drink? Ten minutes only."

Oh, Jesus, a drink, and not alone! . . . Jenny merely pretended to hesitate.

"Oh, all right. Ten minutes. I've got work to do."

"That's OK. I'm truly grateful. What'll you have?"

"Draught stout, if they've got it."

(The wine would be dire, and spirits risky.)

"It'll be waiting for you."

She closed the door and ran upstairs to check that he was crossing the road and not lurking in ambush for her behind the forsythia. He was still on the near pavement, waiting for a gap in the traffic, a large man who carried himself well. He was wearing a Barbour and tweed cap. The look was horsey country gentry, easy for a con man to fake, if he was one.

She counterdressed, for the hell of it, keeping the jeans but changing into her "A woman needs a man like a fish needs a bicycle" sweatshirt and butterfly earrings, and left without hurrying, nearly ten minutes after he had.

She and Jeff weren't regular pub-goers, though there was a pleasant little one a couple of miles across the fields, along footpaths, to which they would sometimes walk out at weekends. The Frenchman across the road was not of that kind. Even out of season there was often a coach or two in its park. There was a bouncy castle behind, and it advertised itself with a gross cartoon of a grinning sausage in a chef's hat serving sausages and mash to a family of salivating sausages.

The man was waiting without apparent impatience in a fake Victorian alcove in the saloon bar. The drinks were already on the table. His was Perrier. He rose and waited for her, smiling. Presumably he recognised her from the TV programme. His face was as military as his bearing, clean shaven, with an outdoor ruddiness. His grey hair, sparse but not balding, was cut short. His eyes were pale blue, with the stony, unimaginative look of a caste accustomed to command. They didn't, to Jenny, seem in keeping with his voice, gruff and level but, she thought, too deliberately affable. She didn't respond to his smile. He read the blazon on her bosom and grinned. She maintained the professional chill of her mien, but he didn't seem put out.

"I'm sorry about this," he said. "I know it's an intrusion, Mrs. Pilcher. It's very good of you to spare me the time. My name is Dick Matson, by the way."

He produced a card and gave it to her. He worked, apparently, for a firm in Devon which dealt in agricultural feeds. His home address was near Tiverton. Jenny would have placed him in a considerably posher line of business.

"That's all right," she said. "I've got a few minutes. What do you want?"

"Well, it's a bit tricky, so I'd better make it clear that I'm not making any accusations. This is just something I want sorted out."

He picked up a brown envelope that had been lying on the table, took out a photograph and gave it to her. It was an eight-by-six, black and white on matte paper, and looked fairly old, but the focus was spot on, with every detail exact, the two pistols nestling into their fitted box with tools and paraphernalia around them. There was no mistaking the silver initials on the butts.

"That certainly looks like it," she said. "How did you get hold of this?"

"My mother took it," he said. "Ages ago. She gave my father the pistols just after the war some time. She'd no idea how good they were—bought them for the initials, same as his, you see—but then Dad did a bit of research and found out about Ladurie and all that.

My interest is that Dad left them to me in his will, and then he had a couple of strokes, pretty bad, but he hung on for a couple of years not knowing much about anything, and when he finally snuffed it they'd disappeared. My mother's still with us, but she's past it too now, poor old thing, and whenever I've asked her about the pistols she's thrown a wobbly, so I've been waiting till she passed on before I did anything about it. They were supposed to be in the bank, like I told you . . ."

"You said you'd got the other one."

"Did I? Well yes, but you weren't giving me much chance to catch your attention. Sorry about that, but you'll see why my eyebrows went up when you showed up on the box toting one of Dad's pistols?"

"I suppose so, if that's what it is. I mean, are you sure that one of yours is missing? If you haven't actually seen them, I mean . . ."

"Well, no, I can't be dead sure, but I'd bet my boots there aren't any others. Ladurie didn't make that many guns and his order-books still exist—Dad went into all this—and ours are there just as a single pair. The entry's marked J.M. You see?"

"All right. I'll accept that. Now, before we go on I'll need to know how you got hold of me. The people at the programme promised us total confidentiality, and I'm careful about that sort of thing."

"I was afraid you'd ask that. It's a bit awkward. I'll put it like this. Programme comes from Bristol, right? Well, it just so happens that there's someone there who owes me a considerable good turn. I called them—notice I'm not saying if it's a man or a woman—and said—"

"Had you called the programme first and found out that they weren't going to tell you anything?"

"Not how I do things. If you know someone in the business, you get straight onto them. Networking, don't they call it these days? So I didn't think anything of it till this whoever got back to me and said they'd got what I wanted but I mustn't let on how I'd found out or they and a good friend of theirs would be really in the shit. Of course if I'd known that's how it was in the first place, I'd never have asked them. You see?"

"In that case, I'm afraid—"

"Hold it. Hold it a moment. As far as I can see we're in much the same boat. We've both got hold of something the other one thinks we've no right to, and neither of us is willing to say how we got it. The difference is—now, don't get me wrong, I'm dead sure you're doing it in all innocence—but the difference is that all I've got is a name—I looked your number up in the book—it had to be somewhere near the Maidstone and there's not that many Pilchers around—the difference is that what you've got is worth quite a lot of money, once the pistols are back together again, which they bloody well ought to be in any case, and one way or another, Mrs. Pilcher, I intend to see that it happens. I don't want to have to go to law over it, if I can help it. Bloody expensive, lawyers are, in case you don't know . . ."

"I'm one myself."

"Are you now? Are you now?"

The blue eyes had come to life and were twinkling with factitious charm, but Jenny guessed that this was his response to being for the first time mildly taken aback. She didn't much like Mr. Matson and was far from sure how much of the truth he was telling her. A good deal, she guessed, but neither the whole, nor nothing but. He had, however, two holds on her of which he was unaware. The minor one was that she was enjoying her drink and now wanted the other half. The major one was that at all costs the thing should be sorted out without troubling Uncle Albert.

Jenny had been looking through the boxes in the attic for clothes for the Oxfam sale while she waited for the engineer to service the washing machine. She'd had to take the whole day off because they wouldn't tell her when he was coming. She'd found the box beneath some strange old cricketing whites—wrong shape and generation for Jeff, and he'd never been a games player, but she had found no end to the weirdness of the objects he'd hung on to. (She herself was a ruthless thrower-out, except in the case of cotton socks. Her bottom drawer held nothing else but favourite pairs, now worn so thin that they would have been in holes after one more use, so she had not been able to bring them to that point. Typically, Jeff had never queried this quirk.) When she'd opened the box and seen the pistol she'd thought it was the same kind of hoarded curiosity as the cricket whites, but beautiful. Then the doorbell had rung, so she'd carried it downstairs and put it on the hallway shelf as she opened the door.

Her caller was the engineer she'd been waiting for, a cheery oaf who apparently expected to be admired for the simple virtue of being male, and became openly contemptuous when Jenny didn't respond. They had parted in mutual loathing, leaving Jenny feeling that she couldn't move comfortably around her own kitchen until it was aired and decontaminated of his presence.

Then Anita Verey had shown up to collect the Oxfam clothes, but also carrying an absurd clock ornamented with stuffed finches which bobbled around at the strike, a series of bird-like twitters. She was on her way to ask about it at this TV programme which happened to be in town. She'd wanted someone to chat to while she queued. Jenny had felt the need to be out of the house for a bit. Anita was good company, and it would be pleasant to get to know her better. Thus it was that Jenny had taken Uncle Albert's pistol to *The Antiques Roadshow* last summer.

She'd told Jeff when he came home.

"Oh, God!" he'd said. "It's all right, darling. You couldn't have known. Let's just hope the old boy doesn't get to see the programme. When's it on?"

"Uncle Albert? Why? What's up?"

"You remember I had to sort his stuff out when he went into Marlings? He was a bit more on the spot then than he is now, but he was pretty bewildered all the same. He sat in the middle of the room while I did the packing. He wasn't interested. Anything I asked him about he said, 'I'm through with that. Chuck it out.' I'd noticed he was clutching this box on his lap and I assumed it was something he was set on taking with him, but when I'd finished he pulled himself together and handed it to me.

" 'Now you've got to take care of this,' he said. 'Seeing I don't know who's going to come poking around this place you're sending me to. You put it somewhere safe and don't you go showing it around nor telling anyone about it. Right?'

"I took it from him and without thinking I started to open the box and see what was in it, but . . . well, remember me telling you how I was brought up scared stiff of him, though as far as I know he'd never laid a finger on anyone, or even raised his voice to them."

"He's got the most beautiful manners still. That's how I'm going to raise ours, if I can."

"You probably can't see it, but it's pretty well in my genes, being scared of the old boy. I'd thought I was past it, but by God, no.

" 'And what do you think you're up to, my lad? Did I say open it up? Did I? No I did not. Put it away somewhere safe, I said, and don't you go showing it around nor telling anyone about it. Right?' "

Jeff had got the old soldier's voice and manner spot on. He then laughed and shook his head, as if trying to come to terms with his having let himself be so dominated.

"You did look, all the same," said Jenny. "You knew it was a pistol."

"Well, yes. I was putting it away and decided I'd better check, but even then I felt guilty. God, I bet there was more than one recruit who pissed himself when Uncle Albert picked on him for dirty boots or something. Let's just hope he doesn't see the programme. When's it on?"

"Next winter sometime. They shoot miles more than they use, so they'll probably leave me out."

But they hadn't. She'd watched the programme with Jeff the Sunday before he'd left for Paris. All other reasons for watching were instantly forgotten in her fascination by her own appearance . . . nothing like the mirror of course, but not much like photographs, or even the odd glimpse on a wedding video. This was the Jenny strangers seemed to see, the chilly little bitch. (She had actually overheard that phrase after a case conference, from a QC who had tried to chat her up.) Yes, there was more than a touch of that on this apparently neutral occasion, when she hadn't at all been aware of turning it on deliberately . . . and anyway she must stop wearing that denim jacket. It gave her a curious hump in profile . . .

"Well, let's just hope he's missed it," said Jeff with a worried sigh, as he switched off.

"He can't still do anything to you, darling."

"It isn't really that. Or not just that. He hasn't got much grasp of what's going on these days, but that doesn't stop him being pretty shrewd at times. I told you he was talking about selling his medals to help with the fees at Marlings . . ."

"He can't. You've got power of attorney."

"That isn't the point. I think he's worked out that I'm paying some of it—he's no idea how much, of course, but he still doesn't like it. He hates the idea that he might be dependent on anyone. He's saved all his life for his retirement, and he thinks that and his pension and the little bit he gets from the Cambi Road Association ought to be enough to see him out. Of course it isn't, anything like, not at Marlings anyway. He likes it there. He's got friends. The staff think he's great. But if he decides that I can push him around and do what I like with his stuff because I'm paying the fees, he's going to try and insist on moving out and going somewhere he can afford on his own. It would kill him, for a start, and anyway there's no such place. Besides, I just don't want the hassle, I get quite enough of that at work."

"Suppose I went and talked to him. I could tell him it was all my fault, and you didn't know anything about it . . ."

"It's a thought. Look, I'll call Sister Morris now and tell her we've just seen something on the box that might upset him, and could she just check if he's OK without letting on that's what she's up to . . ."

Sister Morris had said that the residents had been having their tea during the programme. The TV had been left on, but it was much more likely to have been ITV, and anyway Uncle Albert had had his back to it. He was fine. So that had seemed to be that.

Until now.

Jenny finished her drink, taking her time. Mr. Matson didn't seem to mind waiting. If he was telling anything like the truth, he, or at least his family, obviously had a good claim on the pistol. For herself, she wouldn't have had any hesitation in handing it over, given reasonable proof of ownership, and she didn't imagine Jeff would either. But she was pretty sure he wouldn't do so without consulting Uncle Albert, who'd then be extremely upset, try and insist on leaving Marlings, and so on.

Fortunately, Mr. Matson didn't know about any of that, and otherwise he was no great problem to deal with. Apparent cooperation without any concessions—the lawyer's stock-in-trade. So, since the company wasn't particularly enjoyable, she concentrated on not wasting her pleasure in the stout, relishing both the mild alcoholic kick and the way the smooth creaminess contrasted and combined with the slight harshness in the flavour.

"What about the other half?" he said as she put her glass down.

"My turn," she said, rising. "What's yours?"

He glanced ostentatiously at the slogan on her bosom and chuckled.

"If you insist," he said. "Another of the same, thanks. I'm driving to Devon."

"We had a cook once, used to drink stout," he said when she carried the drinks back to the table. "Mrs. Moffet. Little nut of a woman, henpecked poor Moffet stupid, but she made a wonderful roly-poly. I've never tasted anything to touch it. Well, here's mud in your eye, Mrs. Pilcher, and I'll drink your health for real as soon as I'm home."

"How long will that take you?"

"Bit under four hours, coming, but it's Friday evening. I might be in by midnight if all goes well."

"You drove all this way, just on the off chance of seeing me?"

"They matter to me, Dad's pistols. The old boy was potty about them. I want the other one back. What do you say?"

"It's not as straightforward as that, Mr. Matson. As I've told you, the pistol doesn't belong to me. I found it one day in the attic, when my husband was at work. A friend asked me to go with her to the *Roadshow* programme and I took it so that I'd have something to show too. I told my husband when he came home and he said it wasn't his, either. It had been given to him for safekeeping by an elderly relative whose affairs he looked after, and he'd been asked to put it away and not talk about it or show it to anybody."

"A bit fishy, do you think?"

"Not if you know the old man in question. It's not just that he's an ex-soldier—that doesn't mean anything—but . . . well, no. I'm absolutely certain he came by it honestly, so all I can say is I'll talk to my husband about it. Jeff's in Paris at the moment, but he may call tomorrow morning and if he does I'll tell him what's happened, and then he or I will get in touch with you. That's really the best I can do."

"All right," he said, with surprising resignation. "I get you. You talk to your man. You keep my card. Now, I'll tell you my offer. You're obviously straight, Mrs. Pilcher, and I'll take it your man is too—Jeff, did you say his name was?"

"That's right."

"So this is what you—"

He stopped abruptly. He had been looking into her eyes, all sincerity. The look changed to one of astonished revelation. He gave a silent laugh.

"Tell me," he said. "This old soldier, the elderly relative you've been talking about—are we by any chance speaking of RSM Albert Fredricks of the Second Derbyshire Regiment? It's all right, Mrs. Pilcher. You play your cards as close to your chest as you please, but last time I visited Sergeant Fred—that's what we used to call him when we were kids—he was full of this nephew of his who kept his papers in order. Wasn't he living with his sister near Aldershot someplace? Grand to know he's still alive and kicking. RSM Fredricks, salt of the earth. I remember him since I was knee high. Tall and skinny—looked as long as a flag pole to a kid my age, with this bony great nose sticking out at the top. That was before the war, of course, then he went east with Dad and the Japs got them a week after they'd landed, and then they were on the Cambi Road together. And that pretty well did for them, except that they both had what it took to haul themselves round. Well, well, well, how is the old boy?"

Jenny hesitated. Presumably once again Mr. Matson was telling her something very like the truth. She couldn't imagine how else he might have made the connection, or known what he appeared to about Uncle Albert, but in the end both professional habit and her own continuing distrust won out.

"I'm sorry," she said. "I can't even tell you that, until I've talked to my husband. He told me his possession of the pistol was confidential and I'm not in a position to decide for myself what's relevant to that and what isn't."

"Lawyers, I love 'em," said Mr. Matson, shaking his head. "You're not in court now, Mrs. Pilcher. You've told me, and you know you have. But you talk to your man and tell him this. What was it the fellow on the telly said the pistol was worth, as it stood? Three or four thou, wasn't it? Let's split the difference, call it three-five. We'll make a date and I'll show up with the other gun in its box, with all the trimmings and a copy of Dad's will—you couldn't ask for clearer proof it's mine than that—and I'll hand over three thousand five hundred in cash for the one he's got, no questions asked about how he came by it. Now that's a very fair offer, he couldn't ask for a better, and Sergeant Fred could do with the money, I dare say—it's no joke what it costs looking after an old buffer like that—I don't like to think about what my old ma's costing us in nursing. When is your man back? Thursday, you said. We'll give him another week to think about it, so if I haven't heard from him by the end of the month, I'll be coming after him. Right?"

Jenny finished her glass and put it down. It hadn't given her anything like the satisfaction of the first one.

"I'll tell my husband what you've said," she said, rising. "After that it's up to him. It won't be any use getting in touch with me, so please don't come again without first checking that he's in and is willing to see you. You understand?"

"Only too well, my dear. It's none of your business, and you want no part of it, and nor would I if I were in your shoes, so I don't blame you. Well, it's been a pleasure to meet you, and thank you for sparing the time. Good night, Mrs. Pilcher, and give my regards to Sergeant Fred next time you see him."

3

When she was alone in the house, especially at night, Jenny kept the CD player turned up as far as she thought the neighbours could stand. She wasn't musical—wouldn't even have described herself as a music-lover—but the sound provided a sort of magical companionship, a force field that kept at bay the little insinuating monsters of silence and darkness. Human voices were more potent than instruments, and foreign languages better to work to because the words were mere noise, without intrusive meanings. She had no strong feelings about styles or composers. Handel was as good as Wagner, but it happened to be Verdi that evening, with the Anvil Chorus going full blast, so she never heard the key in the lock or the movement of the door, and the first she knew was when the clamour suddenly muted and Jeff's voice said "Hi."

Her whole body jerked with the bounce of shock. She shoved the laptop aside, staggered to her feet, and round the sofa and into his arms. Behind her eyelids, as they kissed, pulsed a dark red rectangle, the counterimage of the screen she had been staring at.

"Why aren't you holding me properly?" she mumbled.

He pushed her away, brought his other arm out from behind his back and gave her gift-wrapped box.

"Paris nightie," he said. "I don't know how terrific it is. I just had time to grab it out of a shop on my way to the station. You're cold."

"I've been working. What's the time?"

"Half past one."

"What's happened? You said . . ."

"I've lost my job."

"Great! So've I—or I'm just going to. Let's go and celebrate. Have you had anything to eat?"

"Later."

They got up and made scrambled eggs at five in the morning, then went back to bed till noon.

"I'm not sure Billy didn't push me into it on purpose," he said. "It was yesterday morning, and we were having the usual sort-out over breakfast, and Simon asked about the deadline—he's got a family holiday booked—and Billy shrugged and said, 'If I've got to stretch it again, I'll stretch it. I trust you've all got that.' And then—this is what makes me think he saw the chance to set one of us up—not necessarily me—it was the way he did it, looking slowly round the table, forcing us to answer in turn. Anyway, people started mumbling things like 'I suppose so,' except for creeps like Neil who tried to sound all eager to carry on for another month—that's what pushed me into it—Neil—because I was next and I came out with what we'd just been talking about, you and me—you coming over to Paris and so on. I gave Billy plenty of slack to treat it as a joke, but he didn't. He gave me that stare of his and said, 'If that's your line, I don't want you on my team.' And I said, 'That's my line, Billy,' and picked up my stuff and walked out.

"I don't know whether he'd expected me to back down, but I don't think he cared. It's not that I'm irreplaceable, but I really know the stuff, and without me they'd be stuck for—oh, call it a fortnight—and there's no way the Kazakhs are going to wait that long.

"That suits Billy fine. The deal was on the rocks already, and it was Billy who put it there, and he knew it. Sir Vidal set it up in the first place, remember—it's his baby—so walking out the way I did gives Billy the chance to put someone else's head on the block.

"I worked that out on the train. All I thought at the time was that he was trying to show me, publicly, that I belonged to him, body and soul, and I wasn't having it. I'm sorry darling."

"They can't just fire you for walking out under stress. It would be constructive dismissal, at the very least. If you were my client . . ."

"That's not how it will look in Billy's report, and he carries a lot of clout. Our industrial relations setup is palaeolithic."

"I'm rubbing my hands. Just the sort of defense client I like. Seriously, darling, they can't fire you, not without whopping compensation. How long have you been with them? It can't be worth it. They know you're good—OK, it'll be a black mark on your CV . . ."

"Billy will still be there."

"You won't be working for him."

"He'll be out to get me, all the same. I don't mean just casually. He'll make a point of it. Your turn."

"My . . . Oh, well . . . I haven't actually walked out yet, but . . . Did I tell you about Trevor having to be rushed into hospital and Jerry asking me to clear up anything on his desk I could deal with, and pass on anything I couldn't to him? It was a pretty good mess—surprise, surprise—though Millie usually keeps him on the rails. It makes me sick. He takes home four times what she does because he's a partner and she's just a secretary. But even so there was quite a bit of stuff—contracts he should have sent on to clients weeks ago and he obviously hadn't even read yet, that sort of thing—and then yesterday morning I found a letter from a client about a case we'd lost last year. I think I told you—the one about the fun fair ride. I did a bit of work on it but then I went and married someone and by the time I was back from the honeymoon the case had come up and we'd lost it. I was a bit surprised, but I gathered our QC had made a hash of it and that was that."

"The one about the ride that collapsed and a couple of kids got killed?"

"That's right, and eleven others injured. It was big stuff, in the papers, whacking damages. We were acting for the fairground owner. He was insured, but there was a clause in the contract which effectively meant that if the fairground owner was at fault then he was liable for the first five hundred thousand. It all turned on a maintenance docket. Our client's case was that the fault was caused by an unsatisfactory repair by the original manufacturers, which our client couldn't have known about. The manufacturers said that the ride hadn't been properly maintained. The crucial docket was missing. The fairground owner was a blind old man called Colin McNair. He had this amazing memory. He could, literally, reel off the dates and details of the maintenance of every machine in his fair for the last three years. He swore the maintenance had been done, and the checks made, and the docket had been among the papers he'd provided, but it wasn't, and the inference was that the reason it was missing was that the maintenance had never been done. So we lost, and Mr. McNair went bankrupt.

"Well, among the stuff on Trevor's desk was this pathetic letter from the old boy, eight pages long. He'd had to dictate it, of course, but it was totally coherent, as if he'd worked it up from notes on a PC. I mean he'd been brooding, of course, but it wasn't at all crazy. When he got to the docket he didn't just list what was in it, he tried to show how clear his memory was, so he told Trevor about the day he'd brought the papers in and gone through them with him, what the weather was like, and what kind of biscuits Millie had brought with the coffee and so on. And a telephone call Trevor had had to make about a butcher's business someone was buying, and the name of the client and what Trevor had said to him. There was a whole page of that.

"Trevor had written a draft answer, fobbing him off, of course, saying what a shame it was and how he understood the old boy's disappointment but there wasn't anything more to be done. Just generalities. The only actual point he answered was to insist that a thorough search had been made for the docket and he was quite certain that we hadn't got it, and what's more that we'd never had it. He had rephrased that bit a couple of times.

"Now, I'd actually met Mr. McNair, and I knew Trevor, so if Mr. McNair said one thing and Trevor said another I was pretty sure who was right. And why just that one point? There were plenty of others he could have said something about. I don't believe he'd read the whole letter. I think he just skimmed it, and stuck on that one because it was bothering him. I couldn't possibly have done a full file search— it would take weeks and in any case Millie's far too possessive of Trevor's stuff—but I waited till she was at lunch and went and got out the file about the butcher's business. The docket was in it. Please register amazement."

"Registered. That's bloody awkward for you. What's Jerry going to say?"

"I took it to him yesterday afternoon. He cancelled all his appointments and sent for the files. So he's taking it seriously, but my bet is that in the end he's going to ask me to keep quiet about it."

"I thought Jerry was all right."

"Oh, I like him. And he's certainly everyday all right, if you see what I mean. Decent, but . . . look, if we come clean about this, we're dead. It's a partnership, not a limited company, so ultimately the partners are liable."

"You must be insured."

"Yes, of course, we have to be. There's a limit, though I don't know how much in our case. A few million, I should think."

"That would pay for a fun fair, wouldn't it?"

"I should think so, but it isn't just Mr. McNair's losses we'd be in for. His insurance company had to pay out for the deaths and injuries—I told you there were whacking damages—and they could come after us because if we'd won it would have been the manufacturer who'd have been liable. That'd take us well beyond our insurance limit."

"So how's Jerry going to put it to you?"

"I expect he'll—"

The telephone rang. Jeff answered.

"No. I'm back," he said. "Our affairs came to a crashing halt. You can certainly say that . . . I'll hand you over."

"Jerry," he mouthed as he passed the handset across. Jenny felt her heart contract but spoke unflurriedly, her outer persona closing automatically around her inward self.

"Hello."

"I gather you've got him back early. You'll have been missing him."

"To put it mildly."

"So you won't be too keen on having a bit of lunch with me tomorrow."

"Well . . ."

"I need a word with you. Away from the office, for preference. Thing is, it's about that stuff you dug up yesterday afternoon. We're going to have to sort something out, but the fewer people who are involved at this stage the better all round. You follow?"

"Yes, of course. Hold on a moment."

She put a hand over the mouthpiece.

"He wants me to have lunch with him tomorrow. Can you bear it?"

"Better get it over."

"How did it go?"

"Take me somewhere where nobody can hear me if I scream. I mean that. Literally. Please."

He thought for a moment.

"Do you mind getting wet?"

"No."

They drove in silence. The rain sluiced down. He pulled in at the entrance to a forestry plantation.

"All right if I came along?"

"If you want to."

She didn't wait for him. The skirt of her Sunday-lunch-with-the-boss suit constrained her to a stupid mincing run along the squelching track. A shoe was sucked off, but she didn't stop. The track curved out of sight from the road. Another track crossed it. She slowed to a walk. Leafless branches dripped onto dead and sodden bracken. This was the place.

Where the four ways met she stopped, raised her arms like a priestess at a shrine, summoned Norma into being and let her rip, waiting for each scream to fade into the drenched, indifferent trees before she screamed again. Her throat was really painful before Sister Jenny told her that that was enough.

Jeff was waiting a few paces back, with the big umbrella up and her shoe in his other hand. She took his arm and they walked down to the car and drove home, still in silence, with the heater full up. He made her a linctus with honey, scotch and lemon, and then joined her in the shower. They went to bed again and forgot about everything but each other. After awhile she fell asleep, waking several hours later to find him still beside her, reading a Tom Clancy with the same rapid but exact attention that he would have given to an oil policy analysis.

"How's the throat?"

"Better. Thanks, Jeff."

"I didn't know you could do that."

"Nor did I. It was a sort of experiment. I mean I hadn't tried using her like that before, not since I was a kid."

"Who?"

"Norma. You don't know about Norma."

"You don't have to tell me."

"I want to. I didn't before, because I thought I'd given her up, but yesterday, after you telephoned . . ."

She told him slowly, whispering to spare her throat, and absent-mindedly fondling his forearm as she talked.

". . . of course a lot of little girls have screaming fits," she said at one point. "But I started again after Dad walked out, and Mummy started drinking, and that meant I had to do stuff for Grandad because she was snorting on the sofa. I would have been about nine."

"Didn't Sue help?"

"She did it for a bit but then something happened. No one told me what, but she was very upset and I heard Mum screeching at him later. After that Sue wouldn't go near him and Mum told me I'd got to do it. She gave me a wooden ruler and told me if he tried anything I must hit him across the knuckles with it. I hadn't any idea what she was talking about, but she must have said something—I don't remember what—something about him being as good as dead, or he should've been dead by now—something like that—but I got it into my head that the horrible old man actually *was* dead, only . . . I'm all right, darling, I want to tell you . . . just . . . He had a sort of chuckle . . . oh, God, this dead thing . . . only he wasn't . . . Listen, before that, when he was in hospital and Mummy took us to visit him, there was this nurse, Sister Somebody, in her blue uniform and her starched pinny and cap, and a wide belt with a big silver buckle, all clean and strong and alive among the dirty, smelly, falling-to-bits old horrors in the beds, and they couldn't touch her, they couldn't infect her with their mess and nastiness because her uniform was sort of magic . . . Anyway, that's how I invented Sister Jenny, and I gave her an imaginary uniform and while I was wearing it in my head he couldn't do anything to me, he couldn't touch me, he couldn't come and get me and make me dead like him . . . Do you understand, darling?"

"There was something going on, wasn't there, when I took you to meet Uncle Albert first time?"

"It wasn't that bad. You were there. It wasn't my responsibility. I don't know if I could've done it alone. Anyway, being Sister Jenny got me through dealing with Grandad, but really it was a way of bottling up the other stuff till I was out of his room, then when it was over I'd go out into the barn where there was no one to hear but the pigs and get rid of it by screaming and chucking things around. That's Norma.

"I've never told anyone else about Norma. Sister Jenny's the one people get to meet. They don't like her much. Mummy invented Norma, not me, to try and get me out of my tantrums. She was supposed to be a joke, only she wasn't. Not for me. Kids get things into their heads, you know. Like Grandad being dead. So I was two people. I don't mean I'm clinically schizophrenic, or anything. It was just a way of coping, but it got a bit stuck, that's all. Well, now you've met Norma."

"Hi."

"You aren't worried?"

"Why should I be? Tell her to come in and make herself at home, if you feel like it. Unless you're bothered about being married to a bigamist. Though I must say I don't quite see what Jerry's got in common with your grandfather."

"It isn't Jerry. It's me being stuck with a filthy mess which isn't anything to do with me, except I've been landed with it . . . No, I could cope with that. And Jerry himself couldn't have been nicer. I mean he didn't try to tell me the docket didn't exist, or it didn't mean what I thought it meant, and he was furious with Trevor for being so idle and incompetent, but he must have been ill for a while before anyone realised, including himself, and now he's dying . . . Oh Jesus! I don't know why this is getting to me so badly. People keep dying all the time, don't they? It's all right, darling—I can cope. It was just I had a sudden picture of him lying in hospital with all these tubes in him . . . It's some kind of marrow cancer you have to catch early, and they didn't. Jerry didn't make a big deal of it, actually. I mean he said it was ghastly for everyone, of course, but it didn't affect the principle of the thing, which is to do the best we can for old Mr. McNair. Jerry says he doesn't think the docket would have made all that amount of difference, it's just what Mr. McNair has fastened on because he's known all along he was right about it. But what really lost us the case was that the manufacturer'd got hold of a much better expert than we had. I don't mean he knew more about it, but he put on a much better show, and so did their QC, so we'd have lost the case anyway. But suppose Mr. McNair was told about the docket now, he's not going to get the case reopened. All he can do is sue us for the money he lost. But he couldn't stop his insurance company coming after us too—I told you about that—and the way these things are set up they'd have first claim on all assets and there wouldn't be anything left for Mr. McNair, and he'd still have his costs to pay and they'd be a packet. So actually it might be kinder not to let him know."

"A bit specious?"

"No. I mean, I think Jerry genuinely thinks that, and he's probably right, except that in the meanwhile Mr. McNair is going crazy with the knowledge that he gave Trevor the docket and no one believes him. And then—Jerry didn't make a big thing of this, apart from telling me that it was only fair to warn me that it was bound to come out that it was me who started the thing off, and it was an unfair world but people really weren't that keen on hiring someone who'd pulled the rug out from under their firm in however good a cause—but he didn't say anything about the firm going down the tube, or Trevor having a rather hopeless wife and three young children, or Millie with her mother to look after, or Selina's bloke walking out on her and the kids—but of course he knew I'd know all that—it's a very friendly office, and that's mainly Jerry's doing. He really is everyday decent . . . so all I could do was sit and listen and say helpful things and try not to think about Trevor lying in hospital . . ."

"Sister Jenny. With his mess to clear up?"

"That's right."

"And then go into the wood and scream? If you'd given me a bit of warning I could have arranged for some pigs."

*   *   *

Later, lying on his back at some unknown hour, he said in a dreamy voice, "You were being persecuted by a dimwit. When I called from Paris."

From time to time since he'd come home it had crossed Jenny's mind that she should tell him about Mr. Matson's visit, but she hadn't, and she understood why, without having to think it out. This last—how long? Less than forty-eight hours—had been extraordinary. Nothing, not their first physical explorations of their passion for each other, not the boost of renewal on the honeymoon, had been like this hunger, endlessly satisfied, endlessly aching back into life, her whole body like a soft, faint bruise, delighting to be touched. Their need for each other was their only need, though their world, their assumptions, their lifestyle, everything, melted away around them. The stuff they had so far been talking about and dealing with, Jeff's trouble with Billy, hers over Jerry, had been part of the melting, part of what allowed them to seal themselves into this capsule and watch the process with indifference. Only in the capsule could Jenny have brought herself to tell anyone, even Jeff, about Norma, and done it with such ease and such relief.

Mr. Matson's visit was different. It concerned Jeff alone, she had been merely an agent, an intruder, who had made the first mistake and then compounded it. The event wasn't, somehow, part of the melting process.

"I needed a drink," she said.

"Everything is explained. And forgiven, where appropriate."

"I may need to hold you to that."

Adjusting her head on his chest she told him what had happened.

"He's lying," said Jeff when she'd finished. "Aunt Clarisse looked after Albert's affairs until she had her heart attack. That's when I took over, when I had to move him to Marlings . . . It sounds to me as if he knew about Uncle Albert all along."

"Oh . . . I suppose he might have. He did ham it up a bit when he made the connection. And he was lying earlier on, telling me he'd got the other pistol. But I think a lot of the other stuff was true, or nearly."

"It doesn't matter, actually. The only thing that matters is whether he can prove he's the rightful owner. If he can then I suppose we've got to hand the thing over. But I won't say no to the money he's offering if it'll help tide Uncle Albert over for a few months."

"You don't think Mr. Matson's father could have given it to him as a keepsake?"

"Splitting the pair up? And in any case, Uncle Albert would have had it hanging on the wall and told everyone about it, instead of . . . No, I don't buy it. Hell, Uncle Albert isn't going to like it. But I'll ring this man tomorrow and tell him . . ."

"I think it is tomorrow. We're wasting time. Come here."

But the seal on the capsule was broken, and the late night trucks fumed past on the Ashford Road, and love was no longer any more than love.

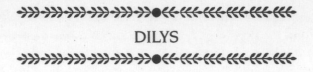

DILYS

I

Soundlessly she opened the door and slipped into the room. She liked to find a patient still asleep, so that she could stand by the bed in the dimness and study the altered face. It spoke to her of things the waking mask didn't, mostly just the peacefulness of being free for a little from the dreary indignities of waiting to die, but sometimes more than that. Sometimes there was a sort of translucency through whose mist she seemed to be able to make out what the face had been twenty, forty, sixty years before—as a child's even. At other times she saw no more than discontents and rages at the betrayal that had so cynically abrogated the freedom and respect and command that had once seemed written into the contract.

Dilys thought no worse of a patient for that; such feelings were human, and therefore proper; even those whose spirits grovelled and whimpered and pleaded had her respect. But there were others who, though their minds might be almost wholly gone, seemed still to register that there were no ears to hear the whimpers, no eyes to perceive the abasement, no court to consider the pleas. In their faces as they slept she believed she could see that these old things were heroines and heroes, and she felt proud in their pride. Her job, her mission, was to make sure that until the moment they carried it into darkness that flame still burned.

She had never had a lover. As a girl she had let herself be kissed and fumbled with a bit, because that had been the way of things, but she'd found it an uncomfortable pastime, arousing sensations that didn't seem to belong to the Dilys she knew and understood. She had not been handsome enough to provoke real eagerness and so had had little trouble in persuading the fellow to desist, and before she was thirty had recognised, with some relief, that unless a crazy took it into his head to rape her, she would die a virgin.

She had sometimes been asked, since she had what people thought a motherly look, whether she minded not having had children. Not wishing to appear heartless, she had answered that she supposed so, but in truth, as far as she could see or feel, she had missed nothing she wanted. In her training she had done a routine course in the obstetric wards and—again because it had been expected of her—she had cooed and admired like a good 'un, but inwardly she had never been able to think of babies as anything more than the main symptom of a common female complaint which she had luckily been spared.

These weren't coherent, verbalised beliefs, but unformulated feelings, and of course she had never talked about them to anyone, being sure that her life would be considered arid and repressed. It wasn't. She found her work utterly fulfilling. When, in the ripeness of time, a patient died, she didn't grieve. If anything, she glowed. A life had run its full course. Over the years she had seen a lot of television which she wouldn't otherwise have bothered with, because patients often liked a companion to whom they could comment about the programmes they chose. It helped keep them perky, which was one of her main objectives. Ladies liked soaps and gentlemen liked sport. That was how she'd come to see a programme about a sprint relay team, and the gentleman in question, Admiral Poskett, had suddenly cackled and said, "That's what you are, Dilys. You're my last lap coach." He'd been right. When the coach had talked about the satisfaction of seeing his team run at their peak he had put into words many of Dilys's own feelings as she closed the eyes and laid the body straight. She had helped her patient live those last months and die that death as well as they could be lived and died.

Not that she was ever impatient for the death. It was the living that counted. Once she had connived with a doctor to allow a patient to escape from endless pain. Once she had, effectively, permitted a strong-willed old man to starve himself to death. But once she had fought by every means she could against a family and doctor who wanted to make an end, when Dilys herself was sure that the patient, stone blind, four-fifths deaf, and in pain, still raged against the necessity. It was fourteen years since Dilys had lost that fight, and she still minded.

This morning, before she was fully into the room, Dilys knew that for the third morning running Mrs. Matson was already awake after a bad night. Her nose told her. She didn't find the inevitable reeks of old age offensive—how could she, after all these years?—but she didn't let habit blank them out. They were useful. To her, there was an obvious difference between the odours produced by someone contentedly wetting and soiling themselves in their sleep, and those that arose in the miseries of wakefulness. There was a particular sourness among the mix of smells—acids or something, but no one would have done the research. It was the sort of thing nurses knew and doctors weren't around to notice. She was already tutting as she opened the curtains.

"We've not been sleeping, have we? You should've let me give you that pill—drinkie before I see to you?"

She eased the withered body up and tilted the glass against lips that were dry as paper, giving them time to sip and sip and sip.

There was a microphone suspended above the pillow that amplified every whisper into Dilys's room. Other patients would have called for a drink several times in the night.

"Thank you," Mrs. Matson whispered. "Pills make me stupid next day."

"There's that," said Dilys. "Now let's tidy you up. Brooding about Mr. Matson, still, were we?"

"Not brooding. Thinking."

"Brooding's just thinking and not getting anywhere, so you may as well stop, only you can't."

"Got somewhere. Perhaps. At last. When you've finished. Filing cabinet. Top drawer, near back. Cambi Road. C. A. M. . . ."

"I remember, dearie—that address list, came a few weeks back, you were telling me where to put it only Mrs. Thomas came in and she said she knew."

"Yes. Bring the list."

"Soon as I've done. Amazing they've kept it going this long, getting out a proper address list every year, and all. My dad's lot—I told you he was in Shangar, didn't I?—they used to have get-togethers for a bit . . ."

She rattled purposefully on, as she always did when she was cleaning up, to distract her patient's attention from the shameful need—they all minded, and rightly so—at the same time with another part of her mind attending to her task, not allowing it to become an automatic process. You could miss little signs . . . yes, tsk, that was a bedsore trying to start—it'd be those acids again—nothing like that for weeks now . . . and the trip all the way to London, seven hours in the coach, '54 that would have been, just finishing at Caernarvon General. Of the thirty-odd in the coach there'd been eight who, like Dad, were still on full disability, and more than a dozen others on half—and not one of them over fifty, including one poor fellow barely ten years older than Dilys herself—which was why they'd taken a real nurse along with them to look after the crocks. Sad as sad it might have been, but they'd sung the whole way to London and the whole way back—"Like a moving chapel," someone had said, what with a reverend from Llanfairfechan in the party, and hymns as well as the camp songs—they'd made Dilys stop her ears for the rude ones . . . But well before Dad had died, even, there hadn't been any of that any more, local fund-raisings for a bit, and a Roneoed newsletter, and then only a few gaunt-faced men among the others on the Armistice Day parade.

"There we are, dearie. All done, and we'll be comfortable. Now I'll go and see what they've done about our breakfast, shall I?"

"List first, please."

"My, we're in a hurry. All right, then."

The corridor was a long space lit by skylights, narrowed from its original generous width by a set of bookshelves that ran along the wall backing onto Mrs. Matson's room, which had been the old nursery. The door of Dilys's bedroom was directly opposite Mrs. Matson's, with her bathroom and sitting room beyond. All the books on the shelves were photograph albums, identically bound in green cloth with green leather backs. Mrs. Matson had learnt book binding in order to make them the way she wanted. At the end of the bookshelves stood a four-drawer filing cabinet, with the card-index to the albums on top of it.

Dilys didn't have any doubts about finding the address list. Mrs. Matson knew where every file was, as well as every album. And yes, the Cambi Road file was exactly where she'd said. The list wasn't in it.

Dilys checked the files on either side in case Mrs. Thomas had put it into the wrong one, but it wasn't there either. She went back and reported her failure.

"Oh . . . but Flora . . ."

"Now don't you go getting upset, dearie. They'll be having breakfast too, won't they? I'll look in and ask Mrs. Thomas, shall I? Perhaps she's borrowed it for something."

"Please."

Dilys left smiling confidently, but shook her head as soon as she was clear of the room. This sort of thing wouldn't do. She'd long ago learnt that the most important part of keeping her patients perky wasn't any of the obvious things like making them as comfortable as poss, or seeing their food was what they liked, or jollying them along; it was allowing them to feel that they still had some control over their lives and their surroundings. Control is life, because it's freedom. From the prison of her inert body Mrs. Matson could still reach out and have her say over what mattered to her. The files and photographs were specially important because she was the only one who knew her way around them and what they meant. Even when the list was found she would be upset, still, that it had not been in its place. We can't have that, Dilys thought.

She was still tutting to herself when she reached the stairwell. She paused, and looked at it with new eyes. It was so odd, and at the same time somehow familiar, though she had never quite been able to lay her finger on what the "somehow" consisted in. The well itself was a square space, the area of a large room, running the full height of the house, with a glass roof overhead. At each floor there was a sort of balustraded balcony the whole way round, with rooms and corridors opening off it. The oddness consisted in the staircase itself. Dilys had worked in large houses, and some of them had had a central hallway and stairs something like this, but in those cases the stairs had been long, handsome flights, there to be looked at as much as walked on. These were a kind of shaft made of wooden pillars and rails, like the balustrades of the balconies, with short flights running down through a series of right angles to the floor below. They looked as if they should have had a lift going up the middle of them, or had been made to fit into a square turret, only here they were standing right out in the open, like a scaffold tower or something. And yet the really funny thing about them was that they didn't look wrong, they looked right.

And now, this morning, Dilys knew why, because there'd been a photograph of them in the album Miss Anne had done for her schoolwork, and opposite a sketch she'd made of some iron stairs at a mill somewhere, and they were just the same. Dilys even understood why they had seemed familiar, because she'd worked in old Victorian hospitals where there'd been courtyards like the stairwell, with iron balconies round them, and a fire escape running down, the way these stairs did.

It was surprising, she thought, as she started down them, how pleased it made you feel when things suddenly made sense when they hadn't a little before, even when they didn't matter to you a bit, like the whys and wherefores of this staircase didn't. And when they did matter, my! That was why Mrs. Matson was so upset about the business about whatever it was in the box—a pistol, she'd let out at the end, one of Colonel Matson's, and it had something to do with him being a Jap POW, and it hadn't been there, by the sound of it, and that dratted list was missing too . . . It wasn't just that they weren't where they should have been, it was that it didn't make sense . . . Let's hope Mrs. Thomas knew about the list, at least . . .

Mr. and Mrs. Thomas breakfasted in the morning room, which faced east and so was full of thin, spring sunshine. There was shiny silver and mahogany, and white table napkins, and smells of coffee and bacon, as well as last year's lavender and this year's hyacinths, not shop-bought but raised in batches in one of the greenhouses by Mr. Worple, a dozen at a time so there'd be a succession of them for the house. The wealth of Dilys's different employers made no difference to her. If anything she respected those who needed to skimp to afford her more than those who could do so and barely notice, but what really mattered to her was their attitude to her patient, as merely a problem to which she was the solution, or as a real person with a right to the best that could be done. Anyway, she liked the Thomases.

Now Mr. Thomas looked up as she entered, rose a polite inch from his chair, saying, "Good morning, Dilys," as he did so, sat back and returned to the letter he'd been reading. Mrs. Thomas laid hers aside.

"Trouble?" she asked.

Dilys explained.

"That's right," said Mrs. Thomas, "about the end of January it must have been, in that cold snap, because I was coming up to tell her about Annie Pinkerton, that's an old friend of hers, we always used to call her Aunt Pincushion, catching the burglar. He was trying to steal the lead cupid from the goldfish pond under her window. There were two of them, burglars, not cupids, but she only caught one, and they'd put a ladder across the pool to get at the cupid and Pincushion was tottering off to the loo in the middle of the night and she saw them, it had snowed, you see, and there was a moon so it was bright as day so she saw them quite plainly, and she flung up the window and threw—Tommy Baring says it was a bust of Shelley, but it wasn't, it was just the dictionary she keeps by the loo for the crossword—it was quite brave of her, really, seeing she's alone in the house—or stupid, I suppose, depending how you look at it—but they'd got the cupid and were almost off the ladder when she yelled and they tried to hurry and one of them slipped on the ice and the other one dropped the cupid on his leg and broke it and he was still there when the police came, and of course Pincushion had gone out and covered him with a rug so he didn't die of hypothermia."

"So it was January," said Mr. Thomas, not looking up from his letter.

"That's right, because of the snow," said Mrs. Thomas. "I wonder what's happened to it. I know I put it in the file and threw the old one out."

"I thought perhaps you or Mr. Thomas . . ."

"Not me. You haven't been at Ma's files for anything, have you, Jack? I can't think who else. Anyway, I've got to take Jack to the station because his car's in for a service, but I'll come and have a good hunt for the thing as soon as I'm back. I'll be about forty minutes and here's something to take her mind off it while you're waiting. You know how to work the video, don't you? I don't know where the bit about Da's pistols comes, so you'll have to play it right through . . ."

"It's a videotape, dearie. Mrs. Thomas said there was something in it you wanted to see, but we're going to have to play it right through."

Carefully Dilys didn't mention the pistols, though Mrs. Thomas had spoken as if she didn't think there was anything secret about them. No point in worrying Mrs. Matson about things like that. The tense look on the old face eased a little.

"Breakfast first, shall we?" Dilys coaxed.

"Please."

It was kedgeree, one of Mrs. Matson's favourites, and usually she was an excellent eater, concentrating on her food to get all the enjoyment from it that she could, and on her difficult days really working to swallow it. This morning she was at first distracted and after a few spoonfuls closed her lips and waited for Dilys to withdraw the spoon.

"The tape," she whispered. "Set it up, then wait for Flora. Don't go away. You watch too."

"Just as you like, dearie, but we'll finish our breakfast first, shall we? Forty minutes, Mrs. Thomas says, and she's always longer."

Obediently Mrs. Matson opened her mouth and did as she was told, but Dilys could sense the inner impatience, so unlike her usual steadfast acceptance of all that she could no longer command, and it didn't seem to ease until the tape was in place and running, just to check, and the title and credits of *The Antiques Roadshow* appeared on the screen. Oh, that, Dilys thought. A lot more interesting than some, anyway. She busied herself with her morning chores until Mrs. Thomas knocked and came bustling in, already voluble.

". . . queue from here to eternity at the Post Office. Well, Ma, what do you make of it? Wasn't that quick? Only three days since I rang Biddy to ask. Is it really one of Da's pistols?"

"We've only just finished our breakfast," said Dilys. "We were waiting for you."

"Well, here I am, all eager. Can you see, Ma? Sure those are her right specs, Dilys? Isn't this perfectly fascinating?"

Dilys finished adjusting Mrs. Matson's pillows, put her middle distance spectacles in place, switched on TV and video, started the tape,
and settled into the chair that she had put ready so that she could
both watch the programme and keep an eye on Mrs. Matson. She
knew *The Antiques Roadshow* well. Some of her patients had liked to
watch it and then reminisce about knickknacks they had once owned,
which would have been just as valuable as the ones on the show if they
hadn't had to be mended after some parlourmaid had knocked them
off the whatnot. The presenter was barely into his usual smooth piece
about the privilege of doing the show in this particular town and
building when Mrs. Thomas said, "Maidstone? Stop the tape, Dilys.
Dick told me Salisbury, not Maidstone. What did he tell you, Ma?"

"Vaguer. Somewhere like Salisbury."

"But Salisbury's nothing like Maidstone."

"No."

"What's he up to? Something, as usual. Carry on Dilys."

The programme got into its customary stride, a painting of a lot
of sick-looking cows, a big brass cobra made into a lamp, a horrid-
looking blunderbuss—"Keep an eye open for that chap," said Mrs.
Thomas. "He'll be the guns expert."—some very ordinary-looking
teacups which the expert said were wonderful and worth thousands of
pounds and the lady who'd brought them in kissed the gentleman
who was with her and everyone laughed, and some chairs and another
picture and a toy train and then a pair of hands in close-up holding
an old pistol, the sort that highwaymen used in films to make the
people in the coach stand and deliver . . .

"That's it, Ma. Look, that's one of Da's Laduries. It's got to be.
There's the initials. How on earth did she get hold of it? Has anyone
ever seen her before? Stop the tape, Dilys. Rewind. Here, I'll do it."

Mrs. Thomas was too excited to notice that Dilys was perfectly ca-
pable of managing for herself, but she handed the remote across without resentment. The rapid images blurred and bounced with the
rewind, stilled onto the toy train, blurred again, and settled.

". . . a very interesting gun, really beautiful. It's one of a presentation pair, of course—you don't have the other one?"

"I'm afraid not."

"Well, it would have come in a box with . . ."

More flickers, and then the picture froze to show a young woman. The camera had been on her only for the instant of her answer. She had, Dilys, thought, a sort of in-between look, dark hair, small nose and mouth, good skin, but she wasn't exactly pretty. Not plain either, mind you. Neat, a bit stiff . . . her voice hadn't been bored or excited. It had just answered the question, not letting you know anything else about her.

"Never seen her in my life," said Mrs. Thomas. "Doesn't remind me of anyone either. What about you, Ma? No? All right, on we go."

"Well, it would have come in a box as one of a pair, with its own tools and ammunition—I'll be coming to that in a moment. Now there are several reasons why this is a very interesting gun. First, it is made by René Ladurie—See here, in the chasing under the butt, his initials. Laduries are extremely rare. This is the first I have ever had in my hands, and I have to say it's a thrilling moment for me. What's more, I can tell you here and now that this is a genuine Ladurie, made with his own hands, because of the sheer quality of the workmanship. There were three great gunsmiths working in Paris at the beginning of the last century, Pauly and Pottet and Ladurie, and it's generally agreed that Ladurie was the best of them. They were all after the same thing, which was a gun you could load and fire quickly and accurately, and be sure it would go off. Just imagine, before that you were in a battle and your life depended on this contraption . . ."

The expert was a small, eager, quick-talking man, not old but almost bald, the sort who tells you everything you could possibly want to know about a subject and a lot more that you don't. He explained, acting it all out, about using an old-fashioned gun, and then about what an improvement this pistol was. The young woman listened attentively but without any of his excitement, as if he'd been a salesman telling her about his wonderful dishwasher.

". . . you needed to do was lift this catch here, open the breech, so, and . . . oh dear, black powder is terribly corrosive. At some point somebody has fired this and then left it, maybe two or three days, before cleaning it, but . . . well, we must get on. Now the third point about this gun is these initials, here. This gun was evidently made for somebody and judging by the care Ladurie put into it, it could well have been someone important. If you could find out who that was, and if it were a person of some historical interest, well . . . so I expect you'd like to know what it's worth. I'll start at the top end. Suppose you had the other gun and the box and the fittings and suppose—I'll be fanciful for a moment—you could prove that it was made for one of Napoleon's Marshals—there was Massena, wasn't there, and Murat, and who was that other chap? . . . then we're talking about something over forty thousand pounds. Now you mustn't get too excited . . ."

(The young woman seemed in no danger of this.)

". . . we aren't anywhere near that. With only the one gun, and the pitting in the firing mechanism, and no box and fittings, well, it's still a Ladurie, and an important one. I'd say between three and four thousand."

He handed the gun back and the young woman thanked him as if she'd been telling the salesman she'd think about his dishwasher, and the programme moved on to other objects. Mrs. Thomas pressed the mute button.

"I don't know what to say," she said, "but that's Da's pistol all right. And didn't the funny little man know his stuff. He actually mentioned old Murat. Anyway, we've got to get hold of that girl somehow. I'll try asking Biddy again. There's far too many people living round Maidstone—Salisbury would have been much easier, but Maidstone . . . Oh, Ma, the Cambi Road list! That's why you wanted it! That's brilliant! I mean it's still a long shot, but . . . I'll go and have a look in the files, shall I? It can't have gone far . . ."

She flurried out.

"Dilys?"

"Yes, dearie?"

"Fast-forward. Quick. The names at the end."

Dilys took the remote and found the place after a couple of tries.

"Stop," whispered Mrs. Matson, and after a pause to stare at the list of names, "Thank you. Turn it off. Wait. I'll tell her I'm tired. I'm not. When she's gone . . ."

She closed her eyes as the door handle clicked. Dilys slid the spectacles from her face and bent to crank the bed down to the resting angle.

". . . know I put it there," Mrs. Thomas was saying. "I can't think . . . What's up Dilys? Been a bit much for her?"

"I'm afraid so, Mrs. Thomas. I think it's time for a wee rest."

"So sorry, darling," whispered Mrs. Matson. "Stupid."

"That's all right, Ma. It's very upsetting seeing one of Da's Laduries all of a sudden like that. I'm absolutely outraged about it. Anyway, don't worry about the stupid list. I'll ring Simon Stadding— he's not been too well, poor chap, something wrong with his liver— and get him to send us . . . no, better yet, I'll ask him if any of the old boys are living around Maidstone now—he'll know. And I'll ring Biddy again. It would mean telling her about the pistols of course, but . . ."

"No. Please."

"Of course not, if you don't want me to, darling, and I'll be careful what I say to Simon too. I simply can't believe Da would have given one of them away, not to anybody . . . You'll give me a call when she wakes, won't you, Dilys? I'll see that Ellen knows where I am. Sleep well, Ma, and don't worry. We'll get to the bottom of this somehow."

As soon as Mrs. Thomas was clear of the room Mrs. Matson opened her eyes and smiled, purse-lipped, like a child certain of forgiveness for some naughtiness. Dilys smiled back. Nice to see her like that, she thought. Always works wonders, bit of conspiracy against the family. Perks them up no end.

"Saturday off?" whispered Mrs. Matson.

"That's right, dearie, not that there's anything much I fancy doing. I thought I might try a bit of shopping in Nottingham, maybe."

"See niece in London?"

"No, dearie, they're both . . . oh, I get you. Well if there's something you want . . . I'm not that good at London."

"London directories. Ellen's office. Grisholm. Ebury Street."

"Wait a minute, dearie—I'd better write this down."

She did so, spelling the names aloud to make sure, and then went down to the room where Mr. Thomas's secretary had her office. Now fully into the swing of deceit, she told Ellen about her niece, who would be staying at a hotel with a name like Gribbins, only when she'd tried to ring it it was an undertaker's and she was supposed to be meeting her niece there Saturday. To her relief there was no such hotel, so she dithered and flustered until Ellen told her to take the book away and bring it back later. She carried it upstairs chuckling inwardly because of course there had been an undertaker called Gribbins, in Cheltenham, wasn't it . . . ?

"Here we are, dearie. Grisholm and Son, antique weapons, armour and militaria—do you want me to go and see the gentleman?"

"Call him. Wait till ten. Tell you what to say."

"Grisholm and Son. What can I do for you?"

Dilys recognised the voice instantly. She was entirely used to this kind of intermediary role on behalf of her patients. It happened time and again, for different reasons. Mrs. Matson listened on the small speaker propped by her pillows.

"Is that Mr. Hugh Grisholm?"

"Speaking."

"My name's Dilys Roberts. I'm calling for an old lady who can't manage the phone. She can hear what you're saying but then she's got to tell me what to say. It's about a pair of Ladurie pistols . . ."

"One moment. I have to tell you, I'm afraid, that since last week when a Ladurie pistol was shown on a television programme, I have had several similar calls. I don't like raising false expectations, so I must start by telling you that it is very unlikely that yours are genuine Laduries. Before we go any further, would you give me some indication of what makes you believe they may be?"

"Wait . . . Yes, dearie? . . . There's just one pistol . . . in a box with all the equipment . . . the other pistol's missing . . . the arms on the box belonged to Marshal—you'd better spell that, dearie . . . M.U.R.A.T . . . don't tire yourself, dearie . . . and it's not for sale. She just wants me to come and show it to you. Are you open Saturday?"

"Not normally, but . . . What time do you suggest?"

"Wait . . . She says I can get there by twelve."

"That will suit me very well. I'll see you then."

2

It didn't look like much of a shop. The one next door had beautiful polished furniture in the window, laid out like a room, the sort of stuff anyone would have loved to own if they'd got that kind of money. This one had a clutter of guns and swords and pikes and armour which you couldn't see properly because of the dirty glass and the grille, and the name board needed a fresh paint. The bell rang as she opened the door. Inside was the same kind of clutter, and the air smelt of leather and oiled metal and dust, like a storeroom. A man came out of the back room, the one who'd been on the programme.

"Miss Roberts, is it? You made it, then. I'll just put up my 'Closed' sign and we won't be disturbed. In here, then . . ."

He held the door for her. The back room was also a clutter of stuff for killing your enemies or trying to stop them killing you. There was just room for an old rolltop desk and a couple of filing cabinets and a small easy chair, which Mr. Grisholm moved slightly, not for any reason except to show Dilys where he wanted her to sit. He seemed surprisingly shy, not at all like the self-confident expert who'd talked about the pistol on the TV programme.

"Well, now," he said, settling and resetting himself behind the desk. "Um. I suppose the first thing is for you to show me what you've brought. That will, uh, establish your credentials. If you follow me."

Dilys took the envelope out of her shoulder bag and put it into his reaching hand. She hadn't even peeked into it since taking it from its hiding place that morning. Now she watched Mr. Grisholm remove the box and study it for a while. He picked up an open book from his desk and compared it with the coat of arms on the box. Then he undid the catches, raised the lid, and again simply looked for two or three minutes without saying anything, holding the box tilted in his hands. At last he laid it on the desk and delicately picked out a pistol, which, as far as Dilys could see, looked exactly like the one on the TV. He peered at the base of the butt through a magnifying glass and inspected the rest of the pistol inch by inch, before clicking a catch and hingeing it open in the middle. Using the glass again, he studied the mechanism.

"Yes," he whispered. "Yes."

He closed the gun, put it back in its case and looked up. His manner had changed, become much easier. Dilys wondered if he'd been afraid he might have to tell her that the gun was a fake, or something, and he hadn't been looking forward to it.

"Well, well, well," he said. "Before anything else I want to thank you for coming, and I want to ask you to say thank you to the person on whose behalf you've come. Will you do that for me?"

"Of course I will, Mr. Grisholm. And I'm sure she'd want to say thank you to you for bothering to come in on a Saturday and look at her gun, when you've got better things to do with your time off."

"No. There's nothing in the world I'd sooner have done, and I want you to assure your friend that I fully understand that the gun—or guns—we'll come to that in a moment—anyway, they're not for sale, though of course if they were to come onto the market I'd be delighted to make an offer for them. Next—"

"Excuse me interrupting, Mr. Grisholm, but it isn't really that I'm her friend. Well, not exactly. She's paralysed and bedridden, and I'm the nurse she has to look after her. She's got her wits about her, mind you, much more than some you'll meet out on the street."

"I see. And I take it she saw the *Roadshow* programme in which a young woman showed up with what seems to be the other gun of this pair? I assume she had been aware that it was missing?"

"She didn't exactly say. Far as I can make out she'd put the box away and not looked at it for years. That's why she's so upset."

"And she wants the other gun back, no doubt. This is all very awkward. I have to tell you that I've reason to believe that the ownership of these guns is in dispute. Last week—Thursday afternoon, it would have been—I had a visit from a gentleman who wanted a valuation on the basis of a photograph he showed me. I have no doubt that the photograph was of these guns, both of them, in this box, with these tools and accoutrements. He said that the guns were his, but he hadn't brought them because it would have been inconvenient to get them out of the bank.

"Naturally I asked him if he'd seen the TV programme, and he said that that was what had aroused his interest, and he assumed that Ladurie must have made two identical pairs. He told me that the guns in the photograph had been found by his mother in a junk shop in Nottingham just after the war, and she'd bought them and given them to his father on account of the coincidence of initials, J.M.

"Now, I happen to be able to corroborate this point. My own father, who is now retired, also watched the programme, and he called me that evening in a state of some excitement and told me that his father, my grandfather, had been shown an exactly similar pair of pistols, in their box, in 1949 by a gentleman who had brought them in and said in passing that his wife had given them to him because they carried his initials; and later the same gentleman had come in again and told my grandfather that he had traced the coat of arms on the box and found it to be that of Joachim Murat, who was one of Napleon's marshals, subsequently King of Naples. The gentleman had had no interest in selling the pistols, of course, but my father remembers my grandfather talking about them as the finest pair he had ever seen, and wondering what had become of them.

"Despite this, I didn't fully believe all my visitor told me. It is inconceivable that Ladurie had made two sets of pistols for the same man, and the photograph he showed me had clearly been taken many years ago. Either he must know that one of the pistols was missing or he wasn't in a position to find out if that was the case. Furthermore, he wanted me to help him get in touch with the woman who'd brought the gun to the *Roadshow*. I told him to write to the programme in Bristol and they would forward any letter to her, as all names and addresses are strictly confidential. If I'd wanted to talk to her myself, I'd have had to do exactly that. Despite that, he spent some time trying to get me to tell him more about her than had appeared on the programme, which I of course refused to do. And I'm afraid if your patient is hoping that I'll be able to help in that way, I shall have to take exactly the same line. I'm sorry about that. I'd like to help. I've very little doubt you're telling the truth, and besides that it's essential, in my view, that this important set should be reunited as soon as possible."

"That's how it goes," said Dilys. "It was Mr. Dick Matson, I suppose the one who came along with the photo. I've only met him just the once, and I must say I didn't fancy what I saw."

"Well . . . No. I'd better not say it straight out. This is a messy sort of business, so I'll be a bit careful. Now, is there anything else you want to know?"

"About it being fired and then not cleaned right," she said. "You're sure about that?"

"Quite sure. This one has also been fired and left for a while—a few hours perhaps—and then very carefully cleaned. But the other one was left for two or three days and, well, it looks as if the chap did his best—I'd guess he knew how to clean a modern gun, but there are vulnerable spots on an antique pistol which he seems to have missed. This is all guesswork, you understand . . ."

"I see. Well, I'll tell her all that. Oh, dear . . ."

"You were hoping for more?"

"She's a really lovely old thing, brave as brave in spite of everything, but she's worrying herself sick over all this. It isn't just wanting the gun back, that's not even the most of it, I reckon. It's how it come to missing, and why. That's why she perked up after the programme. I didn't tell you, we didn't see it when it was shown—Mrs. Thomas had to get hold of a tape for us—we'd only heard about it before that, and from Mr. Dick too, which didn't help, and now what you've just told me, I don't know much about it, but it sounds like just a load of worries for poor Mrs. Matson . . ."

"I'm sorry. I wish I could do more to help. I wonder if they've had cases of disputed ownership before now—at the *Roadshow*, I mean. I'd have thought that if the enquiring party could make out a sufficiently clear claim, they might be legally forced to put them in touch with the current possessor of the disputed object . . . Look, I'll try and find out. Here's my card—I'll put my home number on the back. Call me in three or four days' time and I may have some news for you."

He had been nestling the pistol back into its place as he spoke. He placed the card on top of it, closed the box, slid it into the envelope and handed it to Dilys. They rose and thanked each other yet again, delicately balancing formality against effusiveness, the sort of precise social interchange you sometimes achieve by the end of a first meeting, which then allows you to part feeling altogether better about the world you live in. Out on the pavement he hailed a taxi for her and helped her in. As it did its U-turn to take her back to King's Cross he was locking the shop. I hope he's going home to a nice wife and kids, Dilys thought. He deserves them.

She bought a pad at the station bookstall, and on the train north thought and remembered, sucking her pen, scribbled a bit and thought and remembered again, so that she wouldn't leave anything out. She had it all down and in order by the time she reached Matlock station.

3

Mrs. Matson listened with closed eyes, looking as peaceful as the dead, and after a whispered "Thank you, Dilys," stayed like that for some while.

At length, still with closed eyes, she whispered again.

"Albums, please. Second shelf, far end. Letter J. Nineteen forty-eight."

"I know, dearie. Shan't be a mo."

Dilys hurried out, both pleased and intrigued—pleased because Mrs. Matson was so obviously much less fretful now that she'd found a loose end to tease at in her tangle, and intrigued because this was an album she'd never been asked to bring before. J. was Colonel Matson, of course. Jocelyn. Pity him having a girl's name like that, when he was such a big, strong man—and he'd called Mrs. Matson "Ray" too. It was short for Rachel, but still it was a boy's name, really. Dilys knew that because once or twice in the albums there'd been photographs where Mrs. Matson had set the camera up so that she'd got time to get into the picture herself, and "Ray" was what she'd written underneath. She'd several times asked for the J. albums from before the war, but not this one. Interesting that it didn't start till '48 too. Perhaps she hadn't wanted to take pictures of him until he'd got over what they'd done to him in that Jap camp.

Back in the room, Dilys cranked the bed up, slid the reading table into place, adjusted the lamp, got the reading specs comfortable, opened the album and started to turn slowly through the pages.

A shooting party, eight men in plus fours, with guns, and a row of dead birds and three hares laid out on pale stubble. She picked the Colonel out at once, him being the tallest. Anybody, any nurse, at least, would have spotted he'd been ill and was getting better. He had that newly fleshed appearance. Dilys really liked the way he looked, the way he stood. With pride. Not thinking about it, not working at it, not stuck-up about it—she remembered miners and farmhands who'd held themselves that way—no wonder Mrs. Matson had been so keen on him. She turned more pages. She guessed Mrs. Matson wanted to look at one special picture, but she was very kind about letting Dilys go slowly so she had a chance to see the other ones. Each pair of pages had a sheet of tissue between them, so the photos didn't lie against each other. Sometimes there were two or three on one page, sometimes just a single larger one, like the shooting party. That had been posed, obviously, but most of them hadn't. Still, they weren't exactly snapshots—not like other people's snapshots, anyway. There was something about them. They weren't careless—no, they were somehow *meant*, even when you couldn't guess what the meaning might be. There was a copy of the one on the bureau, with the Colonel standing by his car. Underneath in silvery ink it said "Jocelyn. The Rover. November 1948."

A few pages later the tissue came up sticking to the left hand page. Opposite it was a picture of Colonel Matson out on the lawn with the big cedar beyond him. He had his right arm up and was taking aim with a pistol—no, he was actually firing, because you could see the puff of smoke against the dark of the cedar . . .

"Stop," whispered Mrs. Matson. "Other page."

The tissue was sticking to something, four spots of old gum which had once held a photograph in place. At the bottom of the page it said "The Laduries. October 1949."

"Dick," whispered Mrs. Matson. "Let you in. Stayed out there. He took it. And the list."

JENNY

"For heaven's sake! Not that tie with that shirt! Here, this one."

(Left to himself, even when not in a hurry, Jeff would have dressed in whatever was out—yesterday's clothes or something, perhaps still slightly damp off the bathroom clothesline—rather than go to the trouble of opening a drawer and choosing. His ensembles tended therefore towards the random.)

"And stop worrying. I'll be all right. He won't have a clue who I am, anyway."

"I was thinking if you took the bloody thing with you, it might jog his memory. Look. Take it, see how it goes, and if it looks—"

"Jeff! Stop it! Your lace-up shoes, not those horrible brown things. And your good coat. You've got three minutes. I'm doing your thermos."

He came down the stairs like a falling boulder. She had the door open, locked it behind him and ran for the car. All the way to the station he rabbitted on about Uncle Albert, but she was too busy making time through traffic to pay attention. They reached the station with forty-five seconds to spare. "All right," she said. "I'll see Sister Morris first. I'll take the gun and show him if I think it'll help. I'll *cope*, right? And this evening you'll come home and tell me that Sir Vidal has ordered Billy's public disembowelment. Kiss me."

He did, and loped away. She watched him out of sight, and drove home to make herself breakfast feeling weirdly unresentful that a tycoon's whim should have cost them one of these free days together.

*   *   *

Marlings Retirement Home had originally been built, apparently, by a successful tea planter when he had returned to England with his family just before the First World War. Jenny was unsystematically interested in that kind of thing. She had never been to India, but she felt she might have guessed about the house—wide-eaved, with a deep verandah of dark brown wood, occupying the crest of a low ridge, with dense rhododendrons all along the drive, and behind them droop-branched conifers that might as well have been deodars but presumably weren't. Anyway, it didn't feel as if it really belonged in England. Perhaps it wouldn't have felt right in India either, because it didn't actually belong anywhere. This made it a bit depressing for the kind of place it now was, full of people sitting and waiting, sitting and waiting, the way one does in airports when one's flight's delayed. There's nothing to do here and nowhere else to go.

Sister Morris was a heavy, dark-skinned woman with a faintly scowling look which Jeff said didn't mean anything.

"I was hoping to see Mr. Pilcher," she said. "Thing is, we've had a bit of bother about Albert. There was a gentleman came a couple of days back—no, I'm a liar, Friday it would've been—said he thought he'd look in seeing he was passing so close. Matson, he said his name was, and his dad had been in the war with Albert. Be that as may be, he sounded all right, but when I told Albert he pulled me up sharp. It was Colonel Matson, he told me, and anyway he was dead and Albert knew that 'cause he'd been to the funeral. I told him, no, that must've been this Mr. Matson's father, and Albert went all stubborn the way he does, and said he didn't want to see him, but I persuaded him. They get things into their heads, you know, but seeing the gentleman had come all this way, from Devon, he told me . . .

"Turned out Albert was right and I was wrong, 'cause I'd not left them alone five minutes when Albert was shouting from the top of the stair to me to come and show the gentleman out. He can shout too when he puts his mind to it. So up I run and there's the gentleman trying to calm him down but I could see it wasn't any good so I had to tell him he'd better go."

"Did you tell him anything about Jeff looking after Uncle Albert's affairs?"

"No, I didn't. I was just set on getting shot of him quick as I could, and he'd lost his rag and was trying to put it over me in that hoity-toity voice of his and I wasn't standing for that. Good as a play it must've been for the other old dears by then. Should I have told him about Mr. Pilcher?"

"No, I'm sure Jeff would say you did right. It was just that he came and saw me, later that evening, and pretended he didn't know anything about Uncle Albert living here . . . I wonder how he found me . . . Never mind. Anyway, I know what this is about. Mr. Matson is trying to get hold of something belonging to Uncle Albert. I can't tell you any more. I'm sorry."

"Well, I'm not letting him come bothering Albert again, and that's for sure. The poor old boy's been that fussed since it happened, not wanting to come down for meals in case the gentleman showed up."

"I'm sorry. I'll see what I can do, but I'm not sure he'll listen to me. He doesn't usually remember who I am, especially with Jeff not here. Is he up in his room? I'll go straight up, shall I?"

From her first visit Jenny had been impressed by how they did things at Marlings. The stair carpet was thick, the elaborate dark woodwork dusted and polished. There were cyclamen and heavy-scented narcissi in pots on sills and landings. The staff had time for you. Jenny had merely appreciated these things on earlier visits, but this time she saw them not under the pleasant glow of civilised be-haviour towards the elderly, but in the more acid light of cost. Uncle Albert's pension, with the annuity from his savings, didn't make up half the Marlings fees. Jeff supplied the rest. This hadn't been diffi-cult out of one excellent salary and one reasonable one, but it would be impossible with both jobs gone.

She went down a corridor, passing two fire doors, and knocked at a room labelled "Mr. Fredricks."

"Who's that?" snapped a voice. Even without what Sister Morris had told her Jenny might have detected the note of anxiety. She opened the door and put her head round.

"It's me, Jenny, Jeff's wife," she said.

He was sitting in an upright armchair with a newspaper across his knees, a gaunt old man with a large, high-bridged nose and a thin mouth. He was wearing a suit and tie, and brown laced shoes, polished to a high sheen.

"Thank you, my dear," he said, "but I don't need anything just now."

"Hello, Uncle Albert," she said, paying no attention. "I'm afraid Jeff couldn't come at the last moment. He sent his love. I've brought some fruit. Shall I put it in the bowl?"

"That's right."

She did so, then adjusted the other chair so that she was almost facing him, and sat down. He was only a little deaf, but on earlier visits he had seemed to find the lighter timbre of her voice harder to hear than Jeff's. After the fraught, irrational apprehension of her first visit, when, in spite of Jeff's assurances that Uncle Albert was a nice old boy in excellent health, she had really needed to force herself to go through with it, for Jeff's sake, Uncle Albert's room now held no horror for her. His grasp of present reality might waver, but the habits of order and cleanliness persisted. All his possessions had their exact places. There was none of the reek which pervades the air around some of the old. The visitor's only difficulty was keeping a conversation going.

Jeff's technique was to talk much as he would have to anyone else, a little more slowly but no louder, and if the old boy got hold of the wrong end of the stick, not to correct him, but either to carry on or, if it looked more promising, to go off in the new direction. He said you never knew how much Uncle Albert would pick up, but he would spot it at once if you were trying to make things easy for him.

"I'm sorry Jeff couldn't come," she said. "So's he. It happened only this morning. In fact we were still asleep when the phone rang. The thing is, Jeff had a row with his immediate boss and walked out. Or he was sacked—it depends how you look at it. Anyway, the call was from someone who works for the top guy in the whole company, saying the big man wanted to see Jeff today, in Birmingham, about the row. It looks like being his one chance to put his case . . ."

He was peering at her, frowning.

"Dyed your hair, then?" he said.

"No, it's always been this colour."

"Not since I've known you, it hasn't, and then you were just about so high. You took after your dad, that way. Comes of living in America. They're always messing around with how they look, Americans. Your lad's not coming today, then? What's his name? I'll get it in a minute."

The gnarled fingers groped for the memory.

"Jeff," she said. "He had to go to Birmingham all of a sudden. He sent his love."

"That's right, Jeff. A good enough lad. You've done very well by him, Penny."

Jenny grasped the nature of the confusion, shrugged inwardly, and settled for the moment into the role of being her own mother-in-law.

"I'm glad you think so," she said. "I'm very proud of him."

"Jeff," he said, frowning again. "There's something—you tell him—something he's looking after for me."

He fell silent, staring at her with obvious distrust. Jenny didn't hesitate. If she pretended ignorance now, what if he remembered that when she admitted knowledge later? Anyway, she wanted to get it over.

"Your pistol, you mean?" she said.

The stare hardened to chilly ferocity. He hadn't done this to her before. It was as if an old family myth of Jeff's, a quirk from his childhood, had stalked living and potent into the room.

"What do you know about that?" he said in a quiet, level voice, seeming to bite each word off to separate it from the next. "Who the hell are you, anyway, coming here making out you're my niece. You're not."

"I'm Jeff's wife, Jenny," she said. "Look, I've brought the pistol to show you it's all right, and Jeff's still got it."

She took the parcel out of her shoulder bag and gave it to him. He opened the box, checked that the pistol was there, closed it and put it on the table beside him, all without acknowledgement or comment.

"Do you want me to tell you what happened?" she said.

"If you think you've something to say for yourself, miss, say it."

His tone was unmollified.

"Jeff put it carefully away, like you asked him," she explained. "I found it when I was looking for something else. I didn't know what it was, so I left it out to ask him about when he got home. Then . . ."

His look didn't soften as she told the story. She couldn't guess how much he was taking in, but if she paused he nodded to her to carry on.

". . . so when Jeff got home I told him what had happened, and he said I'd better come and see you, and tell you. I'm sorry, Uncle Albert. Of course I wouldn't have done it if I'd known it was yours."

He continued to stare at her, conceding nothing, but she remained unquelled. She could see how this look might once have awed paraded regiments, but it had no effect on her. It lacked the password to her controls.

"What about Dick Matson, then?" he said. "Put you up to this, did he?"

"No. He showed up on my doorstep the evening after he'd seen you and tried to persuade me that the pistol belonged to him. I didn't believe him. I thought he wasn't telling the truth about several things."

"He's no good. Never was. Scum. What did he say to you?"

She told him, still slowly and carefully, getting the impression now that he was listening with something like comprehension, though for a while he simply watched her as before, in silence. She wasn't expecting it when he broke in.

"Hold it there. She's still alive, Mrs. Matson," he said.

"Yes, but I gather she's not very well."

"I want to see her. Where is she? Still at Forde Place, eh?"

"He didn't say. Where's that, Uncle Albert?"

"Forde Place, Matlock, Derbyshire."

He was heaving himself to his feet, a little tottery after long sitting.

"Derbyshire's too far, Uncle Albert. We can't go now. We'll have to ring up and see if she's there, and ask if she's well enough to see you."

"I'll just get my coat."

"No, Uncle Albert. You can't go today. It's too far."

She took his arm, but he shook her off and started for the door. She ran to bar the way, but the pulse of energy died and he let her lead him back to his chair and settle him dejectedly down.

"Listen," she said. "I've got a few days off, and so has Jeff. I'll try and find out where Mrs. Matson is and talk to whoever is looking after her, and if they say she'd like to see you we'll find a way of getting you up there. Is that all right?"

"Have to be, won't it?"

"I can call Directory Enquiries, I suppose, but . . . Have you got an old address book? Only they'll have changed the number. Can I look in your papers, Uncle Albert?"

"Carry on. Bottom drawer."

He sounded beaten, indifferent, exhausted. Jenny knelt by the chest of drawers and pulled out the lowest one. Most business correspondence came to Jeff, and Marlings redirected anything that came there except the obviously personal. Jeff made copies and then took the originals over on his next visit, went through them with Uncle Albert and then "filed" anything that Uncle Albert took it into his head that he needed to keep. It was mostly pointless, but Jeff said it helped feed the sense of orderliness and control which was part of what kept Uncle Albert in such good shape.

The filing was done in large brown envelopes, each labelled and dated in Jeff's elegant, slanting hand—so much more characteristic, Jenny thought, of his inward self than was most of his outward mien. She tried "Keepsakes." It was mostly postcards, including, she was amused to see, one from Jeff on their honeymoon on Teneriffe. Otherwise it was letters and clippings from newspapers—what, she wondered, had moved Uncle Albert to preserve a photograph and report of an agricultural steam machine rally?

The "Personal" file was no better, but the "Military" produced the goods, a list of addresses, stapled into a booklet, of the Cambi Road Association (Patron Mrs. J. J. Matson). She glanced through it. There were forty or fifty names, and at the end a dozen short obituaries. Everyone was listed by military rank with regiment: RSM A. D. Fredricks, 2nd Derbyshire, c/o Pilcher, 238 Ashford Road, Maidstone. Mrs. Matson was the one civilian. Her address was still given as Forde Place.

"Here you are," said Jenny, showing him. "Just like you said."

She pointed at the line. His eyesight was remarkable. He had spectacles, but could read print without them by holding the paper only an extra few inches away.

"Right," he said. "I'll be taking the train."

Again, but much less decisively, he started to rise.

"No, it's much too late," she said, coaxing him back down. "Look, as soon as I get home I'll ring the secretary—his number's here, Mr. Stadding . . ."

"Major Stadding—he's dead. Saw it happen. No doubt about it. Ask Terry Voss."

There was an odd note in his remark which made Jenny look round at him. Anger or something? His face gave her no clue. She checked the date on the front of the list.

"It's this year's," she said. "I suppose it might be his son, or something."

"Simon. Now, he's a good lad. Going to marry Miss Anne, one point, only he didn't. What about him?"

"I'll call him and see if he'll let me have Mrs. Matson's number and then I'll call whoever's looking after her and ask if there's any chance of you going up to see her, and then, if she says yes, we can work out how and when. All right? But what we'll do now—it's such a lovely afternoon—is go for a drive and have tea somewhere, and then I'll bring you back. Would you like that?"

"If you say so."

"Do you want to go to the bathroom first?"

"Might as well."

He rose obediently and left the room. Jenny made a note of Mr. Stadding's number, tidied the files away, put the pistol in its box and then in her bag. On Uncle Albert's return he looked at her sharply.

"Who are you, then?"

"I'm Jenny, Jeff's wife. We're going out for a drive."

"Going to Forde Place, you mean?"

"Not today, Uncle Albert. There isn't time."

He enjoyed the drive. They stopped at a sports field and watched schoolboys playing soccer, and ate at a tea room below the Downs, after which she shepherded him round a supermarket so that he could buy a packet of ginger nuts. On the way back to Hastings he slept, effortlessly balancing his head upright, unperturbed by the movement of the car.

"Wake up, Uncle Albert," she said as they climbed the Marlings drive.

He leaned forward to stare through the window screen.

"No," he said sharply. "You've got it wrong, young lady. That's never Forde Place."

"We're not going to Forde Place today. There isn't time. But when I get home I'll—"

"If you say so," he interrupted and groped for the door catch. She went round and helped him climb out, slowly and stiffly, looking very much his age. When she'd got him up to his room and settled him into his chair she asked him whether he wanted her to leave the pistol or take it back to Jeff to look after.

"Do that, if you like," he said, and fell asleep.

She looked for Sister Morris, to tell her about the pistol, but she was busy with one of the other patients, so she just told one of the junior staff that she'd brought Uncle Albert home and drove back to Maidstone.

There were two messages on the machine, one from Jeff, saying he would be on the eight forty-eight, and things had gone pretty well, he thought, and the other from Sister Morris, asking her or Jeff to call as soon as possible. She did so, and was told that Uncle Albert had twice been stopped trying to leave, once needing to be chased down the drive. He said he had to catch a train to London, and he was very upset about something he'd lost, but refused to say what it was. They'd given him a sedative and he was quieter now, but they didn't like doing that more than they had to.

"I know what this is about," Jenny said. "I was going to ring you anyway, in case. Tell him that Jeff's got this thing and is looking after it. You may need to remind him that Jeff is Penny's son. Penny is Uncle Albert's niece. He sometimes thinks I'm Penny. He wants to go see an old lady in Derbyshire. I'm trying to get hold of her, to see if anything can be arranged. I'll let you know as soon as I can. With a bit of luck he'll have forgotten all about it by tomorrow. But I don't think he will."

A woman's voice, quavering and anxious, answered the telephone. Jenny asked to speak to Mr. Stadding.

"Could you tell me what it's about?"

"It's to do with the Cambi Road Association."

"Oh, dear. Well, I'll see. Please wait."

There was a long pause, and then a man's voice, slow, weary.

"Well, how can I help you?"

"Mr. Stadding? My name's Jenny Pilcher. My husband—"

"Pilcher who deals with old Fredricks's affairs?"

"That's right. Jeff's away, but I visited Uncle Albert today and—"

"One moment. You're in Maidstone, aren't you?"

"Yes. Why?"

"I'll explain in a moment. Carry on please."

Jenny did so. When she'd finished she heard him sigh, as if her apparently simple request posed immense problems.

"I don't normally give telephone numbers," he said. "The rule is that you have to write to the member in question, care of the Association, at this address, and I will then forward your letter. However, I have reason to believe that Mrs. Matson, or rather her daughter, Flora Thomas, is trying to get in touch with you. She called only this morning to ask if any of the members lived in Maidstone. I told her no, because I send Fredricks's stuff direct to that place in Hastings, and it slipped my mind that your husband is in the list at Maidstone. I think this must be more than mere coincidence, so what I suggest is that I call Mrs. Thomas now and tell her what's happened, and then it will be up to her. So if you'd give me your number to pass on . . ."

"That'll do fine. Thank you very much. Ready?"

The call came through in twenty minutes.

"Mrs. Pilcher?"

"Speaking."

"Now let's get this straight before we start. Are you the one who took a Ladurie pistol to *The Antiques Roadshow*, the one that was shown—Sunday before last, it would have been?"

Jenny paused, unprepared. The voice was sharp, a bit county, bossy in a lively way.

"I'm afraid I'm not in a position to say anything about that," she said.

"Oh, come off it. It's quite simple. You've got my father's Ladurie pistol. I've no idea how you got hold of it, but it belongs to my mother and we want it back."

With her wits now about her Jenny had no problem remaining professionally unruffled.

"I'm sorry," she said, "but what I told you was the truth. The pistol isn't mine and I shouldn't have taken it to the show. I'm not in a position to talk about it. I have no standing in the affair. All I can do is to pass on anything you wish to say to the person concerned, who may then be prepared to discuss it with you."

There was a pause, and a frustrated exhalation.

"Can I tell you why I wanted to get in touch with you?" said Jenny.

"Has it got anything to do with the pistol?"

"I don't know, and if I did I couldn't tell you."

"Bother you. You talk like a lawyer."

"I'm a solicitor . . ."

"Ha!"

". . . but I'm not acting for anyone in this. Really, I'm not."

Another pause.

"All right. You'd better tell me what you want."

"It's about my husband's great-uncle, who's an old man called Albert Fredricks—"

"Sergeant Fred!"

"Yes, he was a sergeant major in the Second Derbyshire Regiment, I believe."

"That's right. Such a dear. Salt of the earth. How is he? Getting a bit doddery, I suppose."

"Physically he's in very good shape for his age, but his memory's pretty erratic. He's in a retirement home in Hastings, and being very well looked after. I took him for a drive this afternoon."

"Good for you. Go on."

"Well, while we were talking Mrs. Matson's name came up—that's your mother, isn't it?—and Uncle Albert took it into his head he wanted to come and see her about something that's bothering him. He wouldn't tell me what, but he got very upset about it. He wanted to start off at once, and to keep him quiet I told him I'd try and get hold of Mrs. Matson and see if it was a possibility. He may have forgotten all about it by tomorrow but I don't think so. After I went he was trying to leave the home to catch a train to London."

"Good for him. This has got to have something to do with the pistol, hasn't it? . . . Oh, all right, you're not going to tell me. Look, my mother's the other way round from Sergeant Fred—I mean she's paralysed and bedridden and can't talk much, but she's absolutely all there mentally. I'll talk to her and see what she says. Then it'll be a question of getting him up here. You could put him on a train . . . No, he'd have to have somebody with him, wouldn't he, or he'd get out at the wrong station. I think we'd better send a car. Would he be up to that? It's three hours plus from London, make it five from Hastings—he'd have to stay the night—does he need nursing? I could arrange—"

"If you're serious, I think he'll have to come with someone he knows," said Jenny. "I suppose I could drive him up. If Jeff—that's my husband—if Jeff's free, he could come and share the driving. I've got a few days off, so it'd have to be this week . . ."

Jenny was uncertain how she had reached a point where she could be thinking about the trip as a possibility. It was something to do with being, for this week only, a completely free agent, free, even, from her own rational needs, with just her whims and desires to satisfy.

"Take a week off to think about it," Jerry had said, but there was no thinking to do. Millie had worked for Trevor for twenty years. Selina's partner had left her and the kids just before Christmas, and not been traced for maintenance. Dave was getting married. Trevor himself was dying. And so on. Anyway, what was the point? The only moral certainty that Jenny had been able to grasp was that she would have to leave. That was fixed. When she'd left, she would try to decide whether to tell Mr. McNair that he'd been right about the docket. But for this week she was in limbo. So was Jeff—not officially sacked, not until this morning working. The car too—theirs and not theirs, for this week only. And the house—there were things to be fixed before they could put it on the market, but the decision couldn't yet be made . . .

Thus it didn't, until she had put the telephone down and thought about it, strike Jenny as odd that she should have pretty well agreed with this stranger that she and Jeff might use one, or perhaps two, of their precious days to take Uncle Albert up to Matlock to visit a bedridden old lady, though when she'd first spoken of it it had been little more than the easiest way to persuade him back into his chair.

"And besides," she told Jeff over supper, "I really want to know about the pistol. I'm inquisitive."

"I'm not," he said wearily. "I just want it out of my hair. Do I have to ring this woman tonight?"

"It's a bit late. Tomorrow . . . Look, I'll do it, if you want. And if she says yes, I'll take Uncle Albert up there and sort out about the pistol with her. I'll do you a couple of lines for you to sign, giving me authority. I'd better look up the law relating to gifts . . ."

"My impression is that Uncle Albert doesn't actually think it belongs to him. None of that matters, anyway, provided he finishes up happy about it. Do you think you can do it in a day?"

"If I can't I'm not going. It's unlucky sleeping apart, I've decided. Bad things happen. You'll be all right for a day?"

"I'll be fine. When you're here, I keep wanting to break off. In fact, one good solid day, when I can really concentrate, would be a help. I've got the stuff on disk, but it's all over the shop and pretty technical. See if you can fix Matlock for the day after tomorrow, then I'll spend tomorrow sorting out what I need—that's just a question of time—and I'll have two days to get it into a shape Sir Vidal can understand. That's going to be the tricky bit."

"I'm worried about him wanting to take you over, sort of absorb you, the way Billy tried. These guys think you're a gizmo, Jeff. There's plenty of gizmos out there, but you're the best, and they want you for themselves."

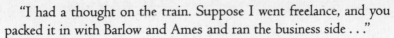

"I had a thought on the train. Suppose I went freelance, and you packed it in with Barlow and Ames and ran the business side . . ."

". . . and get to come with you to Paris and Bermuda as part of the package . . ."

"It'll just as likely be Flint, Michigan."

"Not if I'm running the business side, it won't."

"There's that. Right. I'll take the car back Friday, and clear my desk. But first I'm going to screw Billy."

RACHEL

I

"The most extraordinary thing, Ma! You'll never guess. I was just finishing doing the flowers last evening when Simon Stadding rang—he really doesn't sound at all well, poor man. I wonder if he ever thinks about Anne now. Oh dear, never mind. Anyway all he would tell me was that there was this woman called Pilcher, in Maidstone, wanting to get hold of me. You remember I rang him to ask if anyone in the Association lived in Maidstone and he said no, but apparently he'd forgotten that that was where Sergeant Fred's great-nephew—you remember Sergeant Fred, of course—that was where this great-nephew lives who looks after Sergeant Fred's affairs. Light dawned, you could say. So of course I rang the woman straight away. I thought she'd be asking for money, so I was pretty sharp with her to start with and I didn't say anything about Sergeant Fred. I just tackled her straight off about the pistol and told her we'd got to have it back. She was remarkably cool about it, I must say—she's some kind of solicitor, she says, but she's not wearing her solicitor's hat about this—solicitor's wig, I suppose I mean—no I don't—that's barristers—but she absolutely refused to say anything about the pistol except that it wasn't hers and she shouldn't have taken it to the show, and she'd pass a message on to whoever it did belong to, only it didn't of course because it belongs to you, but you know what I mean. And then she rather took the wind out of my sails by saying that what she was calling about was that Sergeant Fred has suddenly decided he wants to come and see you, and we hummed and hawed about that for a bit but I thought if it means we're going to get the pistol back, and apparently she's prepared to drive him up, with her husband because it's a long way, though we did talk about them staying the night—he's spry as a flea, she says, but his mind's a bit off so he's never quite sure what's what—the other way round from you, I told her—I hope you don't mind—so Mrs. Pilcher says he may have forgotten all about it by tomorrow, but she doesn't think so because he seems to have a thoroughgoing bee in his bonnet about something—she says he was trying to come up here on his own, after she'd gone, and they had to stop him—I must say I rather took to her in spite of her sounding so keep-your-distance about everything. She'd taken Sergeant Fred for a drive this afternoon, she said, and she sounds rather fond of him, so her heart's in the right place. I'd've come up last night and told you only supper was ready and kidneys are Jack's favourite and you know how easily those cream sauces crack—wasn't it good though? She's terrific at the tricky things, only she can't be bothered to get the easy ones right, and really there'd be something indecent about having two cooks . . . anyway, I've been thinking. I bet what's bothering Sergeant Fred is that he's got the pistols, somehow, heaven knows how. I mean if it had been—what was that funny crook's name Da was so fond of? Terry something. Vass?"

"Voss."

"That's right. If it had been him . . . but Sergeant Fred? Anyway, he's got the pistols, and someone must have been messing around firing them and not cleaning them properly, which is a shame because you know what a fuss Da always made about that—and then this woman got hold of one of them—I mean if she'd had the other one and the box she'd have taken them all along to the show, wouldn't she? So now it's all come out and Mrs. Pilcher says his memory's not too good so perhaps he'd just forgotten about them, but now he's decided that he'd better get them off his conscience by bringing them back. Don't you think that's what's happened, Ma?"

"Possibly," whispered Rachel. This was one of her no-saliva days. She couldn't have argued, even if she had wished to.

"So if that's what's going on," said Flora, "wouldn't it be easier all round if I just popped down to Hastings and saw Sergeant Fred and told him all was forgiven and forgotten and he could give me the pis-

tols to bring back to you. I'll be going to London anyway for the Mc-
Nulty bash—think of those two staying married for fifty years! Like
one of those wars people used to have which just went on and on till
that's all anyone knows about them—do you have the faintest notion
what the Thirty Years War was about?—instead of Mrs. Pilcher having to bring the old boy all the way up here. You do agree, don't you?"

"Won't know who you are."

"But I'll tell him, Ma. I'll get Mrs. Pilcher to come too. And I'm
sorry, Ma, but if you get him all this way and he sees you like this,
perhaps he won't . . . I mean, when he used to know you . . ."

"Knows the house. Knows pistol belongs here."

"But honestly, Ma . . ."

"Drink."

"I'm sorry. Try not to talk. Here you are, then. Ready?"

The effort at speech had exacerbated the drought in Rachel's
mouth to a pitch beyond discomfort, not exactly pain, but still with
the true ferocity of pain. And now Flora, overconfident in the conve-
nience of the invalid cup, tried to pour too fast. Rachel forced her lips
to reject the spout just in time to stop herself choking, a hideous experience, convulsing the insensate body while the mind endured, helpless and aware of the ease with which one could suffocate on one's
own vomit. Taken by surprise, Flora poured a generous slop of barley
water over Rachel's chest.

"Oh, sorry, Ma."

She put the cup down and mopped with a towel at the spillage,
using a vigorous rubbing motion, as if drying a spaniel. Rachel's head
joggled helplessly to and fro. The second attempt was more successful.

"Better? No, don't try to talk, Ma."

"Ask her to bring Sergeant Fred."

"Oh, but, Ma . . ."

"No. Listen. Knows what he wants. Doesn't matter how . . ."

Rachel willed the obscenity out.

". . . gaga he is. He knows."

Flora shrugged. Most people would have described her as strong-
willed. She had that manner and usually got away with it. They would

also, probably, have thought Rachel diffident, but even now both still accepted, as they always had, that it would be Rachel who had her way.

She must have smiled without deliberately causing her lips to move (unusual these days) because Flora responded with a laugh. Rachel was aware of feeling peculiarly close to her daughter, the closeness of affection and habit, but not, alas, what she understood by love. Not for the first time she wondered whether Flora had any conscious understanding of how she had been cheated, almost from the beginning. She had been given warmth, interest, help and comfort when needed, all unstinted. But true, deep love from her parents—the real thing, irreplaceable, no other product would do—love such as Jocelyn had felt for Anne and Rachel for Dick—no. Somehow Rachel kept her smile in place, though now weeping inwardly and raging that her stupid arms couldn't stir, couldn't even ache with the physical impulse to stir, reach out, embrace this sixty-four-year-old woman and at last start to atone for all those years of love withheld.

"Darling," she whispered. "I haven't—"

She stopped herself in time and closed her eyes. *Loved you enough*, she had been going to say, but Flora wouldn't have understood, would have protested, distressed. It was too late to explain now, much too late.

"That's right, Ma. You have a good rest, and I'll come up later and tell you what the woman says."

Rachel felt the brush of a kiss on her forehead, heard the movement of door handle and door, and then Flora's rattling syllables receding along the corridor as she moved towards Dilys's sitting room, already explaining herself. Rachel couldn't distinguish the words, and Dilys's softer answers from inside the room, but amid the diversions the gist was plain from the intonation: Mrs. Pilcher's call; Sergeant Fred—who he was and why he mattered; his wish to visit Rachel; Rachel's wish to see him; half-admiring exasperation at the determination of these two old things to meet again; passing mention of the accident with the barley water; and so on. Then both voices moving back towards Rachel's door, the actual words becoming audible as the door opened.

"... could ask Pat to come and give you a hand for the night, I suppose."

"I think I can manage, Mrs. Thomas, really I do. It doesn't sound like the old man's going to be a lot of trouble."

"Well, let's just see . . ."

(Flora now moving away and speaking over her shoulder.)

"... and as soon as I know which day it'll be I'll check with Pat whether she'll be free."

The door closed. Rachel heard Dilys sigh.

"Now then, dearie, we've been at it again, wearing ourselves out chatting, Mrs. Thomas says. You're each as bad as the other, I'm beginning to think. And she spilt your drinkie over you too, she says. Let's have a look. Dearie me, we're all sticky, like a kid who's been at the treacle tin. I don't know. Looks like I'll have to give you your bath all over again. And a clean nightie . . . We're all right, aren't we, dearie? We didn't choke or anything?"

"Nearly."

"Well, a miss is as good as a mile, I always say. She's a very good soul, Mrs. Thomas, and I'd be the last to deny it, but I'll go down on my knees and thank my creator that I didn't have the training of her as a nurse."

Rachel would have laughed aloud, had the mechanism still existed. Years ago, on a nanny's afternoon out, she had watched Flora change one of the children's nappies, talking over her shoulder as she did so, and finishing with a bewildered child wearing a vast but unreliable package of terry cloth wrapped loosely round its midriff.

Still with closed eyes she lay, but for once didn't listen to Dilys chattering away as she worked. She was aware of being in a strange state. Normally, despite the unresponsiveness of her body, not a minute went by, except in dreams, when she wasn't fully conscious of its prisoning reality. This morning there seemed to be a looseness in the connection. She could feel, in the sense that the signals came from the inert limbs, but she was unable to interpret the signals. By the movement of her head she could tell that her torso had been gently lifted so that the sodden nightie could be eased free, but after that, for a while, the eerie disembodiment seemed so complete that if she had known the password she could have slid out of this place, out of this time, out of the inert flesh, away . . .

No. She mustn't do that yet. There was work to be done, tidying and sorting, before she could allow herself to leave. She opened her eyes and found her vision blocked by blurred yellow cloud-stuff, which she discovered to be a clean nightie which had draped itself in front of her as her raised left arm was fed into the sleeve. Then, gently, she was rolled to one side to let the nightie be eased beneath her, rolled back to have her right arm inserted, before the garment was fastened down the front and the bedclothes drawn up.

"Thank you," she whispered.

"It's a pleasure," said Dilys. "And now, what'll we do with ourselves? Listen to our book for a bit?"

"No. Albums."

"Oh, good, ever so interesting, I find them. Drinkie before you tell me? We're a bit dry today, aren't we?"

Typical of her attention, Rachel thought, that she could distinguish between one sere whisper and another. She sipped gratefully, then explained which volumes she wanted. Ostensibly she was looking for pictures that might interest Sergeant Fred, so that Dilys could mark them, ready for his visit. It would have been logical to begin with the early part of the war, before the regiment had sailed for Singapore. Sergeant Fred had barely yet become a friend then, but there were a few faces he might remember. Then there was a whole volume devoted to the Cambi Road Association, and there'd be pictures of the children at various ages. But instead of any of those Rachel chose the final one devoted to Jocelyn. Though the previous album had been less than half full, she had started a fresh one for the funeral.

The rector had been in the parish less than a month. Rachel had done no more than shake hands with him after his first service, until he had called to express his condolences over Jocelyn's death, and discuss arrangements for the funeral. Rachel hadn't taken to him. He had a soft but at the same time domineering manner, and though all he said was impeccably correct she detected no real feeling behind it. He had taken so long to answer her request that she'd thought he was going to refuse.

"Very well," he had said at last. "I will say a few words by way of explanation before the service starts."

"Oh, thank you. Honestly, I don't think anyone is going to think it peculiar. They're so used to me and my cameras."

"That would not have been the problem, Mrs. Matson. You will find that I am not greatly influenced by what people think."

And yet he's lasted twenty-three years in the parish, never putting a foot wrong, but still not much liked by anyone. Sad.

"Ready?" said Dilys. "Oh, my goodness, it's . . . Sorry, dearie, I didn't mean to be rude, but . . . And you can't have taken this one! That's you, there, isn't it?"

Impossible that she should have been able to recognise Rachel, standing at the foot of the open grave, all in black, her face hidden by not only the veil, and the shadow from the hideous black hat, but also by the bulk of the camera aimed down at the descending coffin.

"Tom Dawnay," croaked Rachel. "Local paper. Old friend."

So good a friend that he hadn't submitted the picture for use in the *Inquirer*, who would certainly have printed it. Indeed, it might well have made the national press. It was an image of surreal force, even when stripped of the layers of personal meaning that it had for Rachel. On the left a dark slab, the backs of the mourners, corrugated with heads above and fringed with legs below. Then a strip of sunlit grass, with receding gravestones, then the single black column of the widow, rapt in her rite. The camera that had taken the picture was outside the rite, looking at it, but the camera in the widow's hands was integral, essential to its completeness. Rachel had almost never included photographs by anybody else in her albums, but she had put Tom's here, at the start, because she felt it would resonate through the volume, so that only the most insensitive peruser wouldn't sense, looking at the rest of the photographs, that particular presence, those particular emotions, there behind the viewfinder.

She grunted to tell Dilys to leaf on. Apart from that first picture the album was in chronological order: a line of neighbours, friends, cousins, crossing the graveyard towards the church, the picture taken with a wide-angle lens and the negative cropped to produce a frieze-like strip punctuated by verticals, black and grey, people and tomb-stones; Maxwell in his chauffeur's uniform pulling Dinah Tremlett in her old Bath chair; the children lined up at the porch, Flora pregnant with Ferdie and on the edge of tears, Jack dapper at her elbow and properly solemn, Dick trying to look so and faking it, Anne . . . It was for the image of Anne that Rachel had included this otherwise banal funeral group. Physically she took after Rachel, almost pretty in a fine-boned but still slightly horsy fashion. She had been a lively, amenable child, but around the age of eleven had begun to withdraw, to conceal her pleasures and troubles, to seem to wish to become less part of the family. That was what made the picture of her so instantly shocking, the ferocity of dry-eyed grief that was still half rage, though it was almost two years now since the business about Simon Stadding that had precipitated Jocelyn's first stroke. She had at first refused to come to the funeral, but Jack had gone to Bristol of his own accord and persuaded her.

"Mrs. Thomas hasn't changed that much," said Dilys. "Nor Mr. Thomas, come to that, given he's lost a bit of hair. And wasn't Mr. Dick a well set up lad? Image of his father too. No wonder you're fond of him."

She moved to turn the page. Rachel didn't stop her. No mention of Anne. She must have noticed. Tact, presumably, not to comment on such a glimpse of the raw innards of a wounded family.

Inside the church. The other camera, largest aperture, ultrafast film, then delicate development and printing—the results misty greys, sometimes with focal moments: the jet black of the silhouetted coffin and bearers against the open west door; the coffin at the altar, with candles; the congregation standing for a hymn, Rachel's own place empty, a gap in the pattern of open mouths; Sergeant Fred against the north window (Rachel had almost grovelled to achieve the angle) standing at the eagle lectern to bark the lesson with toneless precision. (Extraordinary—still after almost forty years extraordinary—to think that if Jocelyn had died two years sooner it might have been Fish Stadding reading that lesson. Had Simon or Leila ever heard from him? There's been no way to ask. There was still none. He'd be dead by now, surely.) The last picture she'd taken inside the church was of the front of the coffin in close-up as it had passed her place on its way down the aisle, with the near-side bearer also in close-up, a strong, unreadable face.

Then a gap in the sequence, filled only by a cutting from the *Inquirer*, Tom Dawnay's published picture of the coffin emerging from the porch with Rachel on Dick's arm behind it. (She had handed her cameras to Jack to bring out.) The gap continued for the period she had had to stand, barely holding herself together, accepting the unavoidable condolences. Ten or so blurred awful minutes, the same phrases over and over till they lost all meaning, and Jocelyn dead, dead, dead. No meaning in anything, ever again. Her only solid memory of that phase was of Leila Stadding's face, grief and anger like Anne's but so differently borne; the mouth working almost as if in epilepsy as she tried to speak, but then she had turned away and shoved herself past whoever had been waiting behind her. Rachel hadn't expected any of the family to come, but had hoped that Simon might. He hadn't. Leila's elder son, Bob, had brought her, according to Flora.

And then at last the saving reality of the camera, the light meter, her fingers composedly setting apertures and exposures and changing filters, that composure steadying the whole being.

The graveside—family and servants, Jocelyn's sisters and the Austen cousins, three or four old friends, the Cambi Road Association representatives. Not good of Sergeant Fred, unfortunately. That must be the top of his head behind Duggie Rawlings. Duggie had driven the others from London up in his new taxi. Rachel remembered him coming to her before he left and taking her aside to explain that the reason he hadn't been able to bring Terry Voss was that Terry was in prison again. Of course she'd want to know that, the Colonel having been so thick with Terry all along.

"Thank you very much, Duggie," she'd managed to say. "I'm sure Terry would have come if he could."

And it was true, just as Jocelyn would have moved heaven and earth to attend Voss's funeral, Jocelyn, who, for instance, had refused to shoot again with an old acquaintance whom he'd discovered to be behaving dubiously over the division of an inheritance. But Voss, of course, had been on the Cambi Road. That changed everything.

Finally, completing the sequence, the picture she had been taking when Tom Dawnay had photographed her, the coffin being lowered into its slot of earth, the V of the straining tapes that held it, the surrounding, almost regular patterned frame made by the lower legs and feet of the mourners.

"How sad," said Dilys, closing the album. "But it's wonderful what we can get over, isn't it! Do you want another one, then, or are we finding it a wee bit tiring? How about a little rest now? A drinkie first, and then a little rest, eh?"

"Thank you, Dilys."

"My pleasure, dearie."

2

Horizontal again, Rachel lay and watched the rooks, but today without studying them, though it seemed a waste of a crystal morning, with every twig clear. Absurdly she felt a sense of dereliction at her failure to carry on with her self-imposed task. It didn't even help to tell herself that what she was now attempting to do was a continuation of the task, was indeed the true task, for which the study of nest-building had been a kind of preliminary exercise. Apart from the young man's visit she had not herself witnessed, and would never now have direct evidence of, whatever it was that had happened thirty-nine years ago, any more than she would ever be able to look directly down on a rook's nest in the process of construction. All she had to go on in either case were the side effects, the comings and goings, the shudderings of the structure, the occasional protrusion of objects or events beyond its edge. In one case the distance was in length, in the other in time . . .

Anne banging in through the front door, wholly unexpected, while Rachel was stitching up the hem of one of the hall curtains. No telephone call, no request to be met at the station. No kind of greeting now.

"Where's Da?"

"Hello, darling. What a surprise!"

"Where's Da?"

"In the study, I think. But please, darling . . ."

Anne strode past, blank-faced. When Rachel went to close the door she saw the taxi waiting in the drive. She had guessed it might be bad, but never as bad as this.

And then, of course . . . but there is always something worse that could happen. Mercifully you seldom get to the true worst.

Because there was nothing better to do and it was an excuse for staying nearby, she went back to the dreary job of the curtain. The study was round the corner on the way to the dining room and kitchen, and its door was solid. Jocelyn never raised his voice, spoke more softly when angry, and Anne was no screecher. The first she heard was a single, dull thud. Perhaps she felt rather than heard it, juddering up through the floor. But she sensed it, knew at once what it meant, and ran.

The door of the study opened as she reached the corner.

"Quick, Ma, the doctor. Something's happened to Da."

Then she was in the room.

He must have been standing behind his desk and then have fallen half sideways, heavily, all of a piece. Now he was lying almost prone, with his face in the carpet and his right arm twisted beneath him. Rachel knew nothing about medicine. She took one look, picked up the telephone, dialed 999, was answered almost at once and spoke briefly, keeping her head, to explain the urgency and give directions. Then she flung herself down beside the body and let the dry sobs shudder through her.

"Oh, Ma, I'm sorry, I'm sorry."

"Not your fault, darling . . . Not your fault."

"Is he dead? I suppose we'd better not move him."

"I . . . don't know . . . The ambulance . . . Go and wait for it please . . ."

Voices at the door. Yes, of course. Thwaite and Young Jim would be in for their elevenses in the kitchen. They too must have heard the fall. Her right arm was across his back when she felt the slight spasm. His left hand was beneath her breast on the carpet. She shifted and clutched it. His fingers moved in answer.

Somebody touched her shoulder.

"Now, Mrs. Matson . . ."

Ranson.

"No, don't touch him. Wait for the ambulance men. He's alive. Is Minnie there?"

"Here, Mum."

"Get a bag together for him. Pyjamas. His yellow dressing-gown. His shaving kit, hair brushes . . ."

Things he knew. Things that were his own, part of his being. While she was listing them Rachel eased herself up, never letting go of his hand, so that she could sit nestled against his side and with her free hand gently stroke the back of his neck and head, her own touch, all she could give him to let him know she was there, with him in this pit, this darkness . . .

"They're here, Ma. They've just turned into the drive."

She stayed where she was, waiting. The men were competent and friendly. They let her keep hold of his hand as they eased him onto the stretcher, lifted him and carried him out.

"Do you want me to stay, Ma? I wasn't going to, but . . ."

"Please. For a bit. Ring Flora. Dick, if you can find him. The aunts. Minnie's putting a bag together. Bring it to the hospital. And some stuff for me. I don't know if they'll let me stay. Take the Triumph. The keys are in the hall drawer. Look in his diary and see if he's got any appointments and cancel them if you can. Numbers in his book on the desk . . ."

The hospital was stupidly rigid about visitors. Outraged and distressed, Rachel came home to find that Anne, after coping well with everything within her competence, had worked herself into a pit of her own, in which she was hurled and battered by misery, rage and self-blame. She allowed herself to be held close on the morning room sofa for a while, but rose abruptly and moved away.

"I suppose you want me to tell you what happened," she said.

"Yes, please. Anything. Everything."

"Simon came and told me he couldn't marry me. It was because of something Da had told him."

"Oh, my darling!"

"Did you know he was going to do that?"

"Of course not. Only that Da was going to talk to him about his father."

"About Uncle Fish? What . . . ? And anyway, what bloody business is it of Dad's who I marry? Of either of yours? I'm twenty-three. I can marry anyone I bloody well choose!"

"Yes, of course, darling. Simon didn't tell you what it was about?"

"No. If you want to know there was something shifty . . . I mean, he was upset all right, but it wasn't just about us. He had to get out somehow. I couldn't understand what he was saying. We've always wanted each other. Always. Ever since we were little. Simon's mine. I'm his. I don't want anyone else, and I don't want anyone else to have him. We've been going to bed for ages, whenever we got the chance. Why do you think I was so sweet as pie about putting the wedding off? Because it doesn't make any difference, that's why. We're good as married already, and we can go to a Registry Office and get it made official anytime we want. You can't stop us, Aunt Leila can't stop us, however crazy she's gone. When Simon showed up I thought . . . Oh, Christ! he just wanted to get it over."

"Shall I tell you what Da told him?"

"If you like."

"Fish has run off with the funds of the Cambi Road Association, as well as any of Leila's money that's left. He's abroad somewhere."

"Jesus Christ! Is that all?"

"About forty thousand pounds. Everything Da had raised to help with pensions and so on."

"But . . . All right, Ma, I can see that's pretty awful for you, but it's not enough! It's bloody well not enough! What's it got to do with Simon and me? Nothing. We knew about Uncle Fish doing a bunk, and we knew it had to be something like that, though Aunt Leila won't talk to any of us . . . Look, Simon's always been a bit iffy about Uncle Fish—he says you can't tell where you are with him. But he's always worshipped Da, and if Da came and told him he couldn't marry me because of something *else* Uncle Fish had done—something unspeakable—I can just about see Simon—he's got these stupid ideas about honour . . . Jesus, I'm furious with him! And Da! There's something he told Simon and he wouldn't tell me, though he's bloody well wrecked my life! I'm sorry, Ma. I'm sorry about what happened to Da, and I wish it hadn't, but I came to tell him how furious I was, and I still am, and even if I'd known he'd got a weak heart I'd still have come and I'd still have said what I said!"

A pit had opened into a place which Rachel for the past seventeen days had been schooling herself not to think about. No, that had nothing to do with Fish. She clutched at an irrelevance.

"I think it's a stroke, darling, not heart. You couldn't have known."

"It doesn't make any difference."

"I'm sure I'd feel the same in your shoes. I'm truly sorry for you, darling. I hope you're wrong about Simon wanting to get out of it. I've always loved him. If it's any use to you, Da and I used to tell each other how stupid we'd been, waiting till we were married."

"Not much," snapped Anne, unrelenting. And then, "Oh, God, I'm never going to feel about anyone the way I do about Simon. I can't imagine even being interested in anyone else!"

She covered her face with her hands and sobbed. Rachel rose to stand beside her and hold her close again, but she shrugged herself free and moved away, still blindly sobbing.

"I'm sorry, Ma. Oh, God, I'm being desperately self-centred when . . . I just can't think about anything else. I'd better go."

"Please, darling. Oh, please . . . I . . . I . . ."

But Rachel couldn't bring herself to say "I need you." Not even now, when it would have been for the first time true. For twenty-eight years all that she had truly needed had been supplied by Jocelyn. Even

Dick had been no more than an emotional extra, a luxury, a want and not a need. It was too late for such a demand.

"I'll go for a walk and think about it," said Anne.

She had stayed on, in fact, for three silently dutiful days and then gone back south. A month later a card had arrived saying that she was moving to Bristol, with the address. She hadn't returned to Matlock until the funeral.

Rachel lay and considered the event. The emotions didn't return, however faintly, to confuse her.

All there was was the puzzle for her mind to tease at. She had been aware of it at the time, and Anne had, in effect, stated it aloud, but it had been among the mass of stuff at the periphery of Rachel's concerns, whose centre was wholly occupied with the horror of what had happened to Jocelyn, and then with the obstinate, passionate nurturing of hope when everyone was insisting that there could be none.

The puzzle was that the emotional logic didn't cohere. Fish Stadding had embezzled the Cambi Road funds. When discovered he had fled abroad. The committee had decided not to try and hunt him down. The money was apparently gone on some speculation in the City, so what was the point? Besides, Fish had been on the Road.

The Staddings were old friends, Uncle Fish and Aunt Leila to the children. They had always brought their three boys to Forde Place for a week or so in the school holidays. There had been a lovely inevitability about Anne and Simon deciding to marry. Rachel remembered walking by the river with him—a still, early summer day, a perfect light. She had lagged behind the others, taking pictures, and Simon had stayed with her, unasked, for company. That was Simon, sensitive, considerate, straightforward, very like Leila in that. (In fact it was as if all the good fairies had come to his christening, because he seemed to have inherited his father's quirky intelligence, not to mention the rather oriental good looks of both parents.)

"We didn't fall in love," he'd told Rachel. "I think we were born in love."

The memory simply didn't chime with any picture of a Simon who, on learning that his father was an embezzler who had shamefully betrayed his future father-in-law, had so readily, and apparently shiftily, broken the engagement. Yes, a young man might well have behaved like that, but it would have been a different young man from the one Rachel had talked to by the river. That Simon would have said, "This is tragic and appalling, and I will do everything in my power to make it up, but the first thing I will do is insist on marrying Anne, if she will still have me."

Indeed a Simon something like that surfaced a few years later, when out of the blue he had written to Rachel saying that he had learnt that the Association was looking for a younger secretary, and asking if she would put his name before the committee. He had added in a private note to Rachel that he would like to do something to repair the harm that his father had done to the Association. Rachel had hesitated, but she knew the committee were desperate and Anne was now settled in Canada, so she'd done what he asked.

Surely that Simon would have waited a little while for decency and then gone to Anne and told her he couldn't live without her. As far as Rachel knew there hadn't at the time been another woman. A decade or so later he had married a widow, older than himself, apparently out of a shared delight in bird-watching. He had never brought her to reunions at Forde Place. There had been no children.

No, Anne was right. Jocelyn must have told him about something else. The young man's visit? He certainly couldn't have borne to tell Anne, of all people, about that, and it would have been astonishing if he'd told Simon. Besides, it had nothing to do with Fish.

Unwilled, her lips moved and the dry whisper came.

"He didn't tell me, either."

JENNY

I

"Wake up, Uncle Albert—I think we're there."

Jenny braked inside the gates to give him time to pull his wits together before they reached the house. He had dozed in snatches for almost half the journey, and each time he woke had checked the cardboard box on his lap, raising the lid and groping inside to make sure that nothing had been substituted for the pistol while he slept. It was already early afternoon, but since Mrs. Thomas had insisted that food would be waiting for them on their arrival, they had stopped only once on the way, for coffee and biscuits at a service station. There they had scarcely sat down before Uncle Albert was fidgeting to be off again.

Now he woke and checked the box once more.

"Well, what are we stopping for?" he said. "It's a long way, you keep telling me."

"I think we're there."

Distrustingly he gazed through the windscreen, then relaxed.

"Ah, that's more like it," he said. "That's Forde Place all right. Well done, girl."

It was not at all what Jenny had expected from the picture of well-to-do squirearchy suggested by Mrs. Thomas's telephone voice and chance remarks from Uncle Albert. The grounds were appropriate—not a flower bed visible, but large old trees, cedars and planes and such, rising from several acres of lawn that sloped down to what was probably a river, with a wooded bluff beyond. But the house itself was odd for such a setting, a solid slab of dark red brick with a wide-eaved slate roof and serried windows. It didn't look like a building intended for people to live in. It was utterly different from Jenny and Jeff's own little house, but it had the same quality of being obstinately itself, and the hell with anyone else's ideas of taste and style. Jenny rather liked it for that.

She drove on, stopping a little beyond the front door, climbed stiffly out and went round to help Uncle Albert.

"Lend me your shoulder, girl," he said. "That's right. I'll do in a minute. Legs aren't what they used to be."

"Shall I take the box? It'll go in my bag."

"Might as well, now we're here."

The bell was answered by a middle-aged woman whom Jenny assumed to be Mrs. Thomas, but Uncle Albert spoke first.

"You're new."

"Only been here twelve years," she answered. "Tell Mrs. Thomas you've come, shall I? She's expecting you. If you'll wait just a minute."

She led them into the hall and walked off along a sunlit corridor.

Jenny gazed around. This was more like it—more in conformity with her expectations, that is, though still with something very odd about its proportions. A large space, three storeys high, roofed with glass. Polished old furniture, hyacinths, still lifes, seascapes, display cabinets, never-sat-in easy chairs. An extraordinary staircase, not, as would be expected in such a room, climbing handsomely up in broad flights, but a sort of free-standing shaft, a lattice of pale narrow timbers—satinwood Jenny thought—with stubby flights rising inside the shaft. It was a life-size version of the sort of staircase a hobbyist might model out of matchsticks. It had the beauty of total economy, with no ornament except itself, fashioned from the lightest materials, its obvious strength inherent in the design, in the almost pure idea. Jenny had walked across to look at it more closely when a voice reached her from the corridor.

She recognised it from the telephone calls, though the words weren't distinguishable because, as it turned out when she emerged into the hall, Mrs. Thomas had been talking over her shoulder to somebody behind her. She halted and turned to finish her instructions.

". . . and if he hasn't got them in, ask him to order them. We don't want anything different. We want the ones we've always had."

She turned again.

"Well, well, well! Sergeant Fred! And you're looking wonderful! What a stroke of luck you could come! Ma's so looking forward to seeing you again. You remember me, don't you? I'm Flora. I dare say you think I've changed a bit."

She took both his hands in hers and gazed up at him, openly delighted. She was a neatly plump woman, somewhere in her sixties, Jenny guessed, with blond permed hair unashamedly greying, a little powder, scarlet lipstick prissily applied, scarlet fingernails, green flannel skirt and matching cardigan, cream ruffled blouse pinned with a jade brooch. She radiated a sort of dishevelled but contented energy.

"Ah, Miss Flora," said Uncle Albert, a little uncertainly. "So you've turned out all right. And where's little Anne?"

"She's in Canada, breeding horses. We were over there a couple of summers ago and she seemed fine. And you must be Mrs. Pilcher. How very good of you to bring him all this way. I wish I could have persuaded you to stay the night. I hope you didn't have too grim a journey—it all depends on the M25, doesn't it? Somebody told me such a good joke about the M25 the other day—I wish I could remember it. You know, I could pretty well have told you the first thing he'd ask me about was my sister. She's younger than me and it used to make me mad with jealousy that she was the one everybody was interested in. Well now, I'll show you where the loos are. Can he cope for himself?"

She scarcely lowered her voice for the question.

"Now, this is my niece, Penny," said Uncle Albert. "Penny, this is . . ."

He stopped, frowning.

"Flora. Flora Thomas, actually. I'm married now. This way."

Still talking as if not expecting answers to any of her questions, she led them back along the corridor from which she'd come.

". . . and then we'll go up by the back stairs, and that'll mean Sergeant Fred can use the chair-lift. We put it in for my mother when she could still get about a bit. Of course we'd never have got one in on our ridiculous main stairs . . ."

"I think they're wonderful," said Jenny.

"Oh, do you? I do too, of course, but then we've always loved this house, all of us. You know people used to say how hideous it was—here you are, Sergeant Fred, you'll find everything you want in there—but nowadays students are ringing up the whole time saying can they come and look at it. He's in a muddle about you being his niece, isn't he? I suppose you don't want me to ask you anything about the pistols?"

She asked both questions in exactly the same tone of sprightly candour, though she had glanced a couple of times at Jenny's shoulder bag. The plural was puzzling. It must have been clear from the TV show that Jenny had brought only one pistol, and knew nothing about any others.

"I still couldn't tell you anything, I'm afraid," she said. "But Penny's my mother-in-law. I'm Jenny."

"How confusing for the old boy, but he's pretty wonderful in other ways, isn't he? Do you know, we've got a party of Taiwanese students coming to look at the house next month. Taiwanese, for heaven's sake. Here you are—you must be bursting. Mind you, they didn't come halfway round the world just for us—they were on some kind of tour, but even so . . ."

She laughed at her own amazement and let Jenny go.

Uncle Albert, of course, refused to use the chair-lift and climbed slowly but steadily up four longish flights, resting briefly on each landing. Mrs. Thomas talked the whole way, mainly to him, do-you-remembers about previous visits and encounters—usefully stabilising for him, Jenny thought, though she wasn't sure that she was doing it with that in mind.

At the top she broke off, turned to him and said, "I'd better warn you about Ma, Sergeant Fred. Otherwise you may find it a bit of a shock. She's completely paralysed, poor old thing, and she needs to have everything done for her. She can talk, but it's an effort—just a few words at a time, and only a whisper, so you've got to listen pretty carefully. But she's absolutely all there in her mind—sharp as a needle still. And her hearing's spot on—you don't have to shout or talk slowly, but she doesn't give any sign—she can't—she just lies there, but you've got to remember that she's hearing and understanding, and thinking about what you're saying all the time. You do see, don't you?"

She gazed anxiously up at him.

"I daresay we're all getting on a bit, Miss Flora," he said gravely, speaking her name this time with confidence.

"Well I hope I'm in anything like as good shape as you are when I get to your age. These are all Ma's photos, of course—you remember how potty she was about her cameras—she's looked some out to show you. Ah. Dilys. Here's our visitors. Sergeant Fredricks and Mrs. Pilcher. And this is Dilys, who's been an absolute angel to Ma. All set up?"

A plump, grey-haired woman in a blue uniform had appeared from a door further along the book-lined corridor.

"We're all ready, Mrs. Thomas," she said, "and I've got the table out for when the tea comes up."

"Good for you. I wasn't quite sure what you'd want at such a funny time of day, Mrs. Pilcher, so we're sending you up a sort of betwixt and between kind of meal. How would you like to do this? Ma won't want us all milling around, and Dilys had better stay to—"

"Can't have that," said Uncle Albert. "We've got private affairs to see to."

"Oh, but you see, Sergeant Fred, Ma will need somebody—"

"Penny can see to all that," said Uncle Albert. "She's a good enough girl, though I say it myself. And she's young, what's more, so she's good sharp ears, and you're telling me Mrs. Matson can't talk that easy . . ."

"What do you think, Dilys? Would you mind, Mrs. Pilcher?"

Jenny forced herself to respond. They were looking at her. The sudden wave of old horrors had swept over her without any warning. She had felt no qualms at all about bringing Uncle Albert to visit a bedridden old acquaintance. She hadn't assumed that she'd be able to stay out of the sickroom. She'd need at least to meet the patient, because Uncle Albert would expect her to, and would want to talk later about the encounter. Even the prospect of eating her meal in the room had raised no doubts. Mrs. Matson was clearly very well cared for. By somebody else. Not Jenny. So she wouldn't even need to nerve herself to cross the threshold of the sick room . . .

She blinked and shook her head. Her hands moved downwards, just as they had used to almost twenty years before, smoothing the crisp invisible pinafore into place at her grandfather's door.

"I'm sorry," said Sister Jenny coolly. "I was thinking about something else. Yes, of course I can manage if I'm shown how. I've looked after an old person before."

Her voice sounded perfectly normal in her own ears.

"Well, that's fixed," said Mrs. Thomas affably. "Dilys will show you what to do. Now we won't keep her waiting any longer."

She knocked at the door they had reached, opened it and put her head round.

"Hi, Ma," she said. "Here they are, then, right on time."

She went in and held the door for them. Uncle Albert, typically, stood aside to let the others through, Jenny first. She halted a couple of paces inside the room and saw that they had come too late. The bed was immediately opposite her, placed parallel to the wall beneath a wide window. The dead woman's head was cradled on the spotless pillows, peaked, fleshless, the yellow skin blotched with purple but otherwise almost translucent above the bone. Dead. Jenny had only once seen death before, when she had found her grandfather's body one Sunday morning. Then her magical uniform had vanished at the sight, and the household had been woken by her scream. Now, as she struggled for control, Uncle Albert marched confidently past her.

"Afternoon, Mrs. Matson," he said cheerfully. "Sergeant Major Fredricks, *at your service*, ma'am."

The greeting had the ring of ritual whose repetition invoked the pleasure of previous meetings. The undifferentiated lips of the corpse smiled and moved apart.

"Sergeant Fred," came the dead-leaf whisper.

Still barely in command of herself, Jenny turned away and moved down the room. There was a second, similar window further along the wall. In the space between the two hung a large, framed photograph,

almost poster-size, black and white, of a huge fungus growing out of
the bole of a tree. Jenny stared at it, seeing it first simply as pattern,
but then, as if with the inner click of a switch, suddenly perceiving
what it showed. Logically, it should have reinforced the horror of the
death mask. The fungus was huge, a monstrous symbol of decay, but
for some reason Jenny found it steadying, peaceful, normal. Thinking
about the episode afterwards she was still unable to decide why. It
was something to do with its—she didn't have a word for it—being-
what-it-was?—the fungus was what it was and the photograph was
what it was and they were different things, fungus and photograph,
and there was some kind of balance and tension between the two
things which the photograph let you see and feel, but why that should
make the photograph beautiful, let alone why it should have given
Jenny something to grasp, allowed her to haul herself out above the
tide of horror . . .

"Mrs. Pilcher?"

Jenny shook herself and came to.

"I'm so sorry," she said. "I was looking at the fungus. It's marvellous."

"You do keep saying the right things, don't you?" said Mrs.
Thomas. "Ma took it, of course. She took all of these, and you're
going to help her show Sergeant Fred some of her old albums, while
Dilys and I push off and leave you to it. So if you'll let Dilys explain
to you about anything Ma might need . . ."

"Yes, of course."

Jenny listened with full attention. Those were the reading spectacles. That was the reading desk, all ready, with the first album on it.
She just had to slide it across the bed. Those were other albums, on
the table, and the package was something Mrs. Matson wanted to
show Mr. Fredricks. This was Mrs. Matson's barley water—she'd need
a sip every few minutes if she wanted to talk. The trick was to slide
your other arm down behind her and steady her head in the crook of
your elbow—she didn't weigh anything—and not to pour too fast in
case she choked, and this was how you adjusted the angle of the bed
if she asked you, and that was all really.

"I'm sure I'll manage," said Sister Jenny, coolly. She could almost feel the starch in the imaginary uniform.

"I'll just give her a quick little drinkie now to show you, shall I?" said the nurse. "We'd like that, wouldn't we, dearie?"

Jenny watched the process without alarm. By the time it was over Mrs. Thomas had embarked on a complex flight of reminiscence about old acquaintances, in which Uncle Albert was keeping his end up with astonishing coherence, so Jenny took the chance to walk round and look at the several other photographs on the walls. The room was a fair size, longer than it was wide, and painted white throughout. All the pictures were in black and white, and framed in the same style. This, despite the bits of household furniture—a round folding table set ready for a meal, with two chairs, a really nice old walnut bureau, other chairs, bookshelves and so on—and the bed and sick-room appurtenances, gave it more of the feel of an art gallery than anything else. None of the photographs was of anything particularly striking —a stretch of sunlit paling overtopped by brambles, shadows in a barn, water flowing into darkness beneath two low arches, a white poodle coiffeured as for a show, nibbling its own flank in an ecstasy of pure canine concentration —but as with the one of the fungus all had the quality of instantly communicating their self-hood, why they had been taken in that light, at that angle, developed and printed to these tones and textures, enlarged to this size and these dimensions. That they were also obviously immensely skilled was part of the pleasure they gave, but secondary. She was going round the room, looking at each of them again, now in the light of the others, and paused at the one of the stream flowing away beneath the arches. Despite the stillness of the image, it seemed to have the true, hypnotic quality of moving water. She could remember, as a child, standing on a sunlit footbridge in a park somewhere, rapt, lost. That must have been very early, before Daddy walked out, when she had still been happy . . .

Just as then, a voice broke in, calling her. Uncle Albert. Mrs. Thomas and the nurse were in the process of leaving.

"All right, girl, let's get on with it. We haven't come all this way for just a lot of chat. My hearing's not what it was, Mrs. Matson, so my niece here's going to tell me if there's anything you say and I don't catch it. She's a good girl, now that she's settled down and got a young man of her own. Now, then, there's something . . . the Colonel left it with me, long way back . . . after . . . never mind about that now . . . But it's been on my mind a while, seeing how it doesn't signify that much now—water under the bridge after all these years—so I thought . . . I thought . . ."

While speaking he had turned and reached towards the bedside table, but not finding what he wanted had hesitated and begun to pat his pockets, frowning and peering round the room.

"I've got it, Uncle Albert," said Jenny quickly. "You gave it to me to carry when we were getting out of the car. One moment . . . here you are . . ."

He took the cardboard box from her and stood erect, as if the touch of it were restorative. He laid it on the bed and with untrembling fingers removed the lid, took out the package and slowly unwrapped the yellow duster, putting it back in the box. Grasping the pistol by the barrel he held it over the bed for Mrs. Matson to inspect. Her lips moved.

"Spectacles, please."

Uncle Albert was in the way, so Jenny went round to the other side, between the bed and window, and slid the spectacles into place. Mrs. Matson's gaze didn't immediately return to the pistol, but remained for a few seconds fixed on Jenny, as if seeing her for the first time— which indeed, Jenny realised, she might well be doing. The curve of the lenses suggested a strong correction for near sight.

The slight delay seemed to irritate Uncle Albert.

"All right, then. You show her, girl," he said and passed the pistol across. Jenny took it and turned it to and fro, and moved the catch and opened the breach in the way that the weapons expert had done on the *Roadshow*. She handed it back to Uncle Albert, who laid it down beside the box.

"Thank you," said Mrs. Matson. "Now, brown envelope. By albums. Give it him. Then go outside. Not long. Sorry."

"That's all right," said Jenny. "I quite understand."

She did as she was asked, and left, glad of the chance of a few minutes alone. She found herself unexpectedly upset, or rather upset in a manner that she wouldn't have expected. It was no longer the horror of the dead thing on the bed—even her extreme reaction of a few minutes ago she'd have regarded as a normal, if stupid and shameful, quirk in her own makeup. What had shaken her now was almost the opposite thing, the simple, lively health of the eyes that had studied her from behind the spectacle lenses, both when she'd first put them on and again when Mrs. Matson had slowly whispered her requests. Jenny would not have believed that a pair of eyes, with no facial change whatever to help them, could have sent so clear a message of interest and apparent amusement. One of Jeff's minor oddities was his fanatical interest in the *Star Trek* series, which Jenny usually watched with him for company. Her experience with Mrs. Matson was like some episode in which a team gets beamed down to an apparently dead planet, sends probes into the permafrost and discovers not just a few single-cell organisms that have evolved to survive such conditions, but a whole civilisation, science, arts, sociology, legends, cuisine, religion, hobbies, the lot.

She had no chance to settle down and come to terms with this revelation. The nurse must have been listening for the door, and at once came quietly up the passage.

"She's needing something?" she whispered.

"No, it's all right, she just wants to be alone with him for a bit. I suppose Mrs. Matson took the big photographs on the walls?"

"Indeed she did, and all these here too in the albums. Thousands of them, there must be, and she'll tell you exactly where to look for anything she wants. Amazing she is like that. Other day I was asking about pictures of the house, and, look . . ."

The nurse moved a little to her left, pulled out a blue ring-binder and gave it to Jenny.

"I'm sure it's all right," she said. "She likes people to see. That one's a bit different, mind you, because it was for some schoolwork her daughter was doing . . ."

Jenny opened the binder. The photographs were interleaved with pages of self-conscious young handwriting. There was the house itself, very much as Jenny had seen it from the top of the drive, though later in the year with the trees heavy with leaf. Next a patch of plain brickwork and the corner of a sill, no context, but insistently those particular bricks, seen in that light by those eyes, an effect impossible to analyse but still, to Jenny, obvious. She stared at the picture for a good minute before turning on and experiencing the same trance-like effect from a picture of a fire escape.

It struck her that there might be something wrong with her—sugar shortage maybe. She had had to get up at five, so breakfast had been almost that long ago, and skimped. Since then she'd had just a couple of biscuits and sugarless coffee at the service area . . .

At this point, as if she'd unconsciously willed it to be so, the woman who had first opened the door to them appeared at the far end of the corridor with a laden tray. Her odd mood broken, Jenny put the binder back in its place and explained the situation.

"Just leave it here till you're ready, then?" said the woman, laying the tray down beside the door. Jenny thanked her and she left.

"Your old gentleman looks in very fine shape for his age," said the nurse.

"Yes, thank heavens. Of course his memory comes and goes a bit, but today's one of his good days."

"Wonderful how they can pull themselves together for an occasion. Now, we've got out some of her albums for her to show him so I'll come and settle her down for a rest while you're eating your dinner, and after that your old gentleman will want to go to the toilet, so you can take him out for that while I tidy her up and make her comfortable again. All right?"

It worked out smoothly enough. When Uncle Albert came to fetch her she took the tray to the table and sat him down to eat, which he did with steady gusto. The food was much what Jenny would have chosen, cold chicken, salad, and what seemed to be homemade rolls, cheese and fresh fruit. Meanwhile the nurse dealt with Mrs. Matson and then made tea for Uncle Albert and coffee for Jenny. The brown envelope, Jenny noticed, was back in its place by the albums. The pistol was nowhere to be seen. The box in which they'd brought it was still on the bedside table, with the duster folded beside it. When they'd eaten Jenny took Uncle Albert out to the loo, as arranged.

Emerging, he at once tried to head back to the bedroom.

"Not yet, Uncle Albert," she said. "We've got to wait while the nurse makes her comfortable—you know, cleans her up and so on. She can't look after herself like the rest of us."

"Ah. Right you are. Got it."

He turned and began to study the spines of the albums on the shelves beside him, but almost at once swung round on her.

"What are we waiting for, then?" he said. "We haven't got all day."

"No, Uncle Albert. I told you. We've got to wait. It won't be long."

"Ah, yes, right," he said, but it was obvious that he had for the moment lost the grasp of events he'd so strikingly displayed while talking to Mrs. Matson. To distract him she pulled out an album and leafed through, but it seemed to be devoted entirely to studies of moving water. She tried another from a different shelf. It opened at a cricket match.

Not Forde Place, or anything like it. Some kind of urban playground, with 'fifties high-rise blocks on the further side. The game was not what had interested Mrs. Matson. Only a couple of outfielders were visible to the right of the picture, the centre was a receding curve of spectators in deck chairs or lying on the grass, and in the left foreground, the nearest part of that line, a group of half a dozen young men stood together. They were so perfectly in period, somewhere in the mid-'fifties, that Jenny grinned with pleasure at the inch-soled shoes, the loose-draped, huge-lapelled suits, the exiguous neckties, the fags drooping from pouting mouths, the sideburns, the forelocks greased and curled into a hummocky wave. They seemed unaware of the camera, probably, if they'd noticed it, thinking it was focused on something beyond them, yet they were clearly the subject of the picture. As with the other photographs Jenny had seen, these young men were emphatically what they were.

Uncle Albert was fidgeting again.

"I wonder who they are," Jenny said, thrusting the album under his nose. Obediently he took his spectacles from his breast pocket and put them on.

"Some of Major Stadding's boys, they'll be," he said. "Had me along a couple of times, so I could tell 'em about soldiering and that, in case any of 'em felt like joining up, he said."

He looked at the picture a moment more, and started to close the album.

"A bad lot. A bad lot all around," he said.

Before he could make for the bedroom again Jenny took the album from him and turned the pages. The contents seemed to be character studies, an old man sitting at the door of a cottage shelling peas into a bucket, a small woman in an ugly hat which she clearly thought well of, a seven-year-old girl absorbedly fishing . . .

"Ah, now, that's Miss Anne," said Uncle Albert with a complete change of tone. "Everyone's darling, she was. Wonder what's come of her."

"She's raising horses in Canada, Mrs. Thomas said."

"Right."

He was still chuckling over the photograph when the door of the bedroom opened and the nurse came out.

"We're ready now, if you are," she said.

"Right, then, let's get on with it," said Uncle Albert, tucking the album under his arm and marching off. Jenny might have taken it from him at the bedroom door but decided not to risk unsettling his recovered confidence.

The bed was now cranked up so that Mrs. Matson was in almost a sitting position. She was wearing her spectacles and had a pretty cream scarf round her shoulders. Her hands and arms, fleshless as the leg of a starling, lay inert on the counterpane. The tilted reading stand was in front of her, with a high-seated chair for Uncle Albert beside the pillows so that he could see too, and a stool on the further side of the bed for Jenny.

"Now we're all set," said the nurse. "You'll be all right here, will you, Mr. Fredricks? And if the young lady would go round the other side—you'll have to reach a bit, I'm afraid."

"I'll be fine," said Jenny. "Are these in the right order?"

She picked up the topmost of the pile of five albums that lay ready. The brown envelope, she observed, was no longer beside them.

"That's right—" the nurse began, but Uncle Albert broke in.

"As you were—this here's the one we're wanting."

He plonked the album he was carrying onto the stand, sat and started to turn the pages. Jenny and the nurse glanced at each other. Jenny signalled with her hands to let it be, and the nurse nodded, signalled in her turn that she'd be along the passage as before, and left. As Jenny reached her place at the bedside Mrs. Matson's lips moved.

"Wait."

"Wait, Uncle Albert."

He appeared not to hear and leafed confidently on for another few pages.

"Now, that's what I call a picture!" he announced.

"Anne," whispered Mrs. Matson, or perhaps, Jenny thought, "Anne?" It was hard to tell with the sound so faint.

"A great favourite Miss Anne was with us all," said Uncle Albert. "Never mind her being a wilful little imp. How old would she have been for that, then?"

"Seven," whispered Mrs. Matson. Jenny relayed the figure.

"Seven, eh?" said Uncle Albert. He gazed at the photograph a few seconds more, shook his head and chuckled. Jenny reached to remove the album.

"No. Leave it. Back."

Jenny leafed back, pausing at each page. Mrs. Matson stopped her at the picture of the cricket match.

"Those boys. Who? Ask him."

"Oh, we were looking at that one outside. He said they were some of Major Stadding's boys. Is that right, Uncle Albert? It sounded as if they came from some kind of youth club, or a delinquents' home, or something like that. Uncle Albert?"

He didn't immediately respond. His attention seemed to have slipped now that the remembered child was no longer there to hold it.

"Wait," whispered Mrs. Matson before Jenny could try again. "Third from left. Ask him who?"

"This one?"

"No. Behind. Blond."

The lower part of the face was hidden by the head of a young man nearer the camera. It was in half profile, showing a peak of pale hair, a straight forehead, sunken eye and high cheekbone. Rather than reach right across the bed Jenny carried the album round to show to Uncle Albert.

"Mrs. Matson says, 'Do you know anything about this young man?'" she said.

He barely glanced at the picture before turning his head away, refusing to look any more.

"Never seen him in my life," he snapped.

"But, Uncle Albert, you told me just now, out in the—"

"Now then, young woman, how often have I got to tell you not to go poking your nose in where it's not wanted? None of your business d'you hear me? None. Of. Your. Business."

Jenny looked at Mrs. Matson for guidance. It was some while before the lips moved.

"Drink, please."

Jenny laid the album aside, picked up the invalid cup and went round to her place again. As she did so, her earlier reaction returned, not this time as horror or dread, but as the conviction that just as she embarked on the childishly simple task of placing the spout between the patient's lips and tilting gently, watching the level in the cup so that she could see when the liquid began to flow, the wave would rush up at her, causing her to jerk the cup, and Mrs. Matson would choke, and die hideously in front of her eyes before anything could be done. It didn't, of course, happen. Her hand remained perfectly steady, but she found herself swallowing compulsively as she laid the cup aside.

"Thank you," Mrs. Matson whispered, with her faint but potent smile. Jenny's arm and hand responded as if of their own accord, reaching out and taking hold of the fleshless fingers where they lay inert on the bed just in front of her. This was not something she could have imagined herself deliberately doing, or even bearing to do. The skin felt brittle and empty, like a sloughed snakeskin. She was conscious of the contrasting life and warmth of her own hand. Mrs. Matson smiled again.

"Try and ask him . . . again . . . later," she whispered. "Another album now."

The weird pressure was already slipping away. By the time Jenny had laid the album she'd brought on the stand and opened it at the first page she felt pretty well normal. Relaxed. Confident that it wasn't going to happen again, and therefore able to concentrate on the photographs.

The first was of files of men passing a parade stand, some marching, a few on crutches or in wheelchairs. A very senior looking officer, his chest smothered with medal ribbons, was taking the salute. Jenny thought she might have seen his face in an old newsreel. Not Montgomery, but someone like that. A tall, skeletally emaciated but still unmistakable figure was marching beside the line.

"That's you, isn't it, Uncle Albert?"

He craned, his anger forgotten.

"Right you are. And there's the Colonel, leading us past. Duggie Rawlings that is at right marker—drove a taxi in London after the war. Now, when would that have been?"

" 'Forty-seven. Mons," whispered Mrs. Matson, and Jenny relayed the words.

"Course it was," said Uncle Albert. "Mons Barracks, nineteen forty-seven. The Colonel laid it on for when we set the Association up, so as to show 'em all that we meant it, though there was some of the lads as couldn't walk farther than you'd throw a tram car, or you'ld've thought so, but they all got 'emselves round somehow. I remember Don Kitchens telling me he felt prouder that day than he did when he went up to the Palace for his DSM."

The next few pictures had been taken on the same occasion, three more of the parade, and then the same men, with what were presumably relatives, sitting or standing around at an open air reception. Beer glasses, wine glasses, teacups; cigarettes and pipes; glimpses of a military band. The photographs hadn't been taken with an aesthetic purpose, but as a record of an occasion, but the same thoughtful eye was strongly evident, and the same care for composition. Many of the characters seemed as clearly defined as they would have in a good studio portrait. All the men bore the marks of their imprisonment, a gauntness and frailty, partly masked in some cases by the babyish look of flesh recently put back on. As each page turned Uncle Albert would study it for a while, then name the men he remembered. Occasionally Mrs. Matson whispered an interjection and Jenny passed it on.

"Jack Barnard. Billy Chart, and that's his missus—what was her name? I'll get it . . ."

"Florence?"

"Ah, right. Florrie Chart. Stan Upping—he'd been Mess Waiter. Mr. Graham—went for a curate, didn't he, after demob, and then the police picked him up—choirboys and scouts—and he did himself in. Might've been a bishop by now . . ."

He seemed to speak entirely without blame. Jenny wouldn't have expected him to mention such a thing at all, or else to do so with anger and disgust. There was a striking contrast a few pages later.

"Dickie Fearing; Dickie Brown, Terry Voss—showed up with a couple of thousand fags—black market, of course—rare as gold dust, they were."

"Wait. Back, please. Those two."

Jenny had turned the page, so leafed back. Below the group containing the two Dickies and the man with the black market cigarettes was a picture of two men standing in conversation beside an old muzzle-loading gun on a plinth. Both were in civilian clothes, but bearing and style suggested they were officers. The nearer one had his back to the camera, and the other faced it almost directly. Jenny would have thought him much more recognisable than some that Uncle Albert had so amazingly picked out—darkly good-looking, despite the aftereffects of emaciation, with naturally rounded features, a short but dense moustache, eyebrows and hair of the same apparent texture. Uncle Albert, however, had merely glanced at him and shaken his head, so Jenny had passed on. He looked again with his mouth clamped shut.

"Major Stadding," whispered Mrs. Matson, no louder than she had so far, but before Jenny could pass the name on Uncle Albert spoke.

"Least said, soonest mended. Let the lads down—let us down badly, and the Colonel most of all. That's enough about him. Get on with it, miss. We haven't got all day."

"Wait," said Mrs. Matson. "What happened to him? After? Dead?"

Warned by her earlier rebuff Jenny phrased the question carefully.

"She says do you know what happened to Major Stadding in the end? She wants to know if he's still alive."

"Went abroad, last I heard," muttered Uncle Albert. For an old soldier he was a remarkably bad liar.

"Tell him, come closer. Try to hear me."

"Uncle Albert, she wants to try to talk to you direct. See if you can get close enough. Shall I come round and give you a hand?"

"Stay where you are, miss—I can do for myself," he said, sounding a bit relieved, Jenny thought, by the apparent change of subject. He rose, placed his right hand beside the pillows for support, and craned forward. Jenny could hear the effort as Mrs. Matson struggled for extra volume.

"Please tell me. You brought the pistol. You said. Water under the bridge. Can't matter now. Please. Sergeant Fred."

He pushed himself up from the bed, straightened, turned and strutted off down the room with short, angry steps that suggested he would have liked to march clear away over the horizon. Reaching the table where they had eaten he halted with his back to the bed and rapped the surface several times with his knuckles. He then rounded the table, rapping it twice more as he passed, and came marching back to the bed, where he halted, staring ahead of him, as if being reprimanded by a superior officer on parade.

"Can't tell you anything about that, ma'am," he said. "Don't remember. Fact is, my memory's all to pot—and what do you think you're looking at me like that for, young woman?"

Jenny had indeed stared for a moment in astonishment. She was, of course, used to his lapses of memory, but knew too that they mustn't be treated as normal for him now but as isolated, temporary, wholly uncharacteristic.

There was more than anger in his voice, there was deep shame and misery. Before she could speak she heard the faintest of sighs from the bed.

"Tell him. Not important."

"Mrs. Matson says not to worry, Uncle Albert. It doesn't matter. She just wondered."

He swallowed a couple of times and sat down.

"Let's get on with it, then," he said.

They finished the album and started another one—the same faces at different occasions large and small. There were several pictures of Major Stadding, passed over in silence. Then, to his obvious distress, Uncle Albert's memory started to waver. Mrs. Matson too was tiring, needing to sip more often at her barley water and closing her eyes from time to time, but apparently neither wished to disappoint the other by calling a halt.

"Let's have a rest," said Jenny, realising it was up to her. "I'll fetch the nurse, shall I? And Uncle Albert can watch the TV for a bit, or something."

"Please," whispered Mrs. Matson.

"Time we were off," said Uncle Albert, rising. "It's a long way for the girl to drive, and I've done what I came for. Right, Penny?"

"If you like, Uncle Albert. Is that all right with you, Mrs. Matson? You must be pretty well done for."

"Yes. Say goodbye. Thank you. Sergeant Fred."

"She says, 'Goodbye, Sergeant Fred, and thank you for coming. It's been wonderful to see you again.'"

Uncle Albert drew himself up to his parade stance.

"Thank you yourself, ma'am. It's been a privilege to know you, ma'am. A privilege to serve with the Colonel, and a privilege to know his lady wife."

He ducked his head, turned and marched for the door, which he held for Jenny, as if impatient to make his exit with soldierly smartness.

She started for the door, remembered her shoulder bag, slung on a chairback, hesitated only an instant and walked on.

"I'll just get the nurse, Uncle Albert. Do you want to use the toilet before we go? Hell, I've left my bag in the room. I won't be a sec. Oh, could you show him where the toilet is while I get my bag? The nurse will show you, Uncle Albert."

Without waiting she slipped back into the room, closing the door behind her. Mrs. Matson had her eyes shut, but opened them as Jenny approached.

"Spectacles off," she whispered. "Please. Itch."

Jenny lifted them clear and laid them on the table.

"The nurse is just coming," she said quietly. "I'm afraid Uncle Albert wasn't telling the truth. He really did tell me that those young men had something to do with Major Stadding, and a while ago, when we were trying to find your telephone number, he said that the Mr. Stadding who runs the Association couldn't be Major Stadding, because he was dead. He said he'd seen it happen. He said, 'Ask Terry Voss,' so I think he must have been there too."

"Ah. Thank you."

Jenny waited, sensing that there was more. As the nurse opened the door the whisper came again.

"Anything you can find out."

2

Uncle Albert dozed most of the way home. Jenny spent much of the journey thinking about what had happened, not outside and around her, but within. There had been a moment when everything had changed. Perhaps the change had imperceptibly been preparing for a long while, but this afternoon there had been an identifiable point at which it had taken place, when she had held Mrs. Matson's near-dead fingers in her own. It was as though there had been a knot in the cord of her being only, a simple half hitch which, if anyone had known about it and helped her with it at the time of its tying, might have been freed. But over the years it had been strained so tight that the strands had almost lost their differentiation and it had become a dense little nut in the run of the cord, impossible ever to ease or tease apart. The rest of the cord ran smoothly enough over its pulleys, and long before she was a woman Jenny had become so used to the existence of the knot that without any awareness of doing so she had learnt to adjust her use of the mechanism so that only in exceptional circumstances did it snag. But the cost of being all the time ready for those potential judderings, of not allowing herself to seem to be shaken or troubled by them, had been considerable—an outward wariness and chill, a detachment, a sort of void or buffer zone between that outward and her true inward, a concentration on things rather than people—she belonged to no informal feminine networks, had no bosom friends—especially on things that were stable and controlled, that seemed to her to have confidence in their own selfhood and thus make no demands on her and pose no threats. (That, perhaps, was why she so loved the little house she shared with Jeff, and why Mrs. Matson's photographs spoke so strongly to her.)

But Jeff, and her marriage to and passion for him, didn't come under that heading. They were fluid, dynamic, unpredictable. There were patterns in them that happened to persist, like eddies below a weir, convolutions with much the same structure as the knot, but these could never be traced to any calculable cause, and some minor change in the flow of the stream might at any moment dissolve them completely, re-create them elsewhere or perhaps abolish them forever. Not even the passion could be taken for granted.

So perhaps it was this experience over the past seventeen months that had allowed the fibres of the knot first to soften and then to ease from their taut interlocking so that now with the very minor effort on Jenny's part of reaching out and grasping a skeletal hand, the knot itself should have at last slipped free and gone.

How else was she to explain to herself her betrayal of Uncle Albert's confidence? Mrs. Matson was, and would remain, a stranger, unreachable in the prison of her carcase. Yes, her condition was very sad, and yes, she seemed to cope with it with courage and decency, in a manner that Jenny believed she herself would never be able to cope, should that befall her. But she had no claim on Jenny.

Uncle Albert on the other hand, she knew and liked and admired. Moreover he was family. Family was important to her. Though her own had been an apparent disaster, they had lived together in a series of houses through the almost two decades that had made Jenny what she was. They were part of each other, in a relationship for which there isn't a word, so "love" has to do. The worst horror of her mother's drinking had been that Jenny had continued to "love" her. Her suicide had solved intolerable problems for all of them, but Jenny had sobbed with fierce and genuine grief at the bleak funeral. Now she and her brother and sister communicated only perfunctorily, and never made a point of going somewhere for the purpose of meeting, but when something happened to bring them together the old currents instantly flowed between them, and they parted with a sense of renewal and unvoiced celebration.

Jeff had none of that, apart from Uncle Albert. His childhood had been yet more bereft than Jenny's. His mother had walked out when he was seven. His father, though fairly well off, had placed him in a foster home. His great-aunt, Uncle Albert's sister, had wanted to have him live with her, but his father had rancorously refused permission. The great-aunt was now dead, so there was only Uncle Albert, who must for that reason be cherished and cared for. Jenny didn't merely accept this as a duty, she both thought and felt it.

But despite that she hadn't hesitated to tell Mrs. Matson part of a secret that was sufficiently important to him to be worth the humiliation of publicly pleading his own failing memory. Indeed she was now planning, as soon as she had the chance, to look in his bottom drawer for the Cambi Road Association address lists to see if somebody called Terry Voss was still alive—and wondering, even, if there was any excuse for not telling Jeff about all this in case he should, very reasonably, ask her not to.

The answer, if you could call it that, she decided, was that Mrs. Matson was not after all a stranger. There had been an exchange between them. Something had flowed, and Jenny had been the beneficiary. Years ago, at college, she had known a young man whose legs had been badly damaged in a bicycling accident and who needed a stick to walk. The other noticeable oddity about him was that he was never there on Sunday. He was quietly amiable, and so tended to get included in the activities of the group to which Jenny loosely belonged, but when pressure was put on him to make up the numbers, if the event was planned for a Sunday he always refused. One evening when they were sitting around talking about what they individually believed in he told them why.

After his accident, he said, he'd been confined to a wheelchair and told he would never walk again. His parents had been determined he should, and had tried a series of increasingly weird treatments. Eventually a faith healer had visited them, and had sat alone with Dominic and talked what he described as a lot of stupid guff about spirit and matter and cosmic currents. He had been bored and embarrassed, and longing for the man to leave. He had then been aware of feeling curiously warm, from inside, but without the need to sweat. The warmth had appeared to flow down into his legs, and after a bit the healer had put his hands in his and told him to stand up, which he had done, and then walked across the room, with the healer doing no more than hold his hands to give him confidence, and not supporting him in any way. Though he wasn't completely healed he hadn't needed the wheelchair again.

So now, every Sunday, Dominic made a difficult cross-country journey to be with the cult to which his healer belonged and attend their ceremonies. "I'm not going to tell you what we believe," he said. "You'd think it was a lot of stupid guff, like I did. But when I'm among the Companions I can walk as well as you can. I have to believe."

Jenny felt that something very like that had happened to her as she'd stood by Mrs. Matson's bed and held her hand. She'd been uncrippled. It didn't matter how or why. It had happened, and she was therefore committed. If this included doing what Mrs. Matson had asked and finding out what she could and passing it on, she must, regardless of rationality, do it.

They reached Hastings after ten o'clock. Jenny helped Uncle Albert, very stiff and shaky, out of the car. He leaned heavily on her shoulder for the few paces to the door. She rang the night bell. It was a while before they heard footsteps. A nurse she didn't know opened the door.

"So you've come home to us, Albert?" she said. "Quite the night owl you're getting. We thought you'd be hungry, so there's a tray for you in your room. Had a good trip, then? I'll take him now, miss, unless you want to come in. Come along, Albert."

"Hold it," he said firmly, and turned to Jenny.

"You're a good girl," he said, "and you've done me proud. And I'll tell you this. You made a much better job of it than that other girl would've. What's her name . . . ?"

"Your niece in America, you're talking about?" said the nurse. "Penny, isn't she?"

"That's right, Penny. She'd've got us lost ten times over, for a start. So I'll say thank you, young lady, and good night."

"Good night, Uncle Albert. I enjoyed it."

He let himself be led into the hallway, but before the door closed halted again and turned.

"And ask that husband of yours when he's coming to see me," he called.

RACHEL

I

The footsteps, faint on the carpet, receded. The door opened and closed. An odd young woman, Rachel thought, stranger in the flesh than she'd seemed on television. It would have been a challenge to capture that quality through the lens, the features soft but strong, self-possession with considerable tension, disciplined will constraining something wilder . . .

Voices in the passage, the tone of farewells. The door again. Dilys.

"Well, well, quite a day we've had of it, haven't we, dearie? And what a grand old gentleman, coming all this way at his age, and still holding himself like a soldier. Now, we need seeing to, I dare say— we'll have drunk a bit with all that chat. And then I'll set your bed flat, so we can have a bit of a rest."

"Soon. Album first. One he brought in. Something in it . . ."

"Right you are . . . This one? 'People,' it says on the back. Then here's our specs. Start at the beginning, shall I?"

Dilys settled the album onto the stand and leafed slowly through, commenting here and there.

"Now that's what I call a well set up lass . . . Shouldn't care to meet them in a dark alley . . ."

Already almost exhausted, Rachel gazed vaguely at the passing images. Faces and postures. Strangers, friends, family, that didn't matter, wasn't what they'd been chosen for. The photographs were in this series of albums because when she'd begun to compile them in the second long winter of her widowhood, each had seemed to be, as it were, a passing remark—nothing so solemn as a statement—on what it meant to be a human being.

"Look at that hairdo! And those shoes! You should've heard what my Nan said when I showed up on her doorstep got up like that! I thought she wasn't going to let me over the mat—"

"Stop. That one."

"Teds . . . we had 'em too. Welsh Teds. There was a Welsh word for them, even—*Tedwboi*, was it? Not that I knew more than a dozen words in Welsh myself. What was the point in Bangor? And now my other niece and her hubby—never mind he's from Norfolk—they talk Welsh at home, and the kids too . . . Ready?"

"Wait. Please."

Rachel willed her mind into focus and studied the half-hidden face. Bewildering that she must have seen it twice in the flesh, and then at least four times more in this image—looking through the rough prints, printing it up, and then selecting and reprinting it for the album, and had not then made the essential connection. Only now this ambush.

How long had the intervals been? She could actually remember taking the photograph, pretending to focus on the outfielder so as not to distract her quarry out of their speakingly self-conscious poses, that special uncertain swagger . . . 1955, she guessed. Dick had captained a team against Fish Stadding's Walthamstow youth club (of course Jocelyn had had to do the actual work of getting eleven players together). Rachel had gone along to be with them both—Dick consented to be so little at home . . .

It had been the group, not any of the individuals, that had caught her eye. No reason she should have recognised one of them, meeting him two years later. Jocelyn had died in '59, so it would have been '61 or '62 when she was working on this album. Only four or five years, then, since she'd truly seen him, watched and studied him for an hour or so . . . And she must have looked carefully at the photograph when she was deciding whether to include it. Perhaps she'd still been mesmerised by the group, not to pick him out. Yet now, another thirty-five years on, instantly, on a page half glimpsed as it was turned.

"Thank you, Dilys. Rest now."

As far as possible she blanked her mind while Dilys lowered the bed, peeled back the covers and changed her pad. She was wet, of course, but to judge by the odours had stayed clean. Dilys had clearly been greatly impressed by Sergeant Fred.

"Funny how different they all go," she said. "Not that I've seen a lot of them like that, looking after themselves and everything, just the mind a bit wandery—they don't need my kind of nursing, that sort. There was an old lady I looked after—stuck in a wheelchair she was, and mostly didn't know nor care if she was coming or going, but the family used to take her along Sundays to visit her sister—in a home she was, and her mind gone too, but the two old things would sit together for a couple of hours on end just holding each other's hand, and the family swore blind that they both knew whose hand they were holding, and they were the better for it after. But it wasn't them I was thinking of. There was another old dear in this home—Lettice her name was—and she was spry enough but she was the sort who says the same thing over and over and over, like one of those dolls with a string in its back, only they're all electronic now, I suppose. Anyway, everyone loved this Lettice, but for one or two of the snarky old crabs you always get in a home, biting everyone's heads off 'cause of not being able to bear it, what they've come to, but Lettice was just the other way, she was so happy. And what made her happiest was helping anyone up the stairs, or down them. Opening doors for them and holding them and closing them after they'd been through was better than nothing, but stairs were the best. She'd hang around in the hallway looking at the pictures, which she'd seen over and over and over, but as soon as anyone showed up she'd take a quick peek at them— she knew not to try and help the ones who could manage, but if they were using a frame or maybe just a stick, she'd be at their elbow . . . There, now, that's a bit better. Last little drinkie?"

"Please."

Rachel sipped gratefully.

"Thank you. Flora?"

"Mrs. Thomas said to say she was out saving the children, but she'll look in later if you're up to it. You want me to put your parcel back in its hidey hole before she comes?"

"No. Leave it. In drawer. Not secret. Now."

"Right you are. And she'll be wanting to hear all about the old gentleman too, won't she? You have a good rest, and you'll be feeling perky for her."

When Dilys had gone Rachel lay and gazed through the window. The rooks were raucous and active in the tree, but she was too exhausted to attend to them. Too exhausted for anything . . .

No! It wouldn't do. It was another excuse, another shying away, the latest of countless evasions over the years. The thing must be faced, now, and in detail. If it was there, the answer would lie somewhere in the details, just as the young man's image had lain so long unnoticed in the album.

Buried memory, unconsidered for decades, can't simply be dug up, unpackaged and laid out for inspection. After such a span in the earth, though the shape may still be plain, the individual parts will at first be unrecognisable, compacted, clogged, corroded, some of them of stuff too transient to endure, others readable after careful cleaning. Fragments, though, persist almost unchanged—a coal fire in a half-lit room, the stealthy opening of a door in an empty house, squat fingers uncapping a bottle, the tweed of a greatcoat against her cheek in a dark car park, Jocelyn pausing at the study door, absorbing what she'd told him—from such morsels, with willed persistence, Rachel teased out most of the rest of it. All the essentials she was sure of, though parts she knew to be reconstructions—sequences of minor events, the actual words of a conversation—but even these didn't merely ring true but were flecked here and there with the gleam of metals that burial doesn't corrode.

Twice Dilys came in and took her pulse, but Rachel closed her eyes, pretended to be asleep and waited until she heard her leave. By nightfall she had as much as she thought she was going to get.

2

Begin at the beginning. A mild, dank October day. Late morning. The telephone call. She took it in the hall.

"Hello?"

The clatter of coins being fed into a public telephone.

"Ray?"

"Oh, it's you, darling. What's up?"

"Can't tell you over the telephone. I'll be late back—on the eleven-twelve. Don't meet me. I'll take a cab. Sorry."

"Bother. All right. Shall I keep supper?"

"I'll eat on the train."

"Is it something serious?"

"Afraid so. Tell you when I see you. Look after yourself."

"You too, darling."

"Do my best."

She put the handset down, disappointed for herself because she wanted him home—yesterday's lonely evening had been more than enough—and troubled for him, though mainly about his personal discomforts. The late train was always crowded, the dining car often full for two sittings. Though what was keeping him in London was obviously important and by the abruptness of his tone unpleasant, it would be part of his public world, and he would deal with it as such. He would tell her about it, as he'd said, but by then he would have decided exactly what to do about it, and so would not bring it home in the form of a disruptive worry.

She sighed and went to the kitchen. Thursday was the Ransons' afternoon off. Normally Mrs. Ranson would have set out the makings of a meal, simple enough for Rachel to cope with, before she and her husband went to the bowling club. Rachel told her not to bother. She'd have cheese and biscuits and tomatoes at her table while she finished the Christmas cards. Her afternoon was planned, and that would fill the empty evening.

Those plans for the afternoon. She could remember their existence, but not what they'd been. Had she driven somewhere? Yes, she must have. The trip itself was irrecoverable, but she could remember her sense of utter loneliness as she'd let herself into the house at dusk and locked the door behind her.

The evening, then. About a quarter to seven—the time not memory but reconstruction, since the train—the one Jocelyn should have been on—got in at six-eighteen. The study. Curtains closed and a coal fire starting to glow, not for herself, but so that Jocelyn should have his own warm lair to come home to, where he could sip his scotch and tell her about his day. A pool of light from his desk lamp, for imaginary company: dark, and he was not in the house; lit, and he could just have gone out of the room. Her supper tray at the other end of the desk, so that she wouldn't need to face the ambient emptiness till he returned.

Her own worktable sharp-lit, cleared for her task and then systematically set out: three stacks of blank cards of different sizes; their envelopes; a dozen piles of photographs to be selected and pasted in; her card lists for the past three years; two address books, hers and Jocelyn's; paste; pen; blotter; stamps. Apart from desk and table the room in deep shadow.

The night silent. Neither she nor Jocelyn listened to music, and used the wireless solely for the early morning news. When the Ransons were in you might catch the mutter of their television. The house itself stood rock solid. After ninety years not a floorboard creaked, every door clicked quietly home, and it took a full gale to rattle a window. So the gentle flap of a flame over the coals was enough to mask the opening of the door, which she'd left an inch ajar for air. She merely sensed its movement.

Her heart thumped. Dick? Not the Ransons, home early—she'd have heard the car in the yard. Flora or Anne would certainly have called. Dick was supposedly in Australia, but hadn't been heard from for three months. This would be typical.

She put the paste brush back in its pot and turned. Her heart thumped again. The head that was peeking round the door, though hard to make out with lamp-dazzled eyes, wasn't Dick's. Before she could speak the man stepped confidently into the room, closing the door behind him.

"Hello," she said, now startled but not yet alarmed. "Who are you? This is a private house, I'm afraid."

Without answering he switched on the overhead light and strolled towards her. A young man—eighteen?—slight, blond, with high cheekbones and sunken cheeks. Pale blue eyes and a full-lipped mouth. He was wearing a short dark overcoat with heavily padded shoulders. This, and something in his bearing and look, though his face bore no marks of old blows, suggested he might be a boxer, or perhaps wish to pass as one.

"What do you want?" she said.

"Just a pal of old Joss," he said.

For a moment she couldn't think who he was talking about.

"You mean my husband, Colonel Matson?"

"You're on," he said. "Been a good friend to me, Joss has, a very good friend."

He looked at her half sideways and smiled. She said nothing, only stared. She was aware of her chest heaving, dragging air in, forcing it out unused. Not the words but the look had carried the meaning.

"So when he says to me, 'Why don't you just run up to Matlock, tell my good lady I'll be late home?' I thought, Why not, seeing it's old Joss. 'Here's a tenner for the ticket and the taxi,' he says. 'Tell him Forde Place. And here's the keys so you don't bother the servants.'"

The heaving was replaced by nausea. He was lying, of course. Jocelyn had called. He'd have known the Ransons would be out—he didn't forget that sort of thing. He'd never have sprung something like this on Rachel, or given anyone else his key—he'd even made a fuss about having one cut for Fish Stadding when he'd had a room of his own here . . .

The young man was watching her, still smiling. She saw that he didn't expect her to believe him. His confidence lay elsewhere. In the "friendship."

"Joss didn't want you worrying, really he didn't," he said. "Very thoughtful, Joss is . . . Fag anywhere? No, you stay put, lady."

His right hand, which had so far remained casually in the pocket of his coat, moved as if to withdraw something, and stopped. A flick knife? Rachel had read about flick knives.

He lounged over to Jocelyn's desk, took a cigarette out of the ebony box, and lit it one-handed with Jocelyn's lighter. He inhaled deeply, confident in his own dominance.

"One for you?" he suggested, teasing.

"I don't smoke."

Her voice answered flatly, controlled by some corner of her mind detailed to keep the rest of the system going when the rest was in shock. It wasn't thinking, that rest. It was refusing to think, refusing to imagine, huddling down with its eyes uselessly shut and its hands uselessly over its ears. She had no ideas, no plan. What she had was a vomit-like upsurge of emotions, disgust, jealousy, hate, rage, bottled up in herself for a dozen frustrated years. She had no doubt that her understanding was far more than a good guess. If anything, she should have at least guessed before. Jocelyn was a sensual man. He lived through his body. Younger, she had not believed that of herself, had thought she lived primarily through her eyes and mind. Without Jocelyn she might never have discovered her other self—only, through his captivity and the years that followed, to have to put that self back to sleep, and learn to live again just through the eye and the mind. But it was still there, sleeping, dreaming, dreaming of wakefulness once more. She had shared many of those dreams. But Jocelyn . . . People don't change that much. They don't. Jocelyn was a sensual man still, living through his body. What had changed was the objects of his sensuality. Changed when? On the Cambi Road.

"Well, aren't you going to say nothing?"

The corner of her mind did its duty.

"Sorry . . . I was surprised . . . I wasn't expecting . . . Do you want anything to eat . . . ? A drink . . . ?"

"What you got?"

"The drinks are in the cabinet there."

He opened it and drew the bottles out one by one for inspection, standing sideways on to keep an eye on her. He sniffed a decanter.

"Scotch," he said. "Can't stand it. Rotgut. What's this one?"

The question steadied her.

"It should have a label round its neck. I think it's Marsala. Sweet. A bit like port."

"Port'll do. What's this? Lemon. Well, I'm happy."

He poured a couple of fingers into a schooner, uncapped a bottle of bitter lemon and half filled the glass. He tasted, grimaced, added Marsala and tried again. His hands were small and short-fingered, his movements deft.

"That's something like," he said. "What's yours, then?"

"Scotch," she said. "Not much. Neat."

"I'm surprised at you," he said mockingly, but poured the drink and set it in front of her.

"Thank you," she said, still speaking like an automaton. Jealousy, disgust and fury screamed inside her, but she isolated and contained them. More of both mind and body came under control. She was aware of a change in him, a loss of confidence. He had expected something different.

"You're taking this pretty cool," he said. "I mean me just walking in."

"It's interesting to meet one of my husband's London friends," she said. The absence of emotional colouring made the words seem to hang there, waiting for him to decide how to take them.

He lost patience.

" 'My husband's London friends,' " he jeered. "I suppose you think you know what I'm talking about."

"Yes," she said.

He took a couple of paces forward and stared down at her, leaning his knuckles on the table. She looked up at him, unafraid. There was nothing more he could do to her now.

"Bugger me!" he said quietly. "I don't get it. There was a fat old cow across the road when I was a kid. Been a housemaid or something in big houses, back before the first war, she had, full of stories about life among the nobs, Lord this having it off nine ways with Lady that, and her husband not giving a fuck because he was going with a lot of stable lads. 'Don't you take no notice of her,' my ma told me. 'It's only stories.' "

"Do you want anything to eat?" said Rachel.

He took a look at the tray, sniffed the cheese and made a face.

"There's some ham in the kitchen," said Rachel. "I could make you a ham sandwich."

"What about the servants? He said there'd be servants."

"It's their evening out. They won't be back until ten."

"All right. Got any pickles?"

"I expect so."

All that Rachel could recover from the time in the kitchen was an image of the cooking knives in the jar beside the salt-pot and the scales, and the thought drifting through her strangely will-less mind, Perhaps I could kill him with one of those.

Then they were back in the study, under the ugly, dull illumination of the overhead light. She was at her table again, and he half perched on the edge of Jocelyn's desk, munching. On the plate beside him were the discarded crusts of his sandwiches and a yellow smear of pickle sauce. A fresh cigarette lay on the ashtray, smoke curling up from its tip. He must have helped himself to more Marsala, neat—the glass was half full and the liquid unclouded. He was looking at Jocelyn's lighter, with his initials on it, a thank-you present from Flora and Jack after their wedding.

"Nice," he said. "He'd like me to have that, wouldn't he? Something to remember him by."

"If you like," she said, indifferent.

His eyes widened. Perhaps he had been expecting at least a token resistance. He smiled and dropped the lighter into his coat pocket. His confidence was returning. No doubt the Marsala helped. Rachel wondered whether he would become drunk enough to attack her, and if that would be enough to rouse her from her apathy. Part of her seemed to stand outside herself and consider the question. Probably not, she concluded. She watched him rise, walk round the desk, and sit in Jocelyn's chair. The stimulus of pure anger returned, but there was no eruption. He tried the drawers and found the centre and top left ones locked.

"Where's the key, then?"

"On my husband's key ring."

He nodded, apparently assured that she was too tamed to lie to him, and tried the others. The ones he could open contained little to interest him—writing paper, envelopes, stamps, account books—but from the lowest on the right he pulled out a flat hinged box, opened it, and frowned.

"What's this, then?"

"The ammunition for my husband's antique pistols."

"Pistols, now. Where?"

"On the lower shelf of the table beside you."

He reached down, lifted out the rosewood box, laid it on the desk and opened it.

"Hey! Now that's something!" he said.

He picked out one of the pistols and aimed it at her, grinning. She saw that he was younger than she'd thought. He was a boy, playing with a toy gun.

He switched his aim to other targets, the fire, the portraits of Jocelyn's parents, the fox's mask beside the window. When he pulled the trigger there was no answering click, as the gun wasn't cocked. He put it back in the box and took out the other one, turning it to and fro to study the details. The neat movement of his fingers demonstrated his respect and admiration for the object, something like Rachel herself felt for her favourite cameras.

"Got his initials on them, too," he said. "Only they got to be older than that. His dad's, were they?"

"No. They belonged to a man called Joachim Murat. He was one of Napoleon's generals. The pistols are about a hundred and fifty years old."

"You don't say!"

No mockery now. He seemed genuinely impressed. Rachel could imagine a young man of her own class—one of Dick's friends, say— reacting less appropriately.

He looked up, and his manner reverted.

"Now that's something Joss'd really want me to have," he suggested. "To remember him by, you know? Seeing I've been a good friend to him."

Anger found leverage at last. Her will woke and controlled it, letting her answer in the same dead tone.

"I don't know."

He picked up the other pistol and fought an imaginary skirmish, two-handed, gunning down half a dozen outlaws in rapid succession.

"You'd need to reload between shots," said Rachel.

"Yeah," he said absently, whirling to take a snap shot at the half-caste creeping up behind him.

"Shall I show you how?" said Rachel.

"Oh. Right you are. No, you stay where you are, lady."

He came round the desk with the box and handed her one of the pistols. She picked one of the slugs out of its nest, then put it back.

"We'd better not use these," she said. "They're the original ones, and the paper on the cartridges is very fragile. Will you bring me the other box? Thank you. If you just watch what I do, and copy me, so you know how. You've got the right-hand gun, by the way—it's a little bit heavier. Now you need a slug, and a cartridge and a cap."

She picked out of their compartments two of the elongated lead pellets, about three eighths of an inch in diameter and twice that long, with one end rounded and the other flat; two of the cartridges, tubes of thick waxed paper pinched shut at one end and with a brass base at the other; and from individual slots in the third compartment two caps, squat copper cones with a nipple at the point.

"First you fit the cap into this pit at the bottom of the cartridge. It goes in pointed end first, like this. That's right. Put it down carefully. They can go off at the slightest tap. Now, you have your own loading rod and mallet. Here. You move this catch up—it's on a spring and fairly stiff—and break the gun open. That's right. Hold the barrel in your left hand, pointing downwards. Now drop the slug in, pointed end first. Look and check that it's sitting centrally. Put the loading rod into the breech, this end first—you'll find it just fits— and give it a tap with the mallet. Again—I don't think that was quite hard enough. That's to seat the slug into the rifling. Now drop the cartridge in on top of it, this way round, and push it down with your thumb until you can feel it's flush with the rim of the breech. Let me see. Yes, that's right. Now close the breech—do it firmly, so that the catch clicks. No, take your finger off the trigger. Lay it along the trigger guard, like this. Now with your left hand—you can do it with your thumb, but it's safer to use both hands—cock the gun. That's this lever here. Check that it's all the way back . . ."

While he lowered his glance to make the unnecessary inspection she aimed her own gun at his chest and fired.

Another gap, but of a different nature, because even at the time there had been no memory to fill it. Nothing between the jar of the explosion and her becoming aware of herself sitting in the dark of the hall, shuddering as if with extreme cold. She rose, felt her way to the cupboard and fetched out coats, choosing them by touch, her own camel-hair, which she put on, and Jocelyn's big raglan, which she heaped over herself when she huddled back into the armchair. The movements had been awkward because all the while she had been clutching a hard object in her left hand—the key to the study. That told her why she was here. She was waiting for the lights of the Triumph to sweep across the windows as it took the bend of the drive when the Ransons came home. She would then go down to the back yard and tell them to leave the car out for her to take to the station to meet the Colonel.

There was a taste of cheese in her mouth. She could remember everything that had happened up to the moment she had fired the shot. Her supper tray had remained untouched at the end of the desk, apart from the young man picking up the cheese and sniffing it. She seemed to have no horror of what she had done, but the fact that she must then have felt hungry enough to eat the cheese he had handled struck her as very strange. Strange, but satisfying.

The sequence repeated itself, she didn't know how many times—the waking, the shuddering cold despite the coats, the key, realisation she was waiting for the Ransons to return, the mouth's memory of cheese . . .

*   *   *

Another gap, and then she found herself driving into the station car park and choosing a place well beyond the buildings so that she could be sure of seeing the train come in. She didn't remember speaking to the Ransons, but in her mind's ear was a kind of echo of her own voice, sounding brisk and normal. She must also have driven here. Some part of her mind, disconnected, must have seen to all that.

Perhaps not wholly disconnected, because the thought came to her that she dare not wait in the car, as she'd planned, in case she was in one of her blanks when the train arrived. She got out, went into the station, buying a platform ticket from the machine by the gate, and paced up and down the platform, frowning at the clock sometimes as she passed it, but unable to calculate how long it still was until twelve past eleven.

A porter emerged from a door, saw and recognised her.

"London train's not for another forty minutes, Mrs. Matson."

"Yes, I know. I misread my watch and came an hour early, so I thought I'd wait."

"It's getting parky out here. Be a frost by morning, I shouldn't wonder. Look, there's a nice fire in the porters' room. We're not supposed to, but it's only two of us on, and seeing it's you . . ."

"I was afraid of falling asleep if I waited in the car. And my husband doesn't know I'm meeting him."

"You'll be all right in our room. There's a bell goes off like the crack of doom when it passes the signal box."

"Well, thank you very much."

The blank this time less absolute. Something like warmth beginning to invade her body, something like coherence attempting to piece her mind together as the forlorn minutes dawdled away. Actual thoughts about her situation. One certainty—that she loved, wanted, needed Jocelyn, and always would. An absurdity—that at least it wasn't some other woman. A possible way of thinking and feeling about him: Belinda Daring's cousin, the archdeacon, was married to a woman who couldn't help swearing, wild streams of obscenity, provoked by nothing, in public. Otherwise a pleasant, kind woman, ap-

parently—Rachel hadn't met her—but with this debilitating tic.
There was a name for it, somebody's syndrome. Her husband, his colleagues, her own friends, the parish, simply ignored it among themselves, but led her out when it happened among strangers . . . Perhaps
Rachel might school herself to do the same, to treat what was happening to Jocelyn as merely an unpleasant and embarrassing ailment,
but not despicable or degrading because not his fault, being beyond
his power to control . . . It would be hard, hard almost to the point of
despair, an uncovenanted doubling of the price she had paid for having him home, but still, bitterly, worth it.

The bell. The clarity of full recall. She rose and went to wait by the
barrier. Blotches of light and dark along the platform. The thud of
the big diesel. The train itself invisible, and then a sudden loom in the
darkness when it was almost in. Its slowing rumble along the platform. Arms reaching through windows to turn the handles, the doors
swinging open, tired men getting down, their feet finding the still
moving platform from habit. Others after the train had halted, not
many at this late hour. Jocelyn, unmistakable the moment he emerged,
signalling for the porter and then turning to help somebody with
suitcases. An elderly couple climbing down to join him.

He spoke briefly with them, tipped his hat in farewell and strode
towards her, gesturing to the porter as he passed to show where he was
needed.

"Hello, I said not to trouble. This is . . . What's up?"

"I can't tell you here."

He took her by the arm and led her out.

In the darkness by the car she stopped him with a touch, turned
him, put her arms round him, laid her head against his shoulder and
sobbed. He asked no questions, but hefted his briefcase onto the roof
of the car and held her close, smoothing the back of her head with
his right hand. She remembered standing like this, in the early days of
the war, outside the ward where Anne lay moaning with rheumatic
fever, and the crass consultant had offered them nothing but self-
important mystifications.

When she was ready she gave him the key of the car. The Triumph was hers, but if they were together it was always he who drove. He still asked nothing, and she sat drawn into herself, unable to think how to tell him. He didn't drive down to the yard but stopped at the front door, which he opened with the key on his ring. Still she waited until she was forced to speak, having led him by the wrist to the study door and put the key into his hand.

"There's a man in there," she said. "I think he's dead. I shot him with my Ladurie. I don't know his name, but he said he was a friend of yours. He called you Joss. He had a key to the house."

Jocelyn took a slow breath and nodded, but made no other move. He must have stood a good minute—more—before he turned, said, "Wait here," unlocked the door and went in, closing it behind him. He came out, it seemed to Rachel, almost at once, carrying the whisky decanter and a siphon. He handed the siphon to Rachel, re-locked the door and led the way to the dining room. There were glasses in the sideboard. He poured two drinks, put them on the table, pulled out a chair and settled her into it, then sat cornerwise across from her. He took her right hand in his left and held it.

"Have a drink," he said. "Then tell me what happened, if you can."

She sipped. The bite of the scotch pierced her numbness.

"I was doing the Christmas cards. He just came in. He said you'd asked him to come up and tell me you'd be late home. He said you'd given him a key. I knew he was lying. But he kept saying you were a very good friend of his. He wasn't lying about that. Jocelyn, I knew what he meant."

She'd tried to speak in the same automaton voice she'd used with the young man, but it wouldn't hold true. She found she was crying. She put her other hand over his, and he responded by doing the same.

"I've just got this to say," she sobbed. "It's going to be all right. It's going to be . . . as all right as it can be. Whatever happens, you are still my only darling . . ."

"And you are mine."

"I suppose we'd better call the police."

"No. Go on, if you can."

"Well, we talked for a bit. I wasn't frightened. I was furious—much worse than furious—I've never felt like that about anyone or anything.

But I was sort of numb too. He had one of your cigarettes and a drink—Marsala and bitter lemon. He gave me some scotch. I took him to the kitchen and made him a ham sandwich. We came back to the study. He had another cigarette. He decided to keep the lighter, the one Flora and Jack gave you. He said you'd like him to have it. Then he found the ammunition for the pistols. He didn't know what it was. I told him about the pistols—he was going to find them any-way. He said you'd like him to have them too. I decided to stop him, I didn't know how, but he was playing around with them, and that gave me an idea. I said he'd need to know how to load them, and I pretended to show him. I made him copy what I was doing. When I'd got my gun loaded I shot him. I don't know what happened after that. I must have locked the study door. I waited in the hall till the Ran-sons came back, because I didn't want him coming to tell me they were in. Then I came to meet you. I think that's all."

"All right. Let me think."

She waited for at least ten minutes while he concentrated, sipping his drink. At last he nodded and put his glass down.

"All right. I think that's the best we can do," he said. "First, I've got to ask you this. Are you really sure about what you said just now—I mean that you want to stick with me—in spite of what I am? I don't think I can change that. I would like to, for both our sakes, but I don't believe it's possible."

"I thought about it while I was waiting for you. Yes. I'm quite sure."

"There's not enough I can say, so I won't try. If you want to, we'll talk about it later. And if you want me to go and see psychiatrists and so on."

"Like spinach."

"What do you mean?"

" 'Filthy stuff, but I'll get it down somehow,' " she quoted. "You healed yourself after Cambi Road, darling. I think that for my sake you would heal yourself from this if you could, and if you can't then I don't believe anyone else can help you."

"Well, we'll think about it later. What I want you to do now is to go to bed. Do everything you would on any other evening but don't go to sleep. I'll be up in about three quarters of an hour."

"There's nothing I can do to help?"

"I don't think so."

He rose, picking up the decanter and siphon.

"Oh, put these glasses in the kitchen on your way up, as if you'd taken them in from the study."

"What about his? It'll have his fingerprints on it, won't it?"

"Everything's going to have to be wiped down. I've just got to get the timing right. Off you go, now."

She did as she was told, taking as long as possible about everything. There was no hope of any book holding her mind, but she opened the Angela Thirkell she'd been reading and sat in bed, her eyes scanning the lines, her hands turning the pages, but not a word going in. She refused to look at the clock.

Eventually Jocelyn appeared, came round the bed to kiss her, and started to undress, talking quietly as he did so.

"All right. In a few minutes we're going to smell burning. I'm going down to investigate. I'll yell for you. You put on your dressing-gown and slippers and come down. I'll tell you to go and fetch Ranson and tell him there's a fire in the study, and then to call the fire brigade. You're up to that?"

"I think so."

She watched him go rapidly through his full bedtime ritual, glancing every now and then at his wristwatch. He climbed into bed beside her, put on his reading glasses and picked up his book. He actually seemed to read a page before he said, "That should about do it. We don't want to burn the house down."

Without apparent hurry he got up, stepped into his slippers, picked up his dressing-gown and left, putting it on as he went. With the door open, Rachel caught the whiff of burning.

She did what she would naturally have done in such a case, getting up and following him as far as the top of the stairs. She could hear his footsteps racing down the short flights. His shout rose.

"Ray! Ray! Quick!"

She kicked off her stupid slippers and ran. He was outside the study, with a soaked tea-towel covering his face. He had one of the red extinguishers in his hand. Smoke was pluming out under the door.

"Wake Ranson," he said. "Tell him to cover his face with a wet cloth, get an extinguisher and come here. Then call the fire brigade."

She met Ranson hurrying down the back stairs in his night clothes. She told him what to do, ran and called the brigade from the hall, and then fetched the extinguisher from the gun room at the end of the north corridor and ran with it to the study. Ranson was crouched at the doorway, masked like Jocelyn, directing the jet from his extinguisher into the room. Clouds of smoke and steam streamed out over his head. Crouching beneath them she reached the door.

"Here's a spare," she said. "Where's the Colonel?"

"Over by the window. I think we're winning. This muck is mostly steam. Looks like a spark must've somehow got into the wastepaper basket."

"Out of the way," called Jocelyn—loud, but not a shout—a command.

A moment later he came crouching through the door, choking and gasping.

"Mine's empty. I'll . . . Ah, you've got it—good for you. It's not as bad as it looks."

"Try not to get it on my Christmas cards!"

The mess was merely smouldering by the time the firemen came tramping in to inspect the embers and splash a bit more water around. The patch of carpet where the body had lain was burned right through. The whole room was smeared with smoke, and reeked appallingly. The front of Rachel's worktable was scorched, the envelopes, cards and remaining photographs discoloured. The stack she had completed was gone. Dully she opened the low cupboard behind her chair to inspect her cameras. Several, all her best ones, were not in their places.

She found the cards out on the post table in the hall, where she would naturally have left them. Was it conceivable that she had actually put them there, in that first long blank period after she had fired the shot? The cameras were in her darkroom. True, she might sometimes leave one, or possibly two there, but not five. Jocelyn must have done that. But at no point, except for once next morning, did he say anything to suggest that the fire had been other than an accident, or that the young man had been there at all.

She knew that if she had wanted to talk about what had become of him he would have done his best to comply, but she didn't want—indeed, if he had offered she would have declined. That world was gone. She must learn to live contentedly in this diminished one.

The following morning, then.

Mrs. Ranson brought their tray up as if nothing special had happened. They agreed with her verdict that it was a mercy Rachel had smelt the fire so that the men could get to it in time. Rachel sat up in bed sipping her tea, while Jocelyn stalked half dressed round the room, as he did every morning, fiddling with objects and adjusting them to the precise positions he preferred.

"I'm going to have to go to London," he said suddenly. "It'll take me about three days. I don't want you here alone."

"I can't come with you?"

"Afraid not. No. You'd better go to Jack and Flora if they can have you."

"What shall we tell them?"

"That you're upset about the fire, and you want to be out of the way while the worst of the mess is cleaned up."

"No. That's not me. I'd stay and cope."

"I suppose so."

He rattled a breath out between fluttered lips.

"Right," he said. "It's not just the fire. The reason I have to go back to London is that we've been very badly let down by Fish Stadding. There should have been about thirty-six thousand pounds in the Association funds. It looks as if there's only a few hundred."

"Fish! Is that true? Are you sure?"

"Yes. It looks as if he's been playing fast and loose with some of his clients' money—people I'd put him on to in the first place. Gerry St. Looe was beginning to ask questions. Fish needed to come up with the money fast, so he took what he could get at. We were bound to find out in a month or so, but it was a breathing space—only it wasn't."

"But Leila's rolling!"

"Was rolling, at a guess. He'll have gone through all that."

"Oh, God! Fish! What about Leila? And Anne and Simon . . . ? Oh, Jocelyn!"

"This only came up yesterday. That's why I had to hang on in London, to see what Fish had to say about it. The answer wasn't very satisfactory."

"What on earth can I say to Leila? Does she even know yet?"

"I don't suppose Fish has said a word to her. I was going to tell you about this, of course, until . . . anyway, I don't want it going any further than Flora, and Jack. But that and the fire—do you think it's enough reason for you to go to Flora?"

"Well, I'd want to talk to her anyway, about how we can help Anne . . ."

"If she'll let herself be helped . . . All right, then?"

"I suppose so. But be as quick as you can, darling. Be as quick as you can."

"Do my best," he said, half absently, his mind already busy with necessary plans. But then he put down the stick of never used sealing wax he'd been rearranging on the pen tray, and came and squatted by the bed and took her hand in both of his.

"I need you too, you know," he said.

During his absence Jocelyn called her every day, but naturally couldn't speak of anything of importance on the telephone. After four days he came to Froggatt in the Rover to take her home. There was a large strip of sticking plaster on his left cheek, just above the jaw line.

"Darling! What have you done to yourself!"

"It's not as bad as it looks. I was in Victoria Street waiting to cross, when a damned light lorry swung round the corner, right in the gutter, going a real lick, and a loose end of lashing whipped out and caught me. Just took the skin off, but I bled all over my jacket."

"Why didn't you tell me?"

"Didn't want you to worry."

There was a brief family conference about Fish Stadding. It looked as if over the years he had run through Leila's once considerable fortune, and had taken the Cambi Road Association funds in an attempt to recoup by speculating in titanium options. (It later turned out that he had also taken out a mortgage and second mortgage on their house. That money was also gone.) Fish himself seemed to have disappeared, taking anything that was left.

The immediate problem was Anne's wedding to Simon Stadding, due in six weeks' time, with a big reception at Forde Place. Should this be reduced or postponed, or could it conceivably go ahead as planned, with Fish himself mysteriously absent? Jocelyn had spoken with several members of the Association's committee, and the general inclination was to hush the matter up, partly for Leila's sake, but largely because Fish had been with them on Cambi Road: not that they were inclined to forgive him for what he had done—the opposite, if anything—but because that made even this betrayal something between themselves. Legal action wouldn't recover their money, merely expose their shame. So the question was whether Fish's absence from his son's wedding was likely to produce less questioning comment than the other possible courses of action.

"We'll have to talk to Anne and Simon, anyway," said Rachel. "And Leila, of course. I'll ring her as soon as I get home. I would anyway. I'm worried sick for her."

"There's no point in talking to Anne," said Flora. "She'll just bite our heads off. But Jack gets on pretty well with Simon. He could—"

"I think I'd better have a word with Simon," said Jocelyn.

On the way home he and Rachel talked mainly about Leila, and what could be done for her, and Anne's need for a more generous settlement now that nothing would be coming from Simon's side.

The call to Leila proved extremely painful. She was distraught almost to the point of insanity, and furious, but not with Fish, with anybody and everybody else but Fish. Jocelyn and the "Cambi Road gang" in particular. Fish certainly hadn't done what they seemed to be saying he'd done, and why weren't people who were supposed to be his friends standing up for him, and so on. Rachel barely got a word in. Her attempts at sympathy and consolation were brushed aside in the tirade. There was no possibility of discussing the wedding date. The conversation ended with Leila sobbing wildly and slamming the handset down.

"I'll have a word with Simon when the dust's settled a bit," said Jocelyn.

All this Rachel dealt with just as she would have if the young man had never come to Forde Place. From minor anxieties such as Jocelyn's accident with the lorry, to the near-agony of her call to Leila, her reactions were, so to speak, "normal." During her four days at Froggatt she had occasionally found herself slipping through into that parallel universe with its slightly different history, in which she had been sitting at her table, alone in the house, and sensed the movement of the study door, and turned . . . but she had already learnt to recognise the moment of slippage and to will herself not to let it happen, just as, with recurrent nightmares, one learns to recognise when one reaches it the rocky hillside halfway up which one is going to look back and see that one is pursued, and by what, and so wakes oneself before one sets foot on the path, and then, wakeful, has only the foreshudderings of horror to deal with, not the horror itself. Now Rachel was able to use these discussions, these "normal" reactions and emotions, as present, this-universe realities, to cover over and solidify, layer upon layer, the surface beneath which lay those pits of slippage, until this universe became the only one there was.

One connection, though, remained. She knew what Jocelyn was, and knew—or would have known if she had allowed herself to think about it—how she knew. She didn't allow herself. Though that pit still gaped she fenced it round with "Danger" signs and didn't go near it. So for the next seventeen nights she slept curled into his arms, but made no demands on him, as he made none on her. By denying her own sexuality as they lay together in the dark, she was denying his, and helping him to do the same.

The men had done wonders with the study. Though the reek of smoke was still perceptible it was no longer intense. Everything had been washed down, the ceiling repapered, and the walls repainted. Only the top coat on the woodwork remained to be done. Her table had been taken away and an identical one ordered from the joiners.

When she and Jocelyn moved back in a week later his lighter was on the desk. She didn't see the Laduries, didn't look for them or wonder about them. Only clearing his desk for Jack to use, when he and Flora came to live at Forde Place after Jocelyn's death, she found the box at the back of one of the locked drawers and hid it away in the secret compartment in her bureau, not having opened it and failing to notice that its weight was short by that of one pistol.

3

Once again Rachel heard the approaching pad of feet and felt cool fingers probe gently at her wrist. This time she opened her eyes.

"Well, guess who's slept and slept? And who's been dreaming then! Heart going like a train last time. Any more of that, and I'd've been sending for the doctor. Was it a nice dream?"

"Horrid."

"Tsk, tsk—but funny how they come, that kind. I still have 'em, some nights, no reason at all. Worst is when I'm a little girl again, only I'm grown up inside me somehow, with all I've known and seen, but there I am with the other kids on the footbridge below the pin mill, and we're dropping twigs into the tail of the race, the way we used to, coming home from Sunday School. And then I'm alone and it's getting dark and I look to see where the other kids have got to, but the town's all different, not anywhere I know, so I don't know my way home and there's no one to ask. Then the twig I'm holding gives a sort of kick in my hand and I look and see it's a wicked little lizard, so I go to throw it into the race, only it's all dry, and that's the worst bit, I don't know why . . . I'm sorry, dearie. Maybe I shouldn't have told you that. Don't know what came over me. I've never told anyone else before. It's funny what we've all got bottled up inside us, isn't it?"

JENNY

I

She got home a little before eleven, stiff and trembling after almost twelve hours of driving. Jeff ran her a bath and brought her finger-food to eat while she soaked.

"How have you got on?" she said.

"I've broken the back of it. There's just a bit of tidying up and pre-sentation to get right."

"Are you pleased with it?"

"It's the best I can do—clearer than I expected. But there'll be boardroom politics I don't know about, and Billy's a formidable op-erator at that sort of thing. What about you? Was it worth it?"

"Oh, yes! It's a terrific house for a start. And Uncle Albert seemed happy. There was just one sticky bit—I'll tell you about that in a mo-ment. But he made a little speech and gave Mrs. Matson the pistol—I didn't see what happened to it—she sent me out of the room for that, but it wasn't there when I came back and we didn't bring it home."

"Great. As long as I don't have to bother about it any more. What's the old lady like?"

"Upsetting. No, that's wrong, because she's rather wonderful. She's disturbing, though. They didn't tell us what's wrong with her, but she's paralysed from the neck down, and she can barely speak, but mentally she's all there. Absolutely. You can see it looking out of her eyes. Hell, if I start telling you now I'll get all wound up and I'll never get to sleep. Are we going to have time for a lie-in tomorrow?"

"Nine o'clock? Then you can tell me at breakfast and I'll have the rest of the morning to get my report together, and then we're free."

"Great. Let's have lunch at The Cat and go and walk on the Downs."

The telephone rang as they were leaving the house. Jenny answered.

"Mrs. Pilcher? This is Sister Morris at Marlings. Albert would like to talk to you. He's upset about something he thinks he's lost. He thinks you might have it. Wait. He wants me to go out of the room. Here you are then, Albert."

Sounds of movement, and the closing of a door. Breathing.

"Hello? Uncle Albert?"

"Who's that, then?"

"Jenny. Jenny Pilcher. I'm married to your great-nephew Jeff. Yesterday we drove all the way to Forde Place to give Mrs. Matson her pistol."

"Say that again."

"We drove to Forde Place yesterday. We took the pistol so that you could give it back to Mrs. Matson. She was in bed. You looked at a lot of old photographs with her. There was one of Anne fishing."

His memory snagged on the image, held.

"Right," he said. "So there was. Little Anne, fishing. And that's where it's gone, back in the box with the other one—that's what I wanted to be sure of. Thanks. You're a good girl, Penny. I've been misjudging you, but you're a lot better than I gave you credit for."

"I'm glad you think so. Don't ring off, Uncle Albert. Can I have a quick word with the sister?"

"Listening at the keyhole most likely. I'll get her."

She heard the handset clunk down, and looked at Jeff.

"Could we go on from the Downs and have tea with him?" she said. "I've thought of something that might help."

"Provided we don't hang around over lunch."

"I'll be about ten minutes. You've finished with the computer?"

"For the moment."

It took a bit longer than that, fiddling with typefaces to make the document look authentic. Jeff leaned over her shoulder and made suggestions. The end result pleased them both.

CERTIFICATE

It is hereby certified that on the 9th day of April 1996
SERGEANT MAJOR ALBERT FREDRICKS, M.C., M.B.E.
returned one (I) *LADURIE PISTOL* to MRS. MATSON, of Forde
Place, Matlock, Staffordshire, the said pistol having been entrusted to
him for safekeeping by the late COLONEL MATSON.

Signed   Jennifer Pilcher LLB.
Attorney at Law

"I'll do a couple of copies," said Jenny. "One for him and one for Sister Morris in case he loses it."

"Fine—and I've had a thought. I'll do his filing while I'm there, and that'll give me a chance to see if there's anything about this chap Voss in the old Cambi Road lists."

The obituary was very brief. Terence Voss had died in 1978.

He had been a conscript, so his military career had been limited to the war years, and had consisted of his call-up, training, posting to Singapore, capture and internment. He had remained a private throughout. He was described as a cheerful and colourful character. His next of kin was given as E. J. Cowan, with an address in the Midlands.

As soon as she returned to work, without great hope Jenny wrote on the firm's paper but giving her home telephone number, saying that she would be interested in any information about the late Terence Voss. On the same day she handed in her resignation, but agreed to stay on for a month to clear up outstanding work.

Jeff, meanwhile, received an acknowledgement of his report, with a formal note telling him he was temporarily suspended on full pay. This meant, among other things, that he still had the use of the car.

A few days later, while Jenny was at work, Jeff got a call from Mrs. Thomas, enquiring, with reasonable tact, about Uncle Albert's finances. She told him her mother had asked her to find out.

"I explained we were a bit up in the air at the moment. I said we should be OK for a bit, but we couldn't see very far into the future."

"About till next Tuesday, you mean."

"Oh, it's better than that. Don't worry."

But Jenny felt she had a duty to worry, and to let Jeff see that she was doing so. It took some of the load off him. He wasn't good at worrying, he hadn't had enough practice. He had this image of himself as relaxed, easygoing, taking life as it comes, and to a large extent that was justified. For himself there'd never been much to worry about, and nor did there now seem to be for the pair of them. They would make out. But the sudden responsibility of worrying for Uncle Albert rather threw him. His instinct was to be laid-back about it, but his intelligence was aware that this might not be, in this case, the right response. So, Jenny told herself, if she kept on visibly working at the worry face, he could allow himself to relax.

She still hadn't heard from Terry Voss's next of kin when she left her job and was about to start temporary work with a firm in Sevenoaks. Then a letter arrived, forwarded from the firm she had left, marked "Personal." It was computer-written and cleanly printed, from a church office in West Kent. It referred in formal terms to her enquiry and asked her to call a number. It was signed "Rev. E. J. Cowan."

She called, a woman answered, she asked to speak to the Reverend Cowan, and was transferred. Another woman said "This is the vicar's office. What can I do for you?"

"I'm looking for the Reverend Cowan."

"Speaking."

"Oh . . . my name is Jenny Pilcher. I wrote to you about Mr. Terence Voss."

"Yes, of course. I would like you to tell me what you want to know, and why, before I say anything more."

The voice was light, formal, scholarly in an old-fashioned way, but with something a little peculiar about some of the vowels.

"Well," said Jenny. "It's a bit complicated, and some of it is confidential. I wrote to you on office paper, by the way, because I thought I was more likely to get an answer. I'm a solicitor, but this is a personal matter . . ."

She paused for some kind of response, but none came.

"I got your name from an obituary in the Cambi Road Association newsletter," she said. "I believe Mr. Voss was a Japanese prisoner of war, on the Cambi Road."

"That is so."

"My husband's great-uncle, Sergeant Major Fredricks, was there at the same time."

"Bert Fredricks?"

"We call him Uncle Albert."

"He is still alive then? How is he?"

"Physically fine. He's living in an old people's home near Hastings, where he's very well looked after. But his memory isn't too good, particularly recent stuff. I can't go into the next bit, but he became very anxious to visit somebody called Mrs. Matson, who lives up in Derbyshire. She's the widow of Colonel Matson, who was—"

"I have met the Matsons."

"Well I drove him up about six weeks ago, and he sorted out what he'd come to see her about. She's paralysed, by the way—bedridden—but there's nothing wrong with her intellect. They looked at a lot of old photographs together—Uncle Albert's memory is pretty good for that sort of thing—and he enjoyed himself. But there were a couple of times when he got very agitated, when Mrs. Matson tried to question him about something—it was two things, actually, and I don't know if they were connected. He didn't exactly refuse to tell her, but he pretended to have lost his memory, which he won't normally ever admit to."

"You thought he was lying?"

"Yes. So did Mrs. Matson, I'm pretty sure. This thing was extremely important to her—I don't know why—but she could see how upset he was so she didn't press him. Now, when I'd first been talking to Uncle Albert about making this trip, one of the things Mrs. Matson wanted to know about had actually come up in passing, and Uncle Albert told me he'd been there and so knew about it. He'd added, 'Ask Terry Voss.' So after we'd said goodbye to Mrs. Matson I slipped back into her room and told her, and she asked me to find out anything I could. That's why I wrote to you."

There was a pause.

"Tell me, Mrs. Pilcher, had you met Mrs. Matson before?"

"No."

"What is your general attitude to your husband's great-uncle?"

"I like him a lot. I think he's a wonderful old man."

"And yet you went back and told this almost complete stranger something that he had been anxious to conceal. Why did you do that?"

Ms. Cowan's tone had become marginally less formal since the mention of Uncle Albert's name, and didn't now change, but Jenny felt there was something not exactly brutal, but almost inhuman, in having the question asked so instantly and inescapably.

"Well," she said slowly, "I didn't think about it at the time. It just seemed the right thing to do. But I did on the way home, quite a lot. The answer is that I felt Mrs. Matson had done something for me— she didn't know, and I don't want to tell you what it was—it's very personal—but I felt I owed her something. That's why I wrote to you too—I mean, after I'd had time to think it out."

"And, other things being equal, truth is in itself to be preferred to falsehood?"

"I'm afraid I didn't think about that. Yes, I suppose so. But they weren't. Equal, I meant."

"They seldom are. Well, Mrs. Pilcher, I shall need to think about this. I have not much more time now. But I should very much like to talk to your Uncle Albert. You say he's at Hastings. Where are you? That's a Maidstone number, isn't it? I was wondering whether we could all three somehow meet."

"That would be great."

"I'm afraid that it's not that I necessarily wish to help you or Mrs. Matson. Perhaps I had better explain my interest. Terry was my mother's brother. He was very important to me. The times when he was in prison were the bleakest periods of my childhood. You are not perhaps aware that my uncle was a professional thief."

"No. I'm sorry. He was just a name."

"That is why I was so cautious when you wrote to express your interest. Well, now. From what you tell me, Bert is reasonably mobile.

I'm afraid my own time is extremely taken up. I'm supposed to have Thursday afternoons free, but they seldom are. Let me see . . ."

"I and my husband could collect Uncle Albert and bring him to you, if that would help, but it would have to be at a weekend. I shall be working again from Monday on."

"Unfortunately parish priests tend to be busiest at weekends . . . ah, yes, I could arrange to have an hour and a half free this coming Sunday, before evensong. I could offer you tea."

"That sounds great. I'll have to check with my husband, and the nursing home, but I should think it will be all right. Can I let you know?"

"Of course. I'll pencil it in. Provisionally then, four o'clock, Sunday the 24th. Do you need directions?"

"Not if I can find it on the map."

"We will assume you can. The vicarage is opposite the church, and clearly designated as such. I hope that none of you is allergic to cats."

"Hell . . . Oh, sorry. I'm afraid my husband is. I may have to come without him. I'll let you know."

Jeff decided not to risk the cats, with the hay fever season almost on him.

"I'm sorry about that," said Ms. Cowan, when Jenny telephoned. "But I'm greatly looking forward to meeting Bert Fredricks after all these years. About your other problem I'm not so sure. We may in any case have some difficulty in discussing it in his presence, if he's so unwilling to talk about it."

"Suppose I wrote telling you in confidence as much as I know. It isn't a lot. The main thing this time is to give you a chance to make up your mind whether you want to help at all."

"That might be very useful. I'm glad you see it that way. Till Sunday then."

2

The village—almost a small town—was in that tangle of lanes with which the Kentish Weald is reticulated between the roaring thoroughfares to the coast. It was self-consciously kempt, with old, small-windowed houses, weatherboarded and tile-hung, all in near-perfect condition—this not to catch the tourist's eye and camera, but for the gratification of the inhabitants who had chosen to live in this half-artificial version of the English dream, and had the money to maintain it. The main street curved up a hill—little more than a mound—to a church and churchyard at the top, building and tombstones of the same dark sandstone. The church looked genuinely mediaeval, and was probably fascinating, but Jenny found churches oppressive. She responded much more willingly to the houses of the living.

A woman answered the vicarage door. Several cats wove purring round her ankles. She was about fifty, tall and angular, with a narrow pale face framed by a helmet of dense, shining white hair. She wore silver pendant earrings, a dog collar and a dark grey suit, with the frilled white cuffs of her shirt just visible. The effect, obviously deliberate, was strikingly black and white.

Her smile was thin but not sour.

"Come in," she said. "The kettle is just coming to the boil. Mind your head, Mr. Fredricks—the ceilings are desperately low. You too, Mrs. Pilcher—in fact you'll find the doorways are more of a trap for you, because you aren't used to ducking. This way. I shan't be a moment."

She showed them into a dark room with a lattice-paned window and a beamed ceiling so low that Uncle Albert couldn't stand erect.

"What's going on?" he said. "What's this woman doing, got up like that?"

"She's the parson here. They have woman parsons now, you know."

"It's not right. Not in the Bible—bet you it's not. So what does she want with us, then?"

"She wants to talk to you about Terry Voss. She's his niece. You remember Terry Voss?"

"Terry? I should think I do. What does she know about Terry, then?"

Jenny guessed from his tone what he meant.

"She knows he was in prison quite often. But she was very fond of him. That's why she wanted to meet you."

"Terry's all right. More than all right. Only he couldn't tell yours from mine—never could and never would. Is he showing up here then? She'll need to watch her spoons."

"I'm afraid Terry's dead, Uncle Albert."

"Can't be helped. A lot of 'em are. Most of 'em now, I dare say. Funny sort of room. Looks like it's been got ready for a sale, somehow."

This, Jenny thought, was remarkably perceptive of him. She too had been vaguely puzzled by the oddity of what was clearly a sitting room, with armchairs and a sofa arranged for people to gather and converse. There were upright chairs against the walls, a couple of tables, a bookcase, pictures on the walls, rugs—but nothing seemed to relate to the room or to any of the other objects in it. As Uncle Albert said, it was as if a random collection of furniture had been brought in and arranged wherever it would physically fit, but not because anyone was going to want to live with it.

Ms. Cowan came back with a tray, wading through a moving eddy of cats. She almost knocked the milk jug over as she slid the tray onto a table, but Jenny had moved to help and caught it in time.

"Oh, thank you," said Ms. Cowan. "We're not going to starve, at least. My parishioners rightly consider that I am incapable of looking after myself, let alone visitors, so I have only to mention that I have somebody coming and I am inundated with scones. Now, out you go! Shoo! No laps on Sunday. You know that perfectly well."

She chivvied the cats out and closed the door. They miaowed affrontedly beyond it.

"Weekdays I wear skirts on which the hairs don't show," she explained. "Well now, this is wonderful. So you're Bert Fredricks! Do you mind if I call you Bert? My Uncle Terry always did. It's how I think of you. My name's Eileen, but Terry always called me Nell."

"Nell?" said Uncle Albert, as if instantly, magically unbewildered. "You're telling me you're Terry's little Nell!"

He guffawed with amazement and delight. Jenny had never heard him produce such a sound. It made the effort of bringing him here, even the half day away from Jeff, worth while.

"Yes, I'm little Nell," said Ms. Cowan.

He had risen when she'd brought the tray in, and she now stood in front of him, smiling. With simple naturalness he put his hands on her shoulders, bent and kissed her on the forehead. She seemed to Jenny to hesitate for a moment, but then closed her arms round him and hugged him. The movement was gawky, uncertain, as if long unpractised. After a few seconds she released him and turned to Jenny.

"I'm sorry," she said. "I haven't really introduced myself in the excitement. I'm Eileen Cowan, of course. Nobody except Uncle Terry and his friends has ever called me Nell, but we'll stick to that to avoid confusion. And you're Jenny? Jennifer?"

"Jenny except on cheques and things."

"Jenny, not Penny," confirmed Uncle Albert. "She's worth twice what Penny's worth, if you want to know. Can't think what their mother was doing, calling 'em pretty well the same name like that. It's not as if they'd been twins."

He spoke with the full authority of the head of the imaginary family.

"Well, that's settled," said Nell. "Now if I give each of us a little table. And everyone must have two scones, so that I can say with honesty how much we enjoyed them. The smaller ones are Sharon Smith's and the others are Annie Fletcher's. The jam is Cyril Buck's from his own strawberries. Splendid. Now tea . . . Oh dear, what on earth have I done? And it's almost cold. I know I warmed the pot, and I know the kettle was boiling . . . bother, I shall have to go and make a fresh pot."

"Why don't you let me do that?" said Jenny. "You stay and talk to Uncle Albert—after all that's what we're here for."

"Oh, would you? The kitchen's just along the passage, and I've left everything out."

This turned out to be no less than the truth. The makings of several meals littered the working surfaces, actual food being protected from the cats by being shoved under a couple of old-fashioned meat-safes. When Jenny emptied the teapot she found five tea-bags in it, three round and two rectangular. She deduced that one set had been left in from last time tea had been made, and furthermore, since Nell hadn't discovered them when she emptied the water out after warming the pot, that hadn't been done either.

The cats ignored Jenny as she boiled the kettle and made fresh tea. Two were busy licking the last smears of butter from a wrapping and three others were curled in their baskets. They all looked well and cared for.

Jenny admitted to being mildly obsessive about cleanliness—Jeff said she was a hygienopath. Left by a man, this level of mess would have disgusted and angered her. Left by most women it would have been even worse, not mere slobbishness, but a kind of betrayal. But left by Nell, her reactions were more uncertain. Disgust and horror, certainly—mercifully she had brought out the cup into which Nell had begun to pour, so she could at least get that clean for herself—but the anger was replaced by confusion. To be angry with somebody is to judge them, and she wasn't prepared to judge Nell, both in the sense of not wishing to and of not having enough to go on. Nell's treatment of Uncle Albert seemed to be absolutely honest, from the heart. Did it follow that her method of life was equally honest? Of course not. Nobody needed to be as domestically helpless as Nell made herself out to be—apparently revelled in being, and in her parishioners rushing to her rescue with scones and jam . . . But then again, mightn't that pose, though deliberate, have a quite different motivation? How should a woman conduct herself so as to be accepted as priest to a presumably very conservative parish such as this? Perhaps by letting them believe that she was no more than a slightly different version of a phenomenon they were already used to—the otherworldly bachelor scholar—not many of 'em about these days, mind you—gone with the gouty colonels and the hard-riding squires . . . If so, there was actually something pleasingly subversive about Nell's performance, which she herself might well be aware of.

Then, as she carried pot and cup back to the sitting room, it crossed Jenny's mind to wonder whether Nell might be gay. She knew herself to be imperceptive about that sort of thing. The clerical dress was masculine in effect, and Nell's manner to Uncle Albert had been mildly flirty . . .

She found them sitting knee to knee, bending towards each other as they talked. Both started to rise at her entry.

"Don't get up," she said. "I'll pour. You haven't got all that time."

"You do that," said Uncle Albert, settling back. "Now where was I?"

"You were telling me about Terry giving you all pickpocketing lessons so that you could steal from the guards if you got the chance. Wasn't that dangerous?"

"Dangerous and then some. It was a way of passing the time as much as anything. I don't know anyone was fool enough to try it. Find you at something like that, and morning parade the Japs would tie you to a post and make the rest of us watch while they hammered you unconscious."

"Terry told me about that. It happened to him, he said. It was so bad he didn't remember anything that had happened for days afterwards and when he came round you were in a different camp. The rest of you had carried him there, he said."

"Not exactly carried him—you want me to tell you about that? It isn't party conversation, not to my mind."

"Please. Anything you can about Terry, good or bad."

"Right you are . . . just put it there, lass—two sugars and a good dollop of milk . . . Well, we were building this road, like I told you, and the drill was that when we'd finished one section they'd parade us and march us on to a new camp. Anyone that couldn't stand to for the parade they hammered with their rifle butts and left. No food, no water. I've heard tell of natives come creeping out of the forest and carrying them away and looking after them, but it can't've happened that often—anyway not to anyone I ever ran into.

"It wasn't a long march on, no more than about ten miles, but the state we were in then it might've been from Harwich to hell. And those as couldn't keep up they pulled out of the line and hammered and left by the road—the very bit of road that man might've been building the day before.

"Now our last lot of guards, they'd been a bit soft—bastards still, but sloppy bastards, so we'd been getting away with little things. Then this new lot came, and they were hard bastards. They didn't just crack down, fair and square—they set traps. Day before we were due our next move we were lining up for our ration—mostly it was just boiled rice, but some days there'd be scraps of meat in it, or dried fish—you wouldn't've fed a dog on it, back home—and Terry spotted a bit of fish, as big as my thumb, maybe, lying by the pot, like it could've fallen out of the pot while they were mixing up. It didn't look like any of the Japs was watching, so Terry scooped it up, but of course one of 'em had been keeping an eye on it while the others were looking the other way deliberate, so they were on him, and next morning they tied him to the pole and hammered him unconscious in front of us all. After that they kept us standing out in the sun while they got ready for the move.

"Now Terry was tough. He didn't look it, mind you, a skinny fellow with a big head—big hands and feet too, like he hadn't been put together right, somehow—but by the time the Japs were ready we could see how he was trying to stand up. And just before they gave the order to march Colonel Matson stood out of line, which he wasn't supposed to, and said, 'That man's coming with us.'

"A couple of Japs ran to push him back into line with their butts, but he stood his ground and called out, 'On your feet, Private Voss. Jump to it, man! Attention! Quick march!'

"And then Terry was up and starting to stagger over, and I yelled out the step for him. Left, Right, Left, Right, Left, Right, and the lads joined in, and we hauled him across that way in little dribbles of steps while the guards stood and laughed until we dressed him in line."

He paused in what was clearly a well-worn narrative, stirred his tea and drank.

"I don't know why it is," said Nell. "Heroism ought to be horrible.

The need for it is usually horrible, and so is the event itself. So why is it that when one hears a story like that one feels a need to weep with a kind of joy?"

"It's because we are the way we are," said Uncle Albert. "Mind you, that's just the half of it. We'd got about ten miles to go, and we'd got to get Terry there somehow, though ten miles was about as much as any of us could do, never mind helping a man along who couldn't hardly walk a couple of steps on his own, and the Japs watching out for anyone slowing the line down, ready to haul him out and hammer him and leave him in the ditch. But most of the way they let us drag old Terry along, turn and turn about, one on each side with his arms round our shoulders. I thought maybe they'd eased off a bit because they'd been impressed with Terry's guts, but it wasn't that at all. They were just playing with us.

"All of a sudden, when we reckoned we'd just about done it, they pushed their way in among us and grabbed Terry and started to hammer him again. Of course we yelled at them and broke rank to try and stop them, but they'd got their guns on us before we'd hardly moved, and we could see they meant it. So we fell back, all except the Colonel. He just walked up to Terry regardless and bent down to pick him up.

"And then one of the Japs brought his butt crashing down on the back of his head and knocked him flat and half of them kept their guns on us while the others kicked and hammered the Colonel where he lay.

"Then they shoved us back into line and marched us on, broken men, broken men. Half of us wouldn't have lasted the time we had, nothing like, without the Colonel, and we knew it. And that night, lying in our sheds, I could hear men sobbing in the dark.

"Only somewhere in the middle of the night the Colonel came crawling into the camp with Terry on his back. He'd tied his arms round his neck with his belt so he could drag him along. The Japs just flung them into the shed with the rest of us. And they had them both working on the road next day, but this time they let us cover for them a bit. More than a bit. I met a Jap one time—after the war this was—and I told him about this, and he said it was because they'd been impressed by an officer doing that for one of his men. I don't know, myself. I could never figure the bastards out."

He sat back and drank his tea again.

"Thank you," said Nell. "Terry told me some of that, but of course it wasn't from his own memory. It's never the same as when someone has actually seen it happen. Now we must test the scones. I know the jam to be excellent."

The reminiscence seemed to have exhausted Uncle Albert's conversational energies, but he sat and munched and listened benignly while Nell talked about her own memories of her uncle. Gradually, as she did so, though her diction remained as precise as ever, the underlying oddity of some of her vowels became more noticeable, but at the same time less odd, once the connection had been made to the childhood of which she spoke.

She had been born in Whitechapel, just as the war was ending, into a family belonging to the Elect of God, one of those rigid, highly exclusive millenarian sects, the thought of which gave Jenny the shudders—far worse than the blanketing Anglicanism that her own grandparents had practised, and against which her mother had reacted with total impatience of anything to do with religion.

Nell's family had been very poor. The sect's principles forbade them the use of money that they hadn't earned by their own labour, so they wouldn't accept any kind of welfare payment or charitable help. If they had been permitted, they would have let their children die rather than use the National Health system. Their women were not allowed to work for wages. All this was justified by close reading of the Authorised Version.

They did, however, acknowledge a duty to look after their own. Nell's father was a cobbler, but he died when she was five, leaving her mother with her and two younger brothers and no income at all. The sect, in their own phrase, "took pity on her," that is to say she became a virtual domestic slave in the house of her in-laws, who, when there wasn't work to keep her busy all day, loaned her to other members of the sect in the same capacity. Nell now thought that at least one of the men took advantage of this situation, but her mother had been too cowed to complain.

The mother had converted into the Elect, which was sometimes permitted when no suitable brides were available from within it. Nell believed she had married to escape from her own family, which was a branch of one of the criminal clans which then governed the underworld of the East End. Her father had been a professional hard man and frightener, notorious for his violence, and her only protector in her childhood and youth had been her older brother, Terry. When she was fifteen he was sent to prison for the first time, and offered a way out she took it, marrying illegally, and without the consent of her parents.

They made no effort to get her back. She was one fewer mouth to feed, and was never going to be handsome enough to earn worthwhile money on the streets. On her admittance to the sect she was "made new," and nothing in her past was of any interest to them, so when Terry sought her out on leaving prison he was not welcomed. He was an ingratiating character, however, and managed to persuade the elders that his main interest was in their beliefs. Luckily for him they didn't accept male converts, but had a category of "Tolerables," who, if they remained faithful, would not be fully saved when the Lord destroyed sinful humanity, causing them to die of thirst by removing the sea (Revelation 21:1) but would be allowed to toil in a sort of underheaven, or celestial basement, doing such tasks as emptying the latrines, a necessary consequence of the full resurrection of the body.

("They'd thought it all out, you see," said Nell. "That's the great weakness of systematic religion, the conviction that one can know everything.")

Surprisingly there were almost a dozen of these hangers-on, some of them regular attenders at services and meetings, where they stood behind a rail just inside the door, some more occasional. Moreover their earnings were "purified by faith" and they were thus allowed—indeed expected—to contribute to the finances of the sect. So Terry could help his sister, buying clothes for her and the children, and bringing them permitted treats, such as raisin buns, though not the ones with sugar icing, which were forbidden by a text in Leviticus.

Terry took a particular interest in Nell, declaring from the first that she was a bright kid, and doing all he could to help and encourage her. The sect were forced by law to send their children to state schools, but removed them as soon as they were able to, in those days at fourteen. By that point Nell had won her first scholarship, to a local grammar school, but that made no difference to the sect's plans for her, which were to bring her home, keep her there, and at sixteen to marry her to one of the men to bear his children and drudge for him.

Terry, having told only Nell what he was doing, arrived one morning with a parcel of gifts. As soon as the door was opened to take it in he forced his way through, while two of his friends appeared to hold the door and prevent anyone in the house going to find help. It was all over in a few minutes. Terry collected his sister and the family's few belongings and drove off in the van in which they'd come to the basement flat he had rented for her. He went with her to collect the boys from their school. Nell found her own way to the new home.

A fortnight later Terry was in prison, awaiting trial for robbery with violence. He had left funds with a local solicitor to pay the rent and provide a weekly allowance for the next four years, the sentence he expected and received.

"He never had that kind of money," said Nell, "and he didn't go in for that kind of crime. From things he said later I believe that he took a rap for a man called Dan Brent, whose brother was a major vice racketeer. I doubt the police really believed that Terry was guilty, but he had confessed and they knew they'd get a conviction. I think the money was what Dan's brother paid him for the confession. He didn't do it for my mother or my brothers. He did it for me, so that I could go on with my schooling."

"Were you happy in the flat?" said Jenny.

"Not particularly. I was happy to continue at school, but I missed Terry. My mother cooked and cleaned, to some extent, but she couldn't cope with the responsibility of dealing with money and being on her own. I had to see to all that. And my brothers were too conditioned to the Elect. They had not had too bad a time there. Boys were much more considerately treated than girls. After a couple of years my mother received an offer of marriage from one of the Elect, a widower who needed somebody to keep house, so she moved back and took my brothers with her. I refused to go, and the Elect didn't insist. I think they knew they couldn't keep me, and I would be trouble in the meanwhile. My teachers found somebody to take me in, and Terry's money paid for my upkeep. When he came out of prison there was enough left for him to rent another flat, and I moved in and kept house for him until I went to university. I converted to the Church of England in my first year, and he was the only member of my family who came to the service."

Uncle Albert had listened benignly if uncomprehendingly (Jenny guessed) to Nell's story. The mention of the church service caught his interest. He chuckled.

"So you're a bishop now," he said. "I wonder what odds the bookies would have given me on that—Terry's little Nell becoming a bishop. When's the service, then? I'll come and see you do your stuff."

Nell looked at her watch.

"Evensong's at half past six," she said. "I shall need to go in twenty minutes. Of course you can come if you want to. What do you think, Jenny?"

Jenny had enjoyed the outing, but by now she was beginning to ache for home, alone for the evening with Jeff. And a church service . . .

"Suppose I were to run Bert back to Hastings after the service," said Nell. "I shall need to cancel an appointment, but it isn't urgent. Then you could go straight home after the service, and you would be no later than you had intended. Or you could leave now, and I will find someone reliable to look after Bert until I have 'done my stuff.'"

"Are you sure?"

"I'll be glad to. Bert, Jenny must get home to her family, so you will stay with me for a little and then I'll take you to the church, and when the service is over I'll drive you home and we can talk some more. First I want a quick word with Jenny, so if you will sit where you are and finish your tea, we'll go into my study. It's just across the passage if you need us. Is that all right?"

"You go ahead and do what you want, Nell," said Uncle Albert.

With his usual formality he rose and held the door for them. Nell led the way into a room which, though far more of a mess than the sitting room, was in its very mess more coherent, a room with a purpose, a workplace, with stacks of papers, piles and shelves of books, and a PC on the desk. She turned to Jenny.

"This will take only a moment," she said. "I have thought about your letter, and having seen you both I would like to think about it a little more before making up my mind how much I feel I can help you. I'll write to you in the next few days. I hope this isn't a disappointment after the trouble you've taken bringing Bert to see me."

"Oh, no. It's been absolutely worth it. Uncle Albert's having a wonderful time. Perhaps I can bring him over again one day. And I'm terribly grateful you're taking him home. I never seem to get enough time with Jeff, and it'll be worse now I'm working again."

"You must bring him next time. I will arrange for a cat-free environment. Now, if you will just tell me how to find the place where Bert is living—I know Hastings reasonably well."

3

"What do you mean, unnerving? That's what you said about Mrs. Matson."

"Did I? No, I said she was disturbing, or something. They're completely different. Nell was very friendly and polite and wonderful with Uncle Albert, and she's obviously very bright, brainy, brainy as you are, but . . . I didn't feel easy with her, somehow . . . I think she's probably a bit like me . . . too like. People don't feel easy with me either . . . Has it ever struck you how different we are, you and me? I've been thinking about this. You are you from the inside outwards. You grew that way. Like a tree or something. I'm me from the outside in, like a bit of luggage. There are these bits inside. I've packed them as neatly as I can, and they sort of belong together—I mean they're all mine and they fit me, but they wouldn't be a bit of luggage without the suitcase round them. I've got my name on the suitcase. You can tell me apart from all the other suitcases waiting to be collected . . ."

"Stop there! This one's mine. I'm taking it home."

They were at the sink preparing mixed vegetables for one of his fry-ups. He put his knife down, bent, and heaved her not very gracefully into his arms.

"You should've got yourself a trolley," she said.

"Couldn't get it up the stairs."

"No. Not now. I'm hungry. It confuses me if I keep thinking about food. Anyway, making love to a suitcase is kinky."

"I rather like being hungry."

"Well, you can take yours up and eat in bed. I'm having mine now."

"Typical suitcase," he said, putting her down. "Then Nell's one too? Easy to spot on the carousel, by the sound of it."

"Yes, but . . . I don't know . . . I wonder . . . suppose what's in there isn't just a jumble of stuff. Suppose it's just one thing, and it's alive. And watching you."

"You're telling me you aren't alive inside? Just underwear and stuff?"

"No, of course not. Forget about suitcases. I wish I hadn't started it. She must have had a really extraordinary childhood. It wasn't any worse than mine, but it was a lot weirder."

The letter came on the Wednesday. Enclosed with it was a sealed envelope with Mrs. Matson's name on it.

Dear Jenny,

First, I must thank you again for bringing Bert to tea with me. It was wonderful to meet him, and see him looking so well cared for, and loved and respected. He seemed to enjoy the service, and to remember afterwards who I was. That is to say that without being reminded he told me that I had done very well for myself, and Terry would have been proud of me. I am hoping to arrange for one of my congregation to pick him up sometimes on Sundays and bring him over for tea and evensong. I hope that you and your husband will see fit to join us occasionally.

Now to business. I accept your decision to help Mrs. Matson find out what she wants to know, as far as you can. For my part I propose to compromise. From what you tell me it sounds as though Bert and my uncle may have witnessed Major Stadding's death, and were then asked, or decided, to keep the matter confidential. By your account Bert was prepared to make a considerable sacrifice of his self-esteem in order to do so. Since my uncle, though he liked at least to drop plenty of hints about various episodes in his career, never mentioned the subject to me, except perhaps very indirectly, I believe he would have taken the same line as Bert. I therefore do not feel justified in trying to persuade Bert to break that confidence.

Within those limits, however, on the basis of my own memory of Mrs. Matson as well as what you tell me of her, I am prepared to help. Bert too, when I mentioned her name, was full of her praises, though he spoke as if he had not met her for years. I therefore feel justified in passing on to her a few things that Terry told me that might have a bearing on the matter. They are all trivial and tangential, and though they were in some sense said to me in confidence, I do not feel constrained by Terry's presumed promise of silence.

I have, as you see, written to Mrs. Matson separately, and must ask you to be so kind as to add her address. This is not out of any distrust of you but in order to respect her privacy. I am sure you will understand.

Yours very sincerely.
Eileen (I mean Nell)

"She's been reading too much Jane Austen," said Jeff.
"That's just part of the trim on the suitcase."

RACHEL

I

"The most peculiar letter for you, I'm afraid I opened it—it looked like a begging letter—you know they'll try anything just not to look like begging letters—and that's probably still what it is. I mean it's from a vicar somewhere in Kent—at least he's writing from a vicarage, St. Martin's Vicarage—he was the one with the cloak, wasn't he?— and he's a reverend, or he says he is—the Rev. E. J. Cowan, though he might pronounce it the other way—you can't tell. Have you ever heard of him? I haven't. Jack hasn't. What makes it so peculiar is there's another letter inside, addressed to you too, I haven't read that of course. That's why I'm not sure it isn't a begging letter after all. But listen . . ."

She started to read, interjecting her own comments, with no variation in the gabbling monotone.

"To whoever opens this letter dear friend—a bit pushy, but I suppose it's better than Sir or Madam—dear friend the enclosed concerns a matter which Mrs. Matson may wish to keep private I am aware of her condition—it gets more and more peculiar. I mean the man's a total stranger. Do you think he's mad?—her condition I have therefore written it in large type so that it can be held by another person for her to read—he must have done that on a computer. Everyone has them nowadays, even vicars—her to read if that can be arranged if however having read the first few lines she indicates that she is content to have it read to her I for my part have no objection yours truly E. J. Cowan. At least he doesn't say it isn't a begging letter. If he did, we'd know it was. What on earth is this about, Ma?"

"Don't know. Show me, please."

"You want me to open it? Let's get your specs on first, shall we? Now I'm going to shut my eyes so you know I'm not cheating. I say, isn't this rather fun! Here goes. Help, it's pages and pages. I don't think I've got time now. There, is that the right way up?"

"Yes. Higher. Stop."

The print was as large as a child's first reader. How Jocelyn would have enjoyed a computer, Rachel thought—not just as a toy to be played around with, but as a tool he could use, an extension of his competence to deal with the world.

Dear Mrs. Matson,

Mrs. Pilcher has recently asked me on your behalf about my uncle, Terry Voss. I have no direct knowledge of the episode in which you are interested, but on the other hand I recall an incident that I now believe may be connected. I will describe it in some detail.

Despite the large print the lines filled less than half the page. Presumably the writer had stopped there so that Rachel could decide whether she wanted to keep what followed to herself.

"Too long," she whispered. "Thank you. Dilys."

Dutifully Flora folded the letter and slid it into the envelope before opening her eyes.

"Well," she said. "Is it a secret, or isn't it? Oh, Ma, don't be so provoking! You might at least give me a hint."

"About Terry Voss."

"Terry Voss . . . ? Oh, that funny London spiv Da was so keen on? What on earth has a vicar in Kent got to do with him? He can't still be alive. Can he?"

"Nephew."

"How extraordinary, but I suppose it takes all sorts, even in the Church of England, these days, anyway. I really do try to be broadminded, but I absolutely wouldn't feel comfortable about having my grandchildren confirmed by a gay bishop, so I suppose I can't blame Mr. Cowan for wanting to keep quiet about Voss. It *is* good of you,

Ma, to keep up with these people after all these years, in spite of everything, just because they were on the Cambi Road with Da . . . oh, of course! That one! Da saved his life when the Japs beat them both up and left them by the road. And the first time anyone ever told me about it was Archdeacon Donnelly at Da's funeral, and you said how Da would have hated that, which of course he would, but really it's something people ought to know about. But Voss wasn't there—at the funeral, I mean."

"In prison."

"Oh yes, and you tried to get him let out on compassionate grounds and they wouldn't wear it—doesn't it all seem ages ago?"

"Not to me."

"No, I suppose not. Now I've got to run. I only came up, really, to bring you the letter. Di Grindle's starting another of her Good Works, not as loony as last time, thank heavens—it's getting pets into old people's homes because it's good for them having an animal around, and she wants me on the committee, except she doesn't—she wants Jack, because he's so organised, but he refused to play and who can blame him so she's got me. Shall I ask Dilys to come and help you read the letter?"

"No hurry."

"Right. Then I'm off and you can tell me later if there's anything amusing in it. I do think you're a wonderful old thing, Ma!"

Rachel closed her eyes and listened to the receding monologue. Yes. Jocelyn would have loathed Archdeacon Donnelly. It had to be him because his brother had died on the Road, but the way he had milked the story for heroism . . . Hateful! And made more so by the fact that the trick had worked, even on her, so that she had wept, along with most of the others. Not that it had been the first time she'd heard the story. Jocelyn, of course, had never mentioned it, but she'd picked up hints and suggestions at Cambi Road reunions, often in a tone that suggested that Jocelyn had asked people not to talk about it, so that in the end she'd asked Fish Stadding directly and unrefusably, and he'd told her without fuss, in his own manner, of course—oh how much more tolerable he would have been than the archdeacon to give the address!—so that she was aware of the strong streak of farce that seemed to have been inseparable from the fearsome cruelty of their captivity.

Later, choosing her moment one evening, she said, "I made Fish tell me what you did for Terry Voss."

"Blast him."

"I said I made him. I didn't give him a choice. It's all right, darling, I don't want to talk about it. I'm just telling you so you know I know."

He'd grunted and refolded his newspaper to start the next page, but then had looked up and said, "If Voss had come round before me he'd have tried to do the same thing. He wouldn't have made it, because I weigh twice what he does, and he was in bad shape after his first beating, but he'd have tried. I'm not saying any of 'em would—we'd the same share of mullocks as you'd get in any other grab-bag of humanity—but by and large it was the ones who stuck by each other who made it through. I'd have picked Voss over quite a few of the others, officers among 'em, as a chap to trust in a pinch. I still would."

"I like him too. I wish he wasn't always on his best behaviour with me. He must have some fascinating stories to tell."

Rachel had been thinking, incessantly, uselessly, about Voss since Sergeant Fred's visit and Mrs. Pilcher's brief but desperately unsettling return to her bedside. There was one particular moment, one remark, on which she now felt, everything inexplicably hinged.

She hadn't known Voss at all well—nothing like as well as she'd known Sergeant Fred, for instance. There'd been no reason why she should. He'd been a conscript, and after the war had returned to his own, hidden, alien, way of life, only occasionally attending Cambi Road reunions. Her few conversations with him had been brief and banal. But after Jocelyn's funeral she'd decided to try and visit him in prison, not for anybody else's sake but her own, because it had been something Jocelyn would have liked her to do, and that was what she needed more than anything.

The visit had been surprisingly difficult to arrange. In the end she'd had to tap into Jocelyn's network of influential contacts to be allowed to make it at all. Furthermore, as she'd been dismayed to discover, Voss was now in Parkhurst on the Isle of Wight, serving a longer sentence than usual for taking part in a break-in during which an elderly nightwatchman had been seriously injured. She'd hesitated, but in the end drove down, stayed with cousins near Winchester, and took the ferry over to the island and a taxi to the prison.

Once there she waited for almost two hours among prisoners' families, groups and faces that cried out for the lens, images of despair stoically endured by women who were always tired. Eventually she was taken into a big, bleak room with a kind of counter running its full length. Each prisoner sat on one side of the counter, and his visitors on the other, with a grille between them so that they couldn't pass anything across. Shallow screens gave them a little privacy from their neighbours but a warder stood behind each prisoner to see that the rules were kept.

Once Rachel was seated there was some kind of hitch, unexplained. She waited numbly. She felt in herself the same sort of hopelessness she had seen on the faces in the waiting room. Her man too had been "put away." She too had been betrayed by happenings beyond her sphere, and now she was expected to live and behave like a normal citizen, despite that.

But when Voss was brought in her mood immediately lightened. He must not have been told who his visitor was, but when he saw her his puzzled frown cleared into obvious delight. He looked little different, the same too-large head on a scrawny, hunch-shouldered torso. He'd always been a sharp dresser, and even now had somehow managed to iron and adjust the amorphous prison uniform into something resembling tailoring.

"Why, it's Mrs. Matson!" he said. "Couldn't think who . . ."

His grin faded.

"Ah, he's dead, then?" he said.

She had no idea how he had made the leap. Jocelyn had once said, after a visit from a recent widow formidably in mourning, "You won't wear black for me, Ray, will you? I suppose you'll have to at the funeral, but that's all."

She'd accepted it as one of those odd, strongly held quirks that dotted his apparently conventional outlook. (Detestation of cream stationery was another.) She'd found it no hardship to do as he wished.

Perhaps Voss had seen her loss, visible in her face, or perhaps it was hard for him to imagine any other reason for the visit. Surely he knew that Jocelyn had been ill . . .

"I'm sorry," she said. "I'd have written, but well, there's been a lot to think of and there was a special issue of the Newsletter, or don't you get that here?"

"No one to send that sort of stuff on," he said. "Niece writes to me Sundays, and that's it."

"I hope someone visits you sometimes."

"You're the first . . . lessee . . . six and a half months. Nell—that's my niece—can't come on her own that easy, and there's no one else wants to. Can't blame them. It's a hell of a distance."

"Oh, dear. I'm very sorry. I gather you're here for rather a long time. That's bad luck."

"No such thing, Mrs. Matson. Brought it on myself, didn't I, getting in with a crowd like that. But I tell you I'm not trying anything like that again."

"That sounds sensible. I came because I thought you might like me to tell you about the funeral. I tried to persuade the authorities to let you come to it, but it wasn't any good. Several of your friends were there. Half the Association wanted to come, but there wasn't room in the church, so it was just a delegation and there'll be a memorial service in London next month. But RSM Fredricks was there, and Doug Rawlings . . ."

"Got that new cab he was after?"

"Yes, I think so. He drove some of them up in it."

"So Duggie's got a new cab, and I'm in here. Funny how it goes." He laughed and shrugged, but his eyes were watching her with another kind of look, ironic, almost mocking, as if this was a private reference he didn't expect her to understand.

"Yes, I'm sorry," she said. "Look, I've brought some photographs . . ."

She showed them to him through the grille and told him scraps of news about the subjects, most of it gathered in a long telephone call to the new Association secretary. Voss commented, jokingly disparaging, as if teasing his old mates through her, secondhand as it were.

Time passed much more lightly than she'd expected until the warder looked at his watch, took a pace forward and said, "Sorry, folks, three minutes more and that's it."

"Oh, dear, they don't give you very long," she said as she put the photographs away. "There's just one other thing I wanted to tell you, Mr. Voss. A few years ago I made somebody tell me what really happened that time the Japanese guards beat you and Jocelyn up and left you lying by the road. I know Jocelyn asked everyone not to talk about it, but I'd heard one or two hints and I couldn't help wanting to know the rest. No, wait. This isn't about that. It's about what Jocelyn said to me when I told him I knew."

She recounted the rest of that conversation. When she finished, Voss sat for several seconds sucking at his upper lip and shaking his head.

"Jesus!" he muttered. "I don't know what to say, honest. All right—I wouldn't've let him down—I didn't, neither, when it come to it—but Jesus! . . . Well, thanks, Mrs. Matson. And I'll say this. It goes for you too—right along the line it goes for you. Anything . . . Any time . . ."

"Thank you, Mr. Voss. I'll remember."

"You do that, and just one more thing, Mrs. Matson—if ever it come to your ears how the Colonel got hisself into something he oughtn't of, you can tell 'em straight back it wasn't like that—it was because he had to. Right?"

The warder had stepped forward again as he was speaking.

"Time's up, folks, so just say your tatty-byes."

Rachel, dismayed almost beyond dismay that Voss should bring the subject up, especially after conducting the rest of the interview with such ease and tact, blurted out the first thing that came into her head.

"I think I know what you're talking about and I agree with you."

A look of bewilderment came over Voss's face, but the warder touched his shoulder and he let himself be led away.

Waiting in the drizzle for the ferry Rachel puzzled miserably about it. How could Voss have known? There was, perhaps, a connection: Voss came from the East End, and so, apparently, did the young man she had shot; but Voss's tone and phrasing had suggested both sympathy for Jocelyn's predicament and detachment from it. However much he had admired and respected Jocelyn, was it credible that he would speak in that way of his compulsive involvement with a creature like the young man? But suppose Jocelyn had discovered that side of his nature on the Cambi Road, as she had come to believe; and suppose that many others, not normally that way inclined, had also sought such solace, and been tolerated by the rest—men such as Voss—for doing so, then perhaps there would be no need for Voss to have known about the young man to speak as he had. And perhaps his look of bewilderment, almost of shock, as he was taken away was his reaction to the idea of an apparently devoted marriage that persisted after the man had told his wife that he had done what he had. The young man himself had expressed outrage at the self-same thing, and he and Voss were very much products of the same culture . . .

No, that had not been it. Not at all. She had been wrong for almost forty years. It was something else that Voss had been talking about, a specific occasion, Sergeant Fred also there, and together they'd seen Fish Stadding die, and Jocelyn . . . Jocelyn had "got hisself into something he oughtn't of."

2

"Well, dearie, so we've got a lovely letter to read."

Rachel hadn't heard Dilys come in. Unnoticed behind her reverie the rooks had been making an unusual racket and perhaps that had drowned the movement of the door. She opened her eyes and made her lips smile. Dilys blurred into the usual vagueness as she reached the bed.

"I'm to hold the pages for you so you can read it yourself, Mrs. Thomas says. Sure you can manage?"

"You read it."

"Oh. She said . . . are you sure? All right, then—this'll be it, I suppose. Are we comfortable, dearie, before I start? Here we go, then . . . Goodness, what big letters! Now, she said you'd read some of it . . ."

"Just first . . . paragraph."

"Oh, I see. All right. Here goes . . ."

Dilys, too, read in a near monotone, but very different from Flora's, slowly and with regular pauses to make sure of the next phrase or sentence.

"First, as I have just said, Terry Voss was my uncle, my mother's brother. Our relationship was closer than that implies. As you no doubt know, he was a professional criminal, but he was the only member of my family to show me any true affection, and crucially he enabled me to continue my education when I would otherwise have been taken away from school. I loved him. I also thought of him, and still do, as a truly good man. One of my reasons for writing this letter is that the only other people I know of who seem to have valued him as I did were certain members of the Cambi Road Association.

"During the latter part of my school days he was in prison for a longer sentence than usual, for a serious crime that I do not believe he committed. I think in fact that he had been paid to 'take the rap' for somebody else, and had accepted the money so that my mother could provide a home for myself and my brothers. Be that as it may, though I wrote to him weekly, I barely saw him for several years—"

"Stop. End of letter. Signature."

The pages rustled.

"Mrs. Thomas said it was a parson . . . here we are . . . Oh, goodness me, it's a woman! Eileen Cowan—that's what she's typed, but she's signed it Nell Cowan."

Of course. Not some never-mentioned nephew, but the niece. Voss had brought her once, a rather forbidding young woman, to show off to the Association. A good while after Jocelyn's death, that must have been.

"Go on."

"I did not see him for several years, and when I did I found he had changed. Inwardly, and in his relationship with me, he remained much the same person, but his experiences as a prisoner of war had at last caught up with him, and though he lived for many more years he was thenceforth an invalid. He managed to stay out of trouble until I had finished at university, and at that point, instead of going on to post-graduate work, I took a job so that I could support us both.

"Some years later, my then employment involved me in driving extensively round East Anglia, often to remote areas. My uncle was recently out of hospital, so in fine weather I took him along with me. It was good for him to get out of the house, and it gave him the chance to express his dislike and distrust of the countryside. Other than in his period of National Service he had seldom set foot outside London. He was company for me too, with a fascinating repertoire of criminal reminiscences and lore. Since I was now a seriously practising Christian, he liked pretending to try to shock me with tales of appalling villainy.

"On one of these occasions we drove out to a lonely farm in that strange area of Essex marshland between the Crouch and Blackwater estuaries. I left my uncle in the car, as usual, while I made my visit, and on my return was surprised to find him gone. I waited, and some while later saw him walking towards me along an unmetalled lane that led towards the sea, still a mile or two away to the east. I went to meet him, and then realised from the state of his shoes and the difficulty of his breathing that he must have walked some distance. I helped him back to the car and then remonstrated with him for his stupidity. I will try to reproduce his exact words. You have spoken with him, so will remember the accent.

" 'I wanted to have another look,' he said. 'Been here before, see? But I been and bit off a bit more than I can chew.'

"I drove off, turning the heater full up to warm him. For a while he wheezed alarmingly, but when he had recovered a little I asked him what he had been doing so far from the city.

" 'Losing bodies,' he said. 'Mind you, one of them hadn't been a body, not till we brought him here.'

"For once I was genuinely shocked, so much so that I stopped the car and turned to him. I then saw that he had not, this time, been merely teasing, and realised that the tone of his answer had been uncharacteristically sombre.

" 'That's not the sort of thing you got involved with,' I said.

" 'No more it was,' he said. 'And I don't want to talk about it. Didn't ought to have brought it up in the first place.'

" 'All right,' I said, and drove on, still considerably troubled. I believe he must have sensed this, for after a while he said, 'I don't want you to think bad of me, Nell, so I'll just tell you this. What happened back along that track wasn't nothing to do with villains. Amateurs, more like—which is what they wanted me along for. I'm not saying it was aboveboard, and we'd have been dead in trouble if we'd been caught at it, but it wasn't nothing to be ashamed of. I'd do it again, if the same fellow asked me.'

"I thanked him for telling me. Of course I believed what he said, and still do. He liked, as I have said, to talk about criminal activities, and if he himself had been involved he made no attempt to conceal or palliate his own guilt. The fact that he had never before, and never again mentioned what sounded like a startlingly dramatic episode, and that he was so determined to insist on its ultimate propriety as far as he could, is for me sufficient warranty that whatever had happened out on the marshes must have been very different in nature from anything else he had told me about.

"I think that is all that I can usefully tell you. I would like to add that we have once met, though I do not expect you to remember the occasion. My uncle brought me to a summer reunion of the Association in the garden of your house, and you spoke to me very kindly of him.

Yours very sincerely,
Nell Cowan.

"Only like I say she's written it Eileen underneath."

Dilys sighed deeply as she folded the letter away.

"Well, what a story," she said. "But frustrating, really. Like missing an episode on the telly. And that's what's been fretting you so, isn't it, just the not knowing? And it's something to do with those pistols of yours—got to be, seeing that's what started you off . . . I'm sorry, dearie. I know it's no business of mine. I shouldn't've let myself be carried away like that. Only . . . We're tired, aren't we? Been a bit much for us, has it?"

"I'm all right."

Rachel was in fact exhausted, though not in her usual manner, with the ridiculously small reserve tank on which she now depended for all her energies having run almost dry—though that was indeed the case too. But she was experiencing a kind of spiritual depletion, a feeling that all the extrinsic parts of her self were being stripped away in order that whatever powers were left to her could be concentrated into the central essence, for it to confront and finish with the thing it was here for. In order to reach that moment, other things needed to be done, some practical, some, so to speak, ritual.

She calculated. Voss had been in prison by the time of the funeral. His sentence would have been a year or so earlier. He had "taken the rap" so that Nell could continue her schooling after the age of fourteen. When he had brought her to Forde Place she had been at university . . .

"Albums," she whispered. "CRA. About '64."

"Right you are, dearie. Coming."

Dilys bustled eagerly out.

A ritual, a politeness, that one. The next one, something practical. Rachel continued to consider the problem while Dilys returned, cranked the bed up, adjusted the reading table and light, and settled the spectacles into place.

"There we are, dearie, all ready. I've brought the one from '61 to '66, so that should cover it, easy. Start at the beginning, just in case, shall I?"

"Please."

The pictures ambled past. She had taken as many but kept fewer of these later years. Groups and individual studies of men, and a few women, mostly in early middle age, all wearing Sunday best, styles conservative even in their day, regimental ties, short haircuts, hats and caps—faces and poses caught, embalmed in their instant, by the flick of the shutter. Time at a standstill. Illusion, manifested as such each time the same face recurred at a later meeting, sometimes perceptibly older after the lapse of only a year . . .

"Stop."

The girl was standing with Voss in front of one of the cedars. He was smiling confidently and holding himself with his usual swagger—or attempting to, as he didn't now look well, worse than he had in Parkhurst. Perhaps he was not many weeks out of there, for his long-jacketed, narrow-legged suit looked very new. But for the fact that his arm was round her waist one wouldn't have thought the girl could have had any connection with him. Rachel could see no family likeness. She was barely shorter than him, the narrowness and primness of her face accentuated by a tight bun. She wore a coarse-knitted jersey and patchwork skirt, both so shapeless as to deny any guess at the body within, and she held herself not with the regulation student droop but with stiff unease. There was no sign of the strong affection for her uncle as expressed in the letter. The image of her was in fact uninteresting, but it was good of Voss, and Rachel had few of him elsewhere. Presumably that was why she had kept it.

She closed her eyes and tried to summon energies.

"Thank you," she whispered. "Take it out."

"Out of the book? You're sure? How . . . Oh, it comes quite easily. You want me to send it to her?"

"Yes. Say thank you. Letter very useful. Next. Call Simon Stadding. Number . . . from Ellen. Can he come and see me? Not been well. But try. Let me . . . hear."

"Righty oh. Just put the bed down a bit first shall I, so we can have a bit of a rest. Now don't be naughty. I can tell. We're near done for and we mustn't pretend we aren't."

Rachel tried to protest. Her lips moved, but no sound came. Vaguely she sensed the lowering of the bed as a shift and easing of the pressures on her spine and neck. Her awareness of the change seemed in itself changed—less than she was used to, another loss of the defended ground. A sign that Dilys was right. She was almost done for.

DILYS

I

Deliberately Dilys took her time about putting the album away, phoning the secretary for Mr. Stadding's number and setting up the extension speaker. It wasn't going to be much of a rest anyway, but she would make it as long as she could. She felt anxious. There was nothing to show for it on the chart, temperature and pulse normal, bowels a bit slow, appetite down a little, but over the past few days she had sensed more and more strongly that Mrs. Matson's illness was moving towards a crisis, not drifting towards it, either, as is the case with most really old people as they are eased into their deaths, but being sucked towards it by a strengthening inner current. And night after night Mrs. Matson hadn't been sleeping properly. She was thinking too hard, remembering too fiercely, and all the while digging into herself for any little scraps that might be left there to feed her thinking and remembering.

The doctor was coming this afternoon for a checkup, but Dilys didn't intend to tell him any of this, not unless he asked her directly, and perhaps not even then. She knew what he'd do, he'd prescribe a sedative to calm Mrs. Matson down into a nice peaceful departure. That wasn't right. Mrs. Matson wanted to think. It was really important. It was the only thing left.

But if she didn't let herself rest a bit when she got the chance, she'd be gone too soon to find the answer. That must've been a nasty moment for her just now, when she'd tried to say something and found she couldn't. Frightening.

Having spun things out as much as she could, Dilys made the call.

A woman's voice answered, light, anxious, hesitating over the number she gave.

"Is Mr. Stadding there, please?"

"I'll just go and see . . . Who shall I say?"

"My name's Dilys Roberts. I'm speaking for Mrs. Matson, because she can't use the phone."

"I don't understand. Which of you wants to talk to my husband?"

Dilys explained again.

"It's about the Cambi Road Association," she added.

"Oh, dear . . . well, I'll see."

There was a long pause. Dilys waited, puzzled. This Mr. Stadding was Major Stadding's son, wasn't he, the one in the photographs. He oughtn't to have been much more than Mrs. Thomas's age, but his wife sounded quite a bit older than that, nervy too, used to being looked after, finding even the taking of a telephone message bothersome.

There was the click of another extension and the voice returned, more anxious than ever.

"I'm so sorry, but my husband can't come now. He's not been well, especially these last few days. He says if you could write. Do you have the address?"

"Yes, but . . . you see, we were hoping Mr. Stadding might come and see Mrs. Matson . . ."

"Oh, there's no question of that. I told you he wasn't at all well. No, you'll have to write."

Dilys looked towards the bed. The lips moved briefly, shaping a syllable—inaudible, but Dilys could perceive the weary acceptance. She thanked Mrs. Stadding and rang off. She stood for a little, staring blankly at the handset, still in her hand, while she put her thoughts in order, then turned to the bed.

"Now don't try and say anything for the moment, dearie—you're just wearing yourself out, and it won't get you anywhere doing that. You're going to have a proper rest now, and I'm going to put your book on and you're going to listen to it for a whole side, and then we'll see. And while you're doing that I'm going to write a letter to Mr. Stadding, so you know something's happening and you don't just lie there fretting to get on. Only first we've got to get right what you want me to say. No, don't try and say anything, not yet. You want to ask him something, and it's about his father, isn't it? Trouble is, it's a secret, and he's not going to tell just anyone. It's got to be you, just between the two of you—that's why you hoped he could come and see you. So it's no use you telling me this question, because it's a secret, like I say, and how's he to know I'm telling the truth anyway, about it all being for you, and I'm not going to read what he says when he writes back to you? That's really the first thing we've got to work out. I mean, if he's sure it's you and you can tell him somehow he can rely on me—which he can, if only he knew—and then, somehow, we can get your question to him, do you follow . . . ?"

She paused, not expecting any answer, because that was as far as her thoughts had reached. She saw Mrs. Matson's lips move, again inaudibly.

"I'm afraid I didn't catch that, dearie—you'll have to say it again."

She bent over the bed to hear the faint syllable.

"Tape."

"Tape . . . ? Oh, a tape recorder! That's brilliant! Yes, I can hold the microphone right up close and I'll put my Walkman on so I can't hear what you're saying and I can tell him all that in the letter and he can put his answer on the tape and send it back for you to listen to. You are a clever old thing, you really are! . . . Not like that? But . . . All right, you tell me!"

Again she bent and strained to hear the fought-for syllables, separated each from the next like drips from a tap.

"Write. First. Me. Dead. Soon. Must. Know. Before. Album. Family. Fifty. Seven . . ."

There was a longer pause. Dilys waited, realising that Mrs. Matson was momentarily exhausted and only giving herself time to gather strength again. She wouldn't be at ease, not to rest properly, until she'd finished the message.

"Man. On. Fire. Escape. Send. Say. 'Carrot.' Joke."

"Joke . . . Oh, I get it! There was a joke about a carrot, and he'll remember, so he'll know it's got to be you. That's brilliant! And we can send it to him and ask him to help while we're getting the tape ready . . . You don't think we might as well wait. Ellen's got a recorder sure as eggs. You've just got to have a decent rest, not fretting about it all, and you'll find you're talking normal again. And I'll get that letter written while you're resting, and see Ellen and get it all set up ready, so you can do the tape this afternoon and we'll get it all in the late post. Don't you think that's best? Really?"

"No. Send. Letter. Photo. Graph. You. Take. Tape."

"Me? Well, if that's the way you want it. Just as you like, dearie. Now is that everything? It better had be, 'cause this isn't doing you any good. Best have it off your chest, I know, but it's no use trying yourself beyond what you can manage . . ."

She paused as Mrs. Matson smiled. She had the most beautiful smile, Dilys thought. They were often like that, old people's smiles, holy, sort of, but naughty with it sometimes . . .

"Letter. Lay it. On. Thick. Dilys."

"Do my best, dearie, you can be sure of that. And it'll take me a bit of a while, seeing I'm not much of a writer, so I'm going to make you nice and comfortable, and draw your curtains this end and you're going to have your rest. And I'll settle down at the table there so I can keep an eye on you, make sure you're behaving yourself. I'll just nip out and get that photo first, shall I, so you know I've got the right one."

The photograph was where Mrs. Matson had said it would be, of course. It was of a very handsome young man. Dilys had noticed a couple of pictures of him earlier in the album as she'd leafed through, one of them with Miss Anne down by the river, feeding ducks. Here he was alone on a sort of balcony . . . no, it was the fire escape, of course, like Mrs. Matson had said, only the way he was standing was so poetical you couldn't help thinking balcony . . . you could see he was sending himself up, standing like that, so it was funny already, and then . . . something to do with a carrot—he'd got one and put it between his teeth, like a rose? Something like that. And Mr. Stadding had been there . . . No, of course, the young man *was* Mr. Stadding, so of course he'd remember . . .

She showed the picture to Mrs. Matson, settled her down for her rest, fetched her own writing things and got down to the letter.

It took her almost all morning, with several false starts and endless crossings out. Lay it on thick, Mrs. Matson had said, but she didn't want it to sound soppy or pathetic because Mrs. Matson wasn't like that. She found that the plainer she made it, the more she called a spade a spade, the righter it felt, so in the end it came out a good deal shorter than her first attempts.

Dear Mr. Stadding,

I'm writing to you for Mrs. Matson. She can't write because she's paralysed and she can only just speak so the phone's no use either. She's told me to send this picture along with the letter, so you can know it's from her. She says to tell you "Carrot."

The other thing she said to tell you is she hasn't got long. Motor neurone disease is what she has, and once you've got it you just get worse, starting with your legs and working up. Mrs. Matson's almost gone. I don't know how long it will be, she's such a fighter, but I doubt she'll see another winter.

The thing I want to tell you for myself is she's absolutely all there still, in her mind, I mean. She never stops thinking and re-membering and working things out. So it's no use trying to fob her off. She'll see what you're at, and she won't give up. She'll try and get at it another way.

Now, there's just something she's anxious to get sorted before she goes. She hasn't told me what it is, and I'm not asking, be-cause it's private, but it's got to be something to do with the Cambi Road Association, or she wouldn't be asking you. And I can tell you from me she's not going to go happy without it— she's got herself into such a state fretting about it. She's killing herself, if you want my honest opinion. That's no way to go, Mr. Stadding. It isn't right.

Anyway, she wants to keep it private and so do you, she says, so her idea is I'm going to fix a tape recorder by her so she can whisper into it, which is as much as she can do by way of talk-ing, anyway. And I'll stop my ears so I don't hear anything, and she wants me to bring the tape over for you to listen to, and then you can talk to her back the same way. So you'll know it's only me that had the chance to know anything about it, and you can make up your mind about me when you see me, I suppose.

Saturday's my day off, if that suits you, but we can get the other nurse in different days if you'd sooner. And there's a phone up here, so if you ring the number at the top and ask for the nursery wing, they'll put you through.

Yours truly,
Dilys Roberts (Miss)

Mrs. Matson had actually slept, and when she woke her voice, though feeble, was more under her control. A little reluctantly Dilys read her the letter, but she didn't seem at all put out by its frankness and smiled and said, "Well done," so Dilys parcelled it up with the photograph and put it on the table in the hall to go with the afternoon post. Two mornings later Mrs. Stadding telephoned, obviously reluctant, to say that her husband could see Dilys the following Saturday morning. Dilys, with Ellen's help, had already looked up trains and found that though Market Drayton was only sixty miles away there wasn't anything that got there without taking all day and going all round the shop; and the buses were just as bad. So Mrs. Matson asked Mrs. Thomas if Trevor Sweeting couldn't take her. He was really the under-gardener, but mostly he did odd jobs and stuff, and anyway Saturdays were supposed to be his days off too, but Mrs. Thomas must have got him in a good mood—she had a real trick for that, Dilys had found: everyone seemed to eat out of her hand because it never crossed her mind they wouldn't—so in the end it all worked out.

2

The sixty miles took almost two hours along busy winding roads. Trevor listened to Radio One turned up loud. Dilys sat in the back letting time drift past in a kind of half dream. Looking at all those photos with Mrs. Matson, it must have been, but she found herself supposing she'd spent her life taking pictures of everything that had ever happened around her, so she'd shelves and shelves of albums of her own she could use to fish stuff out of the long ago, the way Mrs. Matson did. Nursing college, say, back at Tredegar. There'd've been an album for that. Who'd have been in it? Di Phillips, for a start, bleached blond hair, pouty lips, always messing around with her uniform to get it a bit tighter where it showed—as if she needed it—and waggling her bum at the senior consultant—a good nurse, mind you, and there'd been a dozen young doctors she could've taken her pick of, instead of which she'd gone and got involved with one of the night porters, old enough to be her father almost, and married him and stuck with him and had three kids, and he'd carried on being just a night porter but she'd gone back into nursing and done very well, heading for matron last Dilys had heard . . . heard how? Somebody must've told her, and the rest, different times, because Di was the sort you talked about . . . but if she didn't know how she knew, how did she know she knew . . . ? And what about that other girl—she was a darling and there weren't that many black nurses back then—but Dilys couldn't remember a thing about her, not her name, nothing she'd said or done, leave alone what happened to her after, only the glossy skin and the big laughing mouth and the sideways glancing eyes, yes, just like one of Mrs. Matson's photos. Bonnie Wincing now—it was the other way with her because there'd been a photo to go on, the one in the newspapers and it had to be her because there couldn't be two people called that. Dilys didn't remember much about her from Tredegar, except the name, but now the papers said she'd given a patient ten times the drug he was supposed to be on and faked a card to make it look like the doctor prescribed it, so she'd be in real trouble when the patient died, which he did. The doctor was a woman, that was the point, and she'd been having it off with another doctor who Bonnie fancied. Looking at the photos in the papers, Dilys wouldn't've known she'd ever seen the face before . . . It was all gone, gone, except scraps, and most of your life is like that, really, if you thought about it, even when you think there's lots and lots you remember. Maybe there were people who had it all sorted and stored away in their minds, like Mrs. Matson had with her albums, but most of us aren't like that . . .

The car slowed right down. Trevor read the name on a gate.

"Looks like we're here," he shouted over the radio. "Fanning, wasn't it? How long are you going to be, then?"

"I don't know. Not very long. Half an hour?"

"Oh, that's not so bad. I'll put the car on the verge there and stretch my legs a bit. OK?"

The house must have been two small cottages once, because half of it had a slate roof and the other half was thatched, and the windows didn't line up—one of them you could see where the other front door had been. There was a tidy plain garden. When Dilys was halfway up the flagged path from the gate, the door was opened by a small, stooped woman, neatly dressed in a wool-knit skirt and twinset. Well into her seventies. Heart condition. Osteoporosis. Might last for years, might go this afternoon, poor thing. Her voice was the twitter Dilys had heard on the telephone.

"You're Miss Roberts? How do you do? I'm Ida Stadding. My husband's expecting you. Please—I don't know what this is about—he won't tell me but I know he's upset about it, and that isn't good for him. He gets so tired."

"That's all right, Mrs. Stadding," said Dilys, on her home ground and armed with her professional confidence. "I don't know that much about it myself, but I don't think it'll take long, and if you want to know my guess is it's something he'll be happy to have off his chest.

And I'm a nurse, remember, so I'll know if I'm taxing him, and I'll be careful."

"All right, then. This way . . ."

The house inside was nothing special to Dilys's eye, but it had that pleasant feel you get when a couple have lived companionably together for many years. Most of the pictures were of birds. Mrs. Stadding opened a door, and a wave of warmth flooded into the hallway. The room was hotter than the greenhouse at Forde Place where Mr. Worple brought the houseplants on. Despite that, the man in the chair had a rug across his lap, a shawl round his shoulders and wore a knitted scarf and mittens. His skin was a dirty yellow, his eyes sunk and his flesh fallen away, but Dilys could still see that she'd been right in her guess, and he'd been the beautiful young man Mrs. Matson had photographed on the fire escape. Liver, obviously. Should've been in hospital, poor man, but by the looks of him it was a bit late even for that.

He acknowledged their entry with a sour little smile.

"I won't get up, if you'll forgive me," he said. "As you see, I am not in very good health."

"Now do be careful, Sim, and not upset yourself," said Mrs. Stadding. "I'll run and put a kettle on for Miss Roberts. Tea or coffee?"

"Don't make it special for me, Mrs. Stadding. Only if you're having some. Tea and milk and one sugar, which I know I oughtn't."

"Count yourself fortunate to be able to make the choice," said Mr. Stadding.

He waited for the door to close.

"Now, what have you got for me?"

Dilys fished in her bag.

"There's the tape recorder," she said. "Put it on your table, shall I, where you can reach it? And I'll plug the microphone in. There's fresh batteries, so you won't need a cord. All you've got to do is—"

"I am familiar with these devices."

"That's all right then. But you're going to have to listen real hard, because her voice is starting to go and she can't talk above a whisper, just two or three words at a time. I was in the room with her to press

the buttons for her and that, but I was wearing my Walkman which
I've got for sitting up with my patients so I don't disturb them, so I
didn't hear anything she said, I promise you that. Now I'll just go outside . . ."

"Go and talk to my wife, if you like. I daresay she could do with a
chat. I am not much by way of company these days. I must trust you
not to tell her the reason for your visit."

"Of course I shan't. That's between you and Mrs. Matson."

Surprised by the sudden affront, she had spoken sharply, but he
merely nodded and waited for her to leave.

From the hallway she could see Mrs. Stadding in the kitchen,
standing by a counter, motionless. She was holding a tea bag by one
corner between fingertip and thumb tip, as if posing for a photo in
an ad. The whistle of the kettle broke her trance. She dropped the tea
bag into the cup and moved out of sight. When she came back with
the kettle Dilys saw that, as she'd guessed, she was crying.

She waited until the kettle was safely back on the cooker and went
in. Mrs. Stadding made no effort to stop her tears.

"Oh, you poor thing," said Dilys.

"I can't bear it. I can't bear it any more."

"It's his liver, isn't it?"

"That's right. We knew it was bad, and we'd been waiting for a
transplant, but suddenly it's got so much worse and he's too ill for it
and they want to take him to hospital but he's made up his mind he's
dying and he wants to die here. I can't bear it. He's so much younger
than I am, so we'd always known I'd go first."

"Oh, that's so hard on you! Of course it is! Why, you've only made
one cup."

"I don't want anything."

"I'm sure you do. Come along now. Tea or coffee?"

"Tea, I suppose."

"There's a good girl. Now you tell me all about it and don't worry
what you're saying because a secret's a secret and I'll not pass it on. I
never think any the worse of someone for what they say when they're
in trouble. Far better have it out, I always say, than bottle it up. Now,
then, not too strong, I expect."

"Oh no, terribly weak. And a teeny bit of milk—I'm not supposed to but I can't stand it without."

"Me too. Now you sit there and tell me about it. No wonder you're fond of him. He must have been ever so handsome when he was a young man."

"Oh, you should have seen him! From the moment I set eyes on him I knew there was no one else in the world I wanted. I hadn't a hope, you'd have said, with me being so much older than he was though I wasn't a bad looker still, if I say it myself, but I wasn't one to give up. I found out he was keen on bird-watching, so I got myself a book and some binoculars and . . ."

Still weeping gently she glanced at Dilys and smiled, and Dilys saw for a moment what a lively little woman she must once have been.

"I've never fancied it myself," she said. "Too much hanging around and getting chilled through for me."

"Oh, no, you can get quite cosy in a hide, you know, waiting for something to happen. I never expected him to love me the way I adored him. There'd been just this one girl he'd loved like that, ever, and ever would, but it had gone wrong, and now he was tired of living alone and at least I'd amuse him and make him comfortable."

"Looks like you did, too," said Dilys. "It's got a nice homey something about it, this house. I felt it the moment I came in."

"Oh, yes, hasn't it? And I've worked so hard for that, and so has he. He didn't used to be like this, you know—it's just his illness. It's eating him up. He keeps saying he's got bad blood—well of course he has, now, but it's as if he's always had it and it's his own fault for being born like that, and now he's being punished for it, and he can't think about anything else. He was always so thoughtful too . . . and we've had wonderful holidays together . . . and been so . . . comfortable . . . and it's not going to be like that any more . . . never any more . . ."

She had stopped crying and now sat staring, grey-faced, at something that wasn't there between her and the Aga.

"You know what's killed him?" she said, biting the words out. "It's the Cambi Road Association, that's what. And that's what you've come about too now. I didn't want him to see you, you know."

"I'm sorry," said Dilys. "I'm only a messenger, sort of, bringing him something. I don't know much about it myself."

"But you wrote, didn't you? The postmark said Matlock. It must have been a photograph of something, but he'd hidden it when I came back. And he was upset—in a funny kind of way, though . . . you aren't going to tell me, are you? It's another of their stupid secrets . . ."

In a sense the situation was familiar to Dilys, familiar enough to know what she felt and what she should do. It happened again and again, younger relatives concealing stuff from her patients on the pretext of saving the old and helpless from unnecessary fret, though in reality, as often as not, doing it to avoid having to cope with what might be a perfectly justifiable fuss. It put her in a false position, and she resented it. Regardless of who was paying the fees her primary loyalty was to her patient, and she disliked being forced to go along with these deceits, as in most cases she was, because now if she told the truth the patient would suffer not only the original fret but also the greater hurt of betrayal. Mrs. Stadding wasn't her patient really, but . . .

"I'll tell you what was in the letter, if you like," she said. "I don't think Mrs. Matson would mind, because she did it that way in case it got opened by somebody else. It was just so Mr. Stadding could know it was Mrs. Matson who sent me. It was a photo she took of him, years ago at Forde Place, on the fire escape, looking all romantic. And she said to tell him 'Carrot,' because it was some sort of joke had happened, and he'd remember and know it must be from her in spite of me writing it. And I was going to bring him a tape with a message on it, and he could send a message back the same way. It was to keep it all secret, you know."

"Don't I just!" sighed Mrs. Stadding. "It's always secrets, and they're killing him. I knew he shouldn't have let you come."

"If you want my opinion, it might help this time," said Dilys. "It might be a chance to get something off his chest after all these years."

"Oh, if only he'd *do* that! If only he'd tell me! I can't ask—I just can't. It's the same with his brothers. There's two of them, and years and years ago us three wives—because they're both married—we got together—we didn't see that much of each other, not usually—but that time we were on our own and we settled down and thrashed out everything we'd picked up, one way or another . . . Do you mind? It's just that I've had it buzzing around in my head all these years . . ."

"Well, I don't know," said Dilys. "In the ordinary way of things I'd say you tell me if you want and I won't pass it on. But this time . . . I'm here for Mrs. Matson. She's not got long to live now and there's something she's desperate to know before she goes, and she's hoping Mr. Stadding will tell her. And it's all to do, far as I can see, with the same sort of secrets, so suppose you went and told me stuff Mrs. Matson might want to know, I'm not going to pretend I wouldn't tell her."

Mrs. Stadding was gazing again at the ghost behind Dilys's shoulder. Dilys wasn't at all sure she'd heard or understood, but she smiled stonily.

"Then we're both in the same boat, I suppose. I'm desperate to know before Sim goes. I've got nothing against Mrs. Matson—not that I've ever met her—Sim didn't want me coming to Forde Place . . . Oh, you tell her what you like, Miss Roberts . . . If it hadn't been for Colonel Matson I'd never have had my life with Sim, anyway . . .

"There was this girl I told you about you see, the one Sim loved. She was Colonel Matson's daughter, and they were all great friends, the Staddings and the Matsons, and Sim and the girl were going to get married, and everyone was very happy about it. But then there was some kind of row between Colonel Matson and Sim's father—I don't know what it was about, but it must have been something Sim's father had done because he walked out. Went abroad somewhere, I mean, and never came back, and took a lot of his wife's money with him too. Leila, her name was—she was my mother-in-law, of course, and Sim used to take me to visit her in Torbay sometimes, where he and the other two had bought a little house for her. She was a sad old thing, and she'd been such a beauty once—that's where Sim got his looks, of course—and there were all these photographs all round the room with bits cut out of them. And it wasn't Sim's father, if that's what you're thinking. There were lots of him, so I know what he looked like, though I never met him. No, it was the Matsons. Any of her photographs had one of them in it, she snipped carefully all round them and put it back in the frame, because she didn't want to let anyone forget that everything that had gone wrong, it was all Colonel Matson's fault.

"Of course I asked Sim about it, soon as we were in the car to come home—it was a terrible drive those days, before the motorways—and all he said was, 'I'm afraid I can't tell you. I would if I could, but I can't. It's something she's done in the last few months, they weren't like that last time I came. And please don't ask me again.' I could tell from the way he said it he was very upset.

"Of course I guessed it was something he'd promised his mother, not to talk about the Matsons, though it didn't stop him going over to Forde Place for the Cambi Road reunions.

"Anyway he'd been in love with this girl, Anne her name was, and they were going to get married. I found some of the wedding invitations at the back of a drawer once, so they'd got that far, and it would have been a big, smart wedding, but their two stupid fathers had this row and it was all broken off. I don't know what it was about. One of us three wives said Sim's father had run off with a woman Colonel Matson had introduced him to, but the other one said no, it was because he'd stolen a lot of money belonging to Colonel Matson, and Colonel Matson had come and told Sim that he didn't want him for his son-in-law any longer. Sim absolutely worshipped Colonel Matson, I should have told you, so I thought that made a bit better sense than the other story, but it still wasn't like my Sim, not if he loved the girl the way I'm sure he did. You can see about cancelling the fancy wedding, I suppose, but what was to stop them waiting a little while and then marrying each other quietly, and bother their parents if they were against it, they were both old enough? And anyway, he was honour bound to marry her, wasn't he, like he was honour bound to the Cambi Road Association, and he wouldn't give it up, whatever I said.

"His father used to be secretary, you see, and Colonel Matson was the boss. And then his father ran off, and somebody else took over, but he got ill and Colonel Matson died, so they were in trouble until Sim went to them and said he'd do the job. I don't know how he put it to them, I expect they were a bit surprised but of course they

jumped at the chance. Only whatever he said his real reason was he
knew he'd made a terrible mistake and he wanted to keep in touch
with the Matsons, just hoping he might pick up with the girl again. I
expect he'd written to her before, and she hadn't answered or she'd
given him the brush-off, but he wasn't going to give up. He's like that.

"Of course that was all before I met him—"

An electric bell rang briefly, twice, from the hall.

"That'll be for you," said Mrs. Stadding, rising. "And thank you for
listening to a stupid old woman worrying away at what can't be
helped."

"You mustn't think that bad of yourself," said Dilys. "You're being
brave about it, you really are. I've seen some make far more fuss when
they hadn't got half what you've got to put up with."

"Only it's so hard to keep going."

"Of course it is."

"And I'll tell you what's the worst of it—it's thinking he should
never have let any of it happen in the first place, and he knows it and
I know it. Oh, why couldn't he tell those stupid old men that their
silly quarrel wasn't any of his business, and just gone ahead and married the girl, if he was that fond of her?"

As she started to weep the bell rang again, longer and more insistently. Mr. Stadding could hear their voices, Dilys guessed. She took
Mrs. Stadding by the shoulders and eased her back into her chair.

"Now, you sit there and drink your tea," she said. "I haven't finished mine so I'll be back in a minute for the rest of it, and we can
talk some more if you want."

She left her dutifully sipping as she wept.

Mr. Stadding was sitting with his head bowed and his eyes shut.
The recorder was in his lap with the case closed and the microphone
unplugged and coiled. After a few seconds he looked up, slowly, as if
just raising his eyelids was almost too taxing.

"I trust you have had a pleasant gossip," he said. "Well, I have
recorded an answer of a sort for Mrs. Matson. I hope it will satisfy
her. Will you make her understand that I have done even this with

considerable reluctance, and shall not respond to any further enquiries. I suppose I must thank you for coming. Goodbye."

Dilys tucked the recorder and microphone into her bag. She was all
too used to the way the old and ill can exploit their weakness to control others. She spoke to Mr. Stadding as if he had been one of her
patients, not letting her anger show, using a quiet, professional tone,
as if she'd been advising him on the management of his illness.

"I've got something to say to you before I go, Mr. Stadding. You'll
think it's no business of mine, but I've been talking to your wife, like
you said to. She's having a very rough time, poor thing . . . No, you
listen to me, and of course you're wishing it wasn't so but there's nothing you can do about it. Well there is. She's got ideas into her head
about the whys and wherefores of stuff that's happened—this stuff I
came to see you about, not that I know much about it myself, but I
know enough to see that some of her imaginings are mistaken. No,
wait. Far as I can gather, you've never told her, not because you didn't
want to, but because you gave someone your word about it, once.
Well, that's all over. It's years and years ago. Colonel Matson's dead
and Mrs. Matson won't be long going and there isn't anyone else that
matters, except Mrs. Stadding. You think it's not got anything to do
with her, but it has. More than anyone else it has, now. You don't want
to leave her thinking worse of you than she need do, do you? So you
go ahead and tell her everything you can. You're a decent man, and
you've been trying to do the decent thing all these years to a lot of
people who don't matter any more. It's her turn now. She's the one
who matters. Don't leave it lying between you the way it is now, and
you'll both feel better for it, really you will."

His answer was toneless with weariness.

"As you say, it is none of your business, Miss Roberts. Neverthe-
less I will think about it."

"You do that. And show her the photograph Mrs. Matson took of
you, and talk to her about Miss Anne. It won't upset her, nothing like
the way she's upset now."

"Goodbye, Miss Roberts."

Mrs. Stadding was still in the kitchen, but she had finished her tea
and cleaned away the traces of her tears.

"I made you another cup," she said. "Yours looked cold and horrid."

The bell rang, a single, longer burst.

"That's for me to go and give him a hand with . . . you know. He can't manage on his own any more. I'm afraid it takes a while, but please stay as long as you want and let yourself out if you've got to go."

"I'll just have my tea and then I'll be off, thank you. I told the driver half an hour, and it's past that already."

"In that case . . . well, goodbye, Miss Roberts."

"Goodbye, Mrs. Stadding. And I do hope things go better for you soon."

"Oh, dear."

RACHEL

I

A voice that has no moisture and no breath
Breathless mouths may summon.

Rachel couldn't remember how she knew the lines, or where they came from, but they sidled often into her mind these days as she struggled with her increasingly erratic command of speech. Today was in fact one of her better days, when she seemed able to put several words together at times and without huge effort. Dilys had returned late yesterday afternoon with the tape, and she had listened twice to the brief message, and had then lain and thought, eaten her supper, watched TV, slept well, and woken full of the excitement of her planned day. It was the excitement, the urgency to get the thing finished at last, that supplied the energies needed for speech.

First, before she started the hunt, the tape again, the two voices from the speaker beside her on the pillow. She had expected Simon to erase her question by recording his answer over it, but he hadn't.

So first, the moistureless, breathless whisper, her own ancient ghost.

"Simon, this is Rachel Matson . . . For old time's sake . . . I must know . . . Before I die . . . Did Jocelyn kill your father?"

Then the more recent ghost, the weary mutter from the new-filled grave.

"I am sorry, Rachel. Memories of Forde Place are among the few sad pleasures I have left to me. I too am dying, and wish it were over. I made Uncle Jocelyn an explicit promise, by which I still feel bound, that I would not answer your question. All I can tell you is that none of the participants would have regarded the event as being, in essence, shameful or iniquitous."

That was all, apart from what might have been a sigh.

She blinked her eyelids twice to signal that she had finished.

The Walkman gave an unfamiliar shape to the blur of Dilys's head as she bent over the bed to switch the machine off and take it away.

"There now, dearie. All done, and I'll take this thing off so I can hear you again. Just leave it on the table, shall I, for next time?"

"No. Wipe it . . . please. Then albums. Life . . . 'Thirty-one . . . to 'Fifty-eight."

Dilys made two trips for the nine volumes she had asked for. There were fifteen in all, Rachel's own deliberately composed autobiography, wordless apart from the brief captions, names, places, dates. She had made the decision to put it together on the train back from London after seeing Dr. Lefanu and persuading him to tell her without palliation the likely course of her disease. He had given her a maximum of four years before she became imprisoned in the total physical dependence she now endured. She had by willpower wrung almost five from the failing carcase, starting the day after her return by getting Farrow and Milligan in from the garden to fetch box after box of stored film down from the attic and stack them in her dining room, once the night nursery, now Dilys's sitting room. For the last three volumes she had no longer been able to work the controls of the enlarger, or to manipulate the prints through the trays, so had hired students, training them to do the job to her satisfaction. Thus the captions to those last volumes were written in a variety of strange young hands. It had been an early exercise in the art of controlling her world from inside a body that couldn't itself be controlled.

Some sections had already been partly composed, the equivalent of diary extracts quoted in a written autobiography, but even here she had not always left the original intact, but had sometimes altered enlargements or interpolated images that seemed to her to adjust a perspective in the light of later understandings.

Begun as a task to see her through the dispiriting process of dying, it had become a wholly absorbing and rewarding occupation, worth doing—no, demanding to be done—for its own sake, a summation of a life and of a way of seeing; like a serious novel, though it could never find a publisher, indeed would never have more than one reader, herself, with anything like a proper comprehension of its meanings, and not many others. Still, fully worth doing for its own sake.

So she had never expected to use it for any practical purpose, as she was now about to do in order to track Fish Stadding through its pages, and study him in the light of what she found there, and thus perhaps, at last, understand him.

The volumes Dilys had brought opened with one of the "diary" passages, composed immediately after her return from India, newly engaged to Jocelyn. She had looked through it at least yearly since then—if you are the only reader of your book, then it's up to you to see that it is actually read now and again—and she still found it satisfyingly remarkable that, though some of the individual compositions left much to be desired, she should have been able, so early in her career, to construct a detached and shaped account of the unbelievable event.

The quay at Karachi. The ship and gangplanks providing a grey-white, sharply angled background. A porter, naked to the waist, staggering on camera under the load of an enormous bale. Leila Valance sitting on a pile of trunks and suitcases and looking straight at the lens. Dear Leila, best friend since earliest school days. In the light of Dilys's report on her visit to the Staddings, Rachel gazed at the image with a sort of bewilderment. She had so long been used to the obvious paradox about Leila, the way in which the looks belied the character. And not only the looks, but movements and postures, all the physical manners—as here, with the glossy, jet black, shoulder-length hair, the almost pearl-pale face, the big, luminous, slightly pop eyes, the luxuriantly languid pose—made people say "very Russian" or something of the kind, implying intellectual, alien, affected, erratic, absurdly emotional and altogether un-English. Not a bit of it. As a close friend Rachel had known her as down-to-earth ordinary, not specially bright but shrewd in her way, loyal and expecting similar loyalty from others, and extraordinarily determined, sometimes to a point beyond pigheadedness. Even the abrupt and, to Rachel, desperately painful shattering of their friendship had seemed of a piece with this reading of her character. Leila's loyalty lay with her husband, overriding all other loyalties, to the extent of refusing to believe that he had in fact utterly betrayed her, and that there wasn't some other explanation for what seemed to have happened. Rachel, though deeply hurt and grieved, had to some extent sympathised. She too, after all, had been almost equally betrayed, and had remained loyal. What if Jocelyn, having done what he'd done and been found out, had then disappeared? Could she have brought herself to believe that he had actually run away? Surely not.

But now, gazing at the picture of Leila on the quayside, she wondered. Had she been wrong about her all along? Or had Leila's inward self, over the years of useless hope, gradually grown to conform to what was suggested by her looks? "Very Russian" it sounded, that to Rachel shocking business of snipping the images of her enemies out of all the photographs she kept on display.

Not yet. That all came later. Back to 1931.

Leila and Rachel had come to India with "the fishing fleet," though unlike most of the other young women on the expedition Rachel had had no intention of finding a husband, while Leila, who with her striking looks and fair-sized fortune could have hooked almost any fish she chose, in any seas, had one particular catch in mind, who merely happened to be in India.

Rachel was there to keep her company and take photographs, Leila paying her passage. For propriety they had attached themselves to a Mrs. Splingford, not one of the regular semi-professional chaperones, but polo mad, and therefore going to Meerut, which was where Leila's fish was to be found. And, as it turned out, Lieutenant Jocelyn Matson. That was why the porter was part of the image. His inscrutable burden portended that future.

"Turn . . . Stop."

Fish.

For at least the hundredth time in her life Rachel felt a pulse, a glow of satisfaction at the complexity hidden in the apparently redundant caption.

"My, what a monster!" said Dilys. "Not that I'd fancy eating it, mind you."

Two market porters faced the camera at a right angle, so that their burden was displayed. Turbans and loincloths, wiry emaciated torsos, looks of baffled impassivity, what could the memsahib want with such a creature? The pole they bore on their shoulders pierced its gills, bowing beneath its weight. Its tail brushed the ground. The individual scales were half a handsbreadth across, the shiny bulging eye yet larger. Leila, in the centre of the picture, had her back to the camera, but her whole stance, the stilled movement of recoil, the raised, spread hands—surrender or rejection—expressed her reaction to the proffered gift, expressed even, Rachel believed (though aware it would have taken improbable perceptiveness on the part of a stranger to read into the image what her long friendship inevitably told her), Leila's simple-minded uncertainty how to take it. Pure joke? A way of moving the courtship on a stage by letting her realise that the reason for her coming to Meerut was common knowledge? A superficially amusing but actually rather unpleasant way of telling her that the metaphorical fish she had come to catch didn't intend to rise? Beyond her, framing the tableau on the right, stood the watching donor, Lieutenant Gregory Stadding, to his intimates henceforth and forever "Fish."

They'd gone, the four of them, to the market, ostensibly so that Leila could look for trinkets and Rachel for subjects for her lens; in actuality to be together, and apart from the other British. Mr. Stadding had disappeared without explanation, returning a few minutes later to confront Leila with an elaborately courtly salute.

"I understand you came to Meerut for a fish, Miss Valance," he had said, and moved aside. The shutter had clicked about two seconds later.

Rachel's eyes searched the figure. It was as if her mind manipulated invisible fingers to adjust to its finest focus the lens through which she captured the world. This was her first clear picture of him, a decidedly handsome young man, slight and elegant, his features, though less exotic than Leila's, having the same suggestion of an un-English sensibility, an intensity of feeling, in his case salted with wryness and irony. Superficially they seemed an obvious match. She already adored him. He behaved as if attracted to her, but so did almost every other man she encountered, and Rachel had almost at once become aware of his far greater intelligence and more complex personality . . .

"Do you think there's any chance they'll understand each other, Mr. Matson?"

"I don't know it matters. People talk about understanding other people, but what do they mean? You can't look inside. It's just guesswork. And in any case you'd have to go a long way before you met anyone, man or woman, who got near understanding Greg Stadding. I'll tell you this though, and you can pass it on to Miss Valance if you want—he isn't a skirt-chaser, as far as I know. And given the chance he'd throw up the army and go home, but to do that he'll need either a goodish job or a wife with money of her own. He's not going to live in a cottage and raise chickens."

"What about you, Mr. Matson? I don't see you raising chickens either."

"Oh, I'd make a go of it if I had to. But soldiering suits me, and I imagine I'll stick with it until my old man keels over and I have to go home and look after things."

She had let the focus blur. Steadfastly she readjusted the lens and gazed. No, not a hint, not in the picture. In Jocelyn's words, possibly.

"Turn . . . Stop."

The Student Prince, put on by the officers at the end of the fortnight with the female parts transposed for tenor voices. The dress rehearsal. Lieutenant Stadding smoking in the wings while he waited to go on as Kathie, wearing not the standard *fräulein* frills but the uniform of a Lyons tea-room waitress, lace cap and white apron, black frock and stockings—the skirt not quite allowing a glimpse of the knees—and high heels, built to male size by a cobbler in the market. To Leila's distress he had shaved his moustache. The calves were a bit muscular, but that apart . . .

"Oh, it's a man! . . . Isn't it?"

"Yes."

Yes? Not a skirt-chaser, confident in women's clothing . . . No, that was hindsight.

"Turn."

A dozen images flipped past. Rachel could have closed her eyes and described any detail in any of them—the polo, a boating picnic, sunset over one of the listless canals, unpeopled except for two striplings working a bucket lift to carry water by those countless thimblefuls up to their father's fields—but she and Jocelyn had walked by the sluggish levels all afternoon (Sunday, and so no polo) and talked for the first time seriously about themselves, without reticence or pretence, revealing and discovering . . .

"Stop."

The four portraits. She had used delayed exposure for her own, and developed them in her hotel room so that each should keep a picture of their lover when they parted.

"Why, that's you! What do you mean telling me you weren't ever that pretty? I tell you I wouldn't have minded looking half so good. You're just putting yourself down, compared to your friend. She was a stunner, mind you . . ."

Jocelyn and Rachel, Leila and Fish. When the album was closed the couples lay mouth to mouth. The portrait of Leila wasn't particularly striking, compared to others Rachel had taken, but the one of Fish was excellent. Clean-shaven, his mouth was fully visible. He had chosen not to smile, but this had the effect of bringing to the surface his odd, ambivalent humour—"He's serious about not being serious," Leila had once explained—and a certain loneliness, or rather aloneness, a state chosen rather than endured. He was such good company that you didn't normally notice that side of him. Rachel thought it one of the best portraits she had ever done, but though Leila liked to cram all available surfaces of her house with framed photographs of her family, mostly snapshots or banal studio portraits, this had never been among them. "I don't like him without his moustache," she'd said when Rachel had asked about it.

"That's all. Thank you. Next one. Please."

The weddings. Rachel had begged off being the sole adult bridesmaid alongside a flock of Leila's little cousins, all of them with the fascinating Valance style. She had gone alone and mostly stalked faces and poses round the sunlit lawns, spending an amusing half hour with the official photographer, a wizened little Scot, a fanatic about his craft, using a superb old full-plate for his work but well up to date with all the latest gadgets and delighted to find somebody else who cared. There were, of course, the standard wedding shots, the couple under the church porch, cutting the cake, getting into the open Lagonda (Leila's gift to Fish) under a blizzard of rose petals—and there were others, more peripheral.

"Stop."

Fish with one of the male guests by an ornamental pond and dribbling fountain. Grey tail suits, wing collars, toppers on the chairs beside them. Fish was Fish, lissom, amused, somehow both tense and lounging; the other man—Lord Something, Rachel seemed to remember—though no taller, must have been twice Fish's weight, stocky rather than stout, with a snub-nosed, shrewd, bucolic air. He was smoking an aggressively large cigar.

"Why, that must be Mr. Stadding's . . . father I suppose. Isn't there a likeness! Funny I didn't see it in the other ones."

"Yes. Do they . . . know . . . each other?"

"I'd say they do. He's kind of teasing the other one, the fellow with the cigar, and he's making out he's hoity-toity about it, but really he's enjoying it no end."

"Flirting?"

"Well, if your friend had been a woman now . . . Is that what you're asking me? Well, now. Not to say yes, that's what they're up to, but could be there's something between them . . . or could be there isn't, not yet, but they're getting interested. Thinking about it, if you know what I mean . . ."

Yes, perhaps, thinking about it. Rachel remembered deciding to use the image mainly because she'd liked it. The balance of shapes was pleasing, the moss-streaked fountain seemed to have an odd menace in the sunlight, the picture of Lord Something was a speaking study of a particular type of man, and the one of Fish was, simply, much better of him than any of the ones with Leila. Rachel hadn't asked herself why, certainly not when she'd looked with satisfaction at the first enlargement, not even when she'd reused it for the *Life*. Now, though, the reason seemed manifest. The picture with Lord Some-

thing spoke of a truth, while those with Leila spoke of, at best, a skil-
ful act, a pretence.

She let Dilys leaf on to her own wedding.

"Why, it's just snapshots, like I used to take with my little
Brownie."

"Yes. Pocket camera."

In the last of her twice-weekly letters to Jocelyn, Rachel had told
him, trying to make her own disappointment sound merely comic,
that her parents had absolutely refused to let her ruin the expensive
white wedding that they had scraped to pay for by carrying "that
hideous black object" around with her everywhere. The letter had
reached him the day before he sailed. He had read behind the comedy
and wired to a school friend in the Washington embassy. The friend
had telephoned around and found in Bloomingdale's, in New York, a
white pocket camera, a ladies' accessory that happened to take snaps,
for use by starlets and such. It had arrived by way of the diplomatic
bag with a day to spare. Pure Jocelyn—the perceived need, the re-
sourcefulness, the contacts. The inadequate images that the trinket
produced were worth their pages, for that reason alone.

As a result, Rachel now realised she had never looked at them with
anything like the attention that she would have given to "serious"
photographs, not even while she was so painstakingly compiling the
Life. They were there for what they were, not for what they showed.
She was certain there was one of Fish only because she could remember the difficulty of taking it in the first place. Yes, there, wolfing a canapé.

"Glass, please."

"Drinkie first, dearie? . . . There. Better now? Which one did you
want to look at? Oh, this one, I suppose, because it's your friend
again. You tell me when I've got it right."

"Higher . . . Left . . . Too far . . . Stop . . . Closer . . . Stop."

The prints were postcard size, the largest Rachel had been able to
make without the images from the coarse little lens dissolving into
their individual grains. That now happened under the magnifying
glass. She could just make out the finger and thumb of the left hand,
a pale something between them piled with a darker mound. Rachel

was fairly sure what it must be, though she was not the sort of bride who could remember, sixty years after the event, the exact list of catered snacks handed round at her wedding reception.

"No good . . . You try . . . What's he . . . eating? . . . What's on . . . other chair?"

"Now, dearie, don't try and talk too much. We've all the time in the world, haven't we? Let me see . . . Perhaps if I take it to the window . . . That's better . . . Well, it's one of those little cocktaily things, isn't it? What's that black stuff called? Caviare? It might be that . . . Isn't that just a serviette on the chair? Oh, no, there's something under it—it might be a bit of a plate . . . And doesn't he look pleased with himself?"

Somewhere at the base of her neck Rachel felt a curious sensation, not itself a tingle, but a blocked impulse to send such a tingle down her spine and along her limbs, to cause the skin to crawl and the body shiver with pure fulfilment, satisfaction at the equation solved, the image perfect on the print, the chaser backed on a hunch nosing home at ridiculous odds. The caviare.

Time and again in his whining old age Rachel's father had reverted to the caviare.

"Want you to meet my daughter, Rachel. Married Jocelyn Matson. What a wedding that was! Best party I've ever been to, though I say it myself. Champagne and caviare."

"You oughtn't to be keeping me in a hole like this, Rachel. You're my daughter, aren't you? Remember what I stumped up for your wedding? Do you know what caviare costs?"

By the end he would bring it up four or five times a visit.

It had been a promise since childhood, at that time easily within his means. But his spice business was one of the early victims of the Depression, when it became an absurdity—except that his hard won status as an English gentleman mattered more than anything else, and a gentleman keeps his promises, whatever the cost.

So there had been champagne, as cheap as could be found, and four plates of little round biscuits spread as thinly as the caviare would cover.

"I'll tell Fish to lay off or he'll wolf the lot," Leila had said. "He'd live on the stuff if we could afford it."

Rachel had no doubt that the order had been given. For twelve years they had been telling each other their private miseries, and Leila knew from many visits the emotional discomforts of Rachel's home. She would certainly have understood how much it mattered that Rachel's father shouldn't be given such leverage to use and reuse.

And yet Fish had taken one of the four plates, carried it, with the two chairs, to a corner of the rose garden well away from the marquee, and hidden it under the napkin. Rachel had spotted him through the rose trellis and photographed him in the act of eating one of the biscuits piled with the scrapings of several others, he unaware of her presence, she of the apparently trivial betrayal. The lens had only three focal settings. The gap in the screening roses was too high for her to be able to hold the camera at waist level and peer down through the viewfinder. She had had to stand sideways on, unable to see him directly, and wait for the moment when the minuscule image looked somehow expressive of him.

Which it did. As with the other image, with Lord Something, his essential nature seemed to speak from the page, a deep satisfaction with himself, independent of anyone else in the world. Dilys had it exactly right. It was himself he was pleased with. The pleasure lay only superficially in the taste and texture of the caviare. (It had, apparently, been of fair quality—Rachel's father still had connections in the trade.) The deeper pleasure lay in his own wishes prevailing over those of anyone else, no matter who.

Since his disappearance, and his leaving Leila so desperately in the lurch, Rachel had come to accept that that was indeed his true nature. But while he had still been there, coming in and out of their lives, such easy company, so useful in odd little ways, so well liked by the children, so continuingly doted on by Leila, it had seemed to be merely the occasional carelessness and thoughtlessness, by-products of an easygoing nature, that had caused the unpredictable let-downs. Jocelyn, a very perceptive judge of men (less so, in Rachel's view, of women), had accepted him fully. Before their marriages they had been no more than regimental colleagues, and would probably not have become friends but for Rachel and Leila's need of each other; even then for a while their friendship couldn't have been called close.

Small chance of that, with Rachel joining Jocelyn in India, and all three children being born out there, and no plans to return permanently to England until the eldest boy, if any, needed to go to prep school. The war had intervened when Dick was only three.

So in the next three albums the only images of Fish had been captured during the Staddings' trip to India in the first year after the marriages, and twice during home leaves, when the Matsons had stayed for a week with Leila and Fish, and a return visit had been paid to Forde Place as guests of Jocelyn's parents. It was there that Rachel had first recorded the bond between Anne and Simon, two three-year-olds, hand in hand, lurking crouched behind a topiary box obelisk, poised to spring out when Fish, already visible on the right of the picture, came strolling towards the ambush, obviously aware of it but happy to play and overplay his role.

Again Rachel willed all her concentration into focus on the image. No, you wouldn't have guessed. However closely you'd watched him then, you wouldn't have guessed. For one thing, how could you suspect anyone whom children liked so readily? He was wonderful with them, full of jokes that stretched but didn't exceed their understanding, and so were especially delightful to them; inventive of amusements for them to learn and then play on their own; patient with their bad moods—able indeed to coax a tot out of a tantrum faster than anyone Rachel had ever known, and without conceding an inch over the cause of the uproar.

He had been just as good with Jocelyn's parents. They were well mannered with Rachel, but couldn't help her perceiving that they thought her nothing like good enough for Jocelyn; and not unreasonably they detested her father. Unable to express their feelings openly, they had displaced them into highly exacting rules about the behaviour of the grandchildren, incomprehensible to toddlers used to the tolerance of a doting *ayah*. It had been a considerable concession that Leila and Fish could bring two further brats for their first visit. By the end of it not only had the rules been greatly relaxed, but Rachel's own

status and worth seemed to have improved, and this had been Fish's
achievement as much as her own.

Before their '37 leave her mother-in-law had written, unasked, to
say that the Staddings would be welcome for as long as they wished
to stay.

Then the volumes spanning the immense hole of the war, and the
two more years before she could bear to photograph Jocelyn again—
or, naturally, any of the other Cambi veterans.

"Oh, that's the one you've got on the desk."

Jocelyn and the Rover. Not in fact the first picture she'd taken of
him since his recovery, but it was here in the *Life* because it was the
first that seemed to her to carry the full charge of her love for him,
and of her relief that he was himself again . . . And the later knowledge that he wasn't? Should that have been there, to eyes unblinded by
affection? How should she know, even now, with the blindness undi-
minished?

The page turned. Ah.

Jocelyn and Fish. Another instance of the trick that still worked,
that could still, despite repetition, in some sense surprise—even herself, though she had contrived it by placing it immediately next. Again
there was a car with its bonnet gaping, again Jocelyn was poised beside it, caught in the action of turning towards the camera at her call.
The echo was so strong that everything else in the picture seemed for
an instant wrong—wrong setting, the stable yard; wrong car, the
Staddings' Bentley; an intruder, Fish, smiling, his greeting to her.
They had been there so that Jocelyn could make some minor engine
adjustment—something Fish wouldn't have dreamed of attempting
for himself—but they must have finished with that because when
Rachel had come into the yard they were simply talking.

About what?

That, though it could never be answered, was the central question,
and the photographs were where they were to ask it. For the real trick
was not the superficial one of the echo, but a deeper and darker arti-
fice. She had, of course, been wholly unaware of it for long after she
had taken the photograph. She had done so, no doubt, in the hope of
capturing a sense of a deep intimacy born of comradeship through

dreadful times, times expressed in Fish's still slightly unwholesome look—he had come through less wasted than Jocelyn, but had recovered more slowly. That comradeship had seemed to Rachel the only good thing to come out of the ordeal, because it balanced her bond with Leila, making the husbands equal partners in the family friendship.

But by the time she had composed the *Life* those friendships were gone, dissolved by death, and disappearance, and the residual acids of Fish's treachery. The picture expressed a premonition of that change, a pivotal moment at which one kind of past began to become a different kind of future. Fish's stance gave nothing away, but comparing the images Rachel believed she could perceive a difference in Jocelyn's. In the one with the Rover it had expressed not just competence in the task, but assurance about the world and his own place in it. In the one with the Bentley there was a touch of uncertainty, of doubt of his own worth and need. Rachel had found it among the rough prints, having rejected it, presumably because when she'd first seen it it hadn't seemed to her to present the "real" Jocelyn. The camera can deceive in that way. Sometimes it may picture a self which the subject would prefer not to display, but just as often the apparent self is an illusion. Looking through the roughs, Rachel must have thought the picture was of the latter kind. By the time she composed the *Life* she could see it was of the former.

She let Dilys leaf on through the remaining volumes, the world acquiring its postwar pattern: the girls becoming women; Dick becoming yearly more and more like Jocelyn in appearance, and less in actuality; Jocelyn settling into his role in the county—the High Sheriff year, and so on—and the Staddings coming in and out of the story, once on a Greek cruise, but mostly on visits to Forde Place.

Sometimes Fish had come with them, sometimes not, because he had been working. But he had often shown up on his own, using the house as his northern base. Before the war he had worked for a large insurance agency, but now he had his own business, specialising in the needs of the owners of country houses and estates, undercutting the big general agencies by insuring direct through Lloyds. Not much was said, but Rachel was well aware that Jocelyn was crucial to the success of the business, because Fish's natural clients tended to be conservative in their ways, sticking with the insurers they had always used until the suggestion for a change was presented to them in a way that they felt comfortable with. Jocelyn's introduction was the sort of thing such people trusted. Fish, in return, had taken on the chore of running the Cambi Road Association, though of course his secretary did all the work.

There was nothing in any of the images, and nothing in Rachel's own memory, to suggest that Fish had been in financial trouble. Certainly he had had his extravagances, but his business had seemed to be prospering and Leila, surely, had plenty of money. She had happily let him run her affairs since their marriage. The camera had caught the well-to-do, contented surface, but nothing of the underlying hollowness.

What it had caught, if only for the eye of hindsight, was the curious, paradoxical relationship between the two men. There were not that many pictures of them together—Rachel was not the sort to pose her travelling companions on the ramp at Delos—but no one glancing at them as they happened by would have doubted that Jocelyn was the dominant one of the pair—not just for his greater size, but the stance of command, the self-assurance, keenness of look and definiteness of gesture, all so much more emphatic than Fish's elusive, lounging, ironic personality. Jocelyn dealt seriously with the world. He had the energy and intelligence to achieve. Fish, potentially had them too, but made little use of them. It wasn't that he lacked the will. He willed the negative.

But now, for Rachel, the cumulative effect was different. Perhaps she had sensed something of it when she had originally compiled the albums, but at last she could see it clearly. Now the series of images seemed to her to portray something very like the history of a marriage, in which there is one busy and active partner, and a quieter one; but it is the quieter one who makes all the major choices, with which the other then copes. In this case the chooser had been Fish.

Just before the end of the final album there was a picture of Jocelyn taken after his second stroke, in a wheelchair on the terrace in the October sun, seemingly content. Beside him stood the glass of champagne he was unable to lift to his lips. Rachel remembered willing herself to take the photograph, a record of continuing love, in sickness and in health. It had been Jocelyn's sixty-fourth birthday.

Last of all Tom Dawnay's picture of Rachel herself, photographing the coffin as it descended into the grave, only the second time her own likeness appeared in any of these fifteen albums.

She closed her eyes.

"Enough."

"I should think so too! You must be quite worn out! My, though, it's been interesting, looking at them all the way through like that. Quite a story they tell too—but I don't have to tell you that."

"Thank you, Dilys."

"And now we'd better have a wee rest, hadn't we? If I just get you all comfortable and settle you down."

"Please. Flora?"

"Oh, she'll be looking in this evening as usual. She'd have told us if she wasn't."

Rachel caught the note of mild surprise and anxiety, and understood it. It wasn't like her to ask that kind of question, to need reassurance. She relied on her own memory to know what had been arranged. But it was important that Flora should come today, when speech was still minimally possible. There weren't going to be many more such days. She could feel the change in herself, mental as well as physical, an acceptance that the time had now come to let go, to fight no more. Almost everything that needed to be done was done, and understood that needed to be understood. After Flora's visit it would be over.

"Curtains open or shut, dearie? Can't see the rooks so well, can we, now that the leaves are coming?"

"Shut."

"Right you are."

2

Deliberately Rachel emptied her mind and waited while Dilys dealt with her, tidied and left. For some time after that she rested, suppressing thought and memory, waiting for the necessary energies to renew themselves. Then, calmly, for the last of many times, but with fresh hope, she thought the whole thing through.

Most of it she had known for weeks, allocating each detail to its place, twisting it to and fro and finding out how it could best be fitted to the structure, as the rooks did when they brought another twig to their nests. Large pieces of the structure had seemed to acquire coherence, allowing them to be manipulated and joined to other such pieces. But the whole would never cohere, falling always into its two halves, the two betrayals, Jocelyn's of their love, Fish's of their friendship, with no connection between them beyond the coincidence of time.

Perhaps she had been blind. Perhaps even before the event she should have seen. It wouldn't have been easy. When she and Leila had been alone together they had talked still just as they used to, as openly, as trustingly. It had been natural for Rachel to tell Leila about her sorrow at Jocelyn's waning physical interest in her, and Leila had told her in return that Fish was still sometimes wonderful when he was in the mood. On their Greek tour, indeed, it hadn't needed a lot of perception to see that she, at least, was having that kind of a good time, though Fish had remained as unreadable as ever.

The other cause of her blindness had been of her own making. It was as if she had all along been trying to build the nest on the wrong bough. To her the overwhelming event of that dreadful evening had never been her killing of the young man. He mattered to her not because of that, but because he had been the annunciating devil, informing her of her own betrayal. Though at the intellectual level she knew the horror of her crime, she was numb to it. If Jocelyn had said to her, "Yes, we must tell the police," she would have accepted that as legally correct and morally justified, but she wouldn't have felt that she had done anything she wasn't compelled to. She would have told the court as much of the truth as she was able to, without at the same time telling the world of Jocelyn's betrayal of her.

Even now, just as it had first done in the numbness of the act, her whole emotional being resonated to the clapper-blow of revelation, drowning all other vibrations.

Thus, though over the last three weeks she believed that she had again and again thought through every detail of the young man's visit, that had not been the case. Much of what he had told her she had set aside as unimportant or untrue. He'd known Jocelyn for some while, she'd guessed, and had been given money by him. He must then have decided, or had it suggested to him, that there was more money to be earned by blackmail than by sex. Jocelyn—how could he have been so infatuated?—must have told him something about his home life— he'd known there were servants—so he had also realised that Jocelyn's one truly vulnerable point was his relationship with Rachel. He had presumably purloined Jocelyn's keys long enough to have copies made, and learning that Jocelyn was delayed in London had taken the chance to come to Forde Place, not intending to precipitate an immediate breakdown in the marriage but to show Jocelyn that he could do so if he chose. He had then misplayed his hand.

That would do as an explanation. It became a structured element in the puzzle, which she took for granted and tried to locate in its en-tirety each time she attempted a solution.

It fell to pieces only after Sergeant Fred's visit—the picture of the young man at the cricket match, what Mrs. Pilcher had said, Sergeant Fred's painful lying—with the realisation that the "he" who had told the young man about the servants, and produced the key, had been not Jocelyn but Fish.

Jocelyn and Fish. Two separate boughs, but crossing so close that over the years they had actually grown together. Useless for Rachel to try to build her structure, the random twigs of memory and surmise that she had collected, on Jocelyn's bough alone. Only at the point of intersection with Fish's bough would it cohere and remain.

The beginning was hidden, though Jocelyn had once told Rachel he'd been in a buggers' house at Eton, using the phrase dismissively but without disgust, as if it had been an inevitable aspect of herding growing boys together. He had neither implied nor disowned having taken part himself, but if he had done so, it would have been a phase abandoned as soon as he moved on into a world with a saner distribution of genders.

Then, in some respite from the horrors of captivity, Fish had, deliberately and for his own amusement, seduced him. That was a guess, but it fitted the structure. It was the same thing as stealing the caviare, the real satisfaction lying not in the physical pleasure but in shaping the world however Fish chose, despite the desires and duties of anyone else. Jocelyn would probably have told himself that this was only the same situation that he had known at Eton, a temporary imbalance, something that could be put aside when he returned to the sanity of peacetime.

But he would have known in his heart that was not true. It was altogether different, because this time he had broken faith, and he had done so because Fish had discerned, released and revealed to him his "true" nature.

Furthermore, though he may never have known this, his self-discovery on the Cambi Road hadn't only been of his sexual nature. That was superficial and partial. If he'd been an out and out homosexual the pleasure in their marriage would never have been there in the first place. His nature, presumably, was bisexual, and if that had been all there was to it he should have been able to make love to Rachel as he had done before. Fish could do it, giving Leila pleasure or withholding it as he chose, and getting his own pleasure from the power to do so. But Fish wasn't bothered about honour. What haunted Jocelyn as they lay together was the knowledge that he could no longer make love to Rachel in good faith.

Oh, Christ, if only he could have brought himself to tell her!

Once honour is broken it will not mend. All you can do, all Jocelyn did in the end, is to use your will to hold yourself as near as you can into the shape that honour would have dictated. The result, like a dubbed voice on a foreign film, is never exactly right, and every now and then it is betrayingly wrong.

Sometime in the early 'fifties Fish had started his boys' club, characteristically presenting it not as a public-spirited act but as a chore taken on to please a group of wealthy clients. He would have had secret amusement in telling so much more of the truth than he seemed to be doing, for the clients' interest would have been less in the boys' welfare than in their availability. And, being Fish, he might have got pleasure from the hidden power of pimping for the plutocracy.

But how on earth had Jocelyn allowed himself to be drawn back in?

Man of honour, however willed? Self-disgust, perhaps. No, not quite that. But say to yourself, "I have betrayed the person who is dearest in the world to me. How did I come to do this?" Then tell yourself, "Because it is my nature. That is what I am. It can't be changed." "Prove it." "Very well, if I must." Let there be an overwhelming reason for the broken faith, retested and renewed on visits to London, rather than the self-knowledge of honour needlessly lost forever. And let it not be an attraction towards a particular person, an intellectual and social equal, a long-term mistress as it were, who happened to be male. No, let the need be for nothing emotional or companionable. Let it be purely and explicitly physical, nothing to do with the inward self that still, in its way, loved Rachel more than anyone or anything in the world. Hence the rough trade, the young man.

Well, perhaps.

Fish, in the end, had run through Leila's money and started to take his clients'. Questions had begun to be asked, and to clear himself in the emergency he had turned to the Cambi Road funds and then, because he'd needed to act in a hurry, been found out sooner than he'd planned for. Perhaps all along he'd intended to turn from pimping to blackmail—it was the obvious next step—but he wasn't yet ready. The urgent need was to let Jocelyn understand what Fish's exposure would cost him, so he'd delayed him in London and sent the young man to Forde Place on the earlier train. "Don't tell her anything," he'd have said. "All I want is for her to start asking questions when the old boy gets home. Here's the key." (Yes, the one that Jocelyn had niggled about having cut for him.) Perhaps, again, such a move had been part of the long-term plan, but in the rush to act there had not been time for full preparation and rehearsal.

So the young man had got it wrong. Fatally.

And so too had Fish. He had pushed Jocelyn to his sticking point: Rachel herself. It was not because she had killed the young man, though this, if he had learnt of it, would have given Fish a monstrous extra leverage for blackmail. It was that Fish had tried to involve Rachel in Jocelyn's own loss of honour. One way or another, an end must now be made.

The details were unknowable. What had Jocelyn said to Sergeant Fred and Voss? Surely he couldn't have told them everything, but he had the young man's body to explain as well. (Sergeant Fred had recognised him from the photograph, but that didn't necessarily mean that he'd seen him alive.) That Rachel herself had killed him? No, for then Voss wouldn't have said what he had to her in Parkhurst. But none of that would have been necessary. He could simply have said, "I am in trouble, and I need your help. I can't give you reasons, so I must ask you to trust me. There is a dead man to be disposed of, and there is Major Stadding to be dealt with. The trouble I'm in is his deliberate doing."

They would have taken him at his word. Voss, after all, owed him a life.

So between them they had collared Fish. How? It didn't matter. But Doug Rawlings might have had something to do with it. There'd been that odd look from Voss when his name had come up on her prison visit. Ah, had Jocelyn helped him buy his own cab, by way of reward? Possibly. And then Essex, and a place Voss knew of where bodies could be lost, for a price. Two prices. First, Voss's own four-year imprisonment, paid to the man called Brent for the use of the facility. Second, what Jocelyn had given Voss to allow him to rescue his niece from the Elect of God, and provide a home for her and her family.

And there they had killed Fish Stadding.

When it was all over, after Jocelyn had come back to Rachel with the plaster on his cheek and dealt with what else needed to be dealt with, he had gone to see Simon Stadding and told him that he had killed his father (oh the willed attempt at honour, rather than the integral thing!).

What else had he said? He must have given more reasons than he had to Voss and Fredricks, but not that Rachel had killed the young man.

Had he simply said that Fish had been trying to blackmail him, through Rachel, and for her sake one of them had to go? And then, "Well, I am in your hands. You may go to the police if you want. I won't deny the charges."

That would have been nonsense, of course. Jocelyn must have been almost wholly confident that Simon would keep his silence, if only for Leila's sake, and Anne's. But the honourable thing would have been to keep his secret to himself, and when the day came to take his daughter down the aisle at his proudest pace—except that it wouldn't have worked out like that, with Leila's intransigence after the disappearance of Fish.

But in any case that was not enough. It would, perhaps, have been a reason for not telling the world what had happened, but for not telling Anne . . . ? No. Impossible.

And now Simon kept complaining that he had bad blood, as if he'd always had it—had been born with it, inherited it. What did that mean? It meant that Jocelyn must have told him how far his father's baseness had extended beyond mere abuse of funds. Told him in such a way that he had then decided that his own blood was tainted . . . Oh, heavens! Jocelyn had adored Anne almost to the point of obsession. Was it conceivable—he wouldn't have done it consciously, surely—but was it conceivable that at some hidden level he had taken the chance to satisfy his own unacknowledged jealousy by breaking the engagement, done so by explaining the leverage that Fish had attempted to use on him, something that Simon would feel he could never tell Anne? Oh, God! Let it not have been so!

Poor Simon, poor Anne. They were like chance passers-by—a couple on their honeymoon, perhaps—caught in the blast when a car bomb explodes, detonated in a cause that has nothing to do with them. For a while Rachel lay and grieved for them, a loss unmitigated by time. It might have happened yesterday.

Then, thinking about what had now become of Simon—how the Simon she had known, witty, charming, thoughtful, sensitive, seemed to have gone completely, to be replaced in the same body (altered by illness, but still the same body) by a dreary and exploitative old whiner—it struck her that there are many ways of dying before the nurse comes to close your eyelids and lay your body straight, and that her own way was by no means the worst, nor Sergeant Fred's, though most people would have thought of those as deaths-in-life: she trapped in her only just not yet purulent carcase; he . . . oh, it was strange, Rachel thought. What made her herself, Rachel and no one else? What but the shelf upon shelf of ordered memories of all that had composed and shaped her life? To take those away from her, that would be the true death. But Sergeant Fred still moved, talked and held himself in a manner that asserted the living essence of who he was and had been and would remain, like some saga-hero, living flesh still, but riding his skeleton horse among the wraiths of the under-world.

Whereas Simon, though his mind was still his own, did not. Yes. That was worse.

And Jocelyn? Honour dead, but willing himself into the modes and speech of honour, and to such disastrous ends? No. Rachel loved him too much, loved him both before that death and after, loved him even now. She would not bring herself to judge him.

Instead she returned to the conclusion of her earlier thoughts and began deliberately to compose the event into visual images, as definite and solid as she could make them. It felt necessary to do this, in order to be able to put the whole thing aside and have done with it. She knew her imaginings to be invention, but they were all that she could now have, so it was up to her to give them the kind of inward truth that was there in the photographs in her albums. Those two-dimensional black and white and grey shapes on paper were none of them the thing they showed, but its essence was in them.

So, now, the marshes. Early morning, a salty wind off the North Sea. Gulls. A flat landscape crossed by dikes. Smoke from some town on the level horizon. A car crawls down a rutted track on the top of a dike and stops. Four men get out, two of them holding a third by the elbows. They climb down the dike to a squelchy patch of turf. One man, tall and athletic, stands aside. A second, taller but bonier, paces out a distance, marking each end by digging his heel several times into the turf. He has a rectangular box under his arm. The third man guards the prisoner, an elegant, well-fed figure who watches these proceedings with curiosity, like a passing stranger who has stopped to see what's up.

The tall man goes to the burly one and opens the box. The burly man takes out a pistol, loads it methodically, puts it back and repeats the process with the second pistol. The tall man takes the box to the prisoner, who chooses a pistol and allows himself to be led to one of the marks. The burly man goes to the other and takes the second pistol when it is brought to him. The two duellists face each other. The tall man moves to one side, halfway between them, and the guard stands opposite him, so that the four of them mark out the four corners of a square. The tall man raises his right arm. The duellists level their guns. The arm falls. In the silence of her imagination Rachel hears no shots, but sees the smoke fluff suddenly from the muzzles, and the prisoner stagger back and fall.

Nobody moves for a while. Then the tall man goes to the fallen body and inspects it. He picks up the pistol, puts it in the box and takes it to the other duellist. Blood covers the lower half of the duellist's left cheek. He stares at the box, takes it and closes it, then hands the pistol he has used to the tall man, speaks briefly and turns away. Rachel hears no words, but knows what he has said. He never wants to see it again.

Why? Because it is the weapon he has used to kill a man to whom his life has been bound for almost thirty years, whom he had thought his closest friend but found to be his secret enemy?

In that case, why the absurdity of the duel? (Forget the apparent frivolity of using the Laduries. Fish was a reasonable shot, and had often played with them on visits to Forde Place. What other pair of fairly matched weapons was available?)

Honour gone finally mad?

Not in that way, no. But it was a final, despairing attempt at the recovery of lost honour, an acknowledgement that Jocelyn's own shame was in some ways equal to Fish's, or greater, and that he couldn't therefore kill the man as an executioner. Each must be given an equal chance. (And no doubt he had plans laid out for what was to happen if he was the one who died.)

And only when it was done had he discovered that honour was still unsatisfied, could never now be satisfied, because it was dead. Long dead on Cambi Road.

Poor darling.

Rachel fell asleep to the imagined yelping of the gulls.

3

She slept peacefully, a huge stint, and woke in the middle of the afternoon. Dilys cleaned her up, made her a delectable cup of Oolong, fed her, and put on the new talking book, about traumatised soldiers during the First World War. Worth listening to, but Rachel barely did so.

All that, fact or fiction, was over and done with, past. There was only a scrap of future left for her. She thought about that. First, today, while her voice still worked . . .

Flora came, cheerfully fussed about one of her dozen godchildren.

"Hello, Ma. Do you remember Zelda Warkley? The one with the pointy ears, and her kids have got them too—it must be one of these gene things. Of course you remember, they came here when they were small and we had to fish Donald out of the river—he'd actually got through the netting—and he's still like that. Zelda was just the same, but it doesn't stop her worrying about Donald. I got a letter from her this morning. Apparently he's in Brisbane—is that Australia or New Zealand?—not that it matters, provided he's on the other side of the world. He went out there to sell this new sheep dip, and I do think somebody might have asked first, but they'd already made it illegal—it's terrific for the wool, but the shearers started getting Gulf War syndrome—so Zelda's writing round all her friends asking if they know anyone who could give Donald a job—anything to get him out of England, really. I don't suppose you can think of anyone who might have a job for a totally charming layabout with pointy ears? What's up, Ma? You've got one of your teases brewing—I can always tell, you know."

"Bureau. Bottom drawer. Brown envelope. Big."

"Told you so! Like wrapping our Christmas presents up to look like they weren't, remember?"

She disappeared out of Rachel's line of sight. The drawer scraped. Papers rustled.

"This what you mean? . . . Oh, good heavens! You remembered where you'd put them? No, you didn't. You'd known all along, you wicked old thing! That's wonderful. I'd better take them straight along to the bank tomorrow, don't you think?"

"Wait. You don't . . . need . . . money?"

"Lord, no. I don't know how Jack does it, but we seem to get more disgustingly well off every year. I'm really ashamed to think about it."

"Anne?"

"She's all right. It's those quarter horses she breeds, tough as old boots but such sweeties, and they keep winning championships so everybody wants one now. And anyway, I'm not at all sure she'd accept . . . Oh, Ma! You're not going to give them to Dick after all! I couldn't stand that! I'd make a really shameful fuss! Please, Ma . . . Oh you are an old tease! It isn't fair at your age!"

"Send Dick . . . something . . . My . . . trust."

"Well, I suppose, if you must. I'll ask Jack. How much? It was five thousand last time, and a darned sight too generous, to my mind, though he didn't seem to think so."

"Same?"

"Oh, all right. What about the pistols?"

"Grisholm . . . Ebury Street . . . Ask him . . . sell . . . Money . . . to Sergeant . . . Fred . . . Trust . . . You and . . . Mrs. . . . Pil . . . cher . . ."

"Don't try and talk anymore, Ma. You're wearing yourself out. I think it's a terrific idea. I'd been wondering if we oughtn't to do something about Sergeant Fred. And you want me and Mrs. Pilcher to be trustees, is that right? No, don't try and talk. She's a funny little thing but I rather took to her, she was so sweet about the house—I mean it's not everybody's cup of tea. And apparently both their jobs are a bit iffy at the moment, and they've been subsidising Sergeant Fred at this home he's at, and they don't know how long they can go on doing that—you remember you asked me to find out if he was all right that way? Oh, good heavens, wasn't Grisholm that funny little man on the antiques programme? You think he'd be interested? Oh, Ma, don't tease! You've been up to something, going behind my back again. And I bet Dilys is in it too. What a pair you are! Thick as thieves."

JENNY

Mrs. Matson died in August. Flora Thomas telephoned next day with the news. Though she seemed to have elected Jenny as a kind of honorary chum during the process of arranging the trust for Uncle Albert, it still for a moment seemed surprising that she should have found the time to do so.

"Oh, I'm so sorry," said Jenny.

"Best thing that could have happened, really. She was absolutely longing to go."

"That doesn't stop it being hard on you."

"No, it doesn't. Still . . . I try not to think about it. Look, I was talking to Ma about the funeral—she couldn't talk any more, poor thing, just blink her eyes for yes or no while you asked questions, like one of those nursery games—she actually managed to make it rather fun, dear old thing—she was a great tease . . . oh yes—Sergeant Fred. She wanted him to come to the funeral. Do you think that's on? We could send a car this time—at least I hope we can. I think you know Eileen Cowan, don't you? She's a parson not far from you, and she's the niece of an old friend of my father's—Ma wanted her too, but she's got a wedding—did I say it was Saturday week, the funeral?— but she's going to see if she can get somebody else to take it—I must say I thought that was a bit much to ask—I mean she didn't even know Ma but she said Ma was the only person who visited her uncle when he was in prison, except herself—so if she *can* come, Sergeant Fred knows her apparently so he'll be all right if we send a car for the two of them, and you don't have to worry about it."

"No, I'll bring him," said Jenny. "Then it won't matter whether Nell Cowan can come or not."

"Oh. Are you sure?"

"I'd like to, if that's all right. I won't come to the service, if you don't mind—I don't suppose there'll be much room, anyway."

"Just as you like, but there won't be a lot of us there, if you change your mind—just us family, and the servants, and a few locals. All Ma's proper friends are dead—goodness I hope I don't live that long—I can't think of anything drearier—being the last leaf on the bough, you know . . . well, that's splendid, if you really want to, but don't forget, if Miss Cowan can come . . . Is that right? It doesn't feel right—but Mrs. doesn't feel right either—not that it matters with everyone using Christian names straight off—who was it tried to call me Flo the other day? Oh, yes, the Deputy Mayor, but you never know where you are with Liberal Democrats—they're such a rag-bag, don't you think? . . . And don't forget, we could easily send a car, and if you want to come you could just hop in and save all that driving . . ."

"No, it's quite all right, really. I'll be glad to do it."

This was the literal truth. It felt necessary that she should make the effort. It was as if her original visit to Forde Place had started vibrations which would whimper uncomfortably on, like the dwindling notes of a rapped wine glass, unless deliberately stilled. Repeating the journey would perhaps do that.

"Well, if you say so," said Flora.

By now Billy Cochrane was merely an exorcised demon, gone with his golden handshake. Jeff, on a recommendation from Sir Vidal, was deep into his first heavy consultancy contract, but insisted on coming to the funeral. To share the driving, he said, but Jenny guessed that it was at least as much that he wanted to be with her, in case she found the event unsettling. He worked at his laptop whenever she was at the wheel. They dropped Nell Cowan and Uncle Albert at the church gate, drove the hundred yards back to Forde Place and parked with the other cars halfway down the drive.

"I'm going for a walk," she said.

"Want me to come with you?"

"It's up to you. But I'll be all right. I'm fine, darling. Really. This is all—I don't know—all the way it's supposed to be. Sorting itself out. OK. You carry on with your stuff, and then you won't be up half the night getting it finished."

"Sure?"

"Yes. Funerals don't last that long. I'll be back in forty minutes and then we'll go and find a pub while they're all at the reception."

She left him juggling equations and walked down the mown grass beside the drive. A caterer's van was parked in front of the house, with last supplies being carried in. She followed a path round to the south side and on, still downwards, past a couple of terraced lawns, and then along the outside of a walled garden to a small meadow with a river beyond it. A mown grass path led to a footbridge.

Still without any particular purpose, beyond a sense of peace and well-being and vague, unformulated expectation, Jenny climbed the four steps and onto the worn grey timbers of the bridge. It turned out to span only an arm of the river, which at this point ran in two channels separated by a narrow island. Trees partly obscured the further channel, but Jenny could see no sign of a second bridge by which to reach the far bank.

She stopped halfway across and looked around. Upstream the river, shallow at this time of year but still fast-flowing over a rocky bed, was visible for two or three hundred yards. Several more gardens, some with boat houses, lined its bank. But downstream the view was blocked only thirty yards away by a curious industrial structure, with small buildings both on the island and the shore, and between them a sort of dam, brick, pierced with two low arches to let the water through. It looked Victorian, but not contemporary with the main house—some kind of primitive hydroelectric device, perhaps.

Jenny stared at it, puzzled. Though she had never before stood on this bridge, there was a resonance, an echo in her mind of something else she'd seen, something that had spoken strongly to her . . . In a dream, perhaps . . . No . . . The sunlit brickwork, the impenetrable shadows beneath the arches, the water steadily flowing out of light into darkness . . . a photograph, on the wall of Mrs. Matson's sickroom . . . She had turned away from the bed, engulfed in her own private horrors, and been rescued first by the photograph of the monster fungus, and then by other images of life and death, including this view, cropped down to include nothing but the dam and the river.

She stood for several minutes, simply gazing at the moving water, then turned and walked back to the meadow. A clump of wild ox-eye daisies was growing close to the path. Using thumbnail and fingernail she nipped off two of the flower heads, carried them up onto the bridge, leaned on the rail and held them out over the water, side by side. She waited a ritual moment, then whispered their names.

"Norma. Sister Jenny. Thanks."

She dropped them, saw them settle onto the current and race off towards the dam. They vanished in ripple-glitter before they reached the darkness.

"It isn't over," she told Jeff later. "I don't think it ever will be. But from now on I'll manage on my own. Just me."

Jeff took the first stint of the journey home. He regarded ninety-five as a sensible cruising speed on the motorway, so they were booming south through the shimmery, fumy harvest sunlight when Uncle Albert spoke suddenly from the back seat.

"Had to do it, didn't I?"

"Do what, Bert?" said Nell, sitting beside him.

"None of your business, miss."

"Are you sure? It sounds a bit like something you'd like to get off your chest—that's part of my job, you know. Think about it, Bert."

He was silent for several minutes. Jenny had the sun visor down to mitigate the glare and could see him in the vanity mirror. His eyes were open but he was nodding drowsily, as if he was about to drop off any moment.

"You're wrong about that," he said suddenly. "It's never bothered me that much. Something's got to be done, then it's got to be done, that's all. Terry didn't like it, mind you—not from the first. Kept trying to talk us out of it . . . All right, I suppose I might as well tell you, now I've started . . ."

"One moment," said Nell. "Do you mind turning the radio on, Jenny? I'm sure you'll understand. Music, if you can find it."

Dutifully Jenny tuned to Radio Three and adjusted the volume to give them the privacy of the confessional.

"Can't have that," said Uncle Albert. "Let me hear myself think, will you, miss."

"You don't mind them hearing too?" said Nell.

"What's the odds any longer? They're all dead and done with. Dead and done with. That's how it goes."

He fell silent again and settled back into the corner. His eyes closed but his lips moved from time to time, and when he spoke it was in a matter-of-fact tone, quiet but confident, suggesting that he had now ordered his thoughts. Jenny strained to hear, but could catch only snatches through the noises from the motorway.

". . . didn't like it at all, like I was saying. 'Suppose the bugger gets you, stead of you getting him.' . . . got it all worked out . . . boat business at Brightlingsea, and Ben kept a couple of yachts . . . lost overboard . . . note to give to Mrs. Matson . . . not like it was with crooks. Crooks don't go running to the police soon as someone goes missing . . . got an answer for everything, so we talked Terry round in the end. It wasn't only that, of course, it was knowing we couldn't've done it without him. He's got the contacts. There was this big fellow—forgotten his name—began with a B, didn't it? . . . he'd pay whatever it took, but the B fellow . . . take the rap for the fellow's brother as long as he could hang on to the money . . ."

The road surface changed to corrugated concrete, setting up a resonant drumming that vibrated through the bodywork of the car, drowning speech. In the mirror Jenny could see Nell leaning right across to catch Uncle Albert's words. There was a brief switch to tarmac as they crossed an interchange, and a few more words came through.

". . . drove his own cab—he'd been on the Road too, of course— so I told him time and place he was wanted . . ."

Then they were on the concrete again. Jenny saw Nell put her mouth to Uncle Albert's ear. He nodded understanding and stopped speaking. Nell settled back in her place, out of Jenny's line of sight. Uncle Albert closed his eyes and slept until they stopped at a service station for Jenny to take over the wheel.

At first as they drove on he seemed to have forgotten what he'd been doing. Jenny could glimpse him now in the driving mirror, and thought he'd fallen asleep again, but then he began to speak, picking up the story almost where he'd left off, but in a very different voice, a kind of dreamy monotone, like that of a subject under hypnosis, not addressed to Nell or to anyone in particular, but slow and clear enough for Jenny to catch almost every word at her quieter pace of driving.

". . . Must've been about one in the morning before we got there. Sort of a farm place, by the smell of it, right out at the end of nowhere. No one around, which there wasn't supposed to be, of course. There was a big shed we could drive the car right in, and we tied Stadding up and let him lay on a pile of straw and we each took a go of watching him while the other two kipped in the car. He never said a word all night and slept better than any of us, far as I could make out. Then soon as it was getting light I did a recce and found a place and we marched him out along the track. Like the end of the world, it was . . ."

He paused. Glancing in the mirror Jenny saw that he was leaning back into his corner with his eyes closed, a look of contentment, like an old man basking in a deck chair. The story, Jenny was sure, was coming to no good end, but he seemed to have removed himself from it completely. Nell didn't prompt him, but after a while he did that himself.

"Yes, like the end of the world," he said. "Dead flat, but for these dikes, and reeking of dried-out mud, and salt in the wind, and gulls, though you couldn't see the sea, but you could tell it was there all right. I'd picked a flat bit of field in a corner between a couple of dikes so we were well down out of sight. We'd no reason to hang around, so I paced out the distance and we stood Stadding at one end and untied him and gave him a couple of minutes to move around a bit and rub himself where the cords had bit. I'd got the revolver on him, of course, in case he tried anything, but he didn't act that interested, more like we were setting up to play a game or something and he thought it was a waste of time but he was going along with it to keep us happy."

He paused again, but went on almost at once, still in the same sleep-walking tone, but more firmly, as if his memory were shedding the last vaguenesses of dream and coming into instant-by-instant focus.

"The Colonel was loading up the pistols and checking them over and when he'd done Terry brought them and showed them to Stadding and he took one, not thinking about it or anything, and Terry took the other one back to the Colonel. I told them the regulations and the signal I'd give, dropping my arm for them to fire, and then I said to raise their weapons, only Stadding didn't do it right, taking aim like he was supposed to. Stead of that he put his pistol right up against his head, like he was making to blow his brains out, and his lips were moving like he was praying and I thought bugger me—he's going to get it right in the end.

"Like you'd expect I took a look at the Colonel to see what he wanted, and he'd lowered his weapon and was just watching like I'd been, when I saw from his face something was up and before I'd time to look Stadding had fired, and the Colonel jerks his head aside—I've seen men do that as the bullet took them, and I thought he'd got him, but he yells, 'Stop him,' and Terry's yelling, and Stadding's running for the dike, only he catches his foot in a tussock and down he goes, and Terry's on him before he's up, and then I'm there with the revolver, close enough he can see I won't miss, and he just nods and lets me march him back to where he'd been.

"I stand him up so the Colonel can take his shot at him, and then I move back not to get in the line of fire. The Colonel raises his weapon. There's blood running down his face but he's not noticing.

" 'So you're going to shoot an unarmed man, are you, Jocelyn?' says Stadding, teasing, and the Colonel lowers his weapon.

" 'We'll start again,' he says. 'Bring me that pistol, Voss, and I'll reload it for him.'

"Terry picks up the pistol and takes it over and I move in round behind Stadding and I let him hear me cock the revolver so he knows not to try anything, but that's not what I'm at, not really. He's had his chance, and it isn't right him having another one, not after all he's done. Soon as I'm near enough I let him have it in the back of the head, and that's that.

"I look and see the Colonel's just standing where he was, staring, like he doesn't know what's up.

" 'All over, sir,' I tell him.

"It's like he hasn't heard me, so I tell him again.

" 'Right,' he says. 'Thanks, Fredricks,' and he goes off and sits down at the bottom of the dike.

"I leave Terry to keep an eye on him and go back to the farm. There's a sort of a handcart in the shed, and I load it up with the weights we've brought, and the young fellow's body out of the boot of the car, and shove it back out to them. Terry and me, we pile Stadding's body on top—the Colonel's still sitting where he was, so we let him be. We shove the cart along to this bit of bog, which is why Terry's brought us there in the first place. There's wire round it, and signs saying it's a quicksand only it's black as tar and stinking. High tides the sea comes in, Terry says.

"Terry doesn't like what we're doing, mind you, not at all. It's not exactly that he's scared, but there's too many of them in there already, he says. But he knows the drill, so we lash the bodies together and tie the weights on, and we put a rope with a slip knot round their ankles—that's the kind of stuff you're taught on exercises—and we haul them out across the bog and I pull the other end of the rope to loose the knot, and in a couple of minutes you wouldn't know they'd been there, ever. Wiped out. Gone."

A long pause, as if the subterranean memories had exhausted their flow. But no. He began to speak again, now in a mutter so low that Jenny caught only the odd word. It was about the drive back to London, with Colonel Matson still apparently in shock. ". . . like getting a drunk back into barracks past the guard . . ." she heard. Another, briefer silence, and a snorting laugh, and then, louder . . .

"We could do with a drink, Terry and me, after all that, so we took the first pub we came to. Fellow jostled Terry in the doorway, shoved him up against me, so I felt this great hard lump in his jacket pocket.

"Soon as we were settled I gave it a poke.

" 'What've you got in there, lad?' I asked him. 'Let's have a look.'

"Tell you the truth I thought he'd latched on to the Colonel's revolver—there'd be a price for a gun like that among some of Terry's pals—but when I reached in and pulled it out far enough to see with-out showing it around, I saw it was one of the old pistols. Terry'd been taking it over to the Colonel, remember, when I shot Stadding, so he just dropped it in his pocket and didn't let on and I hadn't thought to ask him.

" 'Shame on you, Terry,' I told him.

" 'Just a bit of a souvenir,' he says. 'He's not going to want to see it again.'

" 'No harm in asking,' I told him. 'I'll take charge of it now.'

"I was meaning to take it up to Forde Place on my next forty-eight, but when I called about that Mrs. Matson said how the Colonel had had this stroke and wouldn't be seeing anybody for a bit. I went up a couple of times before he died, but he wasn't in a state to be both-ered, so I let it be."

Jenny glanced and saw him shaking his head gently, like any old man thinking about times long past and things long done with, but the movement must have startled him. When she next looked he'd pulled his shoulders back and was frowning and looking around, as if he had no idea why he should be in a car humming along the M25.

"Thank you for telling me that," said Nell. "It's a terrible story, but I'm glad to know about it."

"You think I did wrong, then?"

"It's a long time ago, Bert, a very long time."

"Well, you're right there," he said. "Water under the bridge. Best place for it."